KUXTAL ACADEMY

THE FIRST SPARK

NELLE NIKOLE & MIKAYLA D. HORNEDO

Published by GXLD Page Publishing & Primal Instinct Publishing

Editing: EJL Editing & Editing by Phil

KUXTAL
ACADEMY

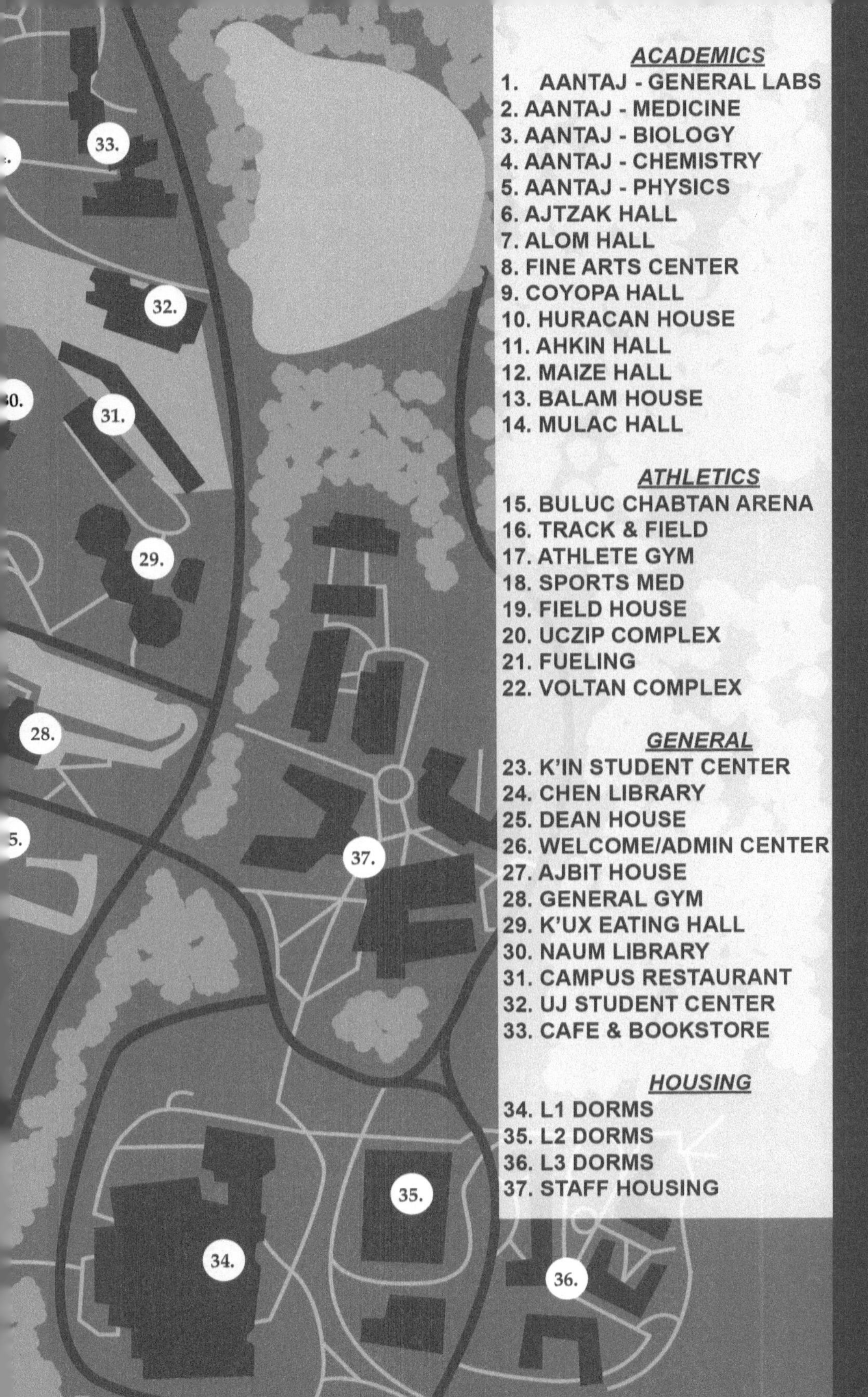

33.
32.
31.
30.
29.
28.
5.
37.
35.
34.
36.

ACADEMICS
1. AANTAJ - GENERAL LABS
2. AANTAJ - MEDICINE
3. AANTAJ - BIOLOGY
4. AANTAJ - CHEMISTRY
5. AANTAJ - PHYSICS
6. AJTZAK HALL
7. ALOM HALL
8. FINE ARTS CENTER
9. COYOPA HALL
10. HURACAN HOUSE
11. AHKIN HALL
12. MAIZE HALL
13. BALAM HOUSE
14. MULAC HALL

ATHLETICS
15. BULUC CHABTAN ARENA
16. TRACK & FIELD
17. ATHLETE GYM
18. SPORTS MED
19. FIELD HOUSE
20. UCZIP COMPLEX
21. FUELING
22. VOLTAN COMPLEX

GENERAL
23. K'IN STUDENT CENTER
24. CHEN LIBRARY
25. DEAN HOUSE
26. WELCOME/ADMIN CENTER
27. AJBIT HOUSE
28. GENERAL GYM
29. K'UX EATING HALL
30. NAUM LIBRARY
31. CAMPUS RESTAURANT
32. UJ STUDENT CENTER
33. CAFE & BOOKSTORE

HOUSING
34. L1 DORMS
35. L2 DORMS
36. L3 DORMS
37. STAFF HOUSING

Author's Note

This book reflects and was written by the perspectives of individuals with anxiety and dyslexia. We understand that these conditions manifest differently for everyone, that's what makes life experiences so unique! We hope some readers find representation here and kindly ask for respect towards those whose journeys differ.

This story was inspired by Mayan mythology, and while not a direct retelling of any of their stories, many of the names of the magical orders, the gods, and some of the places are 'real.' We understand that this is not a widely known mythology, and have provided a magic guide and pronunciation guide. The nahuales (magical orders) are hyperlinked to the magic guide if the reference is needed. The explanation typically follows the name, for example: "*Kaban*, an earth elemental." We've done lots of research, so if you have any questions or want to learn more, reach out to our teams!

Please find the up to date list of content warnings at https://mikayladhorned o.com/kuxtal-academy-the-first-spark/

Take a look inside
our heads

Pinterest:

Playlist:

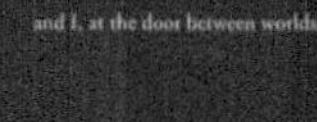

Pronunciation Guide

People

Koa Benício Canek [Koh-ah Beh-NEE-syo Kah-NEK]

Mira Elara Canek [MEE-rah EE-lah-ra Kah-NEK]

Sienna Monroe Hayes [See-EN-uh Mun-ROH HAYZ]

Wren Ikari [REN EE-KAH-ree]

Aurora Canek Tecun [ah-ROH-rah Kah-NEK Teh-KOON]

Emeric Canek [Em-eh-reec Kah-NEK]

Katia Carvalho [KAH-tee-ah K-AAr-Vaa-lyo]

Iris Whitlok [EYE-ris W-IHt-Lahk]

Vitória [vee-TOH-ree-ah]

Zélia [ZEH-lee-ah]

Atlas Ikari [AT-luss EE-KAH-ree]

Zane Ikari [ZAYN EE-KAH-ree]

Jed Mercer [JED MUR-sir]

Adler Mercer [AHD-lur MUR-sur]

Hagen Noh [HAH-gehn NOH]

Ixchel [EESH-chel]

Chaac [CHAHK]

Kukulkan [koo-kool-KAHN]

Places

Herta [HEHR-tah]

Inecha [ee-NEH-chah]

Kuxtal [kooʃ-TAHL]

Balamku [bah-LAHM-koo]

Chan [CHAN]

Chichen [CHEE-chen]

Jayna [JAY-nah]

Jundi [JUNE-dee]

Kuello {koo-EL-oh]

Yaxumi [yah-SHOO-mee]

Abysmi Noctis [uh-BIZ-me NAHK-tis]

Mentiria [mehn-TEER-ah]

Magic Guide

Nahaul - the intrinsic spirit of a fae that defines the unique powers and abilities, ultimately influencing their magical potential and identity

Level 1

Kaban - earth manipulation

Kib - fire manipulation

Chikchan - basilisk shifter; stone gaze, venom, healing, camouflage, psychic or psyche meld

Imix - dragon shifters of different variations (storm dragon, water dragon, etc.)

Ix - jaguar shifter; night fire, night vision, enhanced speed and agility, accelerated regenerative healing

Ok - wolf shifter; advanced senses, extreme empathy, charisma

Ajaw - coercion and manipulation of time

Kimi- soul manipulation

Level 2

Ik - air manipulation

Kawak - storm and water manipulation

Muluk - shadow manipulation

Eb - tooth jaw; mystical knowledge, mind manipulation

Xtabay - siren shifters; enchantment, illusions, empathic connections

Kan - half-shifter feathered wings with soundless air bending flight

Men – harpy half-shifters, extreme speed, claws

Manik - deer shifter; horns can be used for powerful spells

Level 3

Akbal - unknown

Ben - unknown

Etznab - immaculate aim and predatory fighting skills

Lamat - light manipulation

Dedicated to those who rise when silence is easier, who risk all to confront tyranny—may your courage write the future.

1

MIRA

Philosophers theorized that life and death were one. A delicate balance. As I teetered on that edge between the two, I wondered just how true that was. With my gift, I felt the string pulling like a game of tug-of-war. I strummed it with my finger, tipping toward death, then life, before settling in the center of the two.

Delicate wasn't accurate. It was a force, the will to live palpable and inexorable. People always feared death, an uncontrollable end to what little they had authority over. Here, in this liminal state, I was endlessly powerful. I had no desire to topple over to the dark, ruinous space I knew to be death. My family and friends were waiting for me in life. I let the energy of this place fuel me as I pushed toward the light.

A voice, sweet and smooth, whispered my name, a warm caress brushing against my cheek. It was too late. I couldn't turn back; I couldn't see who it was. My nahual recognized it, which meant it could only be one person.

I love you, Tía.

My eyes shot open, my surroundings too bright, so blurry that I wasn't sure where I was. The only thought that came to mind was the intense *need* for air. Breathing was never something I had to think too much about, but right now it was the only thing I was able to focus on. Each gasp for oxygen was more painful than the last, to the point that I wanted to stop trying if only to avoid the discomfort. But as I had just witnessed, our bodies weren't too fond of letting us die, so I persisted until it was a dull ache.

The next conscious thought I had was that the water expelling from my mouth was absolutely vile. It poured out of me with every heave, the coughs forcing more out each time. Everything came into focus, including the reason I was throwing up the revolting seawater. The fact that I had the ability to recollect—that I could move and breathe—meant the hypoxia didn't fully set in. My brain was still functioning properly, so we had to have been pulled from the sea fairly quickly.

"Fuck, Mira," Wren sighed and fell over my body, catching himself on his forearms before fully crushing me.

The healing magic in his fingers sparked out as his chest heaved and he caught his breath. He must have been working on me for a few minutes. The *Ix* weren't nearly as skilled as *Chikchan*—like my brother—in healing, but they had enough power to mend.

Sienna and Koa. I don't see them.

"Where are they?" I asked.

Wren sat up and pointed across the shore. "They're okay."

Koa held Sienna in his arms, crushing her against his chest. His lips brushed her damp forehead, lingering there while her curls clung in dark, wet spirals. Her clothes sagged heavy and crinkled around her frame, but there wasn't a wound visible. He was still flooding her with healing magic anyway, light pulsing faintly between his hands. If I knew my brother, he couldn't help it. He had to fix what wasn't even broken, just to make sure she stayed whole.

Salt burned the back of my throat, seawater still clinging to every crevice of my body—inside and out. The sense of being trapped under the weight of my cold clothing was overwhelming. Every inhale was sharp, stinging, and scraping against my ribs. We were out and safe, but I had no memory of how we got here. One moment we were sinking, my entire being filled with fear and panic, the next...

I remembered the unnatural and magical quality to the crash; we shouldn't have been alive. That was meant to kill us all. *How long had we been out? Who pulled us out? Who brought us back? How were any of us breathing right now?*

Wren shot to his feet faster than I thought possible for someone who'd damn near just drowned, and in the next breath, Koa was there beside him. Their bodies blocked my view, shoulders squared and tense, cutting off whatever had snapped them to attention.

Sienna's arm looped in mine, and she pulled me off the ground and pushed my hair away from my face. "You good, babe?"

"As good as I can be," I responded.

"What the hells happened?"

I shrugged as I searched my best friend's eyes to see if they mirrored my cocktail of fear and confusion. "I don't kno–"

We both perked up when the sharp click of a safety being released from a gun sounded. Koa and Wren held their ground in front of us, a living barricade.

"Show your fucking face, or I'll put a bullet in the shadows and let the gods sort it out," Koa snapped. "Your choice."

Someone emerged from the foliage with their hands raised. A mask covered their face, but they wore the same uniform as the rebels we'd fought at the dock. I didn't hesitate. I yanked one of the guns from Wren's belt and leveled it at the asshole.

"I mean no harm," they said.

"Not sure that phrase belongs in your vocabulary," Sienna spat.

Wren stepped forward, eyes narrowing. "Are you alone?"

"There are two others in a van by the bridge. We've been waiting for you to come to for over an hour now." They pointed to a hill where an SUV identical to the one Sienna was kidnapped in sat. "I'm going to take my mask off. Try not to get trigger-happy."

"No promises." Koa tilted his head in defiance.

Smooth brown skin lacking scars or age lines, with dark...kind, familiar eyes stared back at us. He couldn't have been much older than Koa. In slow and steady movements, the man removed his weapons and placed them on the ground between us before lifting his hands in surrender. Though the boys' fingers tickled their triggers, his attention fell stuck on Sienna.

He was a *Kawak*. I had absolutely no idea how I knew it without seeing him wield any magic, but I did. I felt it in that same place that ached before my nahual emerged—identifying his soul and the power tied to it.

"I got you all out of the water. I am not the enemy," he said.

"Right," Koa sneered, spitting into the dirt at the man's feet. "Because the rebels who spent hours *torturing* my girl and trying to fucking *kill us* go around playing the hero now?"

"You did take that first shot."

Koa fired a warning shot right over the rebel's head and Wren shot one into the ground next to him. He didn't so much as flinch.

Slowly, the man reached into his back pocket, and all of us refocused our weapons. The realization that he was once again an active target had him twisting at the torso to show the folded paper in his pocket.

"I work for Zélia. She had me follow you all when you left the dock. We understand what it must look like, but again, we are not the enemy. We did not cause that accident. We can, however, tell you who did." He stretched his hand out, offering the paper.

Koa and Wren shared a glance before crossing the space together. My brother didn't give his back to the rebel as he snatched the paper, but Wren still offered him cover. When they made it back to us, he held up the paper for everyone to see.

"Once she saw who you are, or more so, *what* you are...she recognized her mistake," the rebel soldier said, eyes fixed on me. "My name is Strider."

It was a letter from Zélia, that much was clear, but giving it our full attention while being watched by the rebels wasn't smart.

"Okay, Strider," Wren said coolly. "Why should we trust you?"

The rebel smirked. "Saving your life not enough?"

"No," Koa and Wren answered in unison.

Sienna waved her hand in a mocking gesture. "You had me strapped to a table a few hours ago."

"Again," Strider said with an exaggerated sigh. "She realizes her mistake."

"And what is it that you want?" I asked, watching for anything to indicate what he *wasn't saying*.

That was always where the real truth hid. It was practically science. A fidgeting hand, a crack in vocal tone, even shifty or unusual eye movements. Things that were mostly involuntary if you were someone with a conscience. Strider displayed none of these indications.

"First, I'd like to offer you information. If you trust me after that, I'll be happy to tell you what we want."

Koa's telepathic magic tickled my senses, an echo told me it wasn't just me he was talking to.

'Anyone object? Alternative is I turn him into stone and we go get some burgers.'

We all gave varying versions of encouragement to move forward. Extending trust wasn't going to happen, but there was no harm in pretending in exchange for information.

Koa gave him a nod. "Go on."

"We saw who caused the accident." He hesitated, as if gauging how much to reveal. Something I'd seen both Koa and Wren do, measuring how much leverage they could use and what they should keep. "It was the Cynod."

Wren stiffened where our bodies touched, a silent warning running through him. Sienna's glance held more contempt than surprise, her mouth pressed thin. Koa snarled under his breath, fingers whitening around the grip before he finally lowered his gun. Reluctantly, Wren and I mirrored him, though I kept mine loose in my hand.

"You don't seem surprised," Strider said with a crease between his brows. "You are the Canek children, no?"

Koa said nothing, only ticked his jaw left, then right, so I responded for us. "In hindsight, an assassination attempt is probably overdue."

"I'm a pain in their ass and Meems here is starting to take after her brother." My brother winked at me but the sadness in his eyes held a different story.

No matter how much it hurt, it was still the truth.

"I see," Strider responded, his gaze calculating. "Then joining our cause would be even more beneficial."

It was never that simple. Too many threads tangled between us for it to be reduced to one choice. These days, a common enemy did not make you friends, and it wasn't the time to test the theory.

"Is your cause about torturing innocent women…or?" I asked.

"Guess we won't be letting that go anytime soon," Strider mumbled. "We could have let you all drown. Instead, we're handling the Cynod lackey and saved you. Let that be an olive branch. We'd really like for you all to consider meeting us. All four of you," he said with his gaze ending on Sienna. "Zélia says as much in the letter."

The chances of Sienna setting foot back on that dock site were slim to none. My best friend could hold the world's longest grudge, and that was just the tip of the iceberg when it came to spite. Strider walked backward toward the van beside the bridge without another word.

"I'd like twenty-four hours with no weird-ass shit," Sienna said as she squeezed water from her shirt.

"No fucking kidding," Koa replied.

It was funny how peaceful and quiet this area of the sea was. As if no catastrophe had happened here. We were such small pieces of an incredibly large world. As the birds sang and hundreds of cars zoomed back and forth atop the bridge, I was reminded of just how inconsequential the accident might have been. The only evidence was the disturbed patch of grass on the bank where we'd been revived, leading into the frigid current that nearly swept our lives away.

I couldn't help but wonder who would have noticed we were gone first? Probably Katia and the Mercers. They were waiting for us, and we'd have to explain everything that had transpired. Judging from the information we'd gotten, our parents wouldn't have mourned us too much. They'd be more upset about the fact that their heirs were gone, and their string to power gone with us.

Even then, there had to have been a plan set. In the grand scheme, the Cynod would use our deaths for something bigger. Some way to get money for a made-up cause or compassion points among the people. Or they'd use it as a way to change the current lineage laws. That way they could appoint anyone with similar knacks for tyranny.

"How we feeling?" Wren asked with both hands on my cheeks.

He traced every line of my face, seeking out any sign that my anxiety was going to take over. It wasn't always like that for me. Something small could set me off, but often in these significant life-altering events, I was fine. My adrenaline kept me going to ensure I was out of danger. Now, the aftermath was a different story. Later, the smell of seawater, the honk of a horn, or breaking of glass might send me there, but right now I was fine.

"I'm not sure I've fully processed. It's all too much," I responded.

Wren brought his lips to my forehead. "I need to talk to you ab—"

Heavy footsteps closed in again, and three familiar faces broke through the cattails. Relief hit first, then curiosity as more figures followed. I didn't recognize them, though the resemblance to Jed and Adler was unmistakable. Sharp jawlines, the same piercing eyes and frames. I was certain the rest of the Mercer clan had arrived.

"We were tracking your location. Saw all four of you go down at the same time. Thought you were trying to set a record for synchronized drowning," Jed said as he pushed back a loc that fell free from his bound hair. "Thank the gods you weren't. That would've been awkward."

"Thanks, Jed," Sienna said.

"Welcome back to the land of the living for...what?" Jed's hand rubbed the bottom of his chin. "The second time today I hear?"

"Brought backup just in case we were going for a third," Adler added.

Sienna's chuckle was weak. "Wasn't dead the first time but was definitely nearing it the second."

Katia sprinted across the sand toward Sienna and me, her eyes darting over our wet bodies and dripping hair. She squeezed us in a fierce hug, holding Sienna a little longer since this was the first time she'd seen her since being captured. Unnatural wind picked up around us, warming by the second and drying us off.

Koa and Wren showed their gratitude in their own way, each landing a firm slap on the Mercer twins' shoulders.

"I want every tracker of yours off my property by midnight, Mercer," Koa added with a smirk to Adler.

Katia rolled her eyes, turning to us as the men huddled close and debriefed.

"So what happened?" Katia asked.

I let out a long, painful breath.

After filling Katia in on everything, I needed a second alone with my brother. Our thoughts appeared to align. He rubbed Sienna's back, then motioned for me to step aside with him, away from the others.

"Mercers have any information?" I asked.

"Nothing yet. Didn't hear any whispers of the Cynod interfering, but I don't doubt it." Koa pulled his phone out of his pocket. "Encrypted email."

He held the phone between us and double-tapped the attachment. A video played, a man I'd seen on the Cynod security detail, Tommy, with his hands behind his back. He groaned as a rebel soldier punched him in the stomach, and he spat blood onto the floor.

"I'm dead if I tell you what you want!" he yelled.

"You're dead either way," Zélia's voice drawled, uncaring. "You can die painfully, or you can die slowly. Either way, dead is dead. Send our regards to Cizin."

Tommy's head lolled forward, movements sluggish as blood trickled down his neck. His voice was a ragged, barely there whisper. "You're right...it was them. The Cynod...it was them."

The screen went black, and a message popped up reading, 'I'm not the enemy. They are.'

Before Koa could tap anything else, the email vanished from his phone. He swiped to the deleted folder, but there wasn't a single trace of what we'd just seen.

"What was his name? Timmy?" Koa said.

"I think it's Tommy. He was with the Cynod when they came to address the school," I responded.

Koa looked to be recollecting, but he was as bad with faces as he was with names. "Does he work for Mom and Dad or everyone?"

"I don't think he's contracted to only one member," I answered, then turned and yelled for Wren. "You remember Tommy?"

Wren nodded his head. "Shaved head, mustache? Guy's a fucking asshole."

"Not anymore. Zélia just sent us a video of her killing him. He's the one they sent after us."

Wren's jaw ticked as he looked out into the water. "He's not one of their usuals."

Now, to determine whether that was a last-ditch effort from the Cynod or if they were widening their net for jobs like this one. Zélia moved quickly. She must have followed us in the same vehicle as Strider and pulled Tommy into her shadows.

"Well, they can't send your brothers to do the job. He was probably eager for a pay bump," Koa muttered.

"Our family loyalty is how we got into this position in the first place. They know we would have said fuck the contract," Wren agreed.

"Regardless, this proves the rebels were right. Now what?" I asked.

Koa looked at me, then over to Sienna, who was still hanging back. Her arms were crossed, eyes narrowed like she was fighting off a thought before joining us.

"We get away from this damn bridge and back to your condo," she said to Koa, then paused before adding, "and once we're there, we need to talk. Alone. Ixchel told me something."

2

MIRA

Thankfully, the ride back to Koa's was smooth. Suspiciously so. You'd think a full-blown assassination attempt would have triggered at least a little Cynod follow-up. Nothing was out of place at the condo. No dark vans parked on the street. No eyes watching from the shadows.

Koa's truck was a goner, but he already had a new one on the way. Benefits of being a society reject with a penchant for 'entrepreneurship.' His words, not mine.

Every sudden noise sent us leaping into fight or flight. Car horns outside, footsteps pounding down the condo corridor, even the clatter of utensils in the kitchen had us frozen for a beat. Sienna cooked when she was stressed, over-whelmed, or experienced any sort of strong feelings in general. So she was already covered in flour and about four other things I couldn't place. Jed and Wren slipped out to chase leads, leaving only Katia and Adler behind. The quiet around us was almost unbearable in its tension.

We sat in the living room, staring off into space silently, when a buzzing startled us out of our disassociation. It took me a minute to realize the buzzing was coming from my phone. It turned face down in a slow circle atop the glass coffee table. But I knew who it was. She had her own special vibration pattern, one to alert me before I even looked at the contact.

"It's Mom," I said to Koa.

My brother snapped upright, any trace of zoning out gone in an instant as he shifted into both a predator and protector. "Answer it. Put it on speaker."

My thumb hovered, then tapped. I let her speak first.

"Mira?" she asked, her voice breaking slightly.

The air in the room was stagnant, as if a missile was hanging above our heads, and our response would bring it crashing down upon us. Our gazes bounced around, so much white in Katia's eyes. I was reminded that she wasn't accustomed to this sort of game.

No part of me wanted to respond. I wondered whether letting my mother think her mission was successful was worth it. But the chances of her not already knowing we were alive were slim. So instead, I gave an apprehensive response.

"Yes..." I trailed off.

"Solis, our intel was wrong." A sigh followed, and behind it, I caught the faint sound of my father clearing his throat.

Koa leaned forward, speaking straight into the phone. There was no trace of a question in his voice, only accusation. "Hm, you have intel."

"We were advised of a rebellion attack. They claimed they were going after children of the Cynod," our mother replied.

"Convenient." Koa looked at me, deadpanned.

I could practically hear the hesitation on her end. We weren't on mute; shuffling of feet and breaths were still coming through the line. If I had to make a bet, my parents were having a silent conversation with just their eyes. An attempt at quickly reconciling and creating a plan before moving forward.

"We're walking into an emergency Cynod meeting. I'll contact you both later."

I locked the phone and set it down as I tried to return some moisture to my throat. "What are we supposed to do with that?"

"Someone is lying," Koa grumbled, his jaw tight and barely moving. "As much as I'd like it to be the rebellion, I doubt it."

The smells from the kitchen wafted into the living room as a timer buzzed, and I realized Sienna was baking her special pot pies. I should have known that's what she was making; it was one of her comfort foods. She'd said that both the process of cooking them and the feeling she got when she ate them brought her solace. She came back through the doorway, tossing her apron onto the breakfast bar, and plopped down next to Koa.

"Feeling better?" I asked.

She gave a small, unsure nod. "A little."

Light filtered in through the small gaps between the curtains. The realization that we'd been up all night, and it was now morning, hit me. My body was dead tired, but my mind was still trying to piece things together. Koa reached for Sienna's hand, his tattoo sparkling in the narrow sliver of sunlight.

"Wait, you left something out," Katia said as she inspected the tattoo at a closer glance. "What the fuck is that?"

Sienna stiffened. So much had happened in the last few hours, and with our adrenaline finally waning, the solitary happy moment at the docks had been forgotten.

"Fuck, we need to cover these," Koa said.

Adler's brows furrowed as he crossed the room, leaning in. "Is that what I think it is?" He reached to touch Koa, then thought better of it, not even considering trying Sienna, though the resistance was noticeable.

The mate mark was one of the few things that hadn't been entirely erased. The glimmering tattoo was still found in art, in stories, on old statues. It was too...romantic to fully die out.

As much as Koa wanted to be a nonchalant, not love-sick boy, he couldn't hide the beaming smile that overtook his face. "Yeah."

"Congrats, man." Adler clapped him on the shoulder with a grin. It was about as casual an embrace the two would share, but it was nice seeing Koa welcome others into his life again.

Katia shrieked, jumping up and down, which finally caused a smile to break out on Sienna's face too.

"It's more complicated than that," Sienna said, and they both sat back down. "Koa's parents have other plans for him. They want to arrange a marriage. Since they don't even recognize the old gods, I don't think we're in the clear just yet."

"Well, I'm still happy for you," Katia said.

"Can you glamour it?" I asked.

"Maybe, but any well-trained *Ajaw* can see through that, our mother included," Koa responded. "Might need to wear long sleeves until we figure this out."

"Good thing I look great in jackets." Sienna rubbed her temples. "One thing at a time."

My phone buzzed again, but this time I was perfectly happy with who it was from.

> **My family is okay. No new information. Will check in soon.**

"Wren's family is safe. Nothing new yet," I said, and Koa tapped his finger on his leg. We were all exhausted, and as much as Wren had healed me, my body still ached. We didn't have to go back to school until Monday, and if it were up to me, I'd sleep until then.

Katia stretched her arms with a yawn, then nudged Adler with her foot. "We should check on Jed, anyway."

Adler glanced at her, clearly wanting to stay for a meal but getting the hint that the three of us needed some time to process without company.

"Oh. My bad. Yeah," he said, reaching for his keys. "You three probably need a minute."

"Thanks," Sienna said quietly.

Katia squeezed my shoulder as she passed. "If you need anything…"

"I know." I smiled weakly.

The front door shut behind them. I got up to lock it and to get myself something to drink. Water was the smart choice, though I craved something stronger. Like a tequila ginger, light on the ginger.

Sienna slumped into the cushions of the couch. "I know we're all exhausted and whatnot, but there's something else I gotta get off my chest to sleep easy."

I glanced over. Koa's eyes were trained on her.

"When we were pulled into that god realm…for the mate ceremony, Ixchel clarified some things," she followed up.

Sienna and I had been friends for so long, it was rare I couldn't get a solid read on her. I always knew how she was feeling, or really, an idea of what she was about to say. Staring between her and Koa, for the first time, I felt left out. Koa sat intently, waiting for her to speak.

She drew in a breath. "She finished the prophecy—"

I dropped my glass in surprise, and it clattered against the tile in the kitchen. Peering around the corner, I stole another look their way. They both stared up at me, one with annoyance and my best friend with timid humor.

"Sorry," I muttered, finding my way back to the living room.

"She said: *A Manik will spark the flame of rebellion. For death is the beginning and death is the end—its touch will ignite a new cycle,*" Sienna continued, then looked my way. "I think...I think that's you and Tía, Mira. That's the part that seems to have already kicked off."

My throat constricted with loss and fear.

Her eyes flickered to Koa. "Um, Ixchel didn't stop there. *When two halves of the same soul unite, balance shall return to the land. Two branches from the same tree take root for the first of their kind.* That last bit," she added with a whisper, "I think it's about us. You and me, Koa. The bond...two halves of the same soul. You're a Canek, and I'm...well, I'm just a Hayes. We aren't exactly known to be powerful. But *I* am. If we marry...it could represent balance. The lines...the families—that's you and Mira. It's the first time two Cynod lines have crossed."

Splendid.

3

KOA

I t was apparent that I'd overslept by the sheer amount of light blinding me the moment I opened my eyes. The heavy velvet curtains Sienna forced me to hang weeks ago were nothing more than decoration. Allowing the light of day to wake you was good for your health. I knew that—but people did things that were bad for them every day and blackout curtains never killed anyone.

Complaining was hard when I was rewarded with watching her work. She hummed along to the smooth, melodic music playing at a near-muted volume as she kneeled before her canvas. Each stroke was sharp. Her touch was precise, careful where she placed each line of color—different from her usual wild lines of paint.

Things had been rough since she revealed what Ixchel laid on her. That was a lot for one person to carry. Being touched by a goddess was one thing, holding their secrets was another. Yes, she'd shared with Mira and me, but that didn't absolve her of the pressure of figuring out what it meant. Since she'd been trusted explicitly, she took that weight on as if it were hers and hers alone.

We all agreed it was pretty obvious who was who now that shit had played out. Making sense of it all was a whole other beast. Top it all off with the shit my parents were mixed into, and her even gracing the walls of my condo right now was a gift in itself. I wasn't sure how Mira was coping with it. She'd shut me out aside from the 'I'm okay, worry about my friend, please' response she gave every time I attempted to check in on her.

I couldn't even say the shit with our parents hurt, because it didn't. To be hurt, you had to have faith the person hurting you would never strike you in such a manner. I never gave those two pricks that much credit. Sadness, however, definitely sat heavy on my chest. It made me revert to a younger, more naive Koa. A version of me that had died the first time my father had raised his hand and my mother hadn't asked him to stop.

"How are you awake right now?" I grumbled, pushing up on the mattress with a yawn.

Drowning fucking hurt; surviving it didn't take away the searing, burning sensation. Knowing Sienna had experienced every ounce of agony that still stained my lungs days later left me exhausted with despair. Influence of the bond or not, seeing her suffer through the trauma of the weekend pulled at pieces of my soul.

"And waste sunlight? No thanks." Sienna's smirk was there, but it didn't reach her eyes—those haunted, tired eyes that had so recently stared death in the face three too many times. "Besides, I was feeling inspired."

She shifted back, moving away from the center of the canvas. Sienna's magic bled into her work, making the image move, breathe. A gnarled tree stood at the center, its roots thick and untamed, clawing through the surface as if fighting for freedom. The bark rose in jagged ridges, vines creeping along the edges, their leaves unfurling slowly, and catching the light as they stretched awake.

Her fingers hovered over the exposed branches. She circled them with trembling precision. Flowers bloomed in real time, petals peeling open to the rhythm of her humming. It was impossible as far as I was concerned. It was magic.

It was her.

"You did all this while I was sleeping?" My voice came out rough, still weighted with exhaustion.

Sienna's smirk widened into a true smile. "It's not like you were going to wake up and entertain me. You Caneks could sleep until the moon rises, then do it all over again twice over."

"You've been practicing," I huffed a laugh, wanting a closer look. I slid out of bed and walked over toward her, placing my hands on her shoulders and giving them a slight squeeze. She leaned into my touch. "It's beyond words."

The air shifted in the room, all lightness now void. "Don't lie to me, snake." Sienna shrugged me off playfully, staring back at her creation. Confidence with magic took time. All fae knew that. We went through a little over two decades of our lives without it. It was a learning curve—as with many things in life, practice made perfection. "Besides, no time better than the present to master all that comes with being a *Kaban* since, apparently, there's a price on my head."

Hearing those words leave her lips was nauseating. "Comes with being a Canek...and my mate. Hate to say kidnapping is always high on the list of possibilities now that you're in my world."

There was always a price on my head—whether it was from business or being a Cynod heir. My sister's too. With her being Mira's best friend, I suppose the threat had always been there. Now she had a tie to both of us, and being dragged right into the middle of our shit wasn't fair. Life wasn't fair. I was well fucking aware of that. The only thing I could do was make sure she was prepared to fight back on the off chance it was attempted again. She would never go a day without training from here on out.

Despite the blatant danger, Sienna only held her head higher, a sparkle dancing back into her dark brown eyes. She released a sigh and then grinned. "High price but worth it, I guess."

"You guess?" I bit down on my tongue in tease, offering her a hand up.

"Those were the words I chose to use, yep," Sienna surmised as she dropped her paintbrush into a cup of water and took my hand. "Come on, I let you sleep in. I can't be late for this class. Midterms are next week, and my grades aren't exactly great."

"You're doing your best. Need an extension on your readings? I can talk to Inés—"

Sienna whirled on me, brow arched. "Inés? You mean Professor Duarte?"

I scratched the back of my neck, words failing me. Nothing I could say would get me out of this hole—it would only dig it deeper. A hesitant laugh that only Sienna Hayes could bring escaped me. She was aware of my past. But hey, what could I say? Being in love could change a man's priorities.

"Classy," she said, turning her back to me and tossing a dismissive hand in the air as she made her way to the bathroom. "No, I've made it this far in life without the Canek name steering my fate, might as well see it through. Builds character."

She slammed the door behind her, and I sighed. Glancing around the room, I made my way over to the bed to semi-make it the way she preferred. Not too neat that it looked 'snobbish,' but put-together enough to ease her mind when she got back from class and was ready to chill out.

My phone buzzed from the nightstand on the other side of the bed. I unplugged it, reading the text with a roll of my eyes.

NOLA:

> *Was the plan to fake your death and leave The Underworld to me, or can I assume you did, in fact, make it out of that water?*

"Fuck," I muttered. It had been my intention to keep word from getting out. If Nola knew from underground chatter, then that meant the media was only a fe—

The grating chime of a ChismeChak article popped up on a banner at the top of my screen.

Assassination Attempt? Cynod Heirs & Notorious Ikari Criminal Fall From Kuxtal Island Bridge

"Fucking perfect." I clenched the sides of my phone, thumbs slamming against the screen to type out my response. There was a long list of shit I was certain Aurora and Emeric Canek had prepared to say to us. Being caught red-handed in association to a notorious crime family was going to be at the top of it.

Me:

> *We're going to have to discuss how you greet your boss.*

"Is Mira up?" I called out to Sienna.

With the news of the 'accident,' we were going to have to fight the press out of the garage and onto the academy grounds. An aspect of this life I envied Mira for escaping. Everything I did ended up a headline, good or bad, some of which resulted in total harassment from the media. Mira had been removed from the limelight for so long, and after tossing her meds, I didn't want this to trigger her.

She'd been alright so far, but everyone had their limits. I would hate to have to put a hit out on someone for testing hers. It was going to hit her the hardest. And with the media spinning various theories on why an Ikari was caught with the two of us—star-crossed lovers was the most popular story. Being romantically tied to an Ikari would likely give my mother an aneurysm. Not to mention a death warrant on his head from our father.

Sienna poked her head out the bathroom, curls falling from the scrunchie bunched at the top of her head, toothbrush hanging on the side of her mouth. "Um, I was hoping it could just be you and me this morning. Stop for coffee and walk me to class?"

I narrowed my eyes. Her gaze darted too quickly. Not answering the question that I asked. We'd been holed up in the condo all weekend. Wren had left to see his family, said his mom freaked out when she heard what happened. Must be nice, having parents who gave half a shit.

Inside these walls, at least, things felt contained. Safe, in a way. I wasn't letting either of the girls out of my sight until I figured out what was going on. Which was why—for now—they were staying here.

"Where is she?"

"She texted after we went to sleep last night." She spat the toothpaste into the sink, using her washcloth to wipe the toothpaste from the sides of her mouth. "I guess Wren's going dark for a few days on some job and wanted to say goodbye, so she slept there."

That didn't sit right. Any time Ikari went dark, I knew. Well in advance. Always. Even if it were Cynod business, we had a system. Protocol. Wren and I coordinated—Underworld tasks handed off, timelines set. I usually had seventy-two hours' notice before he ghosted. Not this. This was new. Not to mention ill fucking timed.

Another buzz drew my attention back down to my phone.

Nola had never been shy about her faith in the old gods. It was part of her appeal. Solis was a curse word to her. And since I now had indisputable truth that they never really went away, that was probably a damn good thing.

Me:

Even the mere hypothetical of someone of my...status, for lack of a better word, being injured was bad for business. It made me appear weak. Someone could make a big play to fill the spot they believed I was no longer powerful enough to keep. If they thought I was dead...

"Tell her to make her way to campus, *now*."

Sienna spritzed her hair with a spray bottle, glancing me up and down. "Tell her yourself or learn how to ask me nicely."

NOLA:

I crossed the room in three strides, grabbing Sienna by the waist and pulling her close. Her breath hitched, but she didn't pull away. My eyes locked onto hers. "Please, let my sister know to head to campus. News is out. Press knows Ikari is tied to us through the accident. I need to call Nola. Be ready in thirty."

"Have they always been this aggressive?" Mira said, her tortoise-shell sunglasses not doing enough to block out the bright camera light damn near blinding us as we rushed toward the safety of the campus wards.

"Yes," I grumbled as I stalked toward an asshole gunning straight for her, unconcerned about respecting her personal space. Smacking the camera out of his hands, I slammed my boot onto the lens shattering it to pieces, my chest rattled, daring him to protest. "It's worse now because they haven't had free access to you in years."

Sienna walked ahead of us, chin high, chest forward, flipping off the cameras with both hands and a lethal glare. A gap split open in the wall of photographers as Katia shoved through, stepping in beside her. She joined Sienna in disrupting their attempts of getting a shot that wouldn't have to be censored to publish. Their vulgar gestures filled the spaces their bodies couldn't block, and I worked to clear a path through.

"Mama is going to *love* this one," Katia's accent tripped on the words. "Jarrod, how are you? How would you feel about your press pass being revoked in Jundi? Back *off*."

The specific lilt in her voice—something about the sharp consonants and the way she dragged the vowels—caught on the edges of my memory, familiar in a way I couldn't place. Like a half-buried echo from another life. It scraped against something I should have recognized, something important, but the connection slipped through my fingers before I could grab hold of it.

Under the safety of the wards, the press wasn't able to follow us on to the main campus. Their noise quieted the second we crossed through, now nothing more than a muted muffle. Without the permission of Dean Cocum, it was impossible to access campus unless you were a student or staff. The only reason they were allowed at orientation was because the wards were lifted for the day.

"Where's Wren?" Katia asked, scrolling on her phone as we passed by the book store, K'ux Eating Hall now in view. "Ew," she groaned, holding her phone up for us to see.

I kept my distance, the girls leaning closer. As much as I adored Mira and loved Sienna, I had no interest in seeing whatever PhotoPhantom post they were seconds away from talking shit about.

Mira mumbled, zooming in on whatever they were looking at. "He's on a job, had to go dark...what the fuck."

"They're really pushing their luck here." Sienna glanced up at me, concern lacing her features. She didn't want me to lash out. I understood—it didn't mean I would make any promises for my behavior.

Mira sighed and shoved the phone into my chest. The Cynod was coming to campus to address the safety concerns of Inecha. Our *accident* had apparently shaken the nation. Nearly dying was bad for political stability, especially when it involved two heirs to the government's future and the son of a notorious criminal. Guess they didn't think that shit through. With the country's 'brightest minds' and most well-connected elites attending Kuxtal, it was protocol to address us separately.

That meant they had contacted us. Our phones had been off in order to avoid the harassment of the media. Gods forbid we had missed a call from them—we'd pay for the disrespect.

"I'll turn mine on," I said to Mira, and she thanked me with a slight smile.

"We'll catch up with you in a minute." She did her best to politely dismiss her friends, but I could see the anxiety already swelling in her eyes.

Sienna pushed to her toes, kissing me on the cheek and drawing attention from a few onlookers brave enough to meet my glare. They averted their gazes going back to practicing their magic or studying before first classes of the day. The girls squeezed Mira's hand, then turned down the path to K'ux.

Linda, our mother's assistant, number popped up on the screen the second my phone turned on. "Yeah," I said, not bothering with faux pleasantries.

"Good morning, Koa, it's Linda." She always tried too hard, her tone too chipper, attitude far too positive to be working under such a soul-sucking woman.

"Obviously."

Mira gave me a look that said to play nice, but I had no such inclination. They wanted something we had no desire to provide—our time. Our audience. Or rather, the other way around. I'd played their games long enough to know what was coming. We hadn't heard a word from them all weekend. Which meant something was moving beneath the surface.

And we were about to find out exactly what.

Linda released a nervous chuckle. "Yes, well. As I'm sure you heard, your parents will be speaking at the academy in a few hours."

"We're unfortunately aware of this tragedy. Send our regards."

"Linda." Mira grabbed my phone, elbowing me in the side as she started pacing until she settled on a bench on the edge of the greenery along the path. "Is this something we can get out of or not?"

"It's just lunch," she said, but her voice went small. She was cheerful but not oblivious.

"We all know it's never just a meal, Linda. Time and place."

"Campus diner," she answered me, still timid. "At noon, they've excused you from your afternoon classes."

"Fantastic." I snatched the phone back from my sister and hung up. Mira slumped onto the bench. Leave it to them to ruin one of the few places on campus that wasn't tainted with their essence—where I didn't feel out of place.

The campus diner was the only building vaguely untouched by their influence. Before they were the Cynod, before they were the architects of a world I wanted no part of, my parents were just two fae. Young adults who sat at one of those back tables, hands brushing over stolen bites of food, laughter spilling between them like something real. I didn't have many illusions about them anymore, but there—watching fae repeat centuries of history—I could almost pretend. And now they were dragging their politics and bullshit into it.

Mira kicked at a stray pebble, jaw tight. "I hate them."

"Yeah, Meems. I think they hate us too, but at least we never wanted them dead."

4

KOA

Students gawked at the barrier of suits outside the campus diner as if they'd never seen Cynod level security before. Zane Ikari posted up at the entrance, arms uncrossing as we approached. His eyes swept the crowd before holding the door open for us.

Mira's curiosity flickered, barely hidden. We hadn't talked about Wren leaving, and it was clear she hadn't fully processed what it meant, or why his brother had been left behind. Ikaris didn't take jobs alone. Maybe Atlas was with him, though I doubted it; I'd seen him post on PhotoPhantom this morning beachside, looking very much not on a mission. I pressed my hand to Mira's shoulder and shook my head. Now wasn't the time for the questions we both wanted answered.

The usual buzz of the diner had vanished, leaving a heavy stillness in its place. The walls, once rich with sunbaked tones, seemed duller now—drained of the laughter and late-night confessions they used to carry. Even the old woven tapestries sagged in silence, their once-busy threads now dim, as if the stories inside them had gone quiet. All but one corner of the place was empty—the booth typically occupied by the pitz team.

"Mira." Our mother rushed forward, her heels clicking against the tiled floor. Her black suit pulled taut at the extension of her arms when she came to an awkward halt as though she'd wanted to embrace her but thought better of it. The relief on her face was evident. She scanned Mira over, checking for any injuries.

Noticing posture, tension, anything that might hint at a fracture beneath the surface.

Physical injuries could be patched. The rest? Harder to control. And beneath the mirage of relieved parent rested a woman who built her entire life around control.

Unfortunately her next target was me. My mother glanced me over from a distance, her scrutiny bordering genuine concern. "Benício," she said and the name suddenly brought me back to my childhood.

It was my middle name, but it was what she'd affectionately referred to me as when I was a young and dumb kid. Before they'd moved up in the Cynod. When our joke of a family could be considered normal. Named after my grandfather, the one person she'd ever shown an ounce of genuine affection toward, even in memory.

I offered her a tense nod, jaw locking and she motioned for us to follow her to the booth where our father remained—unmoved. He scanned from Mira over to me methodically, boredom flickering in his eyes now that he'd set eyes on us. Our father had better places to be as far as he was concerned. Like terrorizing the country and deciding the next war our troops were 'needed' in. We slid into the burgundy leather seats, our parents on one side, the two of us on the other despite the clear divide within the curved seat connecting us.

"Your father and I used to sit in this very booth as students." Our mother pushed her straightened hair behind her pointed ear, her cheeks flushing at the memory.

I didn't bother hiding my disgust. "We don't care."

The nostalgia act was insulting. She didn't get to pretend this was some warm family reunion. I honestly couldn't say the last time we'd sat down for a family meal. We took family vacations for the press, sure, but once we were there, they went to one side of the four walls, and Mira and I went to the other. No need to play happy family when no one was watching. Plus, I was pretty fucking sure it was easier for them to pretend they hadn't screwed us up when we weren't in their faces. Better for everyone that way. Our mother checked in every month or so, but the only time we heard from our father since moving out was when he needed something.

It hurt Mira. She never said it out loud, but once upon a time, he'd brought her around his troops, toting her as a little warrior. That was before the anxiety set in. Never after.

Our mother reached across the table and touched Mira's tapping fingers with a gentle hand. "Mira?"

"You talk to me, not her," I said as Mira snatched her hand away, the tapping of her fingers changing to the bounce of her knee. She offered our mother nothing more than a heavy stare.

Emeric Canek spoke for the first time, his husky voice a sound familiar in my nightmares. "Enough with the theatrics. This is excessive, even for you."

I let the silence drag. Sat back against the booth, arms folding across my chest—-all the time in the world to waste. Making them late to whatever they had to do next on their 'Fuck Inecha' tour brought me joy. "Just tell us what you want. I assume it has to do with the latest headlines."

"If you could stay out of them, it would make our arrangement easier on us all," he retorted, dumping a pack of artificial sugar into his black coffee.

"Emeric." Our mother interrupted with a sternness in her voice I'd yet to see her direct at him.

She never did that. Not with me. Maybe Mira, sometimes, when she was in the rare mood to parent, but never with me. What happened between my father and I was none of her business for twenty-five years. I didn't give a shit why she'd start putting a stop to the tension now.

I flashed a grin, all teeth, knowing exactly how much it'd piss my father off. "You know how I love the attention."

Mira kicked me under the table.

I barely reacted. "Unfortunately, the blame can't be placed on me for this one."

"Do tell." His ink-stain colored eyes narrowed. "You obviously have some asinine theory you'd love to enlighten us with. Let's hear it. I'm excited to see what the drug-inspired mind can conjure."

The server arrived, setting down our food that I couldn't seem to recall ordering. Mom ordered a brisket sandwich. She *never* ate grease, but she inhaled like she'd worship Solis for another splash of it on her truffle fries. Our father, a

BLT—a predictable lunch for him back home. As a kid, Mira's top dinner request was breakfast. It was no surprise the Solis Supreme Breakfast Platter was dropped before her followed by a mac n' cheese burger in front of me. The kind I used to mash together when they had charity barbecues at the house.

It felt deliberate. Like they wanted us to notice they were making some sorry excuse for an effort. After orchestrating the end of our lives—it was far too late for that sort of bullshit.

Mira poked at her plate. "What is this?"

"Before addressing the rest of the students, we wanted to check in on you."

"And?" I prompted our mother to continue.

"And discuss some family business."

"We're fine." Mira focused on our father, who casually dipped his sandwich into a tin of aioli.

Everything about this interaction had me shift in my seat, waiting for the ball to drop. "So skip to the good part," I said.

Mom dabbed her mouth with a napkin, composed as ever after taking the smallest of bites. "Very well. Mira." Her gaze settled on my sister. "With the stability of the nation in question from your...accident and the involvement of potential rebels, it is important that we mend all relations with other states to ensure a united front."

"You mean Jundi?" Mira hammered, the shaking stopped. "Say what you mean, you want me to use my friendship with Katia to get to her mom. Use their connections to get back in their good graces."

"I am failing to see an issue with such a request," our father's tone was smooth, unimpressed. His dark brown skin caught in the afternoon light, dust dancing in the streams of the sun.

"What happened to you?" Mira stared at him, unblinking. The question was clear. What happened to the fae in him? What killed his soul?

Emeric did not answer.

"We were hoping that your friendship would grant you access to their lands," Mom said, careful, like she was explaining something inevitable. I got it now.

Good cop, bad cop. How original. "To meet with her mother, show there is a future in the Cynod that aligns with their...values."

"It's not a curse word," I huffed a laugh full of regretful, sour pity.

My father spared me no glance. "We will deal with you shortly."

"What the fuck does that mean?"

I should have been more focused on the fact that they wanted to use Mira. Parade her around as proof the Cynod could be trusted, that the Caneks were something *they* never were. But that phrasing—*deal with you*—stuck sharper than glass in my ribs.

Emeric leaned back, unreadable. "There will come a time when you both sit at the head of the table. And then, and only then, will you understand the importance of a state bordering the land that they do."

The Sacred Lands.

I let out a short, humorless breath. "Well, we were one accident away from that relationship never being mended then, weren't we?"

Mira scoffed—half a chuckle, half disgust.

Our mother exhaled, slow and measured, then set her napkin down beside her near untouched plate. "Which is why we have decided to move forward with confirming your engagement. It's time to think about the future," she continued. "The responsibilities that come with the Canek name can no longer be ignored. You'll graduate in a year. An heir will be expected within two. The dalliance with the Hayes girl ends today."

Heat crawled up my spine, slow and smothering, then ignited. The rattle in my chest could not be contained.

She didn't pause. "And before you think to *lecture* me on the values of love, Mira. We are fully aware that Wren Ikari was in the car with you and your brother during the accident. Allow this to be a reminder to you both. People like him can serve us, protect our interests, even join us for a little fun in the privacy of four enclosed walls—but they cannot...mix beyond their place. That line exists for a reason, Koa. And you, of all people, should understand it."

"Like nine hells it does." I shot up from the table, fighting off the pending shift that threatened to emerge at the threat of separation from my mate.

Plates jumped, silverware clattered against porcelain. Mira's pulse thumped in a rhythm I could almost see in her neck.

Only our mother flinched. Emeric gave a single nod to Zane, who now stood at the door to the quiet dining room meant for those deep in study. His shoulders were slightly hunched, eyes flicking toward me with a faint, almost apologetic expression before he opened the door. More members of the Ikari clan appeared inside with Wren nowhere in sight.

She walked in like a force of nature—tall, even by fae standards, with a presence that demanded attention. Her features were sharp, almost *too* perfect in their sculpt. The high cheekbones and angular jawline gave her an air of something that screamed...untouchable, and she knew it. They didn't shove her. Their hands hovered near her arms—she was here by choice, at least, for now.

Her dark, sun-kissed skin seemed to glow with the promise of something dangerous, something that could steal your breath by just existing. The allure to her was unusual, though it was clear she was not *Xtabay*.

Hazel eyes that erred on the side of green lured me in and suffocated me in a feeling that said I may never escape. *Ajaw*—like my mother. The only nahuales that forced me to confront the fact that I was still fae and had fears. She sauntered across the room, her focus directly on me.

My father cleared his throat. "Alanna and you will walk to Buluc Chabtan auditorium. *Together*. Do not embarrass us."

"Koa," Mother warned, "Sienna can be removed from the academy if she will be a distraction."

"Excuse m—"

"The same goes for you, Mira," Emeric's tone was final as he interrupted her. "If the relationship with Jundi cannot be mended by the end of the school year, we will be forced to assume Sienna is a distraction for you as well. If you care about her education, her future, the two of you will complete your tasks and you will do it without further argument. As for the Ikari boy, do not allow yourself to be captured in such a predicament again."

The words landed like a death knell.

I met Mira's eyes. She met mine.

'Fuck them.'

'I don't think we have a choice here, Koa,' Mira responded.

Our mother's stare was sharp. She knew what we were doing, how we were cutting them out of the conversation.

'Warn Sienna for me? Please.'

'Yep.' Mira shrugged her shoulders in defeat. *'I wish us both the best of luck with that.'*

There was no point in pretending, no point in asking for mercy. We were already condemned.

Sienna. The girl I'd promised myself I'd protect—my mate, the one I wasn't allowed to have, the one they couldn't know existed. At the thought, fucking rage clawed its way up my spine. I put that fire out. I could not fall victim to that weakness now. My chest felt like it was caving in, but pain didn't make me falter. It made me fight.

"I'm not your puppet," I growled, but even as the words left my mouth, it was clear they meant nothing.

We were trapped in a cage, no room to move, and they held the key.

Our mother smiled as though it were all settled. "Now eat your lunch and entertain polite conversation. The photographers will be here soon. Mira, move next to me please. Chin up and fix that slump in your shoulders." She flicked her fingers at Mira. "Alanna will sit next to your brother. The two of them should exchange pleasantries before we announce their engagement during our speech. Better optics that way, you'll appear less...rigid."

Linda entered with freshly pressed uniforms, setting them on the table behind us.

"Change before we go." Our mother barely spared us a glance. "I can't believe the two of you leave the house in this state. You should be steaming your clothes. You look disastrous."

Alanna slid in the booth beside me, perfectly composed, eyes bright with satisfaction. Her uniform was oddly familiar though adjustments had been made from the standard. The looseness of the tie, the oversized Kuxtal cream sweater, the rolled-up skirt. It was Sienna's style but on her, it was every bit of wrong. Disgust crept back in and I leaned the opposite direction on reflex.

She turned to my parents first, nodding with rehearsed grace. "Aurora." Then, with a sweetness that made my stomach turn, "Emeric. So lovely to see you again. My grandfather sends his well wishes, he was very saddened to hear about the attempt. The rebel situation is at the forefront of Mentiria's policy docket this year. We're quite accustomed to handling such...disputes. It would bring us much joy to assist."

"Ambassador Osorios is always a joy to have. I trust he traveled well back to Mentiria with the extra security."

"Of course." Alanna set her attention on me. She took me in slowly. Measured. And when she smiled, it was no longer just polite. It was hungry. "I look forward to getting to know you. May Solis bless this union."

The gaze of a Canek was notoriously said to be strong enough to kill. My father's hung steady, unblinking—a leash around my throat that tightened with every breath I took. I could hear his unspoken command in the silence: *Don't push me.*

I glanced toward Mira, a promise sat in her sad stare. We had to play the game and we had to play it right. There wasn't shit we could do about now—except plan. Understand what we were up against and the Cynod's motives.

"Likewise. May Solis bless."

5

MIRA

I typed another text to Wren and watched as the sending bar slowly rolled across the top of my phone. There was a good chance that, like the last five texts I'd sent, it wouldn't go through either. He was off-grid, I knew that, but it couldn't have come at a worse time. I might have felt better if he was more specific about what he was doing. Especially after what we'd gone through.

I'd leaned on Sienna for most of my life, but with the bullshit that they just got hit with, I was trying not to pile my own on her. A theme lately, me trying not to be a burden on her, no matter how many times she said I wasn't.

There was a time our only problems were catty girls and passing our tests. What I wouldn't do to go back to that. We couldn't choose our problems, the same way we couldn't choose the good things in our lives. She was a testament to that today. Shit, so was I. Neither of us would have dreamed of being with the people we were, but alas. Here we were...with criminals.

The one common denominator for 99 percent of our issues was my parents. It was one thing for me to take more responsibility as a child of the Cynod. I was kidding myself to think I'd actually get away from that. But trying to take advantage of my friendship with Katia was taking it too far. In the grand scheme of things, Koa had it far worse, but still. Using my friends was wrong.

The real question at hand was why. Why did they need to make false peace with that land? Katia had told us once that Jundi had a great relationship with the people of the Sacred Lands. Because of their proximity, many of the 'Cynod values,' as my mother put it, weren't relevant there.

They still worshipped the old gods. Residents from the Sacred Lands were common in Jundi, which meant they had to want something more than land and power. My parents weren't stupid, as much as I liked to think otherwise. They were calculated. The trick was staying a step ahead of them, and that was no simple task. Their entire lives had been spent perfecting the art of being untouchable.

I squared my shoulders and lifted my chin as I made it to the Buluc Chabtan arena. Koa was with Alanna, his... fiancée? I was sure he was probably only a few yards behind me. He'd told me to go ahead, no reason for both of us being in her forced company. It took effort not to glance back, but I knew exactly what I'd see. One very fake smile on Alanna's face, and Koa looking as if he wanted to turn her to stone.

I'd met hundreds of 'Alannas'—my own mother was an Alanna at one point. Young, ambitious, ready to take power by any means necessary, and most of all, factitious. Neither of us ever had the patience for false pleasantries, though my ability extended far beyond my brothers.

Sienna hadn't read a single one of my texts, which meant I had to be the messenger in person. Awesome. The arranged marriage issue wasn't exactly breaking news. She'd learned it was an impending possibility after the gala mere weeks ago. Our parents had been pushing potential brides at him ever since. What she didn't know, however, was that in the last twenty minutes, it had gone from hypothetical to official. Koa couldn't reach her telepathically from a distance, so that lovely responsibility fell to me.

Pulling up the FindAFae app we used to track each other's location, I saw that she was still in the lobby of the arena. I tracked her to the exact spot she was standing, finding Katia and her in a very intense conversation, neither of them with their phones in hand. Figures.

"Hey! I need to talk to you," I shouted to Sienna.

For a heartbeat, her face lit with relief at seeing me. The smile crumbled into devastation so raw it radiated in her eyes. Before I could blink, her countenance twisted again, mouth curling into a sneer aimed at the arena's entrance.

I was too late.

Koa walked in with Alanna glued to his side, her arm hooked through his like she'd been born there. Her practiced smile made my stomach turn. If it were someone else, I might have asked how she achieved such faux warmth. The room hushed. Somewhere close, stone cracked. Thin fissures webbed through the granite beneath my feet, vines straining through the gaps as Sienna surged forward, fury dragging the earth up with her.

I grabbed her arm mid-stride. When she whipped her head toward me, I froze. I'd never seen that look on her—rage so sharp it scorched, a storm boiling behind her pupils, hot and wild and ready to strike. They said mates were territorial, and fuck, they were right.

"That's what I was trying to tell you. Just hold on, don't make a scene," I managed, trying to sound calm.

"Mir, her dirty ass hands are on my man."

Vines curled tighter around her legs, thorns sprouting sharp as teeth. The tips gleamed red and dripped with something that promised pain. They swayed at her sides, hungry, restless, waiting for her word. For now, all eyes were on Koa. That focus could shift in an instant.

I folded my hands under my chin in a plea. "I know, but my parents are here and looking for anything against you. Reel in your magic and I'll explain."

Reluctantly, the vines retreated, the crack in the stone sealed, and Sienna finally exhaled. She touched the lavender necklace at her throat, muttering a half-serious "woosah" like it might keep her from exploding.

"I'm as calm as I'm going to get. What the fuck is happening?" Her eyes stayed shut.

"My parents." I shook my head. "You know, they mentioned arranged marriage before. This is the candidate they're pushing. Her grandfather is an ambassador from Mentiria, he rejected every attempt to pay them off. Koa got rid of the others, but this one is here. We're going to figure it out, I promise."

Katia's hand pressed between her shoulders, easing nothing. Sienna cracked her neck. "I know the solution. I'll just kill her."

"Okay, you know I'm ride or die. I'll help you bury a body in a second. With that in mind, let's think this through," I said.

"Mhm."

"This means they don't know about...you know." I flicked my gaze down to her mate tattoo, or where it was beneath her long sleeves. "This also means there is leverage to be gained, if we can figure it out. You trust Koa, right?"

"I do. This thing is only seeing her as a threat to be removed." She lifted her arm.

Of course, the threat was heading right toward us.

"Okay. Well, they're walking this way and my parents just entered, so maybe go to the bathroom and I'll save you a seat?"

Sienna started to turn, instincts already pulling her toward the kill, but I caught her shoulders before she could. Instead of fighting me, she tossed her head back and stared up at the ceiling as if the plaster up there had the answers. "Fine."

Katia lingered for a beat, eyes darting between us, then trailed behind Sienna. I heard my brother call for her a few feet away.

"Don't," I said and lifted a hand.

"Get the fuck off me." Koa yanked his arm away from Alanna's, who only rolled her eyes as though the conversation alone was an inconvenience. "I need to talk to her."

"I told her. She needs a minute. Trust me."

'She knows this isn't me, right?' Koa spoke into my mind.

'She does, but whatever is binding you together doesn't. She wants to kill her...like right now. On sight.'

Koa's eyes wandered toward the bathroom where Sienna hid. 'I'm going to figure this shit out.'

He'd extended the mental bridge; I could feel Sienna there, but she ignored him. Her portion of the connection had a solid wall between them.

'We will, together. I'll take care of her, I promise,' I said.

Our parents were bold with this one. They had vastly underestimated how much he cared about Sienna. In my opinion, they didn't understand the concept. To love someone with every fiber of your being, to experience your partner's emotions even more intensely than they did. To wake up and know that there was at least one person living and breathing who would go to the ends of the world for you. Koa's love for me was instinctual, a brother fulfilling a duty to protect. What he felt for Sienna was pure passion if I'd ever seen it. Truthfully, I didn't even think I fully understood the concept yet. But I did know one thing. Love wasn't something to tamper with, and they'd be learning that very soon.

We didn't sit with Koa this time. Linda had found him and Alanna immediately and put them right in the front row. I effectively hid until she abandoned her search to set up whatever bullshit presentation my parents had. I set my hand on Sienna's bouncing leg, giving it a firm squeeze. Which was odd to say the least. She was normally the one to comfort my anxiety, but I was happy to do any small part I could.

Unfortunately, we were required to attend any Cynod addresses. Our marks were scanned as we entered, and if we left early, there would be consequences. Sitting in front of my parents and listening to their voices for however long wasn't going to help Sienna calm down. That was for sure.

A tune played, and the curtains pulled back from the stage as all five members of the Cynod appeared, already seated in their chairs with my mother at the podium. She had an outfit change too. Another suit but this one in Kuxtal crimson.

"Hello, Kuxtal Academy," she said with a smile.

I was nowhere near my brother, but I swore I heard him groan as everyone began clapping and shouting. Sienna was lucky she wasn't a Kib; she might have erupted into flames. Katia and I both grabbed one of her hands, and she let out a long breath between her lips.

"I'm elated to see so many smiling faces today," my mother said. "Although, I must warn, we are not here in good spirits."

The crowd murmured, people turning to each other with worry about what might have happened.

"I regret to inform you that there has been an assassination attempt on two children of the Cynod. My children," she followed up, touching her chest as if in pain.

I wanted to melt into the chair beneath me. Every head in our immediate area swiveled my direction, and those close to Koa practically leaped from their seats to get a glimpse of him.

"Thankfully, they were not successful, and Koa and Mira are here with us today." She scanned the front row, and her brow furrowed slightly when only Koa was found in his assigned seat. I was perfectly fine at the back of the arena.

"Are we safe?" a student bellowed.

I wouldn't put it past them to have asked someone to yell out these things.

"Well, we are doing everything we can to ensure you are safe," she replied firmly.

"Who did it?" someone else shouted.

Oh, they were for sure part of this performance.

My mother took a deep breath. "For years, we have heard whispers through our networks. People speaking of...a rebellion."

The gasps in the crowd were akin to the laugh tracks in the old movies Tía used to make me watch. They sounded fake, though I knew they were real. Many of these people—children of the elite—would never have heard about the rebellion. They wouldn't have even believed there was unrest. Obviously, Solis, their fair and just deity, wouldn't allow for people to be treated poorly.

My mother raised her hand, and the crowd slowly silenced as the screen above her flashed. I wasn't sure how they did it, or when they did it, but they pulled Koa's truck from the crash site. It was crumpled, the hood and engine folded in on itself, windows were all gone, the doors caved in, and the truck bed split down the middle. I knew it was bad. That was a hard fact to avoid in the aftermath. In the same breath, I hadn't quite realized how lucky I was to walk away from that.

"This is what they are capable of," my mother stated, a single tear sliding down her cheek. She caught it at her jawline with the tip of her finger as she gathered herself. "We did not believe that any fae in Inecha could be this cruel, but we stand corrected. My children only survived because a good Samaritan saw what happened and jumped into action. This should serve as a reminder that even the most powerful can be vulnerable."

It was then that I realized there hadn't been any mention of Sienna or Wren in this speech. I wasn't sure if they truly didn't know Sienna was with us since there'd been no mention of her in the ChismeChak article, or if they were leaving it out intentionally. As for Wren, I was positive they wouldn't admit to him being with us without proof, despite the tabloid's claims.

My father rose, moving with the grace of a predator as he joined my mother and placed a hand on her back. She smiled up at him, and he nodded at her as he situated himself before the microphone.

"Our security and defense are at the forefront of our concerns. Not just for our children, but for each of you," he said, his deep voice such a contrast to my mother's.

The slide switched, and a very clear and concise message appeared on the screen.

"First years will no longer be permitted to leave the campus alone. Many of you have not had enough practice with your gifts and, therefore, are at a disadvantage. All other students living on campus can leave, but you will have check-ins and parameters that you must follow as your families are entrusting Dean Cocum with your care."

My mother leaned forward. "Our intention is not to be cruel, I assure you. Should you have an emergency, you can go through the admin office for a pass."

"Again," my father said the moment she finished speaking. "We need to keep you all safe. Aurora, myself, and the rest of the Cynod will continue monitoring the situation. For those in the junior military program, you will all be asked to assist further. Some of you may be pulled on the weekends, should the rebellion force our hand."

"Bulletins are being sent to all of you later this afternoon with specifications. Those in the junior military, and those who are not, it is our job as citizens of Inecha to help protect each other. Take solace in the fact that Solis and the Cynod cares for each of you deeply. Thank you," my mother finished.

They cared about not creating hysteria. About controlling the citizens further. It wasn't our well-being they were concerned for. They all walked off, waving and stopping for a picture at the edge of the stage with Dean Cocum.

"This is fucking bullshit," Sienna spat. "Can we go yet? I'm still feeling rather murderous."

Katia leaned closer, voice barely above a whisper. "I'm in the junior military now. I got the official notice this morning after I registered my nahual."

Her Imix form radiated barely-contained power. Scales glinted faintly in the light, talons flexing. From the way her shoulders tensed, I could tell she knew exactly what she was capable of. Imix were almost always drafted—their size, strength, and ferocity made them weapons by nature. My father was one.

"Did they tell you what your responsibilities are?" I asked.

"No." Katia shook her head. "I have to switch to a military class, and they said I'll be briefed. I know we're unsure about the rebels, but they did save you. Fighting them feels…"

"Remains to be seen how much we can trust anybody," Sienna said, still very much not on good terms with the rebellion.

"We'll figure it out," I assured.

Although, as I said the words, I wondered just how true it was.

6

MIRA

Bulletin:

Kuxtal Academy Students,

As advised in the Cynod's official address, first years will no longer be able to leave the campus. There will be an event once a month specifically created for your class on the mainland. Entertainment, food, and other surprises are to be expected. This will be a Cynod-sponsored event, so we expect you to show your Kuxtal Academy manners. Should you have an emergency, please contact admin@ kuxtalacademy.edu and your situation will be assessed. Should we find your emergency worthy, you will be granted a pass.

We would be remiss not to mention that our very own Koa Canek is officially engaged! Welcome his fiancée, Alanna Osorios, to the campus, and be sure to offer them both congratulations!

Thankfully, we were outside when we received the bulletin—far away from any buildings or breakables. Sienna, Katia, and I had just made it down to the lake. Many of the students had chosen to go back to their dorms or to eat after the address, but the three of us didn't have an appetite.

Sienna cracked a tree in half, the inside blackening as she drained its life force. She hadn't said a word since reading the message, simply took to unleashing her magic on the world around us. I didn't blame her; I wished I could give her more things to destroy. If it weren't terribly foolish and dangerous, I'd point her straight at the Cynod building. She would've leveled it in seconds.

Now she sat on the ground, knees drawn close, breathing deep and meditating while Katia and I watched her from the other side of the field with concern. The switch from wrathful fury to well-tempered was terrifying. If I had known where the day was heading, I would have told her to bring her crystals and a weighted blanket. Slowly, painstakingly, she mended everything she destroyed, the tree stitching itself together and its blackened core turning brown and bright once again.

"I don't even know how to help right now," Katia admitted.

"Me neither," I said, my own concern prickling. "I'm starting to worry about my capacity to help any of us."

Sienna crossed the field, calmer, but I knew all the rage wasn't quite gone. It simmered under the surface, and one small crack in her exterior would have it pouring out again. Students sporadically came out to the field, books and midterm study packets in hand.

This was a pretty popular common area for the students of Kuxtal. *Ok* pranced through the field chasing each other in their shifted forms. An *Imix* swooped down, its clawed feet brushing the tops of the trees that Sienna had just obliterated and remade. It nestled into some tall grass, spreading out and soaking up the sun.

Made for an entertaining sight to people-watch any other day, but we weren't exactly in the mood.

"I want to take off this jacket so damn bad," Sienna muttered, tugging at her sleeves.

"Why don't we go back to the dorm?" I suggested in an attempt to keep her at this level of calm.

Sienna nodded, and we trekked up the trails years and years of footsteps had made in the grass. Sounds emitted from deep within the cenotes, and somebody with a fuck ton of power must have been down there, because my senses went crazy.

I still didn't understand my nahual yet. With minimal time to dissect it, and the only real experience I had being that I killed a handful of soldiers, I didn't want to play with it too much. But there was something I sensed in every single fae I'd come in contact with since that day in the docks. Their soul, their spirit, something always made itself known to me.

I'd known Sienna for so long that hers was easy to ignore; others, however, screamed and shouted for me to notice. Whoever was in that cenote was overbearing. I'd have periods where I'd forget about it, where it wasn't constantly pressing and present, but other times it overtook my other senses.

Like right now, with the thousands of students going about their day, that sensation inside me kept buzzing.

The girl walking toward me was an *Ik*. She didn't know it yet, but I'd heard her talk about being late to emerge in one of our classes. They said nobody took more than nine months to emerge after the spell at orientation, so I figured she'd be getting it soon if I felt it so strongly. A man on a bike made eye contact with me as we crossed the street, a *Kib*. His soul was...hot, like a furnace ready to blow.

We were always told our nahuales are what made us fae, that they were as intertwined with our beings as our tangible parts. One of those things you thought you understood until you experienced *this* and realized you had no idea before. The difference between being mailed a postcard from our highest waterfall versus actually being there, running your fingers through the water.

Koa had explained how his nahual felt before, how he could sense things inside a body. Said he could almost see the bones, muscles, and organs in someone when he was healing. This was different; it wasn't what was physically inside them I sensed, it was deeper. Something untouchable to most. It was how I killed those rebel guards; I could pull it, manipulate it. And in the case of what I did to Koa, transfer the energy. I was guided by something—maybe the gods—that day. It wasn't something I could replicate on the spot.

My gift, *Kimi,* had always been there. Where before it was hiding away, now it was ever-present. I was a cage, a vessel, for Death.

"Oh," Katia grumbled, biting down on her lip as she attempted to redirect us. "Fuck."

It was too late.

"What are they still doing here?" I muttered.

The Cynod were coming out of the UJ Student Center. It was nowhere near the arena, so they must have done some sort of extra appearance. There were media rooms there, so it was likely they recorded a video for the academy. My parents had their backs turned, thankfully. The priest did not.

He locked eyes with me across the sea of students charging toward them and walking past. My nahual went crazy in my chest, his signature really not sitting well with it. I swallowed and rubbed above my heart. His gaze quickly flitted over to Sienna, the sun beaming off his warm brown skin. He didn't watch her the same way he had watched me. It wasn't just monitoring a problem child of the Cynod, the sneer on his lips, the twitch in his nose; it was much more.

"Why is he looking at you like that?" Katia asked, hand falling to her sternum.

"I barely met him once at the gala. I have no idea. They're all fucking weirdos," Sienna responded with snarled disgust.

I pulled her forward. "Don't let them see it all over your face. Let's go before they come this way."

I glanced back over my shoulder, and we left at the perfect time because Koa and Alanna appeared behind our parents. Trying not to draw attention to it, I kept us moving, pointing out a flower and asking Sienna what it was. She rolled her eyes, but let me know it was part of the scavenger hunt for *Herbology 101,* and I should remember. Katia's phone chimed, and she slowed down to read the message.

"The plot thickens," she groaned as she tucked her phone back into her pocket. "Junior military is going to be patrolling. Mandatory shifts, and we'll need to be on standby for the weekends. We'll have to secure whatever the monthly event is with Cynod security as well."

Five minutes of peace. That was all I wanted.

Tía used to do this thing with me and Sienna when we had spectacularly shitty days. We'd shout out every single thing that was bothering us, talk through the worst-case scenario, and as weird as it felt, it always helped. This time, I decided to bring out the whiteboard I used to write scientific formulas. So far we had:

—KOA BEING ENGAGED TO ALANNA

—ASSASSINATION ATTEMPT

—HAVING TO HIDE MY NAHUAL

—HAVING TO HIDE THEIR MATING BOND

—KATIA BEING FORCED INTO THE MILITARY

—WREN BEING OFF-GRID

—NOT BEING ABLE TO LEAVE CAMPUS

"Koa's condo is technically off campus, and we spend so much time there," Sienna said, her shoulders slumped and tears lining her eyes. She licked the back of a garlic parmesan pretzel, and it seemed to help her mood.

The other thing that helped with spectacularly shitty days was snacks. Not the good, wholesome stuff. The more dyes and preservatives most people couldn't pronounce, the better.

I chomped down on our favorite brand of cheese-covered tortilla chips, covering my mouth as I responded, "He can come here?"

"Please. Can you imagine your six-foot-five, two-hundred-fifty-pound brother in my dorm bed?"

"Ya'll can squeeze in." I grimaced.

Our beds were comfy, luxurious even if I considered what most of Inecha had access to in an academy dorm. They weren't the size of the beds in Koa's condo, that was for sure.

"Worst-case scenario?" Katia asked with the dry-erase marker cap between her teeth.

Sienna's response was instant. She'd clearly thought it through and spiraled. "We have to break up, and he marries the knockoff, less hot version of me."

"Your relationship is backed by the *literal* gods," I said.

Which I knew was only so comforting. But if nothing else, she had been one of two fae to speak to the gods in...a very long time.

"Fine," she amended with a roll of her eyes. "We grow apart."

Katia wrote it down, and I went into problem-solving mode. I knew not everything could be solved like a scientific equation, but it certainly helped to analyze things.

"We can get passes, maybe Wolfe can do something in the system to work around it like he did for temple? Or I can find some leverage with my parents. They want me to play a bigger role. I imagine that will involve going off campus now and then."

"I'm sure Koa would volunteer to turn the admins into stone for the weekend?" Katia suggested, and the fact that he definitely would do that made us all laugh for the first time since we started the exercise.

I rubbed the tears from my eyes, realizing we'd forgotten a pretty big problem. "The rebels."

Katia wrote it in all caps, underlining it.

"They had so much information about all of us," Sienna said as a shadow ran across her features. "Even you, Katia."

It was hard to forget such a sight. Pictures of all of us, notes on locations we frequented, people we'd interacted with. Every single one of us. Even places that were supposed to be safe, like Koa and Wren's club. They were extremely thorough in their research, and none of us was safe.

"But they're the ones who saved you, right?" Katia questioned.

"That's what they said. We saw proof that they had a Cynod lackey, and they admitted to it, but it could have been staged."

"What do you believe?" she pressed.

Wasn't that the golden question? It was easy to blame the Cynod given their history and the shit we knew about them. But was the simple answer the right one...I wasn't sure.

"I have a really bad feeling about the Cynod and my parents, above the general hate and disdain," I grumbled.

"My opinion is obviously biased." The lilt in Sienna's tone was heavily influenced by feyfog. "But I don't trust the rebels either."

I passed my best friend the second bag of garlic pretzels. "I don't think we trust anyone outside of us until we have solid proof. Proof that can't be altered, multiple sources."

"Agreed," they both said at the same time.

I was nervous to bring the next problem up. Katia had been such a good friend, but our friendship hadn't been tested by time. I didn't know if this would make her turn from me. I wouldn't blame her.

"My mother wants me to get in your good graces...to get in your mother's," I told Katia. "They really want Jundi to aid in taking over the Sacred Lands, I think."

"Oh." Her brow furrowed, but she didn't so much as inch away.

"I'd never use anything told in confidence against you. I just felt like it was best you knew that it even came up," I added quickly.

I waited for her face to turn angry, for her to swiftly leave the room. She didn't; she only watched like my intentions were floating around me. The contemplative pinch in her brows relaxed, melting into something pretty damn close to pity.

She put down the marker and sat beside me. "No, I'm glad you told me. This isn't the first time they've tried. When I told my mother I was friends with you, it was the first thing she warned me of."

"Their reputation precedes them," I mumbled. "Were you ever worried about it?"

"I think any smart person would. The closer we got, the more I knew you'd never do anything untoward. Especially after all this." Katia pointed to the whiteboard.

That was a relief, but it still left more questions.

"I just don't understand why they want the lands this badly. I know they're power hungry, but I'd like to think that's not solely the case. Something of this magnitude takes resources, both financial and military. Not to mention the personnel to keep it?"

"It holds many treasures," Katia sighed. "Even if they got in, the magic is different there. The land is almost...sentient. It would protect itself."

"They don't believe the tales, I'm sure," Sienna said.

"And their predecessors have already failed in the task. It's not as if Jundi is not part of Inecha, but we're the only thing standing between them and attempting to venture into the Sacred Lands. We have laws of our own that were put in even before the Cynod that they can't touch. Old, ancient magic that nobody can dismantle."

"Okay," Sienna drawled. "So at the very least, it seems like an impossible task, anyway."

"Science has proved time and time again that what was once impossible might become possible in the future. New technology and discoveries happen every single day," I responded. "Not to mention, knockoff Sienna is from Mentiria, the land on the *other* side of the Sacred Lands. There's more here."

We all sat with that. I didn't mean to sound pessimistic, but we had to be realistic. I was sure the old gods never thought they'd be shunned and turned away from. I was also confident that the people from that time never could have imagined their land looking the way it does now. The Sacred Lands may have been safe all this time, but for how much longer...nobody knew.

"Well, regardless of all of this bullshit, we do have midterms this week. Katia, you might not know this, but Mira has most definitely already created a very strict studying schedule for the three of us," Sienna said, and I laughed.

I did. I most certainly did.

"There's even this new study technique I read about! Oh, I made us all binders with flashcards, hold on." I got up and rummaged through my drawers to find them.

If nothing else, I would help them prepare for this. This one thing, I did have control over.

7

KOA

No house could be considered a home without Sienna in it. She wouldn't answer any of my texts or calls, but FindAFae claimed she was with Mira, so at minimum I knew she was safe. Still, the silence of my condo served more as a detriment to my sanity than peaceful resolve.

Taking the weekend to decompress after all the bullshit that went down had been the initial plan. Anything on the flash drive the Mercer clan had decrypted could wait until after midterms. With the new campus rules in place, the situation had become...complicated on top of everything else. Breaking rules was my thing; finding a way around them was relatively simple—except when the threat of Sienna's well-being and future were hung over my head.

Fuck what happened to me, her situation at Kuxtal could not be compromised. If I couldn't figure out a way out of my engagement, she deserved the opportunity to carve her own path. A path that was infinitely easier in the good graces of the Cynod and with Kuxtal Academy slapped on an application.

This condo was the only space we were guaranteed privacy to figure out what the hells was happening. Whoever it was that put the hit on us—Cynod or the rebellion, whatever—had found the flash drive worth killing over, leaving me with the impression they knew its content.

The more I thought about it, the more I questioned everything. Emeric and Aurora Canek wanting to kill their only heirs was out of character—even under duress. We may have had our differences, disagreements, and overall a general disgust for the lifestyle the other led, but Mira and I were their legacy. And to our parents, that was everything.

Considering the past few years of our aggravated relationship and their attempts to diminish any business opportunities they'd caught word of, I should have expected this at some point. I was, in every sense of the word, a fucking dickhead without remorse when it came to them. It was probably easier to get rid of me than keep me around. But Mira? *That* was the part that made me hesitant. My mother had even texted me, attempting to check in on her given Mira was dodging all attempts of communication.

It wasn't as though they were winning any parenting awards. They'd never really shown any emotion toward Mira other than disdain of her presence at best and extreme inconvenience at worst. The catch was, doubting their involvement meant betrayal to the woman I loved.

The rebellion had beaten, tortured, and traumatized her over the mere thought that she knew what the flash drive consisted of. Not to mention the video proof pointing the finger right at mother and father dearest...proof that could be manipulated by an *Ajaw*.

Which admittedly didn't track. Both Mira and Wren had recognized Timmy...Tommy as one of the Cynod's. And then there was Zélia, sending Strider after us to make sure we cleared the water.

The only way for us to fully understand what the actual hells was going on was to find out exactly what it was everyone wanted to know—and would do anything to keep from getting out.

Thrusting ourselves into the middle of a rebellion was dangerous as fuck. Having Mira or Sienna anywhere near it was the last thing I wanted. Still, this may have been the opportunity to do the work I couldn't do alone from my future seat on the Cynod—not even with Mira's help.

What if taking down the Cynod and dismantling their bullshit system from within was the exact opening we both were hoping for?

Death had become a regular part of my job, but I never allowed innocents to be caught in the crossfire. Not if I could help it. Aiding the rebellion had the potential to limit the amount of lower level fae that would suffer, sparing them from the atrocities the Cynod would commit under their 'Solis' based framework. I wasn't stupid. The rebellion trusted us about the same amount we trusted them. That did not negate the fact that we needed each other to get what we wanted.

Alanna's text message popped up over the *Advanced Runes and Glyphs* study guide with an irritatingly grating chime that made me want to slam my laptop shut. She was exhausting, and it had been less than twenty-four hours of knowing her. Apparently, she and my mother had arranged a 'study date' for the two of us to pretend we weren't taking advantage of the press. It was a photo op, might as well call it for what it was.

She was all talk, and none of it was authentic. There was no substance in her words, and any intelligence in her thoughts was laced with manipulation. The only thing Alanna cared about was ensuring her grandfather maintained the power he held onto, and elevating herself to the position in life she thought she was owed. Of course she'd pretend she was excited to see me soon, in the outfit she or my mother had delivered to my door an hour ago—media approved and steamed.

The mere thought of having to touch her again made my skin crawl. In the moments we were forced to—during what she deemed our 'soft-launch' and the official Cynod announcement—every cell in my body recoiled, an instinctive rejection from my mate mark. It was indisputable that Alanna was beautiful, yes. Brilliant even, with a mind as sharp as her cheekbones. But she lacked three things Sienna carried in every glance, every laugh: authenticity. Warmth. A pulse of something real.

Things I'd never thought mattered until her. Until now. Any future without Sienna beside me wasn't just hollow; it was a sentence to pain so deep I doubted I'd survive it.

Tonight, eating the leftovers she'd poured her heart and soul into the night before, studying for a test I could pass without preparation, I questioned what *my* future would look like. The one where no matter how much I wanted to beg her to stay, I would always be alone.

"Bags by the door, phones on my desk," Professor Ortega bellowed across the transformed lecture hall. A collective groan rippled through the class as students reluctantly shuffled toward his desk. "You all can thank the Mercer clan for this, considering what happened last time."

A soft *ping* echoed off the smooth obsidian walls, etched with intricate glyphs made of jade and flecks of gold. Then another. Followed by a macabre of alerts.

The room froze as though the temperatures dropped to the coldness of Yaxumi. Professor Ortega's eye twitched. "Must we go through this every time?"

He flicked his fingers over the screen of the phone closest to him. He pulled the password with the manipulation of his *Lamat* magic, guiding the light over to the projector screen behind him.

[MERCER CHEATNET 2.0]

> **Dax: Pretty sure table #4 is getting the fertility rune, but it also might mean 'exploding chicken.'**

> **Juno: That's...definitely not the same thing. Not even close.**

> **Dax: You don't know that.**

> **Kian: I sat at table #8 on Monday. It's "Alignment of celestial bodies."**

> **Dax: See?? That could be a fertility thing!!**

> **Juno: Literally how?**

Ortega sighed, his ocher-brown fingers rubbing his temples as we all were forced to confront our guilt. "Since the Mercers aren't here to punish...Juno and Dax, Dean Cocum's office after the exam. Find someone to switch seats with. Now."

Across the room, Juno's watch lit up on her wrist as she pushed free from her chair, looking utterly unbothered. Ortega's eye twitched harder, and presumably both of their screens shattered. "Smartwatches or any other similar devices linked to your phones are *also* prohibited in this classroom."

"Hypothetically speaking," Dax said. "If someone had, say, paid the Mercers to link the entire classroom's devices to a hidden relay system that bounced off the university's ley lines, would that be like, a fail-worthy offense? Hypothetically."

"Dax." Ortega stared him down.

"Right," he mumbled as he switched from my table with none other than Alanna. "Still didn't say if I was right about the chicken."

Of course, she'd been placed in three of my four classes this semester. A gratitude that was owed to my mother, I was sure. Alanna sat in Dax's old spot, shifting her chair close enough for our thighs to touch, and without mercy I visibly cringed. She had been a transfer from Ch'ulel Academy in Mentiria. It was easy for her to slip right into the curriculum, given they were the sister school of Kuxtal, where she had previously attended as a third year. Lucky fucking me.

Wednesday happened to be my favorite day of the week. I had only one class—*Advanced Runes and Glyphs*. The subject was entertaining enough, and Professor Ortega wasn't a complete dickhead unless provoked. Once I knocked out this midterm, I was free to head over to The Underworld. I had business to tend to. Business that my so-called business partner and his brothers hadn't bothered to inquire about my ability to handle. Wren had all but fallen off the face of Herta since Monday, and now so had the rest of the Ikari clan with him. It was fucking weird that I hadn't heard from him. He was susceptible to disappearing for various amounts of time depending on the gig but to not have said a word to me before going was unheard of.

Professor Ortega swiped his hand, bending the light in the room to reveal the relics at the center of the large limestone table. Shadows flickered, stretching over the carved surfaces.

"Today's exam requires you to inspect the artifact on your respective tables," Ortega announced. "I expect you to study the inscriptions and draft your interpretations. Allow me to issue a reminder that context is key—understanding not only what the glyphs say, but how they connect to Inecha's history, culture, and broader systems of meaning. This is not a collaborative effort, although each table will share the same artifacts. Gloves on when touching, I don't need the oil from your hands ruining things. Yes, some of the artifacts taste like salt. No, you may not lick them. Begin."

Chairs screeched across the stone floor as students moved into position, their hushed murmurs weaving through the air.

"Good luck, Benício," Alanna purred, her hazel eyes peering at me under fluttering lashes as she reached for my hand.

I snatched mine away, my lips curling in something that wasn't quite a smile. My chest rattled with the effort it took to keep my temper in check. "The luck is all yours."

It was the only thing I could bring myself to say that didn't start with *fuck off*. Causing a scene in a room full of fae who already dissected my every move would only lead to more scrutiny. More whispers. And right now, that wasn't just a problem for me—it was a problem for Sienna.

I could play the game. I needed more time to *adjust*.

Cracking my neck, I let the sound hang before reaching across the table. The stone tablet scraped against wood as I pulled it into my hands, rough edges biting against my gloves as I took my time examining it.

Then I set it down, sliding it toward Alanna with the best smile I could muster.

The tablet was worn. Glyphs cut deep into the surface stared back at me—shapes I didn't recognize. Not at first glance. But the arrangement of them felt...wrong. Not in the way of mistranslation, but in the way of something I *should* understand but didn't. The pattern was like a song I knew but couldn't hum.

"Patterns, class." Ortega passed behind me. "Tell their own stories, even when the full text is lost."

He weaved through the classroom, watching as we struggled with his exam, as he expected and likely enjoyed. *Sadist.*

The *Eb* across from me smirked as he placed the tablet back down—too quick, too confident. He was scribbling down his interpretation. If he was already writing, then he had already failed. Professor Ortega did not *do* easy, and anyone hoping to bullshit their way through this exam was in for a rude awakening. It was why Wolfe Mercer had started his cheating ring years ago—lore as ingrained in this course as the runes themselves. This exam had broken people.

Choosing between this and *Arcane History and Artifacts* was like picking between a slow death and a fast one. Professor Taran had made it clear *that* particular nightmare was best suited for your last semester. Probably because whatever knowledge he dropped on our way out the door was meant to stick.

I ran a gloved thumb over the carvings, my pulse slowing as something in my mind simply clicked. The arrangement was not linear. Not a sentence, not a story. *That* was what we were accustomed to, but the point of a test was to challenge all that you had learned, not memorization of information. The symbols curved back into themselves, repeating in a way that wasn't just decorative. It was structured. The more I looked, the more I saw a pattern—cyclical, like time folding in on itself.

A calendar...no, something far older than anything I felt equipped to know.

I pressed the pen to the page, scrawling my response in sharp strokes. The kind Mira once said was perfect for a healer because no one but me would ever be able to read them.

POSSIBLE CALENDRICAL FUNCTION?

SYMBOLS SUGGEST MEASUREMENT RATHER THAN NARRATIVE.

It wasn't much, but it was better than faking confidence when I—shockingly and admittedly—had none. Ortega had a way of sniffing out bullshit, and I wasn't about to hand him a reason to flay me alive in front of the entire class.

A flicker of movement caught my eye, and I dared a glance at Alanna. She was still staring at the artifact, her perfectly arched and filled brows furrowed, glossed lips slightly parted in surprise—or maybe recognition. Tapping the end of her pen against the paper, the obnoxiously large engagement ring my mother pretended I'd gifted tilted her hand to one side more than the other. Frustration curled at the edges of her fine-tuned composure as she scribbled down her thoughts.

I added a few final notes—small observations that might make me sound like I knew what the hells I was doing. Nothing definitive, just enough to keep Ortega off my ass for lack of effort, and gave it one last glance to make sure it was at least somewhat legible. Satisfied, I pushed out of my seat and crossed the room, sliding my exam onto the growing stack on Ortega's desk and turning to leave.

His voice caught me mid-step. "Mr. Canek," he mused, the gold flecks in his brown eyes dancing with mischief. "I find it rather interesting how knowledge tends to survive in pieces, don't you?"

I exhaled slowly, acknowledging him with nothing more than a nod, letting the words settle without giving them too much thought. It wasn't until I stepped into the parking garage, the hum of vehicles replacing the silence of the exam room, that the underlying implication pushed through.

Knowledge in pieces. Like the tablet. The way history fractured and scattered, leaving only shards behind for people to pick through.

8

KOA

"I have to hand it to you, Koa. Showing face right now? Brave move," Mira said, swinging open her door, her expression caught somewhere between impressed and exasperation.

Mira's dorm was chaotic and quaint in equal measure. The string lights above her bed cast everything in a gold hue, softening the edges of her otherwise 'lived-in' space. There were study guides and notes everywhere, with some of Sienna's paintings stacked against the far wall, waiting to be hung up. The smell of lavender and rosemary incense filled the air—Sienna's doing, no doubt.

"What are you talking about?"

She held up her phone, and there it was—me and Alanna, walking across campus, hand in fucking hand. In all fairness, my face was its usual brand of miserable, but she was all smiles, chatting animatedly while I carried her bag like some doting idiot. Alanna pushed to her toes in an attempt to kiss me outside UJ Student Center. I barely dodged it, turning in time for her lips to land on my cheek.

Fifteen minutes. That's all it took for this shit to go viral. Social media was becoming the bane of my existence.

I pushed past Mira, already knowing who I'd find inside. Katia sat on the bed, rubbing circles into Sienna's back. Sienna wasn't crying. She wasn't hurt. She was furious.

"Get out," she snapped the second she saw me, her hands warming to a vibrant purple with the power of persuasion.

"Venom—"

She was on me in a blink, both hands shoving against my chest with all the strength she had, her power still emboldened. It shouldn't have moved me. Shouldn't have even registered.

But I let it. Let her push me back like she could actually throw me out.

"I don't want to talk to you."

"I got the hint from my thirty-two text messages left on read and fifty-seven missed calls."

"Okay," Sienna snarked with a snort. "Then act on it."

"Pass," I said, unwilling to walk away from this. From *her*.

Katia let out a low whistle, stretching her arms over her head as if this was just another episode of *Koa Fucking Up*. "Wow. This seems like something I have no business being here for. I have a video date with the boys. Call me if you need me."

Mira lingered by the door, shifting, trying to decide whether she should stay or go. It was her room, but me stepping out of Sienna's would spark too many questions.

"Si?" she asked carefully.

Sienna didn't look at her. Didn't look at anyone but me.

"Five minutes," Sienna said.

I exhaled, slow. "Twenty."

"Ten," Sienna countered.

"Fifteen."

"Fine," she ground out.

The tilt of my head no doubt pissed her off, doubling down with the crossing of my arms. "Funny. That's what I was aiming for."

Sienna let out a strangled, furious sound—half growl, half exasperated screech—biting back the urge to hurl something at my head. Mira's eyes went wide before she took a careful step back, muttering, "Good luck," and slipping out, the door clicking shut behind her.

The second it latched, Sienna whirled on me. "It's everywhere!"

"I know."

She shoved her phone in my face, scrolling through the damage. "*Koa Canek drops gutter-born social climber for a true match.*" Another swipe. "*Balance of the Cynod back in check—Aurora and Emeric promise a powerful heir.* Oh, and my personal favorite: the comments." She angled the screen. "*Finally, someone who looks like she belongs next to him.*"

I reached for the phone.

"Nope. Not finished yet, Koa." She pulled it back, the clipped edge of my name hitting sharper than any insult. She always called me *snake*. Never *Koa*. "We're just getting to the best ones."

I skimmed through them, each one landing like a fist to the ribs.

Glad he dropped that gold-digging bitch.
This one's prettier anyway, so classy, I love her dress!
Thank Solis he found an even match.

It went on. And on.

I shut her phone off and tossed it onto Mira's bed before pulling her in, wrapping my arms around her. She didn't fight it. Didn't fight me. Just sank into the hold like the weight of it all had finally pressed too hard.

The first tear hit my skin, and that was it. I dropped us to the floor, cradling her in my lap, holding her as if I could shield her from the world. Sienna's curls tickled under my chin, exhaling long and deep as she let go of everything she'd been holding in.

Her voice was barely a whisper. "Are we...are we done?"

"I will never be done with you—even if you're done with me."

She let out a breath that sounded painful. "I don't see how we move past this. The future seems pretty set to me."

"What happened to 'over their dead bodies'?"

"I meant that. I still mean that." Her fingers tightened in the fabric over my ribs. "But it's just...I feel like there's no way out of this. They announced your engagement to the entire world. You're with her every day."

"She's insufferable." My voice came out flat, but the anger beneath it simmered. "She has zero redeeming qualities. Soaking my skin in hand sanitizer after a thousand paper cuts would make for a more pleasant afternoon than hanging around her, and I say that from experience."

That was a...painful night due to a slight misunderstanding with the governing brotherhood of criminals, *Noctis Fraternitas*. They didn't take kindly to possible leaks.

Sienna huffed a small, bitter laugh. "That's not the point, Koa."

The only thing Alanna ever talked about was herself, whatever was trending, and ways she could manipulate the power I had once taking my seat within the Cynod. She had ambitious political plans. None of them aligned with mine, and all of them were about Mentiria—her home. Never once had she asked me a question, never once tried to understand anything beyond her own agenda. Not that I wanted her to.

I ran my hand down Sienna's back, grounding myself in the fact that *she* was here. *She* was real.

"You still have to marry her." Her voice broke, and the very sound of it nearly broke me.

"I only have one mate, Sienna." I tilted her chin up, making sure she heard me. *Really* heard me. "Nothing, no one, can fucking change that. And right now, my only priority is playing my part until I can move the right pieces into place—until I can guarantee your safety, your happiness. Anything beyond that is irrelevant. *We* are endgame. You and me."

She was quiet for a beat, her eyes darting to the floor. I could feel the tension in her shoulders, the way the weight of everything was pressing down on her.

"I don't usually focus on the negative," she said, her voice tight, "but damn did the world lose its color that day."

That gave me pause, and I met her gaze. "Please don't tell me you've stopped painting."

"I find little inspiration in despair."

I didn't have words for that, so I kissed her instead. Slow. Deep. Pouring every ounce of emotion into it, letting her feel everything I couldn't find the words to say. I did not lie to her. And right now everything I could say would only be an empty promise until I could work things out. Empty promises were only one step up from lies.

When I pulled back, I pressed my lips to her forehead. "Allow me to make one promise—my lips will never touch hers. You own me, Sienna. In every way. To me, it's you or nothing at all."

She nodded, accepting it, despite the pain of the road ahead. Her curls tumbled in loose ringlets over her oversized hoodie. My hoodie.

I ran my thumb along her jaw, eyes locked on hers. "You can't cut me out like that again. Do you understand? That hurt me, Venom. I thought I lost you for good."

She swallowed hard, then whispered, "I told you that you Caneks are stuck with me forever. I meant it."

"Good."

The door swung open, and Mira stepped in, eyes scanning us both. She must've caught the shift in the air because she grinned. "Okay, I see smiles. Are we all good in here, or do I need to awkwardly pace the hallway again? They started some card tournament and it's getting...aggressive, and not in a hot way."

I glanced at Sienna, waiting for her answer.

She shook her head and pressed a soft kiss to my cheek before standing. "No. We're good."

I stood too, fingers reaching for her instinctively, desperate to keep our touch. "I came to make sure she was doing alright. Now that I know we can move past this, there's something else."

I set the flash drive down on the glass top of her desk, smirking at the photos she'd pushed underneath. Some were of her and Celeste over the years, starting from when she first moved in, her smile brighter than I'd ever seen. Most were with Sienna—each one documenting their adventures together. My favorites were the three of just the two of us. We looked almost normal, like siblings annoyed at the other's presence, but thankful all the same. I had come here to make sure she was okay. Now...it felt as though we were about to uncover something that could shatter everything.

Mira's gaze dropped to the flash drive. "Shit, I forgot about that with everything going on."

"How were your midterms?" I asked, shifting the focus.

"Aced them." She flicked her hair over her shoulder with a smirk. I met her hand with a sharp high-five.

Sienna shrugged. "I mean, I'm not going to get kicked out, so that's good, I guess. Could definitely use less drama and more time getting ahead."

"She literally got Bs," Mira muttered, rolling her eyes at Sienna, whose confidence ran dry the minute school came up.

"Yes, and at Kuxtal that's basically failing."

Mira gave Sienna a gentle shove on the shoulder. "Alright, we'll make study guides this weekend for finals. Start early."

"I've got someone working on an app that uses color-coded overlays to help with letter and word recognition. Plus if you upload Mira's guides, it has a text-to-speech feature. Highlights key points and presents them in short. Digests the information into built-in quizzes to reinforce memory. Don't worry about finals. We got you," I added.

Sienna shot us a look—grateful, but not about to say it out loud. Silence settled over us, eyes fixed on the flash drive.

"Well?" Sienna tapped her red, coffin-shaped nails on the desk, breaking the quiet. "Are one of you going to plug it in?"

"Your laptop," I said to Mira. "You do the honors."

She clicked it in. The screen flickered to life and illuminated the room in a soft blue glow. Lines of text flashed before us. Her hands clenched and opened again, leaving behind nail marks that hadn't been there a moment ago.

"Meems, have you been back to therapy?" I asked, noting her fidgeting since she walked back into the room.

She shook her head. "Monday."

"Good. I know laying off the pills was hard. I'm proud of you. This can't be easy." I watched her, not wanting to push, but needing to make sure she was okay.

Her fingers tightened on the desk, her only response a small nod before her focus returned to the screen. The drive loaded—documents, images, reports. Too much to process at once.

"Oh sh—" I started.

"Shit," Sienna finished, her voice low.

Mira's face went blank. "Um."

We all leaned forward, our attention fixed on the screen.

Hagen Line.

The first file. A family tree.

It wasn't uncommon for the elite to track their bloodline. Our parents had both the Canek and Tecun lineages in their studies. But this went far beyond a simple genealogy chart.

There was information about every single person since Hagen. Entire files on the more recent descendants. This was shit I'd seen the Mercers track down on people. Known locations, jobs, spouses, affairs, aliases, education levels. Things to use against people.

"This doesn't look like Mom and Dad's chart," Mira whispered as she double-clicked another file. "These are from this recent generation."

The Cynod was formed several millennia ago. When all five of the families sat down and decided they were the elite. That they were the ones to rule. I'd seen Hagen in the AstralCodex, a small mouse of a man was how I'd described him. Pale, freckled, and balding. But the array of people who'd sprouted from this one person didn't look anything like him.

We bore a resemblance to many of our ancestors; I'd seen just how much Mira looked like our Tecun ancestor in the Codex. The Canek one was a damn near spitting image of me minus the ink. Both lines had been intentional on how they proceeded with the bloodline—hence my arranged marriage. Hagen didn't seem to have such an inclination.

Which was interesting, given his line ran the church. The first few we'd clicked, maybe a couple thousand years ago didn't have photos. For obvious reasons. But these did. Mira dragged the computer mouse over each one until she scrolled to the very bottom. She clicked the second to last file and something in my gut twisted.

I'd stared into those eyes many times. Mira—the person who probably had stared into them more than myself—flicked her gaze from the screen to me, then to Sienna. Sienna went still. The only sign she was breathing was the rise and fall under my hand at her back.

The man in the photo had skin the same warm sepia brown as hers, with that golden undertone the sun always pulled out of her cheekbones. Dark brows, the same rounded line to the nose. There was no denying it. He looked like her. And not just her. For the briefest second, I swore I saw a shadow of Strider in the tilt of his mouth. Not as a son, their resemblance was not that precise. Same tree, different branches. This man...he carried the unlined face of fae longevity, yet there was weight in it. Not youth. Not like us. Not like Strider.

I could laugh. The 'prophecy' Ixchel shared wasn't so mysterious anymore. *Two branches from the same tree take root for the first of their kind.* 'Same tree' made a lot of fucking sense at the revelation. An anomaly, she was not.

Mira's voice broke through the thrum. "Sienna..."

My mate put her hand over my sister's and scrolled down past the photo.

Thaddeus Collins

Previous partner: Marlie Hayes

Offspring: Sienna Hayes

Sienna's name was hyperlinked, jumping to the next file. Her file. Celeste had died for this. This is what she wanted to protect her from. Because under her name, under her location and education, were three simple words: "Has the gift."

There was only one way they'd be able to link that information: the blood test they'd made us all submit to at the beginning of the year. Something so insignificant in the grand scheme of the hoops they made us jump through at the start of each school year, I'd nearly forgotten about it. Yet, it made sense—it had triggered everything. That was the moment our parents began to pay attention.

This was what they'd been searching for. What they *all* had been after—the rebels included. *Fuck*. They'd known before the rest of us did. Had only waited to grab her until she'd shown signs of coming into her magic.

"Venom. I think they've known about you for a lot longer than any of us realized." My heart was pounding, stomach churning with the sickening reality of it all.

I kept the other thought to myself—the resemblance to Strider I couldn't unsee. No proof meant no point in speaking it aloud. And right now, the only thing that mattered was what sat in front of us, black and white, undeniable.

Mira muttered scientific nonsense that made no sense to even me. "The test didn't just confirm your power level. It presented genetic markers."

She went still, caught in the screen's glow. Her mouth slightly opened like her brain hadn't caught up to what she was seeing. I scrolled up, then back down. No mistake. A bloodline that stretched back thousands of years, an unbroken thread.

Celeste. Could this have been part of what she'd discovered and been intent on hiding? The resentment bubbled up, darkening everything. The guilt of knowing...She could have come to me. Although we weren't close...maybe if I had been more present in Mira's life she would have trusted me. I could have found Sienna sooner and been there to protect her. Maybe Celeste didn't have to die for this had I...

"No." The only word Sienna could manage, whispered and broken.

Mira was the first to speak, after a long stretch of silence. "The Rebels knew that someone from Hagen's line could read the glyphs. All they needed was your name and the confirmation of blood."

Her hand lifted like she might reach for the screen, but stopped short. A flicker ran through her expression—disbelief, confusion. Her fingers hovered, not quite able to bring herself to make sense of it.

"The High Priest," Mira murmured.

I shifted uncomfortably. "What?"

"They knew." Sienna repeated, the words sharp but hollow.

"He knew exactly who you were." Mira's gaze snapped to mine, then back to Sienna. "That's why they were watching you."

Sienna finally moved, stepping back for space to breathe. But the screen was still there, glowing with indisputable proof. Mira scrolled faster, desperate for more—more names, more files. More answers. And then—an image.

Temples, surrounded by what resembled the ruins of the Sacred Lands. The arch. The campus buildings—places we walked through every day, the structures that loomed over us without a second thought. They'd been built on top of something older.

A line of text flashed beneath it.

"The AstralScroll Codex. Professor Taran, you son of a bitch," I muttered, scanning through the images. Every bit of it was familiar—because we'd seen it before.

The old temples. The new ones being resurrected in the rubble. The old gods slain, and a new faceless one levitating above them. He who was never depicted.

It was all right there, staring back at me. A pit formed in my stomach.

The screen flickered. Another file loaded.

Prophecy.

I clicked. Images flooded the screen. Symbols, carvings, markings that shouldn't have meant anything. But I knew them. Sienna could read them. The memory slammed into me—sharp, vivid. The weight of it in my hand, my gloved thumb tracing the patterns.

"This is the same kind of etching from my *Advanced Runes and Glyphs* exam," I murmured.

Mira's gaze snapped to mine. Sienna nodded. "It's not like anything we've ever seen but...it reads almost like increments of time."

I scrolled through the images, my heart thudding against my ribs. Symbols carved in ways that shouldn't have made sense—but they did. A message. A code, a calendar, or something more.

The longer I looked at it, the more I saw it. The same pattern. A measurement. Time.

Mira leaned in, eyes wide. "What the hells does that mean?"

"It means the Cynod isn't just hiding something," I murmured. "They're trying to bury it. They *have* buried it."

Mira's fists clenched. "She knew."

Sienna's face went ashen, her hands shaking at her sides. "She knew."

"She knew," Mira repeated, her voice breaking.

A sickening certainty curled in my gut. This wasn't just a secret. It wasn't just history.

It was a target on our backs. On Tía's, and now on ours.

9

KOA

The Underworld was caught in that limbo between slow and total chaos. Smoke curled through the air, thick with the stench of tobacco and indulgence, seeping into the very bones of the place. Saturday nights were like this. It wasn't a fight night, and it wasn't First Friday. Just the awkward lull before things picked up. The kind of slow hour where The Underworld caught its breath. People were around, but not many. Not until the later hours of the night. When the monsters came out to play.

The bar we lounged around in the far corner was empty save for Nola, half-focused on a deal Ikari had started. One that had stalled with Wren and the others now unreachable. The neon glow of the backlit bottles cast sharp lines across her face, her expression unreadable as she waited for the missing pieces to fall into place.

I leaned back in my chair, cigar perched between my fingers, the slow burn releasing a steady curl of smoke. Across from me, Jed and Adler slid into their seats, envelope in hand—mirror images if you ignored the locs on one and the waves on the other. Two sides of the same coin, polished smooth by a life of indulgence.

"That was fast," I said, tapping ash into the tray.

Jed glanced at Adler. "Do you think he meant that as an insult?"

"Nah." Adler shook his head. "He'd never stoop so low."

"I would," I muttered, rolling the cigar between my fingers before taking another slow drag.

Adler smirked. "You placed a rush order. We followed the two-business-day turnover. Anything less would be unacceptable business practices. Customer service is dying, us Mercers do our best."

I slid the money across the table, leaned back, and took a sip of my drink. The ice clinked against the glass, a sharp contrast to the low hum of music vibrating through the floors. "Your discoveries don't leave this table. Not beyond Ikari. Understood?"

"Copy, copy." Jed let out a quiet laugh, nudging Adler, who slid a manila envelope toward me.

I flipped through the contents. Basic background on the rebellion—another attempt at what had already failed time and time again. The Cynod had crushed every uprising since assuming power, leaving thousands dead, entire families snuffed out to prevent the possibility of retaliation. The cycle repeated, blood spilled, hope strangled before it could take root.

Vitória's file was thick, packed with details—the instigator, the lure, the one who made the first move in the attack. Sienna had confirmed as much. But there was very little on Zélia, and by very little, I meant nothing at all.

I peered up at them over the papers. "Are there pages missing?"

Adler shook his head. "Zélia doesn't exist."

"Try again." My fingers tightened around the cigar.

"Wolfe personally ran the search five times," Adler said. "Covered every base."

Jed shrugged. "She is, for all intents and purposes, a ghost. Figment of our imagination. Poof."

Even in the grainy photo, something about her face nagged at me. It itched at the back of my mind, a resemblance to—what? I could tell by the way Jed and Adler shifted that something was bothering them, too.

"Out with it."

Adler exhaled. "This has only happened once before."

"It's possible there's no Zélia because Zélia was never born. Legally, anyway," Jed said, his voice laced with a playful edge.

I frowned, trying to make sense of it. "As in, a home birth?"

Jed shrugged casually, a smirk playing at the corners of his lips. "Sure. Or—"

"Whoever Zélia was before is dead, and Zélia is not Zélia at all," Adler interrupted, his tone blunt and final.

A waitress set a fresh drink down in front of me, along with a new ashtray and two fresh-cut cigars for the Mercers. They cupped their hands around their lighters, twin flickers of flame igniting in unison as they lit up.

I stared down at my hand, at the ink twining up my arm, blending with the rest of the black-and-gray tattoos that covered me from throat to knuckles. The red glow of my mate mark looped around my ring finger, swirling, shifting in its ever-present reminder as I let the glamour slip. From where I sat, only the Mercer brothers could see, and they were no threat to me. The warmth of the mark was a steady pulse, a tether to something I still didn't fully understand. With every mile of distance between us, there was a pull to stop the tautness of that chord—to come back together.

"We came into some information that essentially confirms the Cynod's involvement in the accident."

"Fuck, man," Jed muttered.

Adler sighed. "Sorry to hear that."

Even though we all existed in the same world, the Mercers and the Ikaris didn't know what it was like to face parental neglect. They had no idea what it meant to be discarded by your own family. They worked with their parents. Trusted them. Spent time with them. Pity lingered in both their gazes, but for once, it didn't make me angry. It just made me tired.

Nola walked over, a sly grin on her lips. "She's here."

"Who the fuck let her in?" I dragged a hand down my face.

Nola clipped a laugh. "Mentiria's princess loves making a scene. It was that or another viral moment—which I know you loved so much."

I shot her a look. "I need thirty minutes. Keep her occupied."

Nola mock-saluted and strode toward the bar, where Alanna was already irritating the bartender, who appeared blankly unimpressed.

Jed grinned. "How's that working out for you, buddy?"

"I'm not having this conversation," I muttered.

Jed raised his hands. "Merely asking. There are inquiring minds—such as mine."

Adler, mercifully, circled back to the initial conversation. I nodded in thankful respect. "This intel. Verified?"

"Let's say it came from an indisputable source."

Adler exhaled smoke, watching me. "I don't envy being in your position."

Only idiots did. And the Mercers weren't idiots.

The crowd had filled in. The murmur of conversation had thickened into a low, steady hum, the scent of expensive colognes and burning cigars mixing with the ever-present smoke that clung to The Underworld's walls. Laughter erupted from a nearby table, too sharp, too forced—someone losing more than they'd expected in a bet. Across the room, movement caught my eye. My next meeting had arrived.

A trio, slickly dressed, oozing confidence they hadn't earned. Their suits were tailored but just a little too new, their shoes polished but not yet worn at the crease. Fresh players. The kind who thought they were about to break into something big.

Their leader—a man draped in a platinum chain with a watch that threw sparks in the dim light—tilted his chin like we were equals. His canines caught the glow, diamonds punched into them. I let my eyes pass over his crew before raising my glass in silent acknowledgment.

A pitch for a new magic-infused substance only found in one of the countries bordering the Sacred Lands up north—something for the upstairs crowd at The Vortex. The kind of people who paid triple for exclusivity, who wanted the rush of power humming in their veins without the risk of losing control. If it worked, it could be lucrative. If it backfired, it would be another problem for me to clean up.

Adler noticed my shift in focus and smirked, exhaling a slow stream of smoke. "Looks like you've got business."

"Always."

Jed tapped the edge of his cigar against the tray. "Think they've got anything worth listening to?"

I swirled my drink, letting the amber liquid catch the light. "We'll see. When Ikari is back, we'll circle back to this. My place." I stood. "Only location I can assure isn't bugged."

Jed and Adler exchanged a look I didn't appreciate. I caught it as I turned.

"Keep digging on Zélia," I told them. "There's something out there. Tell Wolfe I'll double his pay if he finds it. And let *Noctis Fraternitas* know I'm open to negotiations."

Jed let out a low whistle. "That serious?"

I took one last sip of my drink, set the glass down, and walked away.

10

MIRA

My almond-shaped nails clicked against my keyboard at a rate that was probably obnoxious to anyone in my vicinity. Did Professor Marco already give us a detailed cheat sheet for this spell? Yes. Was I still taking my own notes based on his verbal lecture as well? Also yes. You could never be too careful. He could give a tidbit of pertinent information in his verbal lecture that he missed in the cheat sheet. I'd seen it happen before.

"As with any other form of magic, you must give the spell your entire focus. Any wavering in intention can lead to critical disaster. You'll get to a certain point where it comes as second nature. For now, let's be incredibly intentional when setting the spells," Professor Marco said as he pointed to the directions on the screen behind him.

Katia wasn't typing like me, although she was watching him very intensely. Her gaze tracked over his hands as the spell fell from his lips, and he seemed to pick something right out of the atmosphere. A string of light lit, it felt...raw.

The string expanded and spun around his body until it disappeared into thin air. He spoke, even appeared to be yelling, but we couldn't hear a thing he was saying. There was nothing visible, no barrier that we could detect, yet no sound he created made it out. With a quick swipe of his hands, his words boomed in the space, and he smiled at our reaction to the sudden change.

"I'm sure you all grew up with parents who performed spells, but this one I find to be a great starter as you gain your magic." Professor Marco took a seat at his desk. "Any questions?"

"After the spell is set, can you move? Is it set around your body or to the area you cast it in?" someone asked from the back row.

An excellent question, one I had myself.

"Again, the spell works based on your intention. The actual words of the spell grant you access to the magic and create the barrier. When you speak them, if you wish to move about, make sure you hold that in your mind. There are other advancements to the basic spell—making it so that you can still hear everything around you, a wider net of silence, etc. But right now we're going to focus on the foundation of the spell," the professor responded. "Anything else?"

"What is it exactly that you're pulling from the air?" I asked.

"Raw magic. It's in everything around us, the spell brings it forth, makes it something tangible for you to use and guide."

"Can you get it to do anything you wish?" a boy behind me asked. A little too inquisitively for my liking. He knew exactly what he'd do with such a power.

The professor shook his head. "No, everything has its limits. Think of it as a form of assistance. You can't use it to gift you powers of another nahual or anything that extreme. You can guide it to stop sound from escaping, to heal small wounds as a non-gifted healer, cloak an item. When you mix with herbs, the possibilities open up even more. Birth control is one of the most popular mixes of raw magic and herbs."

There were endless theories about how our nahuales functioned. Scientists had been trying to solve that particular question as far back as our documentation went. Part of being an intelligent life form meant you always felt the need to ask, *Why?* and *How?*

Why are we here? How did the world come to be? Why are our gifts divided the way they are? How can you get a better gift? How does a *Chikchan* shift into a basilisk? How does an *Ajaw* alter your reality?

The answer to those big questions was...we weren't sure. We could theorize, look into a program like the AstralCodex, but even those forms of research only went back so far. But as Professor Marco said, raw magic was at the root of almost everything. That was one thing we were certain of. Depending on our gifts, it interacted with us differently. The leading theory was that it reacted with our

DNA in a certain way, and that was how you got your gifts. Something inside of us that held one of the twenty nahuales, ready to be unlocked—either by an academy or a public facility.

Raw magic itself was limitless, but he was right that our access and ability to manipulate did have parameters.

Professor Marco paused and waited to see if anyone else had something to ask. When we didn't, he nodded and motioned for us to give it a try with our partners. I checked my phone again, even though I knew there would be no new messages in my notifications.

"Still nothing?" Katia asked, knowing I'd been checking for a text from Wren.

"He sent an email yesterday, encrypted to let me know he was okay, but with everything that happened, I'm just worried," I responded as I chewed on my nail. Koa's uneasy attitude about the situation wasn't exactly helping calm my nerves.

"We both know he can take care of himself," Katia tried to reassure.

That was before the things working against us were so astronomical. Well, the Cynod was always working against him and his family, I supposed. There was always a threat that they'd be hurt, but the fact that action had been taken escalated things. Regardless, I was worried about him.

"Two of the most powerful people I know ended up at the bottom of the ocean right beside me," I whispered. "Anyway, did your parents do a lot of spells around you?"

"Not a ton. Small things, but I can't say I ever saw them use this one. Doesn't mean they didn't, and the point was that I didn't know," she laughed. "What about your aunt?"

"My tía did a lot of cloaking spells. I don't remember her using this one. She never really hid anything..." I trailed off, remembering that there were quite a few things she hid from me.

Katia just smiled and scooted my laptop closer to her. "You realize 95 percent of this is already on the cheat sheet?"

"The 5 percent matters, or he wouldn't have said any of it," I responded matter-of-factly.

"The more we have, the better," she agreed as she scanned. "Okay, you want to go first?"

I answered with an eager, "Yes."

Katia hit the zoom button a couple times on the notes so only the words of the spell were visible. I'd studied this language plenty, but it wasn't something that rolled off the tongue as well as the other languages I knew. It wasn't the gods' tongue—rather an old, harsh language only used now for spellwork.

I started reciting the spell, "*Obscura silentia, vox manet. Nihil auditur, nihil auditur. In me et hos fines, sonus omnis manet.*" And I felt a spark of...something.

But of course, because why not, my nahual flared to the surface. Every magical signature in the room barreled into me like a wave in a storm. Professor Marco said I needed to be focused, which would help if my focus wasn't everywhere all at once. I could sense every soul, but the ones who were using magic were too...bright. Too strong. I didn't know what the word for it was; I just knew it was all *too much.*

Katia's hand on my arm made me jolt.

"You okay?" She ran her gaze up and down my body.

"Magic got a little intense," I said as I shook it off. "I'm okay."

I waited a beat for the intensity to calm down and took a deep breath as I regulated once more. This time, I focused on one spot beside Katia and me, recited the spell, and pulled the raw magic from it. The magic was tangible, like electric putty in my fingers as I toyed with it and guided it to whirl around both Katia and me. As the glow of the magic disappeared, so did the voices around us.

"Wow, good job," Katia said, the sound bouncing against the barrier and around the space between us.

Part of me wanted to tell Katia about my nahual, but I wasn't sure if it would put her at risk. I didn't know if I should tell anyone. She watched me as I opened and closed my mouth to speak with brows drawn.

I disbanded the silencing spell and the raw magic sizzled back into the universe instead. "You want to try?"

"I've found the only magic I've been immediately good at is my nahual. Everything else is difficult." Katia sighed.

"Do you sense the magic around us? In everything?" I asked.

"Sort of? Did you ever do that weird drunk goggles thing in elementary school?"

"Where everything was muddied and discombobulated?" I said with a laugh.

"That's how it feels. I know it is there, but how to get to it…" she trailed off, her accent getting thicker as she focused on the magic.

It came so easily to me that I didn't really think about the possibility that Katia would have difficulty with it. "Should I get Professor Marco?"

"No." Katia shook her head. "I want to try first."

Her eyes narrowed on the laptop as she appeared to read the spell in her head before trying again. I watched as her lips pulled apart slowly and she fixed them around the first syllable. Holding her hands in the air between us, she kept going, and a spark at her fingers ignited. Katia's face perked up, but before she could get her grasp on it, it flickered away.

"It may take some practice," Professor Marco said as he stepped behind us.

"It's right at my fingertips, no pun intended," she grumbled, adding the last part like it was just too good to miss up on.

"Remember, while spell casting is about using the magic, you also need to give it your whole attention. Like I said in the lesson, your intent is important."

Katia quirked a brow. "Well, I had the *intention* of casting a silencing spell."

Professor Marco chuckled, the sparkle in his eye one that told me he'd seen this a few times. "You are an *Imix*, yes?"

"Yes."

"Have you shifted?"

"I've been close, but not fully yet," Katia admitted.

Professor Marco nodded and looked around. "Alfie, can you loan me some dragon fire?"

A boy with long red hair hurried over and sparked some in his hand. The fire was different from what I would light with a match; it was hotter, wilder. Red and orange similar to regular fire, but deeper and richer in an unnatural way.

"Now, this may not work if you emerge as a water dragon or one of the others, so don't be discouraged. But do you sense something when you focus on this?" the teacher asked Katia.

She didn't answer right away, just got closer than I personally would have to the flames. Katia ran her fingers through the tips of the fire and around the air before turning back and looking at the teacher. "There's an energy pulsing from it. Something familiar and comforting."

Professor Marco moved closer. "Mhm. Think of it like a beacon, dragon fire is part of you, so you are drawn to it. In the same way raw magic is part of you, you should be drawn to it. You have to take the time and effort to *feel*, though." He turned and spoke to the entire class this time. "Too many of us move through life without feeling our connections—emotional and magical. Even after you master this, remember to keep that connection, that sentiment, as if it were the first time you were experiencing it. Give thanks to this world for providing you with something you wouldn't have access to otherwise."

Some of the students dismissed him with an eye roll, marking him as a hippy naturalist, but that wasn't what I got from it. He was right; it was hard to acknowledge these things. To give life to the thought that your control wasn't tied to your skills or talent, but rather because this world allowed us to harness it. We could have easily been humans without the access, and too many of us didn't appreciate that simple fact enough.

Sweat beaded on Katia's brow as she focused, speaking the spell with more confidence than before. Her fingers sparked, and the raw magic pooled. She grabbed onto it, guiding it to move around us as she continued the spell. The smile on her face disappeared as the magic dispersed, but when she looked up at me, there wasn't any disappointment in her features this time.

"I felt it that go around." She beamed, and I squealed with excitement.

The bell rang, and Professor Marco yelled a reminder of today's homework to the class as we all filtered out. Not before he gave Katia a thumbs up for her progress on the second attempt.

We dodged a sea of students hurrying to get to their next class. I'd noticed a slight lull before midterms, and my assumption was that people were realizing they needed to take their ass to class now. Students in Professor Marco's next class were already trying to get into the room as we left. Probably looking for some guidance on how to bring their grades up.

Kuxtal Academy was a place for the elites. Even so, it had a habit of showing exactly who took their education seriously, and who thought they deserved to be here solely based on their status. No matter who you were, there was sure to be at least one class that challenged you.

"Any news on the junior military situation?" I asked as we stepped into the fresh air.

"Your father video called in for our first class, actually," she grumbled. "They are being very vague. Something is up."

I rolled my eyes. "I don't doubt that one bit. You have any friends in the class?"

"A couple, but many of them are the, what's the word...patriotic type?"

"Barf," I responded. Patriotic or so far up the Cynod's ass they couldn't tell up from down.

Katia guzzled down a very impressive amount of water. She'd said that the pitz team encouraged her to drink an entire gallon a day, and she was definitely committing.

"You've got therapy, right?" she asked, wiping some water off her chin.

"Sure do."

Kabans were out in the gardens, manicuring and creating new displays. I hadn't seen them do this yet. There had been a couple times the flowers lining the path were one color, and another one by the time I got out of class. They ran their hands across the lush rose bushes currently displayed, and the petals closed, shrinking until they were buds once more. White dandelions sprouted and took their place, wide and turned up to the sun. They were all so happy to be using their gifts in such a way. It made me think of Sienna. I missed that smile on her face.

"First one since...everything?" Katia flailed her hands in the air as she gestured to, well, everything.

My shoulders sagged. "Yes, and I don't know how much of it I can even talk to her about."

"Even after building trust, it's still hard. Yeah, I understand."

"On one hand, it would feel really fucking good to tell someone else, someone who doesn't have a stake in it all. On another, it's one more person who has the information and can use it against me."

"You mean the stuff with the rebels or something else?" Katia tilted her head like she was trying to read between the lines.

I bit my lip in contemplation. I should tell Katia about my nahual, but saying it out loud made it a little too real. Maybe I needed the reality check, and maybe it was better to tell someone I cared about before I even thought about telling my therapist. Thankfully, I knew just the spell to perform. Katia dug into her pocket to grab her phone, and looked over at me, shocked when the silencing barrier went up around us.

"I got my nahual," I said before I lost the courage.

Her gaze ran up and down my body, searching for proof. "Oh, that's amazing! What is it?"

"That's why I set the silencing spell...I, um...you can't tell—"

"Mira, I do not take our friendship lightly. You don't have to tell me if you don't want to, but I would never ever betray you," Katia said earnestly.

I smiled weakly because while that wasn't exactly the reason I was hesitating, it felt really good to hear.

"Oh, I know that. That's not why I'm hesitating. It's just, I don't quite understand it yet."

As Koa so lovingly reminded me, I was a know-it-all. If I *didn't* know it all, and there was no real way to even begin to fully understand the topic, I shied away from it. There were no answers to any questions she might have, because I had absolutely no idea the extent of my power.

"There isn't anyone you can ask for advice?" Katia asked.

"That's the problem. My nahual is *Kimi*..." I trailed off.

My chest warmed, as if saying it aloud and claiming my gift made it happy.

Her mouth fell open, and she scanned the surrounding people, even with the silencing spell. "You're sure?"

"What I did was a little incontestable."

Incontestable and hard to explain.

"As in?" she questioned.

"Ate rebel soldiers' souls." I grimaced.

"Okay, okay. Well, yes, that can really only be one thing," Katia laughed, a sound between awe and bewilderment. "What are you going to do? What do you need me to do?"

I wasn't sure what I expected from her. It wasn't as if I thought she'd accuse me of lying, or run away; she'd already proven that wasn't a factor. My anxiety sometimes convinced me that my friends didn't truly care, that they were looking for a way out at all times. Even knowing it wasn't true, her instant switch into how to help was...refreshing.

"Nothing right now. I don't know what it means for me, or even for the world. For this to come back after...however many years, it has to mean something. It being *me* has to mean something, too. I don't know."

Not to mention what Sienna told us about the prophecy. The mention of *death* could be me, my gift, or it could be actual dying. Branches could mean family trees, or something completely different. That was the thing about prophecies: they were never black and white. They left just enough gray for people to interpret them differently and believe only their version was the right one. We already had so much division, containing the prophecy and what it meant for all of us was much preferred.

"I understand why you're nervous to tell your therapist, too." Her mouth turned down into an understanding frown.

I spotted Jed near the mental health building and waved, and he tried to hide his excitement at seeing Katia. He pulled out his phone, shoving one hand into his pocket, using the other to pretend to scroll. It was cute, the way the twins lost their 'cool' when she was around.

Katia put her hand on my arm and stopped us, giving her backside to Jed. "Do you want me to wait with you until after your appointment? I can meet him later?"

"No." I shook my head. "Go have fun, I'll catch up with you later."

Katia stared me down for a few seconds longer than normal, waiting for me to change my mind, but I disbanded the silencing spell and pointed my chin toward Jed.

"Text the group chat, okay?" she said as she ran off and jumped into Jed's arms.

The mischievous twin offered me one last head nod before I ducked into the building and practiced some deep breaths. Dr. Puebla would be asking about how I felt off my medication, but that had been the least of my worries since our last session.

There was always a certain calm that fell over me once I reached this floor. Whether it was because of the aroma or if there was some other magic at play, I wasn't sure. The same girl who had asked about Koa before was behind the desk and checked me in without me having to give my name over. So I sat by the windows like I had before, and I let the warmth of the sun bathe my hands and arms.

The golden brown of my skin shimmered, but it only brought the memory of them being midnight black with my nahual. As if I'd dipped my arms into a tub of ink and pulled the color from the world. I closed my eyes, thinking back to the way the world shifted, how my vision changed, and how much more I could see. How much more I could sense.

It was hard to imagine a time when this...gift was widespread throughout the population. There had to be checks and balances, some way to control it. Then again, we were a much more trustworthy bunch at that time. Before things like greed and power struggles took over us.

"Mira," Dr. Puebla exclaimed from the hall.

"Hi," I said as I found her waiting in the doorway.

Sometimes I wondered what exactly her closet at home looked like. She always wore a pencil skirt, a button-down, and some sort of cute but comfy pumps. I imagined all her clothes being folded neatly in drawers, and that it took her approximately two minutes to choose an outfit, thanks to everything seeming to piece together perfectly. Although it was the most put-together people who often had messy closets.

She shifted her braid over her shoulder and gestured to the seats. I chose the same one I had each time I'd come, ever the lover of consistency. Which was unfortunate lately.

"Mira, how are you feeling?" She tapped on her tablet and looked up at me.

"Generally or in regard to the pills?" I asked.

"Always the one to jump right into things," she laughed. "Whichever you'd prefer to start with."

That probably looked suspicious.

"I did stop them completely, a little ahead of the weaning schedule," I responded.

"Hm, okay. Can I ask why?"

"I felt okay, and I don't know...it was giving me more anxiety knowing that they weren't on the market and whatnot."

A half-truth, not the whole, and Dr. Puebla seemed to notice.

"I can certainly understand that. No harsh side effects?"

When I first started the pills, most of my anxiety was internal: the constant spiraling thoughts, the panic attacks, adjusting to my new normal. We tried SSRIs first, a medication that was more of an antidepressant and long-term, and those gave me terrible side effects. So this one was supposed to be more of a short-term solution. Aanteni, the medication I took previously, was believed to be in the benzodiazepine class—a central nervous system depressant. But as we searched for a new long-term solution, we found out that it lacked a dependence quality. In turn, it was hard to see how the medication in specific was helping, and how my support system was impacting. We knew it was a mixture, but figuring out the...percentage of either proved difficult.

Especially now, where coming off of it hadn't had any noticeable side effects.

"Honestly, it's been hard to even keep track with everything that I've had going on. But nothing alarming," I responded.

"Do you mind sharing what has been keeping you busy?"

I picked at my cuticles and squeezed my toes together in my shoe, hoping they were small enough movements that they wouldn't be detected.

"I-I'd like to tell you, but I'm..."

Dr. Puebla set down the tablet and slowly stood from her seat. "Why don't we switch the scenery a bit?"

She swiftly moved her hand across the air, and the wall of flowers and greenery pulled apart into another area I hadn't seen before.

"This is my nursery. I've got it climate-controlled and solar-powered, completely off the grid. You are the only other person I've shown it to." She stepped toward the opening, waiting for me to join.

I inspected the space, and it looked safe. It was actually sort of quaint. Small, maybe just 175 square feet, and she had every inch covered in plants. Shelves lined the walls, a table in the middle with a few shearing scissors and pots of water. Bags of soil and other supplies were found beneath the shelves.

"Why do you have all of this when you have magic?" I asked.

"I like to get back to the root of it all, for lack of a better phrase. It feels good to create something with my magic, but watching it grow as I tend to it naturally, there's something more rewarding about that. Have a seat." She pulled out a stool from beneath the steel table.

I cautiously sat, and she handed me a pair of shears and set a pretty large plant between us. Green ribbon-like leaves spilled from it, varying shades of green and yellow stripes. Some of them were completely straight, others crinkled slightly at the edges.

"This is a Chlorophytum comosum, or to normal people, a spider plant." Dr. Puebla smiled. "Do you mind if I seal the wall to my office?"

She knew about my past of being trapped, the fear of being confined, but...none of that arose in me, and I nodded my head.

"Are you familiar with propagation?"

"I am. Sienna is a big plant person. She's also a *Kaban* like you," I responded and twisted the pot.

"I remember that." She nodded softly. "I have had this spider plant for, goodness, it has to have been decades now. It has traveled with me between schools, jobs, and relationships. I take great pride in keeping her alive all this time without the use of my nahual."

"She's magnificent," I said as I ran my fingers over the firm, waxy leaves.

"She is. Though if I did not prune her, the possibility of propagating, of bringing forth new life and energy, would not have been possible. I think of us a lot like plants, which I'm sure isn't too surprising given my nahual. They are living, breathing organisms, just as we are."

Dr. Puebla sifted through the palms until she found a brown, brittle leaf at the base. "Think of this leaf as negative energy, this lifeless piece is but a small part of the full plant, yes? But if I let it stay here, if I let it fester and grow bigger, spread to the other leaves, it can bring down all those decades of work. I wouldn't be able to spread her love into all of these other pots."

I realized that many of the plants on the wall behind us were spider plants. They all resembled this one on the table, in various sizes, but they all had come from this one. Dr. Puebla snipped the dead leaf and dropped it into a trash can.

"Can you fold a paper towel and spray it with water for me, please?" she asked.

I did as she requested, and she once again rustled through the plant. She smiled as she found what she was searching for and pointed to what looked like a tiny little spider plant hanging from one of the fully formed leaves.

"People have different names for these, but I call them spiderettes." Dr. Puebla carefully examined the tiny plant. I pushed the bowl between us, and she carefully snipped the spiderette and made sure it was making good contact with the wet paper towel. "We'll give it a little while, once it sprouts roots, I'll move it to soil with the other plants on the shelf there. If you'd like, you can take it home with you then."

We sat for a beat, and I could tell it was my turn to talk. To snip the lifeless leaf and let myself flourish.

"I got my nahual," I said.

A simple fact, no emotion attached to it. As if I were spewing out a mathematical equation.

"Not the normal reaction to receiving your nahual. Are you disappointed with what you emerged as?"

"Disappointed, no...unsure of what to do with it, yes."

"Are you comfortable enough to share it with me? Remember, this is a safe space, and this specific room we are in is closed off from everything. School and...government included."

I nodded and lifted the little spiderette bowl. "I'm a *Kimi*."

"A *Kimi*. Okay." Dr. Puebla couldn't hide the shock or confusion about where to go next.

A woman who had never worn this visage since I'd known her. She always knew the right thing to say, and as she gathered her thoughts, I set the propagated plant on the shelf beside me.

"How did this realization come about? Where did you emerge?"

"That part I'm not sure I should say, not because I don't trust you but for your..." I paused, looking for the right word. "Safety."

Another red flag for a therapist who had given me nothing but transparency, but it was my reality. She could get hurt if I pulled her into the world of the rebels.

"You are safe, yes?" she asked.

I rolled my shoulders. "Relatively."

"Okay. Can you explain what happened?"

"It was like I'd been living in this world, but not *here*, until the moment I emerged. Color was different. I could see and sense things I couldn't before."

She went to reach for her journal, but brought back her hands with her mouth pursed. "Did that make you uncomfortable?"

"No, not uncomfortable. Just different. It was as if my body knew that this was normal, and it was waiting for my mind to fully catch up. I can't control it quite yet. I was able to redirect energy from someone meaning to hurt me...into someone who was injured. It wasn't like anything I'd read about before."

"As you know, it has been many years, and what we did know was destroyed by the people who forced us to turn from the old gods," she said.

It was the first time she'd mentioned her stance on it, whether she was an avid Solis worshipper or not. I had it on good authority that most people who were at this level of education, and who didn't benefit directly from the church, weren't.

"I haven't had too much time to look into it yet, but yes, that is what I found initially. I don't know who to trust with the information."

"Nobody," she said quickly. "You know I am an advocate for open communication and transparency. However, in this case, do not tell a single person you don't fully trust. Let me see if I can find anything on my side, and I can share with you in our next session."

"That is what I thought too." I sighed.

"But, Mira, thank you for trusting me enough to tell me. That sort of trust is hard-earned, and I'm glad I can be a safe place for you. I can gather a bit better why the pills may not have been on your mind." She paused. "When was the last day you took the pills?"

"I don't remember the exact date, maybe a month ago? I can check my calendar at home."

Dr. Puebla pushed her vast spider plant into the middle of the table. "And the day you emerged?"

"Two Saturdays ago."

"Okay. I will see what I can find."

It wasn't hope I felt, but something did lift from my chest as I sheared that leaf.

11

MIRA

Classes were out for the day, and it was Friday, so Sienna was meeting me down at the cenotes. We'd found this to be one of our favorite places. Away from eyes and ears, lots to explore, or even just to relax. She was, apparently, running late, and as I spotted her sipping a coffee and strolling leisurely in my direction, I feigned irritation.

"Late and with coffee?" I exclaimed with a hand on my chest.

"Don't worry, I got you one too," she said as she lifted a cup holder from the paper bag she was carrying.

I took a sip. "Oh, fuck yes. You're forgiven."

"Thought so." Sienna smirked and walked into the cave opening.

We'd been through most of the common areas in the caves already. Any other time I wouldn't want to venture too far, but with Sienna's *Kaban* powers I felt much safer. We weaved down a few dark tunnels, using our flashlights to guide us. One of the spots we had to turn sideways to get through. This particular spot had thick layers of untouched dirt and dust covering the ground, our footsteps the only things marring it.

"Wonder why nobody has come this far?" I asked as a chill ran over my skin, and I shuddered.

"Don't know, don't care. Just happy to be away from the bullshit," Sienna responded.

"Any changes since our last talk?" I asked.

She was in a...weird space with Koa. Not directly weird because of him, but entirely because of our parents. They were still very much smitten, but with these external, entirely public forces working against them, it was making it difficult to be anything. I didn't blame her. I'd offered my dorm up a couple of times so they could at least talk. Regardless, it wasn't the ideal situation. That I knew.

"Trying to remember that I love him," she grumbled. "And that all of this will be a funny part of our story later. That doesn't change the fact that I'm still over it all."

"Want me to eat her soul?"

Sienna shuffled a step and paused, as if maybe it wasn't a terrible idea, but she shrugged and laughed it off. "I'm trying to focus on school right now. Can't give your parents any excuses to kick me out."

"You know Koa and I would do everything in our power to stop that," I said.

Sienna's eyes dropped to the ground, something crossing over her features that I couldn't quite read. A look I wasn't familiar with—and I was familiar with all of her looks. It felt like...skepticism. Uncertainty about whether she was worth that.

"Hey, what's goin—"

Sienna's hand jutted out to stop our procession. "Stop."

"I'm just saying, Si, that—"

Her arm stayed firm across my stomach as her eyes scanned the stone walls. "Mira, don't move."

I tried to see what she saw, to sense what she did, but all I saw was dirty rock. If there was one thing I did know, it was that we always trusted each other without question. So I did as she said and waited as she ran her hands across the walls.

"You see that?" Sienna flashed her phone light onto the ground a few feet ahead of us.

I narrowed my eyes. "The scratches?"

The dirt rattled and shifted as Sienna waved her hand out into the air in front of her. Slowly, it piled into a neat heap behind us. Only then did I see what she had. Something had been scribed into the floor, or chiseled more so. It was the gods' tongue, the language that only Sienna could decipher.

"What's it say?" I asked.

"It's a warning," she responded as she kept moving forward.

"We're not...heeding that warning?"

Sienna didn't reply. I shook my head and caught up with her. Her eyes were wide, not in surprise, but in focus as she continued reading symbols on the floor. I concluded that it was some sort of directions. The part of me that needed to know everything about *everything* was getting restless. I definitely didn't want to distract her, so I kept my questions to myself. She suddenly stopped at a dead end wall and ran her finger across one last set of symbols.

She mumbled something as she pressed both of her hands against the stone. The wall, ever so slowly, moved, sliding against the ground until a room appeared behind it.

"I was right," she said as if she couldn't believe it. Her stunned expression melted into a prideful smile as we entered the space, and the wall closed in behind us.

"Where are we?" I asked with my eyes on our only known exit now sealed.

"Some of the carvings had worn with age. I'm not entirely sure. If I deciphered it correctly, this has been here since Herta was young and the stars were still finding their place. It was made by children of the gods."

"Like demigods...as in half gods, half fae?"

The Popol Vuh had spoken of the children of gods. Nobody knew where the original book was. Large portions had been translated over time. There was one small section that spoke of the gods lying with the fae and humans. Advising that the fae were strong enough to carry their children, and the humans didn't come to full term. After that, the next section of the book was nowhere to be found. No translations, no trace of where that part of the story existed. People made up their own stories; it was even a subgenre of fiction romance books, but nobody actually knew what happened.

Sienna put her fingernail between her teeth. "Yeah. Something isn't adding up, though. The spell doesn't let just anyone in."

"Meaning?"

"The Cynod has some explaining to do." She pointed across the space.

Rather than only the gods' language, the common tongue was also found here. Similar to the file we found on the thumb drive from my tía, names filled multiple columns. It felt like a log, making sure every person who used these tunnels was accounted for. The names at the top, however, were shockingly familiar. Tecun, Canek, Aantaj, Noh, and others I'd seen many times.

"This is going to sound crazy as all hells, but...only those with gods' blood are allowed in here," Sienna said as she walked toward one of the tunnels.

"Gods' blood..." I trailed off, my mind going back to the names written on the walls.

The area we were in was wide, ceilings so high I had to wonder how far underground we were, if the sky wasn't showing. The walls were lined with dozens of tunnels, all with symbols arched over the entrances. While I couldn't read the language, it seemed clear that these tunnels led to various places around campus.

"This goes to our dorms," Sienna said before pointing to another. "That goes to the beach near Koa's condo."

"I bet we're too far below ground for the wards to work on the boundary spell," I said with a smile.

"Shit, I think you're right." The impact of the realization fell over her slowly, her mouth stretching into a grin.

We could sit in the positivity of how this could impact us—Koa and Sienna specifically. However, there was more here. More that needed to be analyzed and discussed. The first being the fact that we were in this room at all.

"You know what this also means, right?" I asked.

"Please, if you love me at all, don't say it." She closed her eyes as though she were saying a silent prayer.

"Therapy 101: *Face the brutal facts*. The time to confront it is here, Si. This is official confirmation that you're from Hagen's line."

Sienna's shoulders dropped as she huffed out a breath and nodded. She hadn't said much else about it since we learned, and I was convinced she was completely ignoring it. She didn't know much about her bio dad. She told me once that her mother got really sad when she asked, and she never asked again. Her stepfather had been in the picture as far back as she could remember, so it never felt like she was missing anything. Now, there were some answers that could only come from her donor.

"Have you asked your mom since we found out?" I asked.

"No, not yet. I don't want to stress her out on top of everything else. Plus, who knows if the phone lines are even safe? Though, with a way around the wards, I'm falling short on excuses for why I shouldn't pay her a visit."

I agreed, but didn't want to push her too much on it either. These days, if it wasn't one problem we were dealing with, there were a hundred others waiting in line. I especially didn't want to bring up the fact that we were due for a talk with the rebels.

A flicker of hope danced across her face. "Want to try the one close to Koa's?"

"Sure," I responded, and just as we entered the dark tunnel, something else nagged at the back of my mind. An awareness of something not living, but alive, from one of the other tunnels. Sienna was already a few feet ahead, so I shook it off and caught up with her. There was no way this would be our last time visiting.

We were supposed to video chat with Koa and the Mercers, maybe Wren if he was back. The Mercers had some extra-secure app they used for business like this. One of Wolfe's handy developments.

Some form of magic lapped over my body, and I realized that the shiver I felt before might have been some sort of spell down here. Eventually, an image of the beach, blurred and off-kilter, stood at the end of the tunnel, and before I overanalyzed the situation, we pushed straight into it together. I waited for my academy tattoo to burn, to flash, or to do something to show that we weren't where we were supposed to be, but nothing happened.

"Well, damn," Sienna said as we popped up beside a rocky shore. I looked back, finding no evidence of a tunnel.

"Wait," I said. "Did you get the masking homework from Professor Marco this week?"

Sienna tugged at the end of her hair. "Yeah, good idea."

I pulled out my phone to make sure I followed the spell right. I practiced already in my room, but hadn't really been able to tell if it was working outside of the mirror. Sienna eyed the screen as we both recited the spell and changed our features enough to not be noticed.

"Perfect."

Nobody looked at us strangely as we emerged, not for popping out in a random spot on the beach or for noticing who we were. Thanks to the media, Sienna was just as noticeable as I was now. There'd been endless posts about her once she started dating Koa publicly, and now with Alanna in the mix, they'd all but doubled.

"Where did the other tunnels go?" I asked as we walked over to a trail.

"Looked like every important place you can think of. One of them was to the mainland, so that has to be a long one," Sienna said as she gazed up into the sky, recollecting.

It was sort of creepy thinking that people could have been underground anywhere on campus. I knew far too many shifty fae who would take advantage of that. I wondered if the demigods were fair and level-headed, or if they were more like the people who ran our world now.

"To think that has been beneath us all this time. Didn't appear used in the last couple of generations, though," I said with a shudder.

"Makes sense. Had to be long enough for the truth to be hidden. Then again, if anyone had stumbled down there, they would have had no idea what it was. I think the spell was set for anyone without gods' blood to see only a dead end."

I nudged her with my shoulder. "Lucky for us that we have someone who can read all of those symbols."

"Lucky indeed," she said with a click of her tongue.

"We've got to get to the condo; we were down there longer than I thought," I said as I checked my watch. "Don't need him in a bad mood if he finds out we were exploring creepy tunnels."

"I'm also good at handling that," she retorted, damn near skipping toward the high-rise.

"Barf, what did I say about that?" I responded and ran to swat at her.

Sienna laughed, but stopped suddenly when we made it to the main road. I followed her gaze, seeing a very specific sports car parked on the street.

"Did he tell you he was back?" Sienna asked.

She knew the answer. I would have told her immediately.

"No."

I pulled out my phone and called Wren, watching as he got out of his car, and the line went straight to voicemail. He ducked into a store a few blocks from Koa's condo, and I bit my lip. Jumping to conclusions wasn't going to get me anywhere, *I* knew that. My mind, on the other hand…

"Do you want to go in there?" Sienna asked.

"If he didn't tell me he was back, no. Let's just go to Koa's."

12

MIRA

"What are you doing here? Whoa, where's the fire?" Koa jumped back as I stormed into his condo, the masking spell dissolving as I stepped up to the door.

"No fire," I said. "Everything's fine."

"No offense, but you're shit at hiding your emotions from me. And tell me, how much trouble are you two going to be in?" he responded.

"Says the God of rule breaking himself. Give her a minute. I'll catch you up later," Sienna said as she pressed up to the tips of her toes and kissed him.

Koa looked back over at me once, but did as Sienna advised. "Were you seen coming in?"

"Snuck in like a mistress. Changed my identity, since apparently role play is now part of our relationship." Sienna pulled away and joined me in the kitchen.

It was evident that Sienna hadn't been here since last weekend. There was no food, no leftovers, barely a snack that wasn't a cardboard protein bar. A cough in the living room startled me, and I peeked around the corner to find the Mercer twins sitting awkwardly on the couch.

"They officially in on all this?" I asked.

"Considering they were the ones who brought the information, yeah," Koa answered.

It wasn't that I didn't trust them. If Katia trusted them enough, so did I, but it was hard to keep things under the radar once too many people knew.

Knowledge that the children of the Cynod were in conversation with the rebels was something we needed to keep on a need-to-know basis.

I grabbed a bottle of some sports drink with extra electrolytes and headed toward the living room. Wren didn't call back or text, and I wasn't sure why he wouldn't have. We'd only talked a couple of times since he left, and 'talk' was a stretch. One-sided conversations without immediate response. I wasn't asking for him to be up my ass every second. After everything we'd been through, I thought at the very least I'd get a 'hey, love, I'm back.'

Jed and Adler looked at each other, a wordless conversation passing between them before Adler sat forward and stared directly at me.

"We need to discuss something. Pertaining to you and Koa. Regarding your relationship with a certain individual," he said.

My lip pulled back in confusion. Koa went rigid, nodding for him to continue.

Adler scratched his chin and pushed his laptop to the center of the coffee table. "We've been digging into anyone with ties to the rebels, but we're also tracing anything we can find on the Cynod."

"Okay?" I asked. "We know they're bad people, so that won't surprise us."

"It's not them, it's who is connected to them," Jed added. His tone and face were lethally serious. Which made me nervous, because it was *Jed*. The goofy twin.

The front door slammed shut, and awareness ran all over my body.

"Getting lazy, Canek. Front door was unlocked," Wren said as he entered the room.

Adler pulled back his laptop and narrowed his gaze at him. Wren was holding a small gift bag, fluffed-tissue paper sprouting out of the top. The energy in the room was just...off. And it was all coming from the Mercer brothers.

"Hey, love," Wren said with a genuine smile. "Thought I'd see you after this."

Sienna eyed him, her gaze bouncing between Jed and Wren. She felt what I did. But, regardless, I was happy to see him. I stood up from the couch and gave him a hug, a very feline-like purr coming from his chest as he rubbed his cheek against mine. He handed me the gift-bag and I peered inside, unable to see past the tissue paper.

Jed broke the awkward silence as he quickly packed up his things and stood. "We've, um, got business to tend to. Canek, give us a call when you're...available."

Adler shook his head. "No, we can't. They need to know. Time is of the essence."

Another strained wordless conversation between them, and this time, Koa was losing his patience; I could see it on his face. *Who's bad at hiding emotions now, Koa?*

"Spit it out before I rip it out of you," Koa snapped, even though his body language was a harsh contrast with Sienna's legs tossed over his.

"It's about...Ikari," Jed admitted.

"Ikari as in me or Ikari as in my brothers?" Wren's whole body went tight.

Adler sat up, daggers shooting from his eyes. "He works for the Cynod."

"We know that?" I questioned. "He worked security at the gala we attended."

Wren's face didn't give me much, but his body did. Tension crept up his neck. Emotions were running through him at the speed of light.

"Not the contract with the Cynod and Ikari clan," Adler said. "He's keeping tabs on you," he finished with his gaze on me.

"Wolfe pulled a call from him to the official Cynod office right before the crash. He told them you were headed back to the island," Jed said.

"He's been calling every Friday evening to this one specific line, one that took Wolfe time to decrypt. We only knew it was at the Cynod building, on a secured line they use for their illegal work."

"Wolfe tapped into the line last week and was ready when he made the call in." Adler clicked a couple of buttons on his laptop.

Wren wasn't speaking, wasn't moving. He didn't say it was untrue, didn't fight or defend himself. He stood still as a statue as his voice played out of the speakers, his gaze on me. There was something he was trying to convey. My attention was pulled away at the sound of my name.

The words were muffled as my heartbeat raced, as my skin got clammy, and my head pounded. Everything around me spun, and my knees couldn't decide between buckling or going unsteady.

"Stop it," I whispered.

"No, let that shit play," Koa snapped. He was locked in a death stare trained on Wren.

"Stop it," I said a little louder this time, and I felt Koa's gaze flick over to me. "Fucking stop it!"

Adler didn't wait for my brother to oppose; he slammed the laptop shut. Sienna was on her feet in a blink. She hooked her arm through mine.

"Breathe, Mir," she said.

Her voice was little more than an echo in my mind, lost behind the spiral pulling me down. My feet moved, being guided toward my room by Sienna, and I tried to catch my breath. I stared at my best friend, trying to figure out what had happened and where I had gone wrong.

"What was..." I tried to speak, but Sienna grabbed a cold bottle from my mini-fridge and pulled me close.

Shocking the nervous system was one of my favorite tricks to break an anxiety spiral when I was younger. The cold bit into me now as she pressed the bottle against the back of my neck. My lungs started to settle as I calmed, until the crash of furniture and shouting from the living room snapped them back into overdrive.

"I'll check," Sienna said, and I was already following when she wrenched open the door.

Koa had Wren pinned by the throat, slammed hard against the wall. Jed and Adler shouted, trying to wedge between them, but my brother wasn't listening. His eyes were wild, body thrumming with violence, every muscle intent on snapping bones. The thing that shook me the most was the fact that Wren wasn't even trying to fight back. His arms hung slack at his sides, body sagging under Koa's grip. He took the beating, his eyes closed and...resolve set into his face.

"Koa," I said. He didn't respond. Wren's eyes opened, and only when he saw me did he fight back.

"I can explain," Wren gasped.

Koa pushed further, chest rattling, and his eyes narrowed into reptilian slits. He was seconds away from trapping Wren inside his mind—if not stone.

I sprinted across the room, catching my brother's arm, tugging until his head snapped toward me.

Calmly, I stated, "If you kill him before I get answers, I'll never forgive you."

Koa's jaw ticked as he fought against his own instinct to separate Wren's head from his body. With as much restraint as he was capable, he let him down.

"You have ten minutes and then I want you out of my fucking house. Or you'll be leaving inside a duffle bag." Koa turned, the balcony sliding door rattling in his wake.

Sienna stared at me as she waited for a sign that I was okay with talking to him. I wiggled my fingers, a reminder of what I could do if I wanted to. She nodded, grabbed the smoke jar off the table, and joined Koa, offering him a lit feyfog joint.

My feet shuffled as I turned back to my room, and Wren hesitated to follow me. He held his hand on the doorknob, silently asking if I was okay for him to close it, and I nodded. I moved to the ledge on my window, the one that displayed the coast and the mainland skyline. After all the distance that wrecked me, right now I needed the space between us. Wren stayed planted by the door, his mouth opening and closing.

"You said you can explain, and if I'm tracking it correctly, you have 8.5 minutes left," I said.

"I never meant to hurt you," he said as he took one step and stopped again.

That was always the line. 'I didn't *mean* to.' It wasn't an apology for the action taken, just for the fact that it wasn't their intention to inflict harm. I'd heard it from Forrest ample times, and I was completely numb to it. I wanted an explanation. In detail.

I lifted my brows in anticipation. "That doesn't mean much to me right now."

"They came to me wanting information about you. I don't know who saw or when, but they heard we were...friends. They were interested in how you were doing in school at first, and I thought it was odd. Then they started to ask more in-depth questions. I tried to ignore them, to avoid them in any way I could. When they realized I didn't have any intention of helping, they forced me into a blood bond. If I didn't, they'd hurt you. They showed me how easily they could…" Wren paused, his fists balling. "So I gave them half-truths and small lies. I made sure that you were safe. The blood bond swore me into secrecy."

Blood bonds were unheard of; more than that, they were forbidden. They weren't something an outside party could control, which the Cynod didn't allow. Turns out they were keeping it for themselves.

"That's why you didn't stop them from playing the recording," I whispered.

He hadn't denied anything, didn't attempt to jump across the living room and smash the laptop. Wren had kept his stare locked in mine, with no ill will or deceit, only…something fragile.

"What I told them in that recording was wrong. You were here when I called, and I told them you were at your dorm. I don't know if they caught on, and that's why they tried to kill all of us or what. They haven't asked me for anything outside of the updates since the crash."

"They don't know we're aware it was them." I dragged my hand over my face.

Wren seemed to take my reaction as understanding and strode across the room, but I put my hand up before he got to me. My body instinctively recoiled, falling into a defensive position.

"I—do you think I'd hurt you?" he asked, his face crumpling.

No? Yes? Maybe…my life had taught me to never *ever* underestimate someone. Never think that something is too far out of the question. When it came to particular motivations, some people would do anything. Realistically, how well did I know Wren? I thought I knew him. Even in our intimate moments, my soul had felt at peace with him. There was the factor of his family, of the things he'd done to protect them, but if I was honest, maybe I didn't know him at all.

"I don't know what I think right now." Something came to my mind. "Was it my parents?"

Wren almost appeared excited to answer the question. He perked up, energy radiating off him as he said, "No, it wasn't."

"Who was it?"

Wren's blood vessels bulged as his body went stiff. Dark lines ran up and down his tawny skin, there was pain in his posture, but also that same eagerness.

"You can't say, can you? I have to be the one to figure it out?"

He nodded his head ever so slightly—a move that might have taken things too far in his blood bond.

"The priest?" I asked, hopping off the window ledge.

"No."

"Rowan's uncle? Clyde?" One small step forward.

"No."

That left only one person.

"It can't be him," I said as I shuffled backward and went to my desk. "No, that can't be true. He's looked after me and my tía for years!"

I grabbed one of the framed pictures of my tía and me, one that was taken at Aantaj Labs. I remembered him being there, congratulating her, and making sure she knew how important her work was. I remembered his approval allowing me to be the test subject in her most recent one.

"Why?" My lip wobbled and tears filled my eyes. Not only for me, but for my aunt, for the manipulation and years of lies she had to have been told.

"They wouldn't tell me why. But Mira, I swear—"

I slammed the picture frame down. "I can't right now, Wren. I don't know what to believe. I don't know how to even trust *myself*. How could I not have noticed? Every small moment you hesitated with me, every extra question you asked. Every time Dr. Aantaj watched too closely...I can't see any of it clearly now."

"I'd never—"

Fuck, the look in his eyes. They were pleading, begging for anything but my refusal. The darkness I'd found comfort in pulled at me, and I almost let it. Almost.

"You can go. I'll let you know if I'm ready to talk again."

My vision flickered, my nahual coming to the forefront and showing me a sight I didn't understand inside Wren. Colors like I'd seen before at the dock, but there was more to them. It wasn't just a mixture of hues; they were intentional layers. The blue pulsed, like it wanted me to see it. It faded as quickly as it appeared, and my vision went back to normal. I opened the door, and Koa was already waiting on the other side with his arms across his chest, pistol tucked but visible.

Sienna was propped on the arm of the couch and turned the moment she heard Koa's rattling. Her cold stare mimicked my brother's. Sienna had always been defensive when it came to me. She'd hated Forrest. Every time he pissed her off, she said she added five solits to his 'hit fund.' I imagined for Wren's offense, it would be more like thousands now that she had access to Koa's cards.

"Out," Koa demanded.

Wren looked back at me, one more plea for forgiveness or understanding or anything, but I just turned away in favor of Sienna. Jed and Adler were still here and moved between me and Wren as he slowly left the condo.

I exhaled and jolted as Koa pulled me into a far too tight hug. "I didn't know," he whispered.

"I know," I responded.

"What did he say?" Sienna asked.

"I don't want to talk about that right now. We need to finish the conversation about the rebels," I said.

Everyone stared at each other, and I waited for a retort, but they sat back down as Adler pulled his laptop back out.

"Disclaimer to the obvious elephant in the room. I really am sorry we had to bring that up. We didn't know what to do," Jed offered. "The relationship between us and the Ikaris has had interesting developments over the last few months. This was...a situation we're sad to see."

I nodded and looked to Adler, who double-clicked his trackpad. "There isn't much more information than we had before. They're keeping everything locked down tight. We tracked where the most whispers about the rebellion were, and created this map."

Clusters of red marks stretched across the whole of Inecha, a crooked line from Jundi all the way to Chichen.

"They started in Jundi and worked up to Yaxumi, then down to Chichen. Not much has happened in Chan or Kuello yet, but I think they're working that way," Adler added.

"Nothing on Zélia?" Koa asked.

"No, she's not real. She's a myth, a warrior princess from the south turned into a real live person," Jed said.

I wasn't certain if that was incredibly bold of her or sort of endearing.

"If it were me, I'd ask to meet her somewhere central. The Calle de Exiliados gym, maybe, somewhere you have the upper hand and go from there," Adler suggested.

Koa glanced at Sienna, who bit her lip, then stared back at the map.

"Mira?" my brother asked.

"I agree. It's under the radar. No one will think twice about you going after hours. Plus, she's a *Muluk*. We don't have to worry about anyone seeing her," I said.

Talking about this was certainly helping. A good distraction.

Koa cleared his throat. "Venom?"

"I don't like it. But I'm outvoted, so here we go, I guess."

Koa's hand squeezed her thigh. "You don't have to be there. We can scope them out and make a decision after."

"I'll decide when we get closer," she said under her breath.

Koa dug out the letter that the rebels brought from Zélia, a way to contact her at the bottom.

"Guess we're fucking doing this."

13

KOA

A week had passed since Ikari's secret was leaked by the Mercers. We still weren't clear where he'd pissed off to after the accident. If he'd even been away on a real gig, or hiding out like the scared little pussy he was.

I was a lot of things—a liar though? That wasn't one of them. Some of us held a little tighter to our integrity than others. Ikari and I were involved in a lot of shit, yet lies had never been part of who we were. Omission, sure. Flat out lying through gritted fucking teeth, *never*. It was the weak way out.

Pretending I wasn't deeply disturbed by his antics wasn't going to solve any of our problems, and it wouldn't ease Mira's pain. Sienna had kept me updated day in and day out. It was clear shit wasn't great. She'd missed breakfast and dodged me at lunch every afternoon. With it being First Friday and fight night at the club, I was expected at The Underworld after *Magical Ethics and Responsibility*. No time to check in.

Mira had always been one to appreciate space when she was going through things, and I'd give that to her—for approximately another forty-eight hours and the clock was fucking ticking. After that, all bets were off.

I refused to let her go through this without my support. Part of me felt responsible for the heartbreak even though she'd met Ikari on her own terms. But a good brother would have snuffed out his bullshit before the Mercers even had the chance. A better brother would have killed him on the spot.

Maybe today I could be the better brother.

Students filtered into Ajtzak Hall, filling in the seats left at the bottom as Professor Ugalde cleared his throat, a signal to shut up for the start of the lecture. Sun beamed through the large conclave window behind the slightly raised stage. The streams of it dancing against the intricate wallpaper above the wooden paneling of all four walls. It was interesting, the choice of art for an institution so set on preaching about Solis and forbidding the teachings of the old gods.

To some, the details could be perceived as the collapse of the sky, only spoken about in the Popol Vuh. What the Cynod deemed "a myth". A creation story of how we, as fae, came to be. The result of the old gods failing time and time again to create humans—a flawed version of what we eventually perfected after the Veil was placed. Fitting, I supposed, given the subject discussed within these very walls.

This class had always seemed pointless to me. A waste of time and effort that could have been spent on something more...worthwhile. We'd all heard the rumors, that the Veil did not ever exist, and the placement of it was an old tale steeped in warning. Knowing what I did from the AstralScroll Codex, the rumors were bullshit, and so were any lessons of false morality the Cynod intended to teach. The reality of the power dynamics in Inecha was blatant, need not pretend.

"Seats and silence would be much appreciated, and I mean *now*," Professor Ugalde began, the projector screen slid down to cover the majority of the window, darkening the room. "Julía," he beckoned, and his TA nodded, gently lighting the room's tapered candles that surrounded us.

Ugalde had a way about him that was devoid of all pleasantries and cut to the facts. If we were to ask a question or offer an opinion, he expected it to be well-informed and, thus, not waste any of our time. "Half of the class failed last week's midterms. An embarrassment and something I refuse to attribute to my teachings. Let us rewind and start again with the basics. For those who passed, my deepest regrets and sincerest apologies for the ineptitude of your peers."

I shrugged, not caring one way or another. I'd had Ugalde for all three years. He had his feelings about my parents, that much was clear—much like Professor Taran—but he'd never reflected it in the grading of my assignments. Receiving anything less than a B+ in his class would be a shock to us both.

The screen behind him switched to the scenery of what was certainly one interpretation of the day the Veil was placed. They couldn't exactly show the class the truth, how Ixchel and Chaac had gone through the effort to protect the humans *and* the fae. No, this would be the distorted version. The one that showed the old gods turning their backs on us specifically for no rhyme or reason other than jealousy or our proclaimed superiority.

"What we have here, is the beginning of the turning of society as we now know it. This separation of creations led to a new divide within our species. One determined by the amount of power each of us possesses. When the powerful fae no longer had humans to focus on, the lesser fae became subjected to...Killian, since you received the lowest score on your midterm paper out of *all* of my classes—shocking to none but you—finish my statement."

"Uh," Killian stuttered, flipping through his textbook for answers that would not find. It was a question of morality, not fact. "Extreme manipulation by fae that have the power to influence our minds?"

"Is that a question, Killian." Professor Ugalde yawned as he paced toward the other end of the stage, an unimpressed facial expression permanently etched into his skin.

Killian ran his fingers through his shoulder-length hair, sweat beading at his temple, visible even from a few seats over. "Yes? No."

"It's hardly manipulation when Solis himself gifted it to us," the most grating voice I'd ever heard chimed in. Alanna. I'd purposely arrived late enough to place myself in the middle of other students but early enough to keep her from asking them to move.

Of course she would feel that way, she was *Ajaw*. The topic of today's class was about her.

Ugalde ignored her, moving back toward the center of the stage and pointing toward another student patiently raising her hand. "Naturally, there is an imbalance among our species. The science of nature calls for it. However, how we choose to respond to the forces of nature, determines the level of civility we'll see in society."

"I'm no longer bored," Ugalde stated, though his face said otherwise. "Continue."

"While of course, it is expected that some fae see the unchecked power as an avenue for extreme manipulation of—specifically level threes and some twos. Others could find it to be our true natural order. One that we must fall into in order to stay true."

"True to..."

Another hand shot up, ready to step in where the other girl was falling short of her words. "True to the bounds of society. It's why the Cynod stepped in when Solis appointed them power. It's clear there is an imbalance that exists, even if it is the natural order of things. That said, it's not unchecked. So I disagree with the previous statement. It is illegal for the *Ajaw* to influence the mind without the direction of our government. It's why 90 percent of us are immediately contracted with them upon graduation, and the other 10 percent go to private organizations with government contracts. The same way *Chikchan* are punished with legal repercussions for abusing their...limited yet destructive methods. Well, *most* of them, anyway."

She turned back to glare at me as though I'd personally offended her. I took her in, her face somewhat familiar. Her name, as usual, escaped me on all accounts. Shit, I probably had. That or she'd fallen prey to whatever the media claimed I did outside of the academy.

Between trapping people within their minds and our ability to turn those who could not resist our magic into stone, I suppose we did have an unfair advantage. Jail time seemed a little harsh, but a slap on the wrist would hardly stop someone with an immense amount of power.

"Interesting perspective, yet expected coming from you. I must ask, class, the restriction of power...I'm interested in hearing the argument of whether it should be tied to magical constraints. Monitored through the government—as is, or, should we allow citizens to self-regulate and trust that they will not utilize their power to cause harm?"

Of course, the power level ones were ready, hands shooting in the air. Their responses were all different variations of each other. Alanna spoke up again, a habit she'd displayed in each of our courses together. She loved the attention—whether it came from me or the prospective onlooker who may report back to the media.

"There is already an uneven amount of restrictions placed on us," she said. "It's not our responsibility to limit ourselves further simply because power level twos and threes don't have the means to protect themselves."

Though she spoke the words, the infliction of her tone and her body language felt...off. Like she was repeating back what she'd been taught her entire life yet couldn't quite bring herself to believe them. I brushed off the thought; when it came to people like her, what you saw at face level was often what you got. Nothing deeper to dig into. It wasn't as though she'd shown any sort of empathy in our forced moments alone.

A scoff was the only response I had to give which unfortunately, garnered the attention of both Julía—the TA—and Ugalde, who passed a shared look of interest. His eyes hardened on mine, his thinning brows formed from age arched in expectation. He wanted my opinion, and it wasn't an option to provide it.

"Rules only work when those at the top abide by them." I winked, old habits dying hard. "There's no oversight. That, in and of itself, is self-regulation. So the question isn't *should* our society operate this way, but rather, is it effectively running as intended."

The rustling of students adjusting themselves in their seats accompanied the air of discomfort in Ajtzak Hall. There was the show I put on in front of Inecha, in front of Herta, then there was the Koa Canek that existed at Kuxtal Academy. My cynical nature was expected here, and though I knew some shared the same ideology among me, they didn't have the protections that existed when I spoke out.

Someone cleared their throat, and I followed the sound. Rowan. He ran his hand through his short curly brown hair, a faint dimple barely visible in the shadows of the room. "Agreed. I'd like to also add, *Alanna*, that just because someone is lower ranked in magic, does not equate to them being powerless. I find that an irresponsible statement from someone seemingly attached to a future Cynod member. As an heir to those seats, our perspective must be just and fair, as expected by the citizens we will soon preside over."

Rowan's words pulled me in. Not because they were expected from us—he'd been PR trained since birth with his uncle's place in the Cynod and all, much like the rest of us. Objectively, they could be empty, rehearsed.

I didn't see that when I looked at the redness creeping up the back of his neck, the swallowed anger. He believed what he was saying. That much was obvious. And led me to believe, that maybe, just fucking maybe, he saw the world for what it was. A structure designed to keep power concentrated at the top while feeding into the illusion of fairness to the rest.

The pissy toss of Alanna's hair and the tightness in her jaw made it clear she didn't appreciate his targeted response. It didn't matter; now that he'd spoken, the murmurs had already started, low but building. A few heads turned toward Rowan in speculation, others in agreement. He did not shrink beneath the attention, instead, he met it head-on—gaze steady and forward, shoulders squared.

No. Rowan Rainwater was not like the other heirs at all. I could see that now. He didn't simply regurgitate what we'd been fed since birth; he took the time to think about it. When Mira was finally up to having a conversation, I'd be sure to see what she thought. Where she felt he stood—she'd always been closer to him when we were kids.

A voice cut through the noise, softer than Rowan's but weighted as sharp. "And who enforces justice when the enforcers are the ones who are corrupt?"

Oh *shit*. The words came from a power level three, a scholarship student, sitting in the middle row. Julía shuffled the papers she was grading on the desk, stopping the lecture recording on the device near the edge.

There it was—the real question. The one that had always been buried beneath debates like these but never truly answered. And the kind of question that would get anyone who wasn't Rowan or me in trouble.

Professor Ugalde stiffened. His eyes darted toward Julía as if expecting her to step in. She remained silent, waiting to see how he handled it. He exhaled through his nose and adjusted his stance, smoothing down the pleat of his trousers. "That," he answered carefully, "is a complicated matter. One that extends beyond the scope of today's discussion."

The room sat in silence for a beat before the timer on his desk signaled the end of class. Chairs scraped against the stone floor as students gathered their things. I stayed behind, watching Rowan as he moved toward the exit, his pace unhurried, attention shifting. Alanna and him made brief eye contact as he passed through the exit, where she annoyingly stood waiting for me with a sinister smile painted on her face. He glanced back once more before he cleared the view of the room, a look of understanding landing...on me.

He was watching me, the same way I was watching him. Assessing. Calculating. As if he was weighing whether I was worth considering an ally once we took our seats among the Cynod or just another piece on the board.

Interesting.

Before I could make a move, the heavy doors of the opposing hallway creaked open. A member of the front office stepped inside, their gaze scanning the room before landing on the student who had spoken up.

"Come with me," they said, voice devoid of emotion.

The student hesitated, looking around in expectation of someone to intervene. Alanna took a small, but noticeable step forward and dropped her crossed arms, then glanced up at me, and took another step back toward the exit. They stood, shoulders stiff, and followed the staff member out.

I didn't move. I couldn't, no matter how much I wanted to. No, this game required my compliance, because Sienna's safety depended on it. My fingers curled into a loose fist beneath my desk.

Another name added to the list of those who asked the wrong questions.

The Vortex was business as usual, minus the Ikaris. With most of our First Friday drink enhancement deals set up for the next six months, I figured cutting them the fuck out was future Koa's problem. Or Nola's—most definitely Nola's problem. I trusted her judgment and when Ikari wasn't here during the day or went black for weeks at a time, she was the one who handled that business.

Not to mention with the Mercers now ingraining themselves in half of my business, swapping them out for the Ikari clan would hardly cause a blink in the patron's eyes. If they got fucked up, then that was a successful night in their books—didn't matter the source, only the quality.

I sat with Nola at the bar where Sienna and I had that fateful date at. It was still calm and early enough in the evening that we wouldn't have to switch to The Underworld just yet. Zane and Atlas were lurking down there and I had no interest in answering any of their questions. Ikari would show up soon enough. I wasn't in the mood to answer their questions twice.

"Alright, boss, you wanna tell me why we're slashing all lines of their business, or is that none of my concern."

"None of your concern," I replied, but I knew I could trust her to a certain extent. "They're snakes in the water. I have no interest in doing business with those who defy my trust."

It was something I didn't hand out freely, so to burn that bridge was nothing to me. Trust, at its core, was hard-earned and easily dissolved.

"Heard. And Alanna's business plan? What would you like me to do with that? I'm about to start planning next quarter. Should I factor that in or..." Nola's fingers tapped against her tablet, shuffling down our list of to-dos.

"Haven't read it. Don't plan to. Do whatever it takes to shut her up when it comes to The Underworld."

She tilted her head with a scoff only she could get past me. "Pretty sure you don't want me cutting that check. Do it yourself when you're ready to stop pouting, or whatever *this* is. I assume you're aware that her brothers were your appointment last week when you were meeting with the Mercers?"

Now *that* was news to me. The trio had spoken nothing of their connection to Alanna—which the secrecy of it all raised every alarm I had. I worked to keep the irritated rattling of my chest at bay, but the glass of whiskey shattered under my grip, drawing the attention of the others around us. Nola snapped her fingers, the bartender quickly making her way over with a rag and fresh drink. Waving my right hand over my bleeding left, warmth slid over the wound as it healed.

"I'll take that as a fuck no. Yep," Nola chuckle was laced with sarcasm. "Business plan has already been emailed over as well as the key takeaways—bullet points for your concern, per usual. You deal with your anger, get another drink in your system. I got some feyfog rolled in your office. Try to keep it together when Wren shows face. We really don't have room in the schedule tonight for a side-show to accompany the main event."

And with that, Nola was off, her tablet still in hand as she made her rounds at the club.

I exhaled, stretching my fingers against the cool glass of my drink before setting it down. The music pulsed through the floor, reverberating in my chest, but I barely heard it. The Underworld called to me, a steady drumbeat beneath my feet, waiting.

I pushed off the bar and made my way toward the stairwell tucked behind a guarded entrance, the neon lights overhead casting long shadows against the walls. The descent was familiar, the air thick with something heavier than smoke, something alive.

The moment Wren walked through the doors, I knew it. It was like the suffocating shift in the air before a storm hit. He moved between the crowd, the usual feline arrogance in his step dulled enough to set my teeth on edge. He knew he was walking into a fight.

There was little interest in handling this out in the open. With the tick of my head, I signaled for him to follow me toward his office, not mine. New wards had been set up there. He would not gain entry for as long as I was alive. And given I was the only one with the authority to grant him access—he'd been effectively cut off from the safe where our shipments were stored. Ikari no longer had business here, that would be coming to an end the second I found a way to cut ties.

I sank to the velvet black chair with my back to his open door. He stopped behind me, then leaned down, face-to-face with a lethal glow in his eyes, scanning the drink in my hand before settling on my eyes. "We need to talk."

A silencing spell dropped down around the room, cutting us off from the rest of The Underworld.

"No, we don't. Talk to Nola if you have questions." I leaned back against the chair, taking a slow sip. "The only thing keeping me from cutting you off completely—hells, from killing you where you stand—is Mira's indecisiveness. You think I haven't pictured it? I have. Every detail. How quick it could be if I wanted to make it clean. How long I could stretch it if I wanted you to understand every mistake that led you here. If, and fucking frankly, *when* she makes the decision to wipe you from her life? A task, I am pleased to have Alanna assist with, there is no place you could go or hide, Ikari, that would keep me from making an example out of you. A cautionary tale people whisper when they remember how a traitor dies."

Outside of the clench in his jaw, he gave me nothing. No bite, no smartass retort—just quiet understanding. It pissed me off more.

"Figured as much." His voice was steady. "Personal matters aside, that doesn't mean you need to cut my brothers out of business."

I laughed, cold and sharp. "You don't get to make demands."

Wren's focus shifted the second the private room door swung open across from us. The Mercer brothers walked out, flanking a man Ikari had been making deals with not long ago. The moment the fae and his accomplices caught sight of Ikari, their steps faltered, but the Mercers didn't stop. They walked past without sparing Ikari a glance, ice-cold dismissal written in their movements.

He exhaled slowly. "So, you're working around me now."

"Future-proofing," I corrected. "You're a liability."

His lips pressed into a thin line. "Whether we said it or not, I considered you a friend."

"Your mistake."

And mine—because he was right. We did not say it or admit it over the past few months. For a long time, Ikari had been a business partner, nothing less and certainly not more. But in the recent timeline, he'd been beyond a friend.

I'd considered Wren Ikari to be something of a brother, and now that the delusion of trust had been shattered, I'd address him no more than I addressed my parents. When he was out of sight, he might as well be dead to me.

Wren took a step closer, lowering his voice. "I'll respect your space, Koa. I won't push. But don't cut my brothers out. Contract between us aside, they weren't part of my mistakes. They're trustworthy."

I finished my drink and set the glass down hard enough to crack the ceramic coaster down the middle. "Anyone you trust, I mark as a target. Keep that in mind before you open your mouth again."

He stared me down, nodded once, and left without a word.

14

KOA

I had absolutely zero desire to be at any party that my parents were in attendance of. Much less one where any woman besides Sienna was required to be on my arm.

Yet, here I was, standing under the migraine-inducing camera lights, my hand settled just so against the small of Alanna's back while she spun the perfect story to the press. The touch of our skin was blistering—my palm was burning at the deep cut of her white silk gown, carefully elegant and, no doubt, something she considered sexy.

Alanna was statuesque, her dark brown skin glowing under the artificial lights, sharp hazel eyes scanning the crowd like a predator waiting for the right moment to strike. Her hair had been straightened again, styled almost identically to Sienna's from the gala only weeks ago. A deliberate choice. A reminder—whether by her choice or my parents, the resemblance of who she was to replace was there.

She wasn't my mate though, and I doubted Alanna had what it took to live up to Sienna's quiet fire for life. How she carried truth and chaos in the same breath while still making you feel as though you belong in her world.

"The first time we met?" Alanna echoed the reporter's question with a soft, knowing laugh, tilting her head toward me with a smile as if we were sharing some cherished secret. "It was fate, really."

Fate. That was one way to describe my mother's careful maneuvering. The word in regard to the two of us made me want to fucking throw up. Instead, I exhaled through my nose, keeping my expression relaxed. Soft. That romantic bullshit image she was desperate for me to sell.

Alanna gave my hand the slightest squeeze—a delicate, practiced motion the cameras would interpret as affectionate. I knew better. It was a warning. *Play along.*

I let my gaze drop to her, amusement curling at the edges of my mouth as if I couldn't help myself. "I guess you could call it fate," I murmured, just loud enough for the mic to catch. "My parents really wanted me to meet her, and the charity event at my Calle de Exiliados gym had all the stars align. Common interests and all."

Not a lie, but a total exaggeration. The stars aligning being the check offered from her grandfather and the *common interests* being whatever the hells the Cynod wanted from Mentiria.

A fae lingered in the hallway near the door swallowed in the shadows only a *Muluk* could pull off with such imperceptible grace. No one seemed to notice him—except me. And Alanna. Her eyes were lit with something that rivaled the mischief of half the fuckers I knew. I narrowed my gaze, the distance and shadow work making a snake's already shitty eyesight a liability.

The reporters lapped it up, murmurs of *how sweet* and *so in love* spreading through the crowd.

"And what was it about Koa that first caught your eye?" another reporter chimed in, angling a mic closer. It took everything in me not to smack it away.

Alanna tore her gaze from the shadows without missing a beat. "Oh, you know," she said, flashing a smile that managed to be both flirtatious and vaguely condescending. "The usual—handsome, mysterious, that bad-boy charm with something deeper to him. He's quite the sweetheart, that side of him he usually keeps hidden, but not from me. Don't tell anyone," she added, voice dipping as if this wasn't being broadcast to the entire fucking world. "But he plans the most *thoughtful* dates, really considers what speaks to your soul. Our first date he built a fort and stocked it with junk food. Totally casual, but...I could tell he actually thought about what would make me feel safe. I couldn't believe it."

What the fuck. My attention snapped to her, fingers twitching against her back. She shouldn't know that. *How* did she know that? But she did. Clearly.

"And he's so intense," she continued, shifting just enough for the cameras to catch her fingers brushing my wrist, showing off her immodestly sized ring. "That quiet, musing thing he does? I love that."

I barely stopped myself from laughing. She was so fucking psychotic she almost managed to scare *me*. Instead, I leaned in slightly, tilting my head toward her like she'd said something only I was meant to hear.

'Fine. Let's play, then.'

The cameras would catch the way I looked at her, the slight curve of my mouth, the relaxed set of my shoulders. I could already imagine the headlines. *Koa Canek, completely smitten. The perfect couple—passion and power.*

But beneath it, I let the truth slip, just enough for the one person who mattered to see.

"You know," I said, joining in with more enthusiasm than any of them had seen so far. "It's funny you say that."

Her fingers tightened on my wrist, the only sign that she was aware something was off.

I let my smirk sharpen. "Because I've always been drawn to *venom*. Alanna, I found, is the opposite. *Anti-venom*, if you will. All sweet, pure."

Alanna didn't flinch, didn't pull away, yet I felt the shift in her, the barely there falter before she forced her expression back into something camera-perfect.

The press didn't catch it.

I didn't care. It wasn't for them to understand. *Sienna would.*

She'd know exactly who I was talking about. She'd know exactly who I was thinking of.

Alanna worked the room, playing up the performance—smiling, laughing, keeping her hand on me to keep up appearances. Cameras lapped it up. She set the stage, controlling the space effortlessly. A shift in her posture, the slightest tilt of her head, the kind of practiced motion that promised something intimate. Lips parted just enough. Eyes half-lidded, expectant.

A kiss designed for the cameras.

She turned into me, waiting for me to meet her halfway. I moved, smooth, effortless, my hand catching her jaw as I pressed a kiss to her temples. Protective. Sweet. Granting the press the ability to swoon over our 'undeniable chemistry.'

"These lips are not yours to take," I whispered in her ear, a message that would read as seductive to anyone watching.

Alanna beamed, polished as ever. "Aw. Koa...he's a complete softy," she added, flicking a glance at the cameras. "You wouldn't think so, would you? But behind all that brooding, he's just—" She gave my arm a squeeze, her nails pressing enough to remind me who was in control of this narrative. "Well, let's say he's got a very sweet side too."

The reporters fawned over the moment, and I played my part, slipping a lazy smirk into place. Alanna was selling a love story—I was selling the illusion that I didn't have a knife in my back.

"And his past. That didn't weigh into your relationship?"

"Oh, no. I mean we're young," she waved a dismissal. "If we all took one-night stands and juvenile relationships into account, we'd hardly be able to call ourselves a civilized species. No. What's meant to be, will always be. I have no concerns in that regard. Koa's had his fun and honestly, I'm grateful. It's shaped him into being the male he is. I like to think the maturity on both ends is refreshing for him."

One-night stands.

Juvenile.

The rattle of my breath was damn near impossible to keep quiet, fury pressing sharp against my ribs. *Sienna was anything but.* And Alanna—calculating and careful as she was—knew exactly what she was doing. The image of the woman she was attempting to destroy.

A low murmur started behind the press line, an unsettled ripple that didn't match the saccharine energy in front of the cameras. People gathered near the hallway, headed toward something that hadn't been there before. A poster. Cynod lineage photo, last year's edition. They made us retake them every five years, a show of unity and honestly, a display of power. But someone had scrawled across it in thick, unmistakable lettering—even from here:

YOUR PEACE IS BUILT ON OUR BONES. HOW LONG MUST THE STARVING SERVE THE CROWNED?

Security moved fast, tearing it down before the lenses of every news source and shitty gossip show could capture it, but the tension it left behind clung to the air.

Alanna pivoted like a pro. Not even a flicker of panic. To the displeasure of my gods forsaken ears, she squealed, eyes locked on the ring as if it had come to life. She turned to the nearest reporter, murmuring something about a wedding exclusive. Designers. Covers. Bait they couldn't resist. She held a spotlight. The press turned, hungry for the story she handed them, and the wall of truth behind them faded from view. It was disappointing how easy they could be distracted.

Good journalism had been dead for a while now anyway—ever since they let themselves be bought.

"Tell us about the proposal!" someone called out.

Alanna's eyes gleamed. "Oh, it was *perfect*—"

I let her talk.

Let her shape the narrative.

Let her weave the fairy tale people wanted to believe in.

I just kept smiling, fingers curling slightly against the silk of her dress—as if I weren't already deciding which thread to pull first.

Brunch had barely begun, and already, Alanna was working the room like she owned it. The garden hummed with conversation, glasses clinking as servers wove between clusters of guests. The scent of fresh-cut citrus and jasmine clung to the air—artificial and suffocating. To be frank, it made my ass itch.

I watched her, all smiles and easy charm, as she engaged a group of government officials from Chichen and Chan. I told myself I didn't care. Then, she opened her mouth one too many times, and said something that turned my disinterest to ice. The Chan official I'd blatantly dismissed—the one who'd tried to barter his daughter's hand in marriage—was fishing for weaknesses. And Alanna, in her desperate need to assert control, overcompensated.

She attempted to squeeze past me and move on to the next vulture. I caught her hand, my grip light enough for the cameras, firm enough that she knew better than to brush me off. "A word."

Alanna arched a brow, allowing me to lead her out of earshot with the clear threat of throwing a fit. "You know, there are much more flattering ways to get my attention, fiancé."

I ignored that. "What the hells do you think you're doing?"

"You'll have to be more specific. I do and say *so* many things." She blinked, faux-innocent.

"An heir?" The word curled in my mouth like venom—and not the kind I so desperately wanted to taste. "Have you lost your fucking mind?"

Alanna chuckled, resting her fingers against my cheek as if we were lovers stealing a moment. Her nails bit into my skin. "I'm just doing what I always do—playing along. What's the difference? It's not like you've made any attempt to get to know me, ask any questions, figure out what our future together may actually look like. If you want to sell bullshit, we can do that too, but right now, I'm improvising. Fall into line, or open your mouth and speak either to me or to them—whatever pains you least. I don't care. Give me something other than whatever *this* is." Her gaze darkened. "Or is this really about her?"

I went deathly still.

"Yeah. I'm no fool. I'd place a lifetime's bet that it is. The little gutter rat clinging to you and your sister like you're her last chance at happiness."

My jaw locked. The surrounding air thinned, the garden fading to nothing but the pulse in my ears. Alanna didn't know *me*—didn't understand the weight of the name she dared to drag through the filth. Because if she did, she'd never have the nerve to speak on Sienna in such a way.

I forced myself to breathe, to shove down the instinct clawing its way up my spine. She wanted a reaction. Proof that she had found a weak spot.

Alanna's smirk deepened. "She must be *incredibly* special to have you this worked up."

A misstep. She didn't see it yet, but it was there—clear as blood in snow. And she would pay for it. She thought to have me figured out. Thought she could thread the needle without pricking her own skin. But in the process, she'd shown her hand. Her tell. This wasn't just a power play—it was personal.

Alanna thrived on control, but she hadn't realized who she was dealing with. I was no pawn to be maneuvered or an opponent to be outwitted. I was a consequence. She thought she could pull the leash without losing a hand. Her first mistake was thinking she could manipulate me the way she did everyone else. My patience wasn't infinite.

Her abilities meant nothing against me. As an *Ajaw*, she could twist and weave her influence like silk around others, bending them to her will. But I was *Chikchan*. I had my own gifts. And if she ever dared to test the limits of her power against mine, she'd fear what might happen.

She was fighting for control over this engagement. The more I resisted, the more desperate she became—an animal gnawing off its own limb to escape a trap.

Still, I wasn't the one she feared most.

Speak of Cizin and Cizin will arise. I saw my mother then, standing across the garden. A quiet specter in the chaos, watching. A puppet master ensuring the strings never slipped from her grasp. If she believed the power I would inherit—*her* bloodline—was at risk, Alanna wouldn't last long enough to regret it. Mother met my stare and offered me the strangest, soft smile. It disappeared the second my father joined her at the hip.

Alanna followed my gaze, a soft laugh escaping her. "Poor little Koa Canek, all the riches in the world, but power and money mean nothing to you. Did I get that right?" She reached out, brushing her fingers over my collar in a calculated gesture. "Yes, I think I read you pretty damn well. You'll do anything to keep your hold on what matters most to you, even if that means bending down for *me*. Don't worry, sweetheart, keep following me. I've got my own ways of keeping everything in balance."

She still didn't get it. She never would. For that to happen, she needed a heart, a soul, something to care about. It was clear—she was lacking in all of it.

My fingers twitched, a surge of instinct telling me to rip her hand away. I steadied my breath, forcing calm through clenched teeth. "It's quite clear you don't know what you're dealing with. Let this be your first and final warning."

A voice called from the terrace.

Alanna smiled, tilting her head with an air of mock affection. "Oh, sweetheart, I think I do." She took my arm before I could stop her, all practiced warmth. "Now, be a good fiancé and walk me inside. I believe brunch is served."

The scent of burning copal clung to the air, thick and heavy, sticking to my clothes as the officiant signaled the next part of the engagement ritual. The hall gleamed with gold and candlelight, the air dense with incense and crushed flowers. A spectacle. A performance. Exactly what Alanna wanted.

I sat at the head table, wedged between her parents. Their stiff presence, unyielding and silent, was a constant reminder of the weight this arrangement carried. Her grandfather sat on her other side, stone-faced and watchful, as if he could see straight through me. Across from us, my parents were the same. A wall of scrutiny, unbroken, as though their disapproval could physically press down on me—warning me, reminding me of the repercussions any embarrassment I displayed could bring at a later date.

All three of her brothers were seated at a different table, exiled but close enough to remind me of unfinished business. They'd known exactly who I was when they'd approached me at The Underworld, pitching a deal with the intent to buy their way into my world. They assumed I'd be an easy target for their schemes—underestimating the weight of their own ambition, which, in retrospect, was likely a carefully cultivated tool of their sister. Now, with the full picture laid out before me, I couldn't help but wonder how much of their ambition was truly theirs—and how much of it had been designed by Alanna.

The sound of strings and drums pulled me back, the rhythm slicing through the room as the dance began. Tradition, symbolizing harmony and partnership. The irony practically dripped off it. I rose, extending my hand to her. Alanna's fingers brushed mine in a movement so practiced that it was almost mechanical. Her smile didn't reach her eyes. The guests watched, their approval nothing but background noise to the tension in her grip. We moved toward the center of the floor, but it wasn't the ceremony or the crowd that held my attention. It was her.

Each step we took traced a pattern as old as the land itself—a serpent coiling in on itself, a symbol of cyclical struggle. Alanna moved with a grace that reflected the years she'd spent perfecting this ancient art. I followed her lead, every turn and step a quiet contest beneath the surface, a constant push for dominance masked by the fluidity of the dance.

"You're enjoying this," I murmured, as our hands met again, her fingers warm against mine.

"I enjoy many things, fiancé," she replied, her voice loud enough for the nearest guests to hear. The perfect image of a woman enraptured by her intended. "Though I'd enjoy it more if you weren't so stiff."

"I have a question first."

"Only one?" she teased, her lips curling slightly.

I held her gaze, lowering my voice. "Your latest business venture."

Her grip tightened, just a fraction, before she leaned back, a quiet laugh escaping her lips. "Ah. So that's what's on your mind."

"Why?"

"Why what, sweetheart?"

I kept my gaze steady, the dance flowing beneath our feet, but the tension between us grew with every beat. "Why help the underprivileged in Mentiria?"

Her head tilted, smile never faltering, though her eyes sharpened, a subtle shift in her expression. "You don't think it's a good idea?"

"I think it doesn't align with who you pretend to be."

She clucked her tongue, her nails tapping rhythmically against my back. "You say that like you know me."

"I know the image you want people to see," I said, my tone quiet, but pointed. "And I can see the potential for something much darker."

The silence between us stretched. I watched her carefully arrange her expression into something unreadable. Then, just as smoothly, she leaned in, her voice low and warm. "And what if I said I don't care why you think I'm doing it? That I know exactly what my country needs—better than you know your own."

"You expect me to believe this isn't about appearance?"

She scoffed like it was a stupid question. "Does it matter?"

There was no time for me to form a response, the music shifted, and the rhythm of the dance pulled us deeper into the tradition.

Alanna's hand moved against mine as we shifted seamlessly into the next step, a fluid motion that had nothing to do with the guests or the surrounding spectacle. Her expression was cool, but there was a subtle fire behind her eyes. She didn't break our gaze as we glided across the floor.

"This isn't for show, Koa. Though it certainly is a perk," she murmured, her voice low, barely a whisper over the drumbeat. "Come on, you're sharper than that. You see past the bullshit, bigger picture sort of thing."

The movement of this dance was slow, close—an exchange of symbolic offerings, whispered words lost to the beat of the drum. My hand brushed against Alanna's, the touch fleeting before we turned, stepping in rhythm.

I felt it—for a moment—when she let go of the performance. The tension in her posture softened, and her body moved with familiarity, as if this, too, was part of who she truly was. But then, just as quickly, the mask slid back into place.

I exhaled slowly. "I think you prefer having control of the narrative."

Her lips curved, but the smile was quieter now, tinged with something I couldn't quite read. "And you don't?"

The dance shifted. We turned from each other, circling in opposite directions before meeting again at the center—a balance of forces. A test of harmony and opposition.

Alanna tilted her head, her voice soft but edged with something genuine. "You don't have to like me, you know. But if you're smart, you won't waste your time hating me either."

I held her gaze as the music swelled, the ceremony unfolding around us. This was a game. A battle. A negotiation wrapped in centuries of tradition.

And for the first time, I wasn't sure if Alanna was playing to win—or simply playing to survive.

Emeric cornered me in the darkest pit of the ballroom. The chandeliers didn't reach this far; shadows licked up the gold-trimmed walls. His posture was rigid as he stood shoulder to shoulder with me, watching the party. The celebration was unraveling now. Drunk fae stumbled about, the dances slipping from neat and tight to a wild intensity, their movements fast in line with the beat.

"I appreciate the cooperation, son."

I glanced once to my left, once to my right, then again to be sure he was talking to me. *Son.* I scoffed. Had I really been that to him over the last few years? Not since he realized I wasn't built in his image, but worse. A better version. Our relationship was beyond repair.

"Threats will do that to a person," I muttered, knocking back the last of my whiskey. It burned going down, but not half as much as standing beside him did.

He hummed, the sound almost approving. "Threats?" he repeated. "Is that what you thought our exchange regarding *that girl* to be? You mistake discipline for malice far too often. It's disappointing."

"Discipline," I said, jaw clenching. "You threatened to ruin my m–"

His head tilted, dark eyes lighting as his lips curved into a grin.

"My girlfriend," I corrected. "You threatened to destroy Sienna's life. Call it what it is."

He stepped closer as his hand settled heavy on my shoulder. "And yet, here you stand. Whole. All of you. Safe and unharmed. Because you listened. Good behavior is rewarded, Koa."

I felt my pulse in my throat. "Safe," I echoed, the word cracking. "You think that's what this is? You think any of us feel safe?"

Emeric laughed as though I'd said something truly amusing. Though, the stiffness in my body at his touch was enough to humor him most days. "Escalation is never the goal. You were built to survive, all Caneks are."

The way he said it—quiet, even—made the room tilt. It sounded like advice. Like regret. Or maybe justification.

"Did you know?" I asked before I could stop myself. My voice came out lower than I intended.

"Careful," was his only response.

"That's not an answer."

My mother appeared, her dark gown untouched by the night. "Darling," she said to my father. "Ambassador Osorios wishes for you to meet him in his study for a cigar."

Her gaze slid to me, softening slightly. It made her nearly unrecognizable. "Benício, you look tired."

My middle name almost undid me. I clenched my fists to keep from shaking.

Emeric withdrew his hand, straightening his cuffs. "I will check in with you at a later date," he said.

"Can't wait," I muttered, though my throat ached.

"Go get some air," my mother's hand brushed my arm as she turned to leave with him. Aurora Tecun-Canek returned as her departing words slapped me in the face. "Tighten up."

15

KOA

I sent the message and dropped a pin, making my way over to the L1 dorms to escort her there.

A smirk tugged at the corner of my lips as I read her reply. My Venom—sharp tongued and quick-witted. I moved quickly, letting the camouflage of *Chikchan* magic settle over me like a second skin, slipping into the background of campus. Sticking to the shadows, I followed Sienna from the L1 dorms, my presence no more than a bristle in the wind of a Sunday autumn evening.

She walked with purpose, her curls tousled in her speed, but I caught the way she peered over her tense shoulder periodically as if sensing me. I had to bite back a chuckle. Even when she couldn't see me, she knew.

I kept my steps light, close enough to track her but far enough not to be noticed. My focus should've been on why she was slipping off to our spot alone, but my eyes betrayed me. The sweater hanging loose off her shoulder, the rhythm in her stride—she was a contradiction of effortlessness and tension. A storm rolling in without warning. And gods help me, I wanted to get caught in it.

Fucking focus, Canek. Control. I'd built myself on those things. But nothing in me had been trained for this. Not for her. Not for the pull she had without even trying. Right now wasn't the time for distractions—no matter how tempting they looked in faded jeans and my money on her back.

By the time she reached the cave's mouth, I was already there in her shadow, my steps swallowed by the earth. My phone buzzed in my hand as she sent a simple text:

Venom :

Here.

I closed the last steps between us and dropped the camouflage, one arm sliding around her waist to lock her against me. My chest pressed flush to her back as I bent low, lips grazing the shell of her ear. "I know," I breathed.

With surgical precision, her palm found my throat, exactly the way I'd taught her. The impact jolted through me, a sting that forced my head back. I let it land, let the pain spark across my windpipe as I staggered a step.

A ragged cough tore out of me, but it melted into a low laugh, the sound roughened by the burn she left on my skin. "Damn, I'm impressed."

Sienna squealed, springing up on her toes as she seized my face and crushed her mouth to mine. Quick. Fierce. Enough to send my pulse racing. When she pulled back, mischief sparkled in her eyes. "Anti-venom?" she repeated from the clip of my 'engagement' interview.

I brushed my thumb across her lower lip, savoring the curve of it. "Not a doubt in my mind you'd know it was for you."

Her smile faltered, joy shrinking under the weight pressing between us. What we were. What we couldn't be.

"What are we doing outside the caves?" Sienna's arms folded as she stepped back, retreating into that fragile wall she clung to.

I leaned in, my body unable to resist the pull of hers. Whether it was the mating bond or just the excitement of being graced with her presence again, I couldn't be sure. The reasoning didn't matter in the slightest. "Meems may or may not have told me this is your new favorite place to explore."

Her lips parted, hesitation flickering across her face. "Maybe..."

"So maybe you can take me to the best spot in the house?" I pressed, watching her wrestle with the choice to indulge me or keep me at arm's length. Though we'd fallen back into our routine of texting daily and the new one of falling asleep on the phone, she still had up this...wall. A carefully established distance to protect her peace.

She let out a breath, shook her head, and turned anyway. I followed as she led me into the tunnels. We walked in silence, the cave swallowing us in its cool embrace. The air smelled of damp earth and what we now knew—ancient secrets. Shadows stretched along the walls, shifting with each step as we passed the openings leading to other tunnels.

The cavern reeked of still water and blood before I even saw them. *Xtabay* lounged in the water lazily in the cavern's glow, feeding, sated but never full. Their eyes found mine first, curiosity simmering beneath hunger. Then they saw Sienna. A different kind of hunger stirred. The lure of the power I possessed that they'd never had a taste of and never would. No *Chikchan* worth their shit would ever allow it, least of all an heir to the Cynod.

Sienna didn't flinch beneath their stare. She met it head-on, unyielding, before flicking her wrist. Vines tore through the cave floor, weaving into a barrier that swallowed the sight of them whole.

My lips curved. I stepped in behind her and let my palm crack against the curve of her ass. The sharp sound echoed off the stone. She jolted, cutting me a glare over her shoulder, but I only grinned. "Possessive looks good on you, Venom."

She scoffed, satisfying me as I caught the flicker of satisfaction in her eyes before she turned away. "Not a fan of how they were looking at my man."

Yeah, fuck me. If she thought a line like that wouldn't go straight to my head, she was dead wrong about which head it fueled. I swallowed the response clawing up my throat, mostly because if I let myself dwell on it, we wouldn't make it another ten steps.

The deeper we went, the quieter she got. Her steps slowed as we neared a familiar turn. Just before we reached it, she came to a complete stop.

"It's right up—" She cut off as she turned the corner and froze. "Koa, what's this?"

I stepped in behind her, wrapping my arms around her shoulders, pressing a kiss into the crown of her curls. "A date," I murmured, "with the *real* future Mrs. Canek. Figured it was time we had one where no one bled. Progress."

The cavern had been transformed. Candles flickered, casting golden light against the stone walls. A soft, Kan blue blanket was spread out on the ground, with a spread of food she'd formed the habit of ordering from the diner. Cheese fries, salad with her favorite creamy dressing, fried cheesecake, a milkshake, and of course, we wouldn't be us without a tray of pre-rolled feyfog.

She leaned down, shifting aside a napkin covering a porcelain plate framed in jade. "Is this..."

"Lemon sugar cookies and chocolate chipless cookies? Yeah." I ran a hand through my hair, half amused, half exhausted just thinking about it. "Your instructions were incredibly unclear in your recipe book by the way. Took me three tries, and I was up at five a.m. making sure I got them right...but it was worth it. That smile your fighting off makes it so fucking worth it— Oh, your new stand mixer should be here tomorrow."

Sienna blinked. "Why would I need a new...should I even ask?"

"There were complications."

Her laugh was all sarcasm as she took a bite out of the lemon sugar cookie and her eyes rolled back in pleasure. "Complications like your fist and a lack of any resemblance to a synonym of patience?"

"Allegedly." I shrugged. "Not important, considering it's got that Marta Suárez lady or whatever's autograph on it. Sage green."

"That was—"

"The one you've been stalking, waiting to go on sale all week." Sienna tilted her head, a piercing gaze stared up at me. I grazed my teeth with my tongue, reaching for her chin as I lured her in with an electric touch. "Telling you how I know that won't win me any favors in getting back into your good graces."

She turned, eyes narrowing in that way she does when she's pretending to be annoyed—but her mouth was already betraying her. Soft at the corners. Like she knew exactly who helped me, and part of her hated how much she fucking loved it. "I don't think we ever had a real date that didn't involve tears or crime."

"Let's say I'm hoping to turn things around starting today."

"Koa—"

"I know you were watching," I cut in, catching the way her shoulders stiffened. "Or at least following along on PhotoPhantom. Three posts from ChismeChak went viral within the hour. Nola made sure I was aware. She's already pulling strings with the Mercers to get them scrubbed, accounts banned, the whole thing buried."

She opened her mouth to protest, but I didn't let her. "Not going to tell you to stop watching, because that would be an unrealistic expectation, especially for you," My hand slid to her waist, fingers tightening. "Hear me when I say, none of what you're seeing is real. This"—I tilted closer, brushing my thumb over the warm curve of her skin between us—"this is the only thing that's ever been real to me. Little moments like this. You. Us. So let's not talk about it. Not tonight."

Her throat worked around a swallow, eyes shining, clearly working through it, then gave me that subtle nod of hers. "Deal."

We ate, talked about nothing and everything. I let myself drown in her laughter, in the way her eyes crinkled when she teased me, in the way she stole fries off my plate with no remorse. Sienna wasn't shy about taking what she wanted, and damn if I didn't find that kind of confidence attractive. But the ease of it—the illusion of normal—only made the weight in my chest heavier. Borrowed time.

That's all this was. And I knew it. Sooner or later, the chaos waiting for us would come crashing down. I had to find a way out of this.

But not tonight. Not while I had her sitting here, close enough to touch, close enough to make me forget.

When the conversation lulled, my gaze drifted to the walls, taking in the intricate carvings and detailed markings of what apparently were our godly ancestors.

"I'm going to ask my mom about Thaddeus," Sienna said suddenly.

My eyes snapped back to her, watching the way she traced a crack in the stone with her finger. "Is that...a conversation you think is worth having?"

"Well, I can't exactly ignore it, as much as I want to, given, ya know." She gestured vaguely to the cave, to everything around us.

"Right." I drew in a breath, then let the words slip out before I could stop them. "I'd like to come with you, if that's okay. To meet them."

She smirked, but the wariness in her expression didn't fade. "It's customary to wait for an invitation to meet parents by the way."

"I'm not most people, and you shouldn't confuse me as such." I smirked.

She nodded but hesitated, sighing. "She's not going to like you. Ethan might...but definitely not Momma."

"Smart woman. Most people don't. Starting to think there might be something wrong with you, Venom."

She shot me a flat look. "Promise you'll be on your best behavior?"

I chuckled, letting the sound soften just for her. "You won't even know I'm Koa Canek." The words slipped out effortlessly but there was a part of me that knew it wasn't going to be that simple.

"I haven't seen them since I got here, but they're off next Sunday and asked if I could make it out for dinner and a movie. There are Kuxtal events on the last weekend of the month, so we're free to leave campus."

I hesitated, weighing how much to tell her, then decided honesty was better than illusion. "Wolfe contacted Vitória. The meeting's set for next Saturday, an hour after the gym closes. I haven't told Meems yet, but...I think we'd both prefer you there. No pressure."

Sienna exhaled, a ripple running through her that would have shattered the strongest of hearts. "We'll see. Can we just enjoy the rest of the night? No more serious conversations. Just you, me...maybe you without a shirt." She bit down on her lip with hunger, but it didn't match the distance in her eyes.

I nodded, letting her have this. But as I pulled her closer, I didn't loosen my hold. Something was shifting between us, changing, moving beneath the surface.

And I wasn't sure I wanted to hear it.

16

MIRA

There was nothing to take my mind off the situation with Wren like being so incredibly overstimulated it wasn't possible to think. Every single first-year was supposed to attend this student club event at some point in the evening, and apparently everyone decided now was a good time. It wasn't required, but it was highly encouraged that first-year students find some extracurricular activity to participate in. Somewhere to fit in and be part of something. I'd found out the hard way that when things were highly encouraged, it typically meant they were actually nonnegotiable. Since our after-school activity was currently dealing with a rebellion against the Cynod, I wasn't sure what else we'd have time for.

My nahual also decided to remind me of just how many souls surrounded my body.

Sienna put her hand on my arm, scanning me up and down. "Anxiety attack?"

"No, not exactly." I picked at a zipper on my bag, listening to it rattle and focusing on that instead of everything else. "I'm okay. Where do you want to go first?"

Sienna pulled a baggy of some sweet treat she'd made recently from her backpack and handed it to me. "Sugar in your system always helps. Honestly, I'm not particularly interested in any of it. We can wander around."

There were some rather interesting choices; I would give them that.

The theater group was putting on a mini performance, pulling in random students from the crowd and getting them to do improv. One small, awfully sweaty student stood in the middle, begging her friends to come up with her, but they didn't budge. A theater club member handed her a rake, and she pretended to tend to an imaginary garden. The girl was a natural; any evidence of nerves long gone as the theater club cheered for her. They gave her a red ribbon, and she scribbled her name down on a clipboard.

"Any interest in theater?" I asked Sienna.

"No, my life is enough of a production."

"Wish that weren't so true." I scanned the room. "If we have to do something, I'd rather do it together, with you and Katia."

"Agreed."

The club I'd prefer to join was Aantaj's science club, of course, but they didn't take first years. It was more of an internship, and they only took you seriously if they were sure you'd be emerging as something that fell under their umbrella. Which was a scenario I hadn't fully thought through. In all fairness, I wasn't even sure where my nahual placed me. I wasn't a shifter, and my magic wasn't elemental...as far as I knew. My tía was able to disguise herself as an *Eb* thanks to her intelligence. If *Eb* was a power level one, maybe I could have done the same. With these new advancements in blood scanning and spellwork, I had to disguise myself as something on my level. There were some nahuales that were similar or had overlapping powers. So far, mine seemed to be one of a kind.

I trailed behind Sienna as she absentmindedly swished her cup around. She popped off the top and shook a few of the crushed chunks into her mouth while we surveyed the list of groups. There were a few that might get my mother off my back. Student government, community service, and even a tutoring club would look good. If I were thinking logically about this, these were easy wins that could satisfy their need for me to do more.

"I thought you said you wouldn't be a stranger," a deep voice spoke over my shoulder.

"Hey, Rowan," I said as I turned. "Sorry, I didn't see you."

The last time we'd spoken was when I'd snapped up PR pics for him at Katia's Pitz game. Gods, that had seemed like forever ago at this point.

"Come on, Mira, you see everything." He smirked.

He was right. I was usually pretty aware of my surroundings, but all these faces started to mix together at some point. Rowan was in his casual attire, a worn light blue shirt and even more worn dark jeans. The right level of wear and tear that people considered 'vintage.' He'd obviously gotten some sun since the last time I'd seen him, his skin a deeper golden brown than before. He was probably out helping his uncle on the farms.

If I didn't know him, I'd never have placed him and his uncle as family. Rowan took after his father a lot. The darker features and skin opposed to his mother's and uncle's fair skin and strawberry blond hair. He did get the freckles, though.

"You going to join the agriculture club?" I asked.

Rowan shook his head. "I do enough of that on my own. Think I'll join something else. What are you all thinking about?"

"Ha. Question of the night," Sienna said as she took another mouthful of ice.

"I was just thinking this would be an easy way to appease my parents, Si. Maybe one of the do-gooder clubs?"

She tapped her finger on her chin. "You mean one of the ones that'll make for good PR?"

"Look at you, yes. It would be an easy win. They might lay off us for a little bit," I said as I grabbed her cup and tossed it in the trash. I didn't know how many times I had to tell her that chewing ice was terrible for her teeth. She glared at me, but Rowan pointed across the room and distracted us.

"I was thinking of the community service club. They do some cleaning and upkeeping with the campus. Great photo ops," Rowan said, reminding me of the last time we took advantage of a photo op at Katia's game.

"Yeah, I think the student government might be a little too on the nose. I like it," I responded.

I gestured for him to lead the way, and from the looks of their table, Sienna was actually going to enjoy some of it. They had plants and greenery in an arch, with the words "community service" in yellow flowers and vines.

"Now, I know what you're thinking. When you hear community service, you think of court-ordered mandates. We're just a group of volunteers dedicated to keeping campus and the island as beautiful as possible," one of the members behind the table said with a welcoming smile. She pulled out pamphlets and flattened them on the table as she pointed to all of their goals.

I tried to focus, heard her talk about their new mural project, and watched as Sienna perked up at that, but there was something bugging my senses. I leisurely turned my head to the table right behind this one, trying to be inconspicuous, and my brows drew together at the person manning it.

I hadn't seen her before, and I had to assume she hadn't seen me yet. Iris talked to a student in my and Katia's herbology class, someone who, like me, wanted a path to Aantaj.

"I'll be right back," I whispered between Sienna and Rowan.

I felt every impact of my feet on the ground as I walked around the booths to the other side, everything else going quiet. We hadn't seen Iris since the game, when she told me I had all I needed to figure it out. It was hard not to wonder how much she hid from me, if she knew what we'd have to go through to uncover it.

Iris flicked her gaze over to me, and her eyebrows rose as if she wasn't expecting to see me here. She nodded to the person she was speaking with before asking the other person manning the table to cover for her.

"Hey, Mira," she said as she walked up to me with open arms.

I returned the gesture, giving her a hug, if not just to feel close to my tía. Even now, she still smelled like her. Iris rubbed my arms as she pulled back and focused on my face.

"You look good after..."

"An assassination attempt?" I joked.

"Well, yes." Iris laughed, but the sound was more unsure than anything. "Did you figure it out?"

"We did."

"I wondered if that was what sparked the attempt, but didn't want to reach out if things were being monitored." Her gaze nervously bounced around.

I tried to read her to no avail. Koa had seen one side of her, I had seen one side, and my tía had seen another. It was hard to determine what her true motivations were. Letting her in on the fact that I wasn't so sure also wasn't the best idea.

"Where are you in all of this?" I asked, hopefully vaguely enough.

"I'm where I need to be. Celeste and I didn't agree on some of the methods being used. We're both scientists—she prioritized compassion. I worried about the consequences she overlooked by considering non-scientific reasoning."

Her response only left me with more questions. This seemed to be a habit of hers because it had happened every single time I'd seen her since my tía's death. But I knew which question I needed answered first.

"Does that have to do with my medication?" I asked.

Her eyelashes fluttered ever so slightly. "Not here, Mira."

"Iris!" The woman at the Aantaj table called out, waving for her to come back.

She turned to go. Frustration flared, and I grabbed her arm. The touch wasn't rough, yet it landed somewhere deep. Whatever it hit, it stopped her cold. Her eyes went wide as she looked from her hand to my face, lips parting and closing as she tilted her head.

"If not here, then where?" I asked before she could say anything else.

She relaxed, and if I didn't know better, I'd think it was a show to appease me. Prey in a trap, playing dead when they knew they couldn't get away.

"I'll send you a way to contact me off the record. I promise."

Iris didn't take promises lightly. I'd seen her and my tía promise each other things many times, and they always kept them. I realized then I was still holding onto her, by the arm, and by her...soul, and let go with a nod. When she jogged back to the table, I found Sienna staring at me from the other side. Her gaze flicked somewhere behind me, a subtle gesture to peek in that direction.

Taran watched me, not like he had before, when he had found me curious. He and another teacher stood shoulder to shoulder, their eyes cutting daggers into me. Was it my proximity to the Aantaj table and his hate for the Cynod, or was it Iris that caused this reaction? I looked back as I returned to Rowan and Sienna, and both Taran and the other teacher were gone.

"What was that about?" Sienna whispered.

"I wish I knew."

Rowan bounced his stare between us, deciding to stay out of it and pointing to the sign-up sheet. "We signed all three of us up. First session is next week."

Sometimes I didn't completely understand Sienna's 'woo-woo' stuff. As a wonderful best friend, of course, I always supported it—the crystals, the stars, and whatnot. But I had to give it to her; whatever type of yoga we were doing was actually really working. I felt more centered and at peace than I had in...gods knew how long.

Wren had given me my space after leaving Koa's, and I appreciated it. Not having any other issues added onto the unavoidable ones was nice. There was a traitorous part of me that missed him, though. Missed the assurance he gave me, the protection and stillness he brought when my world was spinning like it was now.

"And a deep breath as we clear our thoughts and rise to a sitting position," Sienna said as if hearing what was going on in my mind.

I did as she said, crossing my legs and feeling her back line up with mine.

"This is called the seated twist. Turn your body to the left side and grab my knee, and I'll grab yours. We should stay connected and smoothly move to the other side after ten deep breaths."

"Sounds good," I responded.

"Deep breath one," Sienna said calmly.

We inhaled in sync. Sienna had taught me how to breathe through yoga positions a long time ago. I didn't realize how important it was during these exercises until she pointed it out. It was very similar to the diaphragmatic breathing my therapist had me do as well. I let my chest and belly expand as air filled my lungs. When I felt Sienna hitch at the top of her inhale, I exhaled slowly with her. I focused on the sensation of her at my back, our connection both physical and beyond that, with my second breath. With my third, we both jolted, and when I opened my eyes, we were no longer on Sienna's dorm floor.

"Mira?" Sienna said cautiously, not breaking from our position.

"Um..."

"Is this... Tía's house?"

It was. We were on the living room floor, somewhere we had done yoga many times. The lamps were on their lowest setting, a dim, warm glow coming from the corners of the room. A crash in the kitchen had me and Sienna on our feet. When the soft humming came, our hands found each other like magnets. Then the smell hit me. The Tecun family's tamales was a recipe passed down from generation to generation. It was a very specific scent; the combination of spices and sauces was unrecognizable. Sienna seemed to notice at the same time I did, and I gulped as we walked toward the aroma together.

The humming, gods, the humming, it made the hairs on my arms stand up. This song had filled these walls practically every day. We turned the corner into the kitchen and froze as if turned into stone.

Tía had her curls pulled up out of her face, a green bandanna holding them back. She was in her comfy clothes, the ones she changed into after work: a soft black t-shirt and stretchy pants with an apron strung across her hips. Slippers that had seen better days graced her feet as she shuffled back from the oven with a steamy ceramic dish.

"Oh, good, I timed it just right," Tía said as she turned around with a smile.

A tear fell down Sienna's cheek while the only thing I could manage was to stare. I dug my nails into Sienna's hand, and she jerked from the pain, but she didn't let me go.

My tía set the dish down and wiped her hands on the dish rag. "Well, come on, my girls, give me a hug."

We dashed over to her as fast as we could, our arms wrapping so tightly around her body as she chuckled. She wasn't as warm as she had once been, but I felt her body press against mine. *Truly* felt, not like in a dream.

"Make yourself a plate and we'll sit down to talk," she said.

We opened the cabinet above the coffee maker and grabbed our plates. She'd already steamed the tamales and was keeping them warm in the oven. I plucked out two for each of us and hurried to the table. My mind was spinning, trying to make sense of it all, but it was her. Whatever I needed to do in order to stay here, I'd do.

"Alright, ask your first question," she said as she sat back.

Sienna and I spoke at the same time, neither of us getting our words across as they became jumbled and mixed together. We both stopped abruptly, and Sienna nodded for me to go first.

"Where are we? How are we here? Are you really here?" I asked without taking a breath.

"We are in a level of the spirit world. Your gifts brought you here, and yes, I'm really here," she answered warmly.

"What do you mean by a level?" Sienna questioned.

"There are levels through death; I'm still in one of the more corporeal ones. I knew you'd be able to contact me soon, so I stayed."

"And the house?" I asked.

Tía tilted her head, a faint smile that felt more sad than happy pulling at the corner of her mouth. "I could have made this any reality, but I loved our reality more than anything."

The air felt thick with our grief, with our love, and tears stung my eyes as she sat forward and said, "You made it here once. I tried to show you, but you hadn't fully come into your gift yet."

"In the therapist's office, I knew it was more than visualization. I can do this anytime?"

"I'm not entirely sure how far your gifts stretch, if you'll be able to get to me as I pass through the other levels. But let's not focus on that. We don't have infinite time. You found my letter?" she asked both of us.

Time was the only thing I needed, and she was right, no matter how badly I wanted, I could feel in my chest that this wouldn't last forever.

"We did, and we also met the rebels..." I looked to Sienna.

My best friend's gaze dropped down to her plate. A question it seemed she didn't want to ask, or accuse the woman who loved us like her own.

"They took Sienna because they thought she could tell them who would decode the glyphs," I said, barely above a whisper.

"I thought maybe you...Well, I thought..." Sienna trailed off.

"I did not tell them what you could do, Sienna." My tía's face pinched as if struck in the chest. "My plan was to make sure they were a safe space, and then ask you how you felt about it. I never would have given you up like that without permission."

Sienna let out a long exhale, finally glancing back up at her. I could see the understanding on her face, the relief that she was still the person Sienna thought she was.

My chest tingled, and I rubbed my palm against it. Tía looked around, sensing it as well.

"We don't have much more time. Know that I did trust the rebels to a certain extent. They are trying to bring the Cynod down for all of the lies, and I stand by that. Remember that their cause is the only thing that matters to them, though."

The room flickered, the lights flashing bright and dimming.

"Wait," I said, trying to hold on to whatever it is that brought me here. "The pills, what were you trying to do with them?"

"They stopped you from emerging. I was trying to stall. It was always you and me, we were the beginning and the end."

I sucked in a breath at the reference to the prophecy. "Why not tell me?"

The lines of her face blurred, and Sienna grabbed onto my wrist as it felt like we were being ripped away from this dimension.

"I didn't think the world was ready. But you were, you both are. I love you, my girls. May the gods protect you on this next stretch of your journey without me."

Her lip quivered, the world around us shaking and going black. My eyes shot open, our bodies back in the dorm with my hand still on Sienna's knee. It should have felt good, seeing her again. But something about her last words had me thinking that was truly the final time.

17

MIRA

I hadn't spent much time at Koa's gyms. It wasn't that I didn't enjoy physical fitness; it was that the patrons of his gyms *loved* that shit. Like, eat, sleep, drink, fitness. A lot of them didn't have many other places to go, so I understood. Koa took care of his gym and the members, but my little 'squat the bar without added weight' workouts weren't going to cut it here.

The last kid left for the day with her coach following right behind, and Sienna locked the door behind them. She was less than excited to see the rebels again. I understood it, but we were getting to the point where we had no other choice.

"Did talking to Tía help any?" I asked.

After my nahual gave me the gift of…whatever that was, we didn't say much. We finished our yoga workout and then watched TV in silence. I'd always needed to process things in my head before I could put them into words. Sienna wasn't much different. She usually didn't voice her feelings unless prompted. She was certainly vocal in many areas, but with these big life-changing things, she tended to stew. Especially when it affected both of us.

"It helps to get her perspective on the parts she was involved in. But no. It doesn't help me understand the rebels or even consider justifying their actions." She pulled the metal looped string so the black blinds shielded any outside eyes. "You know, it's just like, there's a right way to do things, then there's a wrong way. Sometimes the risk was worth it. Koa, for example, and everything he does. But they kidnapped me and beat me, Mir. How am I supposed to look the other

163

way? And what does that say about their methods? They needed me. I wasn't dispensable. What do you think they do to people who are?"

"Did you want to stay in his office? Just watch the conversation from the cameras?"

Sienna shook her head, a dark curl falling free from the messy bun she'd pulled her hair into. "Nah, if I'm here, I'm here. I'll have to get used to it, no matter what, it seems."

"There's power in facing it like you are," I said.

I didn't want it to come off as patronizing, and Sienna didn't take it that way, thankfully. She didn't say anything as we walked behind the counter and through the staff hall. I slowed just enough so that I could take my phone out of my pocket without her seeing. Call it intuition, or the fact that the only people I texted aside from Katia were here with me, but I knew who the notification would be from.

Respecting your space, but I want you to know that I'm thinking about you. No expectations. I miss you.

I quickly swiped the notification and tucked my phone back in my pocket when I heard voices coming from the break room. I didn't have time to respond or even think of a response. The rebels were here. There weren't many places that Koa considered safe outside of his gyms and clubs. Thanks to the fact that Wren was attached to the club, he decided this was a good location. I hadn't had the courage to ask my brother about how they were dealing with it yet. Partially because that meant I had to talk about my part of the situation, and I wasn't ready for that. As much as I loved Koa dearly, he wouldn't be the first person I'd talk to. He'd want to problem-solve, work out a solution. Probably recommend a few options for Wren's death.

No, it'd be a girls' night topic.

I threaded my pinky through Sienna's, one last attempt at offering her strength before we pushed the galley door into the breakroom. Koa waited on the other side, alert, having sensed our approach. His hand rose, thumb tracing the line of Sienna's jaw, his voice sliding into my mind.

'You both okay?'

'As okay as we're gonna get,' I responded, and he turned to the rebels.

Adler was here, one of the few times I hadn't seen Jed at his side. He was on a job a client had already paid for. In their world, that wasn't something you could back out of. We didn't want to bring Katia into this part yet. She wasn't super involved outside of the crash, and we had no reason to expose her more than she already was. Thankfully, she had a junior military drill right now. Since she was going to come over tonight anyway, filling her in was the better option.

I fully faced the rebels; this time lacking their full battle regalia. Without the all-black, the neck gaiters, helmets, and bulletproof vests, they looked like...normal people. The first person I recognized was Strider, the one who gave us the letter at the bridge. His hair was braided into cornrows with just an inch or two hanging at the base of his neck. He was trying his best to appear friendly, with his gaze set on Sienna. She didn't regard him in the slightest; her attention homed in on someone else. I hadn't brought up their potential relation. Neither had Koa. It was one of the few things we didn't have to face right away, so we didn't push.

Another rebel sat beside him, not one I recognized. A woman with unsettling green eyes and a shaved head who didn't appear capable of being friendly if she tried. There was another person in the space; I could feel it. They were watching, walking around the table, and heading toward us. I stepped forward, and Koa shuffled to go with me. Raising my hand, I reached for where I sensed a soul.

Zélia manifested with a smile, my hands around her neck.

"Hm, interesting," she said as she pulled out of my grasp and sat beside Strider. "You met Strider. This is Asha; she doesn't speak. Two of my most trusted."

Asha's gaze bounced from Zélia's lips back to us. I wasn't sure if she meant she was mute or deaf, or if she just wasn't a talker.

"Well, no other introductions needed thanks to the fucking stalking," Koa said as he plopped down in a chair beside Sienna.

Watching my brother battle the desire to do the 'right' thing, whether that was in regard to Sienna or to the whole of Inecha, was difficult. I knew he wanted to say fuck them all, thanks to what happened to her, but for so long, Koa had been looking for these people. Whether he knew it or not.

Every time he rebelled against my parents, every gym he opened to help the people the Cynod didn't care about. Each rant he went on about how things could be better, that the government shouldn't have the power they do, he was searching for the people with shared ideals.

He'd found a certain family in the criminals he associated himself with, people who detested the government in the same way. But Koa took it a step further, whether he wanted the world to know or not. He wanted to be the change. As did the rebels.

Zélia didn't speak, nor did her soldiers. We all stared at each other across the wide table. While our desired outcome was the same, it didn't make any of us instant best friends. Koa was the one leading the charge in this space, as important as Sienna and I were to everything; his need to protect us had him taking the first step.

"I have a couple of questions before we agree to anything," he said as he pulled out a black pill. "What are these, and why were they at your docks?"

Zélia lifted a brow and sat back with her arms crossed. "You're observant."

"Do yourself a favor and keep that in mind," Koa quipped.

"According to my 'stalking', Mira is well acquainted with these pills," Zélia drawled.

"I was. I'm not anymore, and I never really knew what they were. My tía gave them to me, but you know that too, yes?" I responded.

'Not so much information, kid,' Koa spoke into my mind.

Right. Leverage and leaving space for them to expose themselves was his area of expertise, not mine.

"Why doesn't everyone take a nice calming breath?" Strider chimed in. "Loosen up some of the tension in here?"

Not a single chest moved but his.

Zélia's shadows spilled out onto the table, and she wrapped a tendril around the pill to lift it between us. "How familiar are you with pharmaceuticals?"

"It's not our specialty, but we've been around it quite a bit," I said, answering for both Sienna and me.

"There are many medications on the market that have multiple uses. You change the dose, alter the release time, or mix it with something, and it creates an entirely new drug. A small dosage of something like finasteride treats hair loss in men, but if you multiply that dosage by five, it treats benign prostatic hyperplasia. The same medication can be used for diabetes or weight loss."

"And this one?" Koa pushed.

"The generic name for this is Aanteni. According to your aunt, this had an incredible number of applications. It was supposed to be a super drug. Something that would be a cure-all," Zélia followed up, her eyes getting big the way my tía's used to when she was onto something. She must have been a scientist before she started leading the revolution.

"But?" Sienna cut in.

Adler's fingers typed away at his computer like he was taking meeting notes, and not leaving a single word out of the conversation.

"But..." Zélia tapped her knuckles on the table. "There were unforeseen complications. The trials showed a blockage they couldn't explain."

"A magical blockage." I rubbed my chest, remembering what my tía had said in the death walk.

"Correct. It suppressed the trial participants' nahuales when given at a high-dosage extended release. Which is what you were on, Mira," Zélia said.

That checked out. Dr. Puebla was taken aback when she saw how high my dosage was.

Strider cleared his throat. "They were a little overzealous when the trials first began. They put out a study talking about how this would be some miracle medication—targeting arcanoma patients specifically in this case. Your aunt wasn't the first person on the trial; the original scientist died in a 'car accident' after it was published. Then they put your aunt on it for better... discretion. She was the daughter of a Cynod member. My thought is they expected her to be more aligned with their values."

"The psychiatrist?" I asked. "Dr. Garcia?"

"Yes. You know how the *Eb* are, their natural geniuses allow them to have many areas of study."

I remembered when she died. The lab shut down for an entire day, which was unheard of. She was my original psychiatrist for the trial. I racked my brain for any medical journal articles that had come out around that time. For her to publish, she would have needed approval from her superiors. Unless she went rogue and went in a different, less medical direction.

"So what are they aiming to do with this shit?" Koa asked.

"Control, Koa. It is all about control for them. They're controlling half of the population because they've made them believe they're weak. Dose them with this and it's no longer an idealization, it's reality. They can't fight back."

"Our research details an interesting story." Adler took a break from typing to speak. "Your group doesn't have the ability to fight back yet, either. Telling everyone they have power is one thing, but talk is cheap when you don't have the ability to back it."

"Not to mention we've been witness to your tactics," Sienna spat.

Strider tilted his head with a pointed look at Zélia. "*That* wasn't supposed to happen. Trust me when I say we've ensured the parties have been dealt with."

"Unfortunately, that isn't enough for me," Sienna responded.

Strider looked like he wanted to say more, to apologize or set the record straight again, but Zélia spoke before him.

"You're not exactly wrong that we don't have the power—yet. We've got underground systems, rebel chapters in every major city, and we'll be ready when the time comes. But we need you," she said.

"Is it just the pills that you want to stop from being distributed? What are you doing with the shipments you steal?" I questioned.

"We're disposing of them," Strider answered. "It's the whole fucking system. These power levels, these elitist societies. These 'Solis-appointed' governing parties. The people should choose who leads them, not some made-up deity they use to control us."

"Yeah, I want to be real fucking clear in intentions here. You mean kill them?" Koa asked.

Zélia sat forward. "Whatever needs to be done."

She watched in expectation of a reaction. As if saying that was some test we needed to pass.

"Seems like a pattern with you people," Sienna mumbled under her breath.

"Killing them wouldn't do anything. Systematic oppression goes beyond the current oppressors. It means that even if there is nobody with those views in power, the system itself would still oppress. To be successful, we'd need..." I trailed off.

"A full-fledged revolution," Koa finished.

"The people want change. They're too afraid to say it, but we have eyes and ears everywhere. We are aiming to break it all. Everything you just said, we wholeheartedly believe. Come to one of our meetings, we'll introduce you to the team, and we can go more in-depth with our plan," Zélia said.

"As much as we would like you to join us, we can't give everything away without full trust that you're with us," Strider said with a weak smile. "We hope you understand."

Our side of the table stared at theirs. If the roles were reversed, we wouldn't give them anything either. Koa's eyes flicked between us, standing and gesturing for us to follow him to discuss. The rebels stayed seated, and I made sure Zélia wasn't watching us from the shadows.

Koa set down a silencing spell in his office as his hand settled on Sienna's lower back. I could still feel her apprehension and unease threading through him. He was torn, a war playing out behind his eyes: the weight of balancing her trust, her fear, and the unyielding responsibility of doing what was right.

"They didn't say anything we don't agree with," I broke the ice, not making Koa be the one to say it.

"We found everything we could on them," Adler offered. "I don't have any more information on what their plan might be."

That was the Mercers' specialty, so if they couldn't find anything out, we had no other choice.

"We have to agree to work with them to find out more," I said, waiting for Koa's response.

"I don't think we need them. We can deal with the Cynod on our own. We have ins that they don't have," Sienna retorted.

It was a good shot at playing Cizin's advocate. Except we all knew that it was coming from a very biased place within her.

"Sure, but we don't have their numbers," Koa said cautiously. "Venom, they've put time and effort into building this movement. They have the momentum needed to *fuel* a revolution. You're right, we have ins that they don't...but they have the numbers to get shit done. Working with them—"

Before my brother even finished his sentence, Sienna had already pulled away from his touch. I saw the ripple of dismay and maybe even regret overtake him as her nose pinched.

"Are we forgetting what happened to me?" She lifted her shirt in anger. "Do I need to remind you what they're capable of?"

Faint scars covered Sienna's midriff that she refused to let him heal. They sliced through the beautiful red ink of my brother's shifted form wrapped around her body, but Koa kept pushing, lifting his own in response. "I have them too. There's no world where I think what happened to you was okay, but..."

"We can't do it all alone," I offered. "They hurt you, but, Si, the Cynod tried to *kill* us. What can we do?"

"Why do we have to do anything? Why is this our responsibility?" she shrieked.

I thought she'd come around, but being here with them must have triggered her, bringing it all crashing back. She seemed to realize why it *was* our responsibility the moment after she said it. I saw as she fought for some other response, some other argument to sway us, but she couldn't come up with one.

Koa lifted his hand to comfort her, but she stepped back. "Fine. Whatever."

"Venom..."

"I said whatever." She turned and went back to the breakroom.

Placing my hand on my brother's shoulder, I reassured, "She'll come around. I think it's a lot right now."

"Yeah. It is a lot. And it's only going to get heavier the longer we delay. If we start picking and choosing when to actually *do* something based on comfort or perfection of methods...then we're already done." Koa looked over at Adler, who had effectively shut up once Sienna began yelling. Koa shook his head and went to follow behind Sienna.

I knew he didn't mean to sound harsh, and I hated how much I agreed with him. Sienna would come around. She had to. I knew in the back of her mind, her mom and Ethan lingered. How hard they'd worked growing up, all the days and nights she'd spent at our house just to not feel alone. The cause mattered to her, and eventually, the end would justify the means.

Zélia, Strider, and Asha watched us with anticipation, but I wanted to ask one other thing.

"Tell me who killed my tía first," I said.

"You already know the answer to that question, Mira. The same ones who tried to kill you," Zélia said with her hand on her hip.

It was the answer we all didn't want to say out loud, but we knew they were telling the truth. Everything was connected in a big web of lies, disasters, and grabs for power. At the center of it all was the Cynod, watching and waiting for us to make our next move.

We all stood still, the rebels looking to see if that answer impacted ours. Koa cleared his throat and asked, "When's the next meeting?"

18

MIRA

"Well, I, for one, think it's romantic," Katia said as she dabbed the last bit of mask goop onto her face.

"I bet you do," Sienna laughed and handed her a paper towel.

Katia wiped her fingers and tossed her hands up in surrender. "I'm just saying, she's not appreciating him enough! She stabbed him, and he barely blinked. That's real love."

"I'd like to say there's better conflict resolution, but in this fictional world, I'm with you," I said and closed the book.

Our read for this week was enemies-to-lovers. One of those stories where you couldn't quite place the line between enemy and lover until they were fully lodged into lover. The FMC had stabbed the MMC for leaving out a vital piece of truth, and he thought he was only omitting something small. The tension was delicious, and I just knew the romance was going to really take off in the next chapter.

"We'll see if he returns the sentiment after she gets him to the closest healer," Sienna said with a roll of her eyes. "He's a man, Katia. They'll always act in their best interest, no matter how pretty they make it look."

She was in another mood, and I couldn't exactly blame her.

"You know what I think it is? The fact that she could do something so extreme and unforgivable, and he still wants her," Katia said. "Can you imagine that need and desire?"

Sienna and I both groaned, and Katia realized her mistake immediately.

"Wait, I'm just saying—"

I swatted my hand at her with a chuckle. "No, we get what you mean. We wish things were so cut and dry in real life."

"Either of you want to talk about it?" Katia smiled nervously.

Sienna glanced at me, and I stared back at her. She broke first.

"I know why Koa's doing it. Deep down, I understand. Believe me, I can see the logic in a lot of shit that doesn't align with my own personal morals. It's...it's the surface part of me that feels betrayed, the scars and ghost-like pain I can't shake," she whispered.

"Would you have been happier if he hadn't agreed to work with them?" Katia asked.

"I don't know. For the sake of my sanity *and* relationship, I'm doing my best to avoid reviewing the hypotheticals. I also love him too much to ask him not to do what he thinks is right." Sienna's head jerked to the kitchen. "Shit, my cookies."

She got up in a hurry right as the timer went off. A slam of the oven and a pang of the pan hitting the stovetop sounded before she came back.

"Anyway, something about those two in particular makes me feel weird," Sienna followed up.

"Zélia and Strider?" I asked.

She nodded. "Zélia, for obvious reasons, but Strider watches me with too much...caution?"

Ah, still avoiding this, I see.

"He said they weren't supposed to do what they did to you. Maybe he just feels bad?" I questioned.

Even though I'd seen it too. His stares went beyond guilt, like there was a puzzle to decode beneath her skin.

"I don't know." She shrugged. "Maybe."

"What's his last name?" Katia asked as she flipped open her laptop.

"No idea," Sienna answered.

Katia clicked a couple of buttons on her phone, and Jed's voice came through her speaker. "Hey, babe."

"Hey, you're on speaker. Mira and Sienna are here. Can you help us with something really quick?"

"Anything for you."

They were so cute it was actually disgusting.

"You guys did research into the rebels, right? Would you know Strider's last name?" she asked as she hovered her fingers over her laptop, ready to type.

"One second." Silence on his line, then a couple of beeps, and he was back. "Brown. Strider Brown."

Katia made a smooching sound, and Jed chuckled. "I'll pay for your services later. Thanks."

She hung up on him before he could respond.

"Do *you* care to talk about how that's going?" Sienna said with a finger pointing toward Katia's phone.

Katia tossed her head back and laughed, her fingers seeming to type on their own accord. "It's going great. Really great. I thought they'd get jealous of each other at some point, but they haven't yet."

"Have you done both at the same..." I trailed off,

There was a better way of asking that question. Curiosity got me before I could word in a more eloquent way. Besides, we were all thinking it.

"No." She laughed. "Nothing like that. They're so different, you know? Jed keeps me laughing when I'd probably lose my mind otherwise, and Adler is...he's steady. Safe. Together it all kind of balances out. They don't try to compete, they just fit."

"Interesting," Sienna said, her gaze out in the open.

I knew this look was the one where she was picturing something in her mind. Sienna had a *very* vivid imagination, like, scary vivid compared to my mostly dark and shadowy subconscious.

"Ah!" Katia shrieked. "Here he is."

"Time with the Mercers is paying off in more ways than one," I said as I leaned closer to the laptop.

I saw no immediate red flags. With a private account there was only so much to see. There could have been something hidden, but the only way to figure out that would be to send him a friend request.

"He's cute," Katia said with a smile.

"You have enough on your hands," I laughed.

"Don't you go speaking for me now. There are other places to fill," she said as she zoomed in on his picture and then back to his profile. "City boy. Not much info on him at all. Page is private. Less than a hundred followers, looks like he follows the same amount back."

"I'm surprised the rebels allow any sort of socials," I said.

Sienna bit the inside of her cheek. "I assume the minimum requirement is a private page. It wasn't a bad feeling I got from him, just like I'd met him before. Maybe they'd been trailing me longer than I realized."

"If he's the one rebel that doesn't set you off, and he was upset about your treatment, maybe you contact him?" I suggested.

"Um..." Sienna's mouth tightened, and her face twisted like I was saying to jump into the man's arms.

"Not in a suspicious way," I clarified. "Just a controlled scenario to make yourself more comfortable with it all. You've always been very good at judging people's characters. If a part of you trusts him, I'd run with it. You could even tell Koa."

"I agree," Katia said. "And it's an easy block and unfriend if you decide it's a bad idea."

"Okay," Sienna said, sounding convinced enough. "I'll send him a request, but you greatly underestimate your brother's skepticism."

Sienna pulled out her phone, and Katia went to the kitchen to grab the cookies. The candle burning beside me caught my attention, the flame reflecting in the window glass. It stood out against the dark of the night sky, and it reminded me of Wren. The way he'd used his magic to create constellations in my room. The warmth and brightness of it.

I hadn't responded to his text yet. I'd opened and stared at it a couple of times, even though I hadn't typed a response.

Just like I'd done before, I clicked his name in my messages. The conversation a few scrolls above it made me smile, and I had to hide it behind my fist. We'd been texting in the same room with Koa, debating what facial line my brother would get first. I said frown lines, Wren said scowl. He'd even taken a picture of

Koa and drawn it in for effect. My brother didn't notice. He was too busy staring at Sienna like she was the moon and the sun all wrapped up in one. Fuck, were those simpler times. It was crazy what could happen in a few weeks.

"Mira is texting Wren!" Katia screamed from behind me, and Sienna whirled around.

"Wait, no—"

Sienna grabbed the phone from my hand. "You are! Wait, when did he take this picture?"

I snatched it back. "I wasn't. He texted me earlier today, and I was just...looking at it."

"Her thumbs were hovering, I saw it!" Katia said.

"Okay, when did you become such a snitch? You should know the Mercers really don't like that." I put my hands on my hips and couldn't help but laugh at how serious their faces were.

"Oh, baby, you're losing it," Sienna said as she grabbed a cookie. "Here, eat this."

"Out of all the things in my life that would make me go insane, he's not exactly at the top of the list," I said as I bit the cookie and sat down.

They both perched on the couch, waiting for me to continue. I didn't know what to say. Maybe I *was* losing it. I hadn't thought about what I'd seen through the eyes of my nahual before Wren left Koa's condo that day. There wasn't anyone to help me understand my gifts.

"When Wren told me about what happened, my nahual showed me something. His...aura, maybe? It felt like it wanted me to see what his soul was made up of. The blue radiated."

Sienna groaned. "A blue aura indicates truth and wisdom. It's tied to your throat in a way, clear and honest communication."

I perked up. "So that means he wasn't lying, like, for sure?"

"It could mean that, I don't know. I'm just the weird hippie according to your mother," Sienna said with a single shoulder shrug. "'Gutter rat' to my real haters."

Not the answer I was looking for. A resounding 'yes,' or even a 'no,' was preferred. Just so I knew one way or the other.

"Did you feel like he was lying?" Katia asked.

I debated as I chewed on my bottom lip. "No, I didn't. But even if it is the truth doesn't make it hurt less."

"All three of us play roles that we don't necessarily want to. Mira, you play the role of a Cynod heir in public, someone who agrees with them. Is that to be perceived as a lie, hard stop? Sienna, you pretend you aren't Koa's mate. Is that a lie, with no wiggle room? And me, well, every person in Jundi puts on a show for the Cynod to pretend we don't worship the old gods. My parents told me to blend in, not to draw attention to myself. Truths aren't black and white, just as lies aren't. We make these decisions with good intent, knowing that we could be hurt, that our loved ones could be hurt. Maybe he did the same."

"Everyone can't go around lying with good intent and say fuck the consequences," I said.

Impact over intent, that was what I always said. Especially when dealing with people like my parents. They could go on and talk about how much they wanted to make things better, but their actions didn't align with the people. However, when it was all said and done, who was I to decide what lies were permissible, and which ones weren't.

"No, they can't," Katia agreed. "We have to trust that the people who truly know who we are wouldn't betray us. It doesn't mean it doesn't happen. I have a hard time believing that Wren, a man who put his life on the line to save your best friend, did this just to be...evil."

"A snitch *and* wise, apparently," I sighed and looked to Sienna for her opinion.

"You said I'm a good judge of character; remember that you are too. I mean, I'd have to grill the fuck out of him if you forgive him, maybe even test out my power of persuasion." She winked. "But no, I wouldn't hold it against you either."

"Koa is going to tear him in half, regardless." I bit my nail.

The image of him on the verge of killing Wren wasn't one that I'd lose anytime soon.

"Koa cares about you, and he *thinks* he could have stopped what happened. He's mad at himself, too. If Wren makes you happy, he'll get over it...eventually. And don't tell him I'm saying this, but Wren hurt Koa, too. He thought they were friends," Sienna offered.

Katia nodded. "Life's too short. Don't miss out on something purely on principle. The least you can do is talk to him, understand him better. Make your decision from there."

"You're both right," I said as I typed out a message.

Me:

Let's talk.

19

Sienna

Between the insane amount of sugar we ingested and the wine we downed during girls' night, my head was throbbing something serious. Lucky for me, and gods be blessed, I'd get to marry rich one day, and said rich fae had a diabolically comfortable mattress. I rolled over and pulled a five-star hotel-level pillow over my head.

If I never had to emerge from this dark and freezing room, it would be too soon. Koa's blackout curtains eliminated any light that was surely trying to breach through the window. It was nice not having to worry about Bran or one of our other overlords reporting us missing from the dorms. The caves had become a fun, safe space for me, but stumbling through them to see my man for a few seconds was getting old, fast.

With the Kuxtal Academy event today, we'd been free to leave campus all weekend, which also meant it was the day we'd been dreading all week. Koa would meet my parents. And with him missing from my side at what was sure to still be early hours, the nerves must have been eating at him, too.

He'd been wound up all damn week. Between finals next week, handling business, and everything with Wren, no amount of text messages had helped settle him. Somehow, someway, I was going to have to convince him to try yoga or something.

The Caneks siblings were born with anxiety, and only one of them was willing to address it in a healthy way. Rolling over with a soft groan, I pulled my phone off the charger on the dresser and let the light blind me. One voice memo from my snake.

"Morning, Venom. Brotherhood called a meeting. I'll be back by dinner. I love you."

My smile was reminiscent of the love-sick idiots in just about every book I read. Give me fantasy, extra romance, or give me death. I peered up at the time in the right-hand corner: 9 a.m. *Dammit.* I absolutely despised waking up this late; it chipped away at the day.

Scrolling over to PhotoPhantom, I checked my friend request to Strider, still no dice. It made sense. He probably thought I was a weirdo. Sending a friend request to a private account when you're practically a stranger is classic weirdo behavior.

It was time to start my day, anyway. Tugging on Koa's shirt, I opened his bedroom door and crossed the living room to see if Mira and Katia were awake yet. I could hear them passed out and snoring from behind the door. Mira had always slept hard—Katia, however, slept like the damn dead. There was plenty to keep my mind busy while I waited for them to wake up.

Step one: center myself and set the tone for the day with morning meditation. That had really been what got me through each week. Of course, Mira had done her best, but she had her own problems to face. And as happy as I was for Katia and her love life with the Mercers, it was hard to be in tune with my emotions when everything for her was going so great. The thought of that alone made me feel like the shittiest person in the world. Thus, multiple meditation sessions—morning, noon, and night.

I rolled my yoga mat out from the corner of the living room, lit some incense, and dropped into my morning flow. Nothing fancy—only enough to stretch out the nonsense and remind my body it was still attached to a soul.

Halfway through a sun salutation, I muttered under my breath, "Help Momma not curse out Koa today," and followed it up with, "Also, maybe make my glamour not suck?"

The universe didn't answer. *I'll take that as a soft maybe.* I'd toyed with the idea of whether or not to bring up Thaddeus today but decided to play it by ear. It was my first time seeing my parents in what felt like forever. That coupled with introducing Koa...I didn't want to make momma have a stroke.

After a few more deep breaths and one very questionable downward dog, I tossed my curls into a bun. Facing myself in the mirror was hard as all nine hells. Despite Koa fawning over me as though I were Ixchel herself, I found my confidence near zero these days. It was hard when his 'fiancée' did her best to be a near-perfect version of myself.

Any style I played around with, new changes to my hair or experimentation with my makeup, was replicated in a palatable way for the public eye. They fawned over Alanna on PhotoPhantom and tagged me in 'versus' posts, comparing us side by side.

The idea of comparison was strange to me. I was never one to care what the world thought. It was all outside noise. I mean, who gave a fuck?

Turned out, I did.

It was hard not to when thousands of fae took time out of their day to make sure I knew I was less than. A second choice. Another phase for their bad-boy heir. No amount of compliments, flowers, or access to a black card would make that go away. It was up to me, myself, and I to maintain my sense of self. I snatched the positive affirmation for the morning off the mirror in Koa's bathroom and washed my face as I repeated it seven times for good luck.

The air was blissfully perfect—blue sky, that crisp post-summer breeze, and just enough warmth to tease a tan on my brown skin. Not that I'd know. The second I left the house without covering up, I feared the mate mark would flare like a damn neon sign. Still couldn't figure out how to anchor the glamour properly. The old magic that bonded us was too strong, and mine was...let's call it cooperative adjacent.

I tugged my sleeves down and popped in the new earphones Koa got me last week, with the little 'be aware of your surroundings' setting. Which was an effort to avoid a repeat incident from a few weeks ago. The flashcard audio kicked in, and I started walking, letting the calm voice recite the terms I was supposed to know by heart.

Studying this way worked well for me. Reading felt like my brain was in a fight with itself. When it wasn't for fun, the task was beyond daunting. Flashcards only worked if I used a color-coded white board situation to memorize the answer. That wasn't actually learning, so I preferred to save that for emergency situations. But listening? That I could do. I could process with the speed needed to keep up with the rest of this stupid academy I never planned on attending. I could walk and sip coffee and dodge seagulls and still process half of what I needed for finals.

It wasn't that I regretted being forced here with my best friend, and by proxy, her brother. It was just...I had goals for myself that now seemed completely out of reach.

Making a living from my art was going to be hard. I knew that. Opening my own studio one day was damn near a fever dream, but it was still my future to decide, and that alone was enticing.

I wanted to earn it. Not have haters flock there to mock or esteemed critics post reviews simply for the clickbait of someone attached to the Cynod.

The street was chill, mostly locals this early, with the ocean just peeking between buildings up ahead. The promise of caffeine lured me forward. I already knew I'd order the usual—oat milk iced latte, cinnamon on top, and maybe an extra shot of espresso if I was feeling reckless.

I flexed my fingers, the mate mark pulse faintly under the glamour, and sighed. Neither Koa nor I had figured out what that meant. At first, we'd checked in with each other, made sure it wasn't a sign of danger. Then we assumed maybe it was distance, both metaphorical or physical. That appeared to be partially correct, the further away we were from each other, the more that invisible string pulled taut. It hadn't become unbearable—yet. A time would inevitably come, however. Wasn't sure how I'd live through that one. No explanation for ancient magic that no one had seen in several lifetimes.

"Do you seriously have to tingle every time I breathe a little too hard?" I muttered. "We get it. You're all powerful and cryptic. Calm down."

By the time I made it back to the condo, my coffee was nothing more than emotional support ice. I kicked the door shut with the heel of my sneaker and heard the distant hiss of the shower coming from Koa's bathroom. His keys weren't on the counter where he usually tossed them, like everything else he cluttered around this place, so my guess was that Mira was occupying it. One could only assume that meant Katia was busy in ours.

I dropped my tote bag and gave the kitchen a once-over. Koa rarely did anything about groceries—especially with us no longer staying here on the weekends. Lucky for literally everyone here, I was a miracle worker when it came to whipping up something tasty out of nothing for breakfast. Or brunch. Or whatever you call a meal that happened before noon, but after existential dread for finals and life in general.

A simple breakfast, I told myself—promised myself—would calm all the buzzing energy begging to bring me down.

Thirty minutes later, I had cranberry orange muffins cooling on the stove and eggs folded with whipped ricotta. A side of chicken sausage that was crisped perfectly around the edges, plated on the counter next to hash browns, golden enough to impress a breakfast hater. An elaborate tea setup was laid out with cream and sugar, as if I lived in a cozy cottage and not a high-rise condo with mood lighting and blackout curtains.

Mira came out first, hair damp, hoodie half-zipped, skin flushed from the steam. She clocked the spread and blinked. "I fucking love it when you stress cook."

"Who's stressed? Not me. You love it when I cook in general. Your stomach is not picky," I said, already halfway through arranging mint sprigs on the tea tray like it was a competition.

Mira's bedroom door opened, and Katia emerged in her junior military uniform. Her long, dark hair was in a tight braid that emphasized her copper-bronze cheekbones and pulled back her narrow hazel eyes. The kohl smeared around them only adding to her lethal charm. She took one look at the table and whistled low. "Please say this is for us and not your grump of a boyfriend."

"It's for my sanity," I said. "You just happen to be here to benefit."

Mira rolled her eyes and grabbed plates. "Don't argue with her. Just eat."

We fell into our usual rhythm—gossip about anyone other than us, background music humming low from the smart speaker, forks clinking against porcelain. For a second, it felt normal. Like we weren't knee-deep in complicated emotions, ancient magic, and unresolved trauma.

Katia checked the time and stood with a groan. "Alright. I've gotta be on parade duty before the event starts. Junior military wants to flex, and the newbies are the shiny force of power they want to show off since we fully emerged."

"I'm hitting the library before I meet Katia there. Gotta get some extra hours in today since I have therapy tomorrow before I meet with Wren. Doubt I'll get much done after that." Mira pushed her chair back next.

Arching a brow, I gave her a once-over. "You good?"

"I'm managing." She paused at the door, the smile faltering for half a second.

Which meant she wasn't. Mira had levels of denial so refined it could be bottled and sold. Still, I nodded. I could pry, but honestly, my heart wouldn't be in the pep talk, and bad advice would damage more than none at all.

"Call me if you need anything. I'll be here pretending I'm not spiraling."

She smirked faintly, then disappeared out the door, leaving me in the quiet hum of the condo. Citrus and sage overwhelmed my senses, caffeine still low-key buzzing in my veins, and a pile of dishes that felt like a metaphor.

Koa came home as I was finishing the shading on the hibiscus petals. These were a replication of the ones I'd grown, wrapped around the banister of the balcony. When I first emerged as a *Kaban*, I'd feared that the ability to magically grow earth from my hands instead of balancing the knowledge of Herta wouldn't entice me.

There was fun in manual efforts. Knowing you had to get the conditions just right to have a healthy plant. I found that there was joy in both methods over the last few days. Different kinds of joy, but still enough to fulfill that 'fun meter' we all possessed.

The balcony creaked open behind me. I didn't bother to turn as I took another slow pull from the feyfog joint and exhaled toward the sky. He leaned down to press a soft kiss on my temple, the sensation sending more warmth on my skin than the sun beating down from the skylight.

He leaned against the doorway, the scent of sweat and sea breeze trailing behind him like it missed him already. "Miss me?" Koa teased.

"Mm. Hardly." I flicked a little extra gold into the edge of a leaf.

"Don't lie to me, Venom."

The gravel in his voice sent a snaking thrill down my spine. I stood, brushing paint flecks off my thighs, and stubbed out the feyfog. "I hate to sound like your mother, however..."

"You hate what I'm wearing?"

"I mean, no. I love it, which means my momma is going to find a problem with it. It's very..." I fought to find the words.

"Criminal, trouble-making boyfriend who used to be a man-whore that owns a secret fight club and nightclub notorious for not having any rules. Oh, and rides a motorcycle that very publicly almost killed her daughter?" he finished for me, the nerves in his shifty eyes not matching the faux laugh he forced out.

Koa grabbed the feyfog roll-up and relit it, taking an exaggerated drag and holding it in. I scanned him over, my head tilting side to side as I did my best to find the right words. Momma and Ethan were not ones to judge a book by their cover. At the same time, first impressions were everything. We were only fae. Gods knew what I first thought before I got to know deeper than the false persona he let the world see day in and day out.

He never underdressed. Sneakers and Koa didn't see each other unless he was headed to the gym, but perhaps that was the problem. Koa didn't just scream "bad-boy", he always yelled "money". I wanted my parents to get to know him and not allow outer appearances to block their initial judgments.

"I was only going to say you look like an asshole. But sure, your description works too. Maybe, fewer designers, more things Mira bought you?" I offered as I pointed to the outfit worth Ethan's paycheck. "The boots definitely have to go." I squinted, finalizing my assessments, and grabbed his hand, leading us inside.

We reached his closet, and I took a few moments scouring through, then turned, realizing he was still smoking. I smacked it out of his hand, and he laughed with a questioning gaze. "We can't smell like that when we get there. Ethan hates drugs."

"It's feyfog…" Koa said, as if that were excluded.

"Class A, Class E, doesn't matter. Drugs are drugs when you used to work for the IDCC."

"I didn't know that." Koa scratched the side of his head. "Anything else I should be aware of? Like him having my case file or something?"

I shook my head and pulled out a casual linen shirt Mira bought him and murmured a quick de-wrinkle spell this girl on our floor taught us two nights ago. "He quit when he met my mom. She needed help with me, and the hours weren't good. Unless you had a record as a toddler, the only thing he knows is what the press released over the years. His best friend is still on the force though."

"So everything plus the cover-ups. Fantastic," he whistled, pulling on the shirt I picked out and rolling his eyes as I ogled his bare chest. I had to resist the urge to reach out and drag my nails down over the intentionally unhealed marks left from last night.

Tossing the matching sneakers we all had—another gift, compliments of Mira—I watched him slide them on, then offered a nod of approval. We had another twenty minutes until it was time to go, so I needed to move quickly.

My outfit was already laid out on the bed. Momma had gone through hells and back to get it for my birthday—straight from my local favorite shop, paid for with quiet sacrifices I tried not to think about. Cream and rust tones, soft fabrics, and an off-shoulder top that felt like a tiny rebellion against my now usual hoodies. I wasn't sure if I wanted to hide our mate mark or not. It would be another game-time decision, but with Koa there, at least I wouldn't have to worry about my magic sticking to keep the glamour up.

I ran my fingers over the delicate embroidery on the hem. Matching pieces, she'd said. One for me, one for her. *"So you don't forget where you come from, even if you outgrow it."*

I blinked hard and picked up the necklace Ethan had given me as a little girl. Simple gold chain, tiny obsidian charm. Not expensive, not loud, but thoughtful. Protective. I wore it for every special occasion, and today was definitely that. I'd never brought someone home to meet them. There'd never been anyone who lasted long enough or felt important in a way that seemed permanent. Not until Koa.

20

SIENNA

It took us a little over an hour to get back to the mainland, Chichen. The coastline blurred by as Koa's new truck hummed under us, the suspension too high for my personal comfort but perfectly Koa. He'd put some music from my playlist on as we crossed the bridge, our hands tightened at the memory of how cold and dark the ocean was beneath us.

By the time we pulled onto my old street, the nerves and anxiety had subsided, and the joy of seeing my parents had taken over—until we passed Celeste's house. My smile dropped. The shutters were drawn. Grass had grown a little too thick along the sides. It no longer held the essence of a home—what was once a sanctuary was now no more than an empty, hollow shell of what once was.

"I'll come by this week to cast a landscaping spell, then set a reminder to reset it according to the season. Don't worry, I'll be sensitive with garden care...in case you want to come back to it," Koa reassured.

I loved it when he picked up where I couldn't step in. It was nice to not have to always do the thinking, the planning, and the filling in of the gaps. My entire childhood had been that way, at no fault of Momma and Ethan. It was just how things were. Koa was as busy as they were; the only difference was, he had access to resources they did not. Which only made it a touch more meaningful when he offered to do things when Nola usually took care of the smaller matters in his own personal life. Only a nod came as my response, my eyes still glued to Celeste's front door.

Koa glanced at me. "You wanna go in? We've got time."

"I haven't been in there without Mira since..." I said, unsure why the thought filled me with dread. "But it doesn't feel right without her, you know? It's like...even though it's ours, it's not *mine* when she's not there."

I knew Celeste hadn't left half of the house and her belongings to me out of pity. She truly considered me to be her own, just as Mira did. Still, it didn't seem right to breach that barrier for the *first* time without my best friend at my side. I didn't hold it against her for coming back here with Wren before she had come with me. Our needs were different, and I *needed* my best friend for that moment.

He nodded, rubbing the back of his neck. "I get that."

"You okay?" It was my turn to check in on him.

Koa's hand tightened slightly on the wheel. "Yeah," he muttered, then shook his head. "No. I'm nervous as fuck."

The honesty cracked something open in me. Koa wasn't the type to admit a perceived weakness. The words made my chest ache—and made me want to kiss him for both of our comfort. My chuckle released some of the tension brewing in the car. "That's adorable."

He shot me a mock glare, but I leaned in, shutting him up the best way I knew how. A slow kiss that awakened the snake beneath his skin. My hand slid up to his jaw, thumb brushing against the rough stubble he hadn't had the chance to shave before we had to leave. He tilted into my touch, and I pressed in harder, savoring the way he gave in—how every part of him always did, when it came to me. Like I was the only one allowed to reach the soft beneath the steel.

A loud bang echoed against the window. We both jumped, breaking apart.

Koa's hand shot to the gun holster attached to the driver's side door. His slitted eyes gleamed for a flash before he clenched them shut, pushing down the shift. I turned toward the window and immediately gasped.

"Ethan!"

He was not a small man, yet compared to Koa, he might as well have been. Still, if I had to place any bets, it would be a close fight. Ethan, while a teddy bear to me and Momma, had a history of holding his own when it came to his time in the Inecha Department of Domestic Crimes. I flung the door open and scrambled out of the truck, nearly tripping down the step. But Ethan caught me, arms open wide. A grin stretched across his face as I slammed into his chest, hands accidentally pulling on his wavy dark hair that contrasted his sun-kissed bronze skin.

"I missed you so much," I said into his shoulder, words breaking on a hitch of breath.

He hugged me tight, the familiar scent of herbs, wood, and oil wrapping around me like home. I hadn't realized how much I'd needed this exact feeling—safety with a little bit of gruff. I considered him my dad in every way possible, and I knew he thought of me as his biological daughter. Ethan had been one of my first words, and it had always stuck. He was a father-figure when necessary, but always my friend first. Who needed some loser named Thaddeus when you had an Ethan?

The driver's door thudded shut behind me. Weight moved in its wake. I stepped back as Koa came around, clearing his throat as if it would scrape off the edge. He looked too big for the driveway, too sharp under the early dusk, even though I'd 'un-expensived' him. His movements, usually fluid, held the stiffness of someone pulling threads taut. Raw angst shot through me that did not belong. Our bond pulsed and Koa tilted his head, a million emotions probably flashing clean across my face. I cleared my throat, intent on pushing the most recent development of our bond out of sight, out of mind.

"Ethan," I said, lacing my fingers through Koa's. "This is Koa. My boyfriend..."

Well, that word doesn't exactly fly out of the mouth. We were so much more than that, but baby steps, considering I'd settled on hiding the mark for now.

Ethan's gaze dipped to our hands, lingered, and I checked to ensure the glamour remained in place. His sight climbed to Koa's face. A short nod. Not cold, but not generous either. "Nice to finally meet you."

"You too, sir."

I flinched. Koa never said sir. Not to anyone. The word fell clipped from his mouth, awkward in the silence after. Still, he held his ground, hand steady in mine.

"Where's Momma?" I asked, looping my arm through Ethan's, steering us toward safer ground.

"Where she always is when we're home," he said, already moving. "Kitchen."

I herded them inside. The door opened, and the smell hit me hard—roasted squash, fresh bread, cumin, and something sweet. Home, all of it, thick in the air. My lungs tightened when familiar paws shuffled on the tile floor.

"Mistress Pickles!" I dropped to my knees as the elderly tyrant of the house strutted out, her crooked whiskers twitching. Twenty-ish years old according to the vet, half-blind, full attitude. She let out one grumbling meow and climbed straight into my lap, purring loud enough to rattle her ribs.

"She missed you," Ethan muttered, watching us with crossed arms.

"Mistress Pickles thinks I abandoned her."

"She's got a point; that makes two of us."

I grinned up at him, scratching behind her ears, and braced myself for what came next.

Momma in the kitchen. And Koa, who now stood silent behind me, about to meet the woman who could gut a man with a glance. Where else would I get it from?

Steam curled from a bubbling pot on the stove. Momma stood barefoot on the cool tile, hips swaying to the low hum of Rhythm & Blues playing from a speaker tucked behind the spice rack. Her head bobbed gently, braids tied up and tucked under a scarf, a wooden spoon in one hand, tasting something from the edge of a saucepan. The smells increased the closer I got to the source—coconut milk and curry.

"Look who finally decided to visit," she said, eyes flicking up as she set the spoon down and opening her arms. "Get over here."

I melted into her hug—finished far before I was ready for it to end.

"Now taste this," she demanded, already pressing the spoon to my lips. "Tell me if it needs more heat."

It was perfect. I tipped my head side to side anyway, like I was thinking about it, tongue already burning in a good way. Koa stood a few steps behind me, that crooked grin barely holding. Never in a million years did I ever imagine Koa Canek would be standing in the kitchen I learned to cook in, holding my cat, looking out of place.

"Momma," I said, shifting enough to let him into her line of sight. "This is Koa."

She didn't move. Only gave him a once-over, then turned back to the pot with a loud, and extremely clear *'Mm.'*

Oh gods. This was only going to go one way, and it certainly wasn't in our favor.

Momma knew we were dating, was very clear on how I felt, yet whenever we broached the subject, she changed the topic or merely offered displeased mumbles.

"I know who he is."

I bristled. "He's not—"

"Set the table," she said, reaching into the cabinet. Plates landed in my hands a second later.

"Mom—"

'It's okay, Venom.' Koa's voice echoed, cutting me off mid-plea. *'Got all night to make her see my charm.'*

'Imagine if your face matched your personality.' I rolled my eyes.

'Once again, I find myself saying that says a lot about your taste in men.'

Ethan stepped in, glancing between us in what probably appeared to be an awkward stare-off. "Go on, Si. I've got this handled." He winked at me, then clapped a hand on Koa's shoulder and gestured toward the bar. "You drink rum?"

Koa hesitated a breath, then followed. I caught his eye—a quiet apology edged with warning.

Momma came out a moment later, balancing bowls of food with a grace that could only come from muscle memory. Spiced rice, roasted squash and chickpea coconut curry, flatbread still steaming in a towel.

"Be nice," I said with as respectful of a plea as I could muster as I laid out silverware.

"I'll try," she murmured. "But it's hard, having a future Cynod member under my roof after what the current ones have done to people like us. I thought I raised you to have better…I don't know, Sienna Monroe, judgment?"

I turned toward her with some understanding—mostly annoyance. She wasn't being fair, and there was hardly room to argue once she had made up her mind. "Mira's a Canek, too. *And* a Tecun."

"Mira grew up around this house. She knows how we live. She didn't come from power. Well, she does, but not in *that* way."

"Koa didn't either," I defended.

Momma chirped an aggressive laugh I knew so well it had become my own somewhere along the way. "Didn't he?"

"You don't know him."

"His choosing to pretend to do things on his own doesn't erase the power his name provided to get him where he is now. I know enough."

"No, you really don't." My voice cracked, and I winced. I never spoke to her like this. Not once in my entire life. Something about hearing someone judge him without knowing him didn't sit right in my heart—no matter the fact that it was my own mom. "I love him. I want to be with him. That should be enough for you."

Momma looked at me, sharp and still.

"Sienna, this isn't a movie. Cut the dramatics. I might not be on that PhotoGhost site the way you kids are, but I still hear things. I know he's engaged."

My stomach dropped. "PhotoPhantom," I grumbled pointlessly.

Footsteps echoed around the corner, and Momma only stared back at me with a distasteful, pitying stare. It confused me, because there was nothing about my situation that called for pity. Things weren't the best right now, but I knew where I stood in his life and his list of priorities. That was enough.

Ethan's voice cut clean through the thick silence. "Smells damn good in here."

Koa followed behind him, two glasses in hand and a careful smile on his face. Mistress Pickles trotted close to his heels, tail high like she was personally escorting him to his fate. He stopped short when he saw us. His gaze landed on me first, then my mom, and something in his expression flickered as he set the drinks down with quiet precision.

"We ready to eat?" Ethan asked, already pulling out a chair with a pat to his stomach.

I nodded, forcing my limbs to move, to *do* something. "Yeah. Yeah, let's eat."

We settled in, the table full of color and spice. Bowls passed back and forth—rice bright with turmeric, squash softened to the edge of sweet, chickpeas beautifully roasted, a tangy slaw with a vinegar bite.

The food was warm. The silence, warmer—thick, almost sticky. No one spoke at first, like the first remark might crack something open.

Ethan, reliable as ever, jumped in to fill the void. "So, Koa, did Sienna tell you the story of how she forced us to take in Mistress Pickles?"

"No," Koa replied with an earnest smile, the first one since stepping inside. "But I can only assume she was the one to name her."

"Sienna found her in the engine of Ethan's old truck when she was eight," Momma added, surprising everyone at the table with the lack of bite in her voice. "Barely a heartbeat left in her. Nursed her back with a dropper she dug out of Celeste's garbage can and stubbornness."

"She bit me the first three times I tried to help," I added, hand brushing Koa's under the table.

"She bit everyone. But now?" Ethan nodded toward her. "That cat's royalty."

Mistress Pickles yawned wide and slow, as if to agree, then resumed her watchful perch. A chuckle slipped out of me before I could stop it. Even Koa gave a soft laugh, eyes flicking down to the cat now draped dramatically beneath his chair, as if bored by our entire existence.

That laugh cracked the seal. Slowly, things began to ease. Forks scraped plates. Small talk surfaced. My mom said little, but she listened. Watching. It almost felt normal.

The lull didn't last.

Conversation ebbed and flowed—mostly surface-level, mostly safe. Ethan asked Koa about the island's weather, I jumped in with stories about my classes, and even Momma offered a comment or two, usually about the food.

By the time the bowls were scraped clean and the second round of drinks had settled into everyone's system, the table had softened, but only at the edges.

Momma set her napkin down and pushed back from her chair. "Alright," she said, standing with that same quiet command that used to freeze entire classrooms mid-chaos. "Let's clean up and get that dessert out."

Ethan stood too, stretching his back. "Sienna, help me set up the movie."

It was a trap, and I gently stabbed Ethan with my fork for his betrayal.

"Momma," I started, already bracing.

She didn't even glance my way. "Koa can help me with the kitchen."

Ethan gave my arm a gentle nudge. "Come on, Si Si. I need your help picking something that won't knock me out in the first ten minutes."

I looked at Koa. Our eyes met. He gave the smallest nod—subtle, unreadable. Mistress Pickles, traitorous and loyal all at once, trailed right behind him as he followed Momma toward the sink. I hovered in the doorway long enough to see her hand him a towel without saying a word.

"You'll be fine," Ethan murmured, steering me gently toward the cozy den. "She just wants to see if he can hold his own."

"She could ask."

He chuckled. "If she did that, she wouldn't be your mom and you wouldn't be *you*."

21

KOA

I could see where my Venom got her poison from. Mrs. Hayes was both bark *and* bite. I'd met criminals from the darkest shadows who were less intimidating than her shoving ceramic plates toward my chest as she washed them off.

Without as much as a word, I put them away to where she silently pointed, her dark eyes that mirrored Sienna's glared into my soul, not bothering to glance away. Back at the condo, I would've spelled them to stack themselves—easy enough. Not here, though. She hadn't granted me permission to use magic inside her home, and power without invitation was rude as fuck. Even I knew that.

"So," I led, not sure what I was supposed to discuss with her, but wanting to try to win her over anyway that I could. "That meal was great. Is it safe to assume Sienna learned her skills from you?"

"You have to get creative when solits only go so far," she bit out, and I cursed myself for thinking she would respond in any other way.

Or perhaps I would just shut my damn mouth. Telling her I understood clearly wouldn't go well, and explaining to her how I planned to help when I took my seat would probably go over worse. She didn't seem the type to buy into promises, no matter how sincere they were.

"Some of the kids I mentor over at my gyms rave about their mothers' cooking. Called me an old fu—an old man when I told them how lucky they were. I suppose I never thought about the other side of it." I cringed at my honesty—unsure what brought that admission forward.

The Hayes family had that effect on me. Sienna's mom hadn't been warm or welcoming by any means. The best way to describe her was...genuine. There was a part of her that provided a sense of permissible comfort that I'd lacked my entire life. I realized then I wanted her approval, not just for my relationship, but because I yearned for the motherly scolding and warmth I'd seen her provide to Sienna during dinner.

She passed me another dish and turned the water off. I waited for further instructions and then realized none were coming. Mrs. Hayes watched me, stared at me as if she were attempting to read my soul.

"I don't like you, Koa Canek," she said plainly, matter-of-factly. "I don't know what your end goal is with my daughter. I only ask you to respect her enough not to lead her on. This has gone as far as it should."

The kitchen lights dimmed, ambient warding in the house responded to her tone. If I had to guess, it was over a millennium old. Old protection magic lived here. One that bent thick with her will.

I wanted to defend myself, opened my mouth to do so—she cut me off with a hand in front of my face. "I acknowledge that there may be more to you than meets the eye, or what trickles down through the press, and I do not care. Sure, you may be different from your parents. I've lived long enough to know that rarely does the apple fall *that* far from the tree. You will protect your own, and I need to protect Sienna. Love...it makes you blind."

It hurt at first, real fucking bad. The underlying tone of her own pain silenced mine at the understanding that there was more there to share. She spoke as though she came from a place of knowledge. And though it may not be our truth or my truth, it was hers. It put me in an awkward-ass place. I had no experience with this—handling parents that were not as cruel as my own, especially ones where I wanted their approval. A 'fuck your opinion' would get me kicked out of this house, and probably in the ass by Sienna. So I simply folded the hand towel I'd been holding and set it on the counter, at a loss for words.

I could've walked out. Should've, maybe. A stronger, better man would have. But I didn't. Instead, I leaned against the counter and faced her fully.

"Mrs. Hayes." I tried to channel every ounce of patience in my body to keep my tone respectful despite the response our bond sent up the mark at the sound of the challenge. "I know there are a dozen things you've read about me. Hells, half of them might even be true. And I know who I am, who my parents are—that gives you a hundred more reasons to hate me. None of that changes the simple fact that I love your daughter and will always do right by her. I plan to give Sienna my last name one day. I'm not asking for your blessing now; I get that it has to be earned. All I'm asking for is time to prove it."

She didn't blink, only crossed her arms, eyes sharp as knives. "And what about the girl you're already supposed to marry?"

I closed my eyes and exhaled. "That was never real. Political convenience, nothing more. It was arranged without my say. It's complicated, I won't lie. But what I feel for Sienna isn't. She is the most real fae I've ever met, and if I wanted to flatter you further, I'd tell you that you did a damn good job raising her. I'm not going to insult you by doing so, however, because it's clear you know that. The pride is written all over your face—something that matches her ego, and that can't be taught. Only ingrained over the years, much like her appreciation for honesty. Which is what gives me the confidence to say, nothing that happens here will make us stop loving each other, but what happens today *will* affect her happiness. And my preference is to do whatever I can to make her smile, so tell me how fucking high to jump, and I'll do it."

She arched a brow at the curse, and I muttered a quick apology. "Sorry, I'm not used to the whole interacting with a parental figure thing."

"So I've heard." Mrs. Hayes let that sit for a beat before she spoke again. "I was with someone once. Someone powerful. Someone with influence. Said all the right things. Made all the right promises."

There was something different in her voice then. Distant. Worn. Longing.

I glanced at her, trying to read past the glare. Something told me this was lore regarding Sienna's biological father, Thaddeus. This house had been left to them by someone on her father's side, though she wasn't sure who. Only that it had been in his family for generations, with no clues as to *who* the family was. Sienna had only asked her neighbors about it twice; once to Celeste, who hadn't moved in until after them, and the other to the neighbors across the street. Neighbors who had insisted the house had been vacant but well-manicured for at least a hundred years. She hadn't cared to ask more after that.

Now she had some answers, yet the desire to learn more remained nonexistent. "What happened?"

She busied herself, drying her hands on her apron and taking it off as she reached for the tray of brownies on the stove.

I stepped in gently, sensing something more beneath her words. "Does this have to do with Sienna's bio dad?"

She stiffened like I'd slapped her. "Ethan is her father. That's what matters. That's *all* that matters in this house."

I nodded slowly, hands up. "Understood. I didn't mean—"

"You're nosy," she cut in, eyes narrowed. "Too damn curious for your own good."

I didn't disagree. "Curiosity's kept me alive," I said, almost as a joke, trying to ease the rising tension. "That and reading people. Situations. Emotions."

The pity slid back into her gaze, and I knew then either Sienna or Mira had let my history with my father slip. She smirked, and it lacked kindness. "You're not gonna dig it out of me, boy. I like your sister better."

I let out a low, dry laugh. "Yeah, most people do."

It came out harsher than I meant it to, but hells, it was true. I wasn't the one people gravitated toward. That had always been Mira. I was the weight people had to drag around, or more intentionally, avoid—until Sienna.

Sienna's voice rang out from the den. "Movie's ready!"

Saved by Venom.

Mrs. Hayes turned to the pantry without saying a word and shoved the tray of brownies into my hands without sparing me a glance. "You can take these. I'm going to make the popcorn," she said flatly, pulling a handful of golden kernels from a glass jar above the stove. "We're finished here."

It didn't feel like she was simply talking about the dishes. I looked down at the brownies. Comfort food people made with love or obligation. I was nearly certain it was the latter in this case.

"Thanks," I mumbled, turning toward the hall to the den, then stopped under the arch. "For dinner. And...yeah, thanks for dinner."

Sienna

I mean, the movie wasn't terrible, and Momma stopped giving Koa the stank eye after the first couple of minutes. It was some dystopian action movie. Ethan's favorite and the only thing that would keep him awake after a hearty meal. Momma would watch anything, and I'd sit through whatever made either of them happy. Koa and I had watched it a few weeks ago. Zombies weren't really his thing, though he found the politics rather interesting—and I found him interesting enough to distract him about halfway through.

Tonight could have gone worse, but it certainly had the potential to be ten times better. I'd expected awkward, a lot of tension, and a few discouraging glares tossed his way. What I had not placed on our bingo card was the back-and-forth tug-of-war between disdain and mild tolerance Momma displayed.

It was as though she couldn't decide whether to hate him or accept him at my expense. I was proud of him, though. He'd kept his composure despite the judgment placed on me that I knew ate away at his soul. Koa didn't care much about what others thought of him. In fact, he told most people to shove it where the sun doesn't shine when they even muttered an opinion aimed at knocking him down. This was new for him, and he couldn't have handled it any better.

I peered up at him, lifting my head off his shoulder from our corner of the old, tattered couch in admiration. Shit, I didn't think it was possible to love him any more than I already did.

Ethan had noticed my tattoo when I reached up to grab the DVD off the shelf above the TV and eyed me with caution. There was no explanation needed of who or what marked my skin. At least it wasn't the mate mark. All he'd said was that Momma better not see it anytime soon, and he'd promised not to tell—mostly because he didn't want to be in between the argument that would ensue.

Marking my body in such a permanent way for a *man* would send her into orbit. My idea of romance was her worst nightmare and no doubt something she'd try to commit me to a mental hospital for. That was a conversation I had no interest in having for a very, very long time. Preferably after "I dos" were exchanged.

She could have her opinion of our relationship all she wanted. It wouldn't stop me from pursuing it or rejecting the bond post-ceremony...if that was even possible. Her blessing would be nice, sure. That didn't mean I'd allow it to become yet another thing that kept Koa and me apart. I knew Ethan would be on board for whatever made me happy; it was just how he operated. *Life is too short* was something he'd taught me from a young age—why I was so carefree.

Fae lives definitely were not short, though when placed in the perspective of the next day never being promised, they could be. *Especially* when power level twos and threes were in such expendable positions at work, I'd taken his stance to heart.

I caught myself smiling, head against Koa's shoulder, his arm slung over me with a possessiveness that wasn't for show. The couch sagged beneath us, worn and soft from years of use, its cushions lumpy and fraying at the seams.

The movie carried on—guns, explosions, political metaphors mocking the Cynod disguised as plot—but the sound barely reached me anymore. Across the room, Ethan had drifted into the early stages of sleep, lips parted to let out a soft breath. I shook my head, not upset in the slightest. He deserved the rest, and I was only glad to be in the same room with them again. Momma hadn't moved, her eyes still on the screen, her hand resting over his. Their fingers were tangled.

Time had never been on their side. Work. Life. Sacrifice. They took what slivers of peace they could find and turned them into moments worth remembering. A quiet night. A shared blanket. That one glance across the room that said everything without a word.

I watched them, my chest tightening with something tender and raw. They'd been through storms. Survived things no one talked about anymore. Yet here they were, still choosing each other, even when the world kept pushing in from every angle.

A part of me ached at the sight. That was what I wanted with Koa.

I did not envy them. But I *hoped*. That Koa and I wouldn't lose this—the closeness, the warmth, the bone-deep knowing that someone was choosing you, even when the world refused to make it easy. That time wouldn't chip away at us until we were just two people sharing space instead of building something together.

Even if it got ugly. Even if it already had.

Would Koa and I survive the weight of the world, the politics, the bloodlines, the past neither of us chose? Would we still laugh, still reach for each other, when everything else tried to pull us apart?

I sank deeper into him, needing his closeness to ground the thought. The room dimmed around the edges, the flicker of the TV dancing across the walls in erratic flashes. Koa's breathing stayed steady. His thumb traced the edge of my wrist, absent and instinctive.

A sharp vibration cut through the moment. I blinked, glanced down at my phone still half-tucked under my thigh.

[Strider accepted your friend request.]

I didn't know what I had expected. Maybe for it to go ignored. Maybe for the universe to grant me silence and save me from having to feel anything about it. If I ended up talking to Strider, it meant I had to face the truth about a lot of shit when I was far too comfortable sitting in the lies.

Another notification lit up the screen before I could process the first.

Strider:

If you ever want to talk, I'm here.

An open door.

My fingers hovered over the message. I didn't open it. Not fully. Just enough to see and read, to let the words settle somewhere they didn't belong.

I adjusted my posture before Koa could notice, shifting my weight so my phone was angled away from him. His arm stayed draped over me, but I felt the subtle shift in his body—alert without seeming to be. He noticed everything, even what I tried to hide.

"You okay?" he murmured.

I nodded once, shortly. "Yeah. It's nothing."

He didn't press. And he wouldn't unless he deemed it necessary. I appreciated that about him—the space he provided until I'd gone too far and put real distance between us—as unintentional as it may be. Or intentional at times. Guilt curled tight in my chest. It wasn't as though I'd done something wrong. But because hiding anything from him, even a few words on a screen, felt heavier than it should.

I glanced at the message again.

If you ever want to talk, I'm here.

Simple. No pressure. But it burrowed deep, tugging at some part of me I didn't know was still raw. Strider wasn't a friend. Adding him had been a moment of weakness.

"That wasn't supposed to happen." Were his words that day by the water.

What the hells *was* supposed to happen?

I didn't know why I believed him. I just did. That scared me more than anything. Because whatever this was—whatever Strider saw in me, or thought he saw—I felt it too. Not with logic. Not with memory. Rather, it was something older, something buried in my bones.

And I didn't know how to tell Koa that.

A thread tugged too tight inside me. Familiarity wrapped in confusion.

The end credits rolled. Ethan stretched with a groan and declared bedtime in that half-joking, full-dad tone. He nudged Momma with his shoulder, and she shook her head, muttering something I couldn't hear as she gathered the dishes on the coffee table.

Koa straightened beside me as a reminder that the night was winding down. Soon, we'd step back into the real world—the one waiting outside this fragile little bubble of family and almost peace.

I tucked my phone back under my thigh. Strider's message still burned in my mind. I wasn't going to message him. Not tonight. Momma avoided Koa's eyes as we said our goodbyes, while Ethan gave him a half-hug and a gruff "drive safe." I kept thinking about it. About the way Strider had looked at me—like I was a memory he hadn't expected to find again.

And despite every reason not to...I was beginning to wonder if I should ask him what it was he saw.

23

MIRA

I knew it wasn't the most popular opinion, but I loved testing. There was something validating about seeing my knowledge in a tangible way. To know that I really did retain the information, and that I could keep it forever.

Which was why I was studying by myself. I'd already forced Sienna and Katia into study sessions, and if I made them look at these flashcards one more time, they might have burned them. Not to mention that Sienna typically used her audio program for studying outside of our sessions. So here I was, sitting in the K'in Student Center and going over the cards again.

There was a recent study about detailed versus conceptual flashcards. It suggested that making cards less detailed and more compare/contrast or process related was helpful, and I was testing their hypothesis. I wouldn't know for sure until after the test, but right now it seemed to be working.

This set of flashcards was for Herbology, and I had to remember what the Mountain Ash Berry's magical qualities were. Some of the tests would be more hands-on, and the spells we'd have to perform accurately. Things like herb qualities would be in the written section. I blew air between my lips, guessing the answers in my mind, *strong magical connections, meditation, protection, mind clearing,* and smiled when I saw I was correct.

I looked up from the study pod—one of the kinds that are meant to provide some privacy. Apparently not enough because through the gaps in the canopy roof, I spotted Alanna. Even worse, she spotted me. Koa and Sienna filled me in about the 'engagement party,' and all the bullshit that came with it. We hadn't had

213

any one-on-one time, which I, for one, was thankful for. Koa was media-trained, and I was to a certain extent, but not enough to hide most of my facial expressions.

"Hey, sister-in-law," Alanna said as she put a hand on my study pod.

I really shouldn't work myself up *right* before therapy. *Deep breaths, Mira. Deep breaths.*

"Hello, Alanna," I responded through tight teeth.

"My brief said you were studious," she said as she wiggled her fingers toward my books. "Seeing it in person is cute."

Alanna didn't move, so I decided to feed into whatever it was she was trying to say.

"Brief?"

"My people weren't going to send me into a pit of lions without any knowledge. I know that you weren't raised with Koa; your aunt who did raise you died recently; you love a good textbook; and you're friends with the little...ex-girlfriend."

Ex-girlfriend was hilarious. I did my best not to laugh in her face.

"I'd like to think I'm more than a few bullet points, but sure." I scanned the room for a way out, which I quickly realized wasn't possible. "Did you need something, or...?"

"We should do a girls' day. It would be great PR and show that the family is accepting me, you know? Pedicure maybe. Somewhere with a lot of windows..." She trailed off, the thoughts seeming to take over her speech for a moment.

"I'm going to have to pass. Lots of responsibilities, finals coming up, all of that," I responded just as my alarm for my therapy session went off.

Alanna crowded into my space, an intimidating energy radiating off her that didn't quite meet the mark. "This is inevitable, Mira. Loyalty to your friend won't stop that. You should do what you can to stay ahead of the game. We're all lions here, but unlike them, we don't fight in a pack."

Even with her pursed lips and arched brow, she sounded genuinely concerned. Which I didn't know what to do with. I didn't owe her anything, and neither did she. No matter how much research she did about me, there were things she never would have known. Like the fact that I could spot a lion miles away.

"I've known it's every fae for themselves since I was a child. Thanks for the advice, but again, I'll pass."

Alanna raised a single shoulder as if to say 'suit yourself' and left with a toss of her straightened hair. She was...more complex than I might have deemed her originally. I wondered what environment created someone who felt the need to take what she knew didn't belong to her. To encourage me to turn on my best friend in favor of good publicity and a pat on the shoulder from the Cynod.

Shit was fucked here, but if there was one thing that was rewarded and respected, it was loyalty. Whether that be loyalty to the Cynod, to Solis, to your family, loyalty was at the root of our society. I shoved my flashcard binder back into my backpack and weaved around the bodies. The student centers were typically packed, and with finals coming, they were even more busy than usual. While being sure not to run into anybody, I pulled out my phone and typed out a quick text to the group chat. This one had Koa, Sienna, and Katia in it. Koa was only added because he was tired of us laughing at our phones together, so we let him in as a joke. He could have removed himself, but he didn't, and I think he secretly loved it.

Me:

Run in with Alanna. She's...interesting?

Sienna:

Did it end with a sharp object? That would make it interesting.

Katia:

Only stab the ones we love. Didn't we learn anything from the book club book?

Koa:

What the fuck did you read this week?

Me:

Koa sent back a GIF of a flashing middle finger, and Sienna and Katia laugh reacted.

"I've got you checked in," the girl at the front desk said.

I didn't realize I'd made it here already, so I slid my phone into my pocket and nodded my appreciation. There were a few other people in the waiting room today, one girl looking particularly distressed. She picked at her cuticles and bounced her leg rapidly. If I had to guess, finals were getting to her. It was well-known that the mental health facilities were used more during midterms and finals.

I dug a fidget clicker out of my bag and reached to hand it to her. "This helps to distract from the picking. It's saved my nail beds and my eyebrows quite a few times."

"Oh." Her mouth fell open, a sudden realization that she was indeed destroying her cuticles. "Thank you so much."

She took the clicker, and I saw as she tested the weight in her hands, acclimating to the fidget before clicking. It might have driven someone else crazy, but it was soothing to me. I saw a sense of relief fall over the girl; she'd still need to heal those cuticles. The bad pain never hit right away; it waited until you felt a little better—a physical reminder.

"Mira," Dr. Puebla spoke from the hall.

I smiled at the girl, and she lifted the clicker in thanks as I passed. The scent of this room had been added to my bank of comfort smells. There were only a few: the kitchen at my tía's, Sienna's hair products, and the expensive ass incense in Koa's apartment was a recent addition. I took my usual seat, and Dr. Puebla sat in hers.

"How are you doing today?" she asked.

"I'm good. It's finals week, which is basically my version of a pitz championship. How are you?"

"Doing alright as well. Oddly enough, finals week is also a championship of sorts for the therapists." She chuckled warmly and opened her tablet. "I have a few things I'd like to discuss. First, I'd like to see if there was something you wanted to start with?"

"We can start with yours," I replied.

She stood up and pulled out a stack of books from behind her desk. "Okay, this is all I could find about your nahual. There was almost nothing available digitally, but thankfully, the teachers here have a stash of books the academy no longer deemed...safe."

"That would be where you'd find the information. That's for sure," I said as I scanned the tomes.

Their age was evident in every loose stitch, in each curled, tattered edge of the parchment. The last time this leather had been used was...maybe a thousand years ago. Skin from a beast now extinct due to us driving them from their homes to create our own.

"There are a few old textbooks from the beginning of the academy. A couple of journals, some of which are in a language I don't understand, but others have translated copies. I'm thinking we should take a field trip. Turn to page 237." Dr. Puebla leaned forward.

She passed me a double-sided book, one side the original text and the other a translated copy bound to it. I opened the side I could read and scanned the index, finding Kimi toward the bottom of the list.

"How old is this one?" I asked as I flipped to the page.

"One of the oldest. It was banned a very long time ago. They wanted it burned, but thankfully, one of the old professors who believed in preservation saved it. Goes without saying..."

"I trust you. You can trust me. I promise."

Dr. Puebla nodded and leaned into the text when I found the page. *KIMI* was in bold and capitalized letters, *Death* beneath it. Internally, I was trying not to freak out about the fact that I was holding a book this old. I wanted to study it, to commit it all to memory.

There was a note bracketed by asterisks: *It is important to disclaim that during this time, death did not have a negative connotation. Death was life, life was death. In both of those, there is a transfer of soul. From the spirit world to the physical and vice versa. The soul is the root of life and death, and in the original text, they were used interchangeably. I tried my best to translate in a way that would help the reader at this time understand.*

That tracked. I'd also seen that in my research. I'd seen it in the way I saved Koa. My gift wasn't only taking, it was giving—balancing.

"I think the next section is what I wanted to focus on," Dr. Puebla pushed.

"Next section is..." I ran my finger to the first paragraph. "Here. A *Kimi* is one of, if not the most, powerful of the fae. Their ability to manipulate a soul grants them one of a kind access. The most powerful ones can transfer energy from one to another, and travel into the spirit world. Kimi's were used in battle to fight, and as healers of sorts."

"Does that match what you know to be true?" Dr. Puebla asked.

"It does. I pulled the souls, or energy, from the...people trying to kill us, and I think I saved Koa's life because of it." I bit my lip before reading more. "*Kimis* have a special connection to their surroundings. When they first emerge, they may need to avoid large crowds. The souls can be overwhelming if they are unable to extinguish the connection. A tip from a *Kimi* when writing this book was to sit in a jungle and feel for the animals. They have souls that are easier to manipulate than fae."

"I have a feeling jungles were a little more accessible at this time. I'm thinking we can go to a park?" Dr. Puebla suggested.

"Yeah, maybe." She stood, and I followed up, asking, "Oh, you mean now?"

"No time like the present. Our last out-of-office session went great. As long as you have the time? It may run over a couple of minutes."

I shot up, bouncing on my heels with energy. "I absolutely have the time."

There was a garden on the very edge of campus, one that students and teachers could reserve for various reasons. Some clubs used it as a place for their meetings, others for birthdays and gatherings. Thankfully, Dr. Puebla was able to reserve it for us on the way over. Tall hedges offered privacy, and there wasn't much in the general area either.

"Okay, I see quite a few critters around here," Dr. Puebla said as she set herself up on a bench.

I closed my eyes. "Any tips on what to do next?"

"Do you remember how you tapped into it before?"

My brother was threatened, Sienna was beaten, and it was all about protecting my loved ones. The other times I've had minor uses, I was out of control. Yoga had been the closest I'd been to any sort of understanding.

"I'm going to try to meditate," I said as I sat in the thick, lush grass.

Dr. Puebla stayed silent, and I squeezed my eyes tight. I listened to everything around me. The whistling of wind through the trees and flowers, the water rushing out of the fountain, and the sweet song the birds sang. Our stillness and quiet seemed to advise the animals that it was safe to come out of hiding. The shuffling of tiny paws came from my left, then scratching against tree bark to my right. I tried to imagine what they looked like—created an image in my mind. By the second, more and more tiny lives made themselves known to me. Their souls felt...gentle. Untampered with the weight of rectitude.

I willed my nahual to uphold the connections as I opened my eyes, and my vision went technicolor. Dr. Puebla was in her own meditation, wholly still with her eyes closed. She emanated yellow and green as I'd seen before in the soldiers, but then my chest warmed, and purple overtook the other colors. Taking a deep breath, I blinked, and she returned to yellow and green. There were levels to this. One to identify that there was a soul, and the one to better understand it. The purple in her was calm and...intuitive. I had a feeling purple was common for her.

I shifted to see the animals I'd sensed earlier, being sure not to move too quickly and scare them off. The scratching I'd heard against the tree was a squirrel, the tiny paws a rabbit in the garden. Small birds filled the branches like precious jewels on a crown. Even the tree felt alive, not necessarily a soul, a connection to the life force of our world.

The next part, I wasn't sure how to initiate. To manipulate their soul and maintain enough control to avoid hurting them. I noticed now that Dr. Puebla's eyes were open, and she remained still and quietly watched me. She didn't make me nervous; if anything, she gave me an—albeit false—sense of security.

Just as I was about to aim at the squirrel, something else in the garden caught my attention. Not a fae, but another animal bigger than the others. It moved slowly, short and sure motions telling me it was most likely stalking something. By the time I finally spotted the fox, I realized the rabbit was its prey. My initial reaction was to save the rabbit, but there was no malicious intent from the fox, simply an animal looking for a meal.

I lifted my hand steadily, figuring this was as good a chance as any. Just like with the soldiers, I was able to grasp onto the invisible string connecting us. As I felt before, their souls were different from a fae, certainly more malleable. One could assume that while the soul wasn't something a person without my gift could tap into, intelligence played some factor in fighting against my hold. The fox twitched as I pulled at his soul, and the rabbit went still.

It was difficult to understand whether my grasp on their soul was stopping them or if I was puppeteering. I tried to will them to move forward. Their steps were choppy, but it seemed like I was the one in control of them.

Panic ran through the rabbit—from me or the realization that they were being hunted, I wasn't sure. I lifted my other hand so that their connections were handled separately and loosened my hold on the fox. It shook its head as if gathering its bearings before it focused back on the rabbit. The tall grass rattled, and a pair of chipmunks darted toward the cover of a thick bush. I kept the connection to the rabbit as the fox pounced, and its powerful jaws snapped around the animal's neck. At the moment it began slipping, I yanked on the rabbit's soul. Green and yellow barreled toward me, a smaller stream than when I'd pulled on the fae soldiers.

Instead of an intense impact, this one gently caressed my skin and seeped into my chest. Energy buzzed through me as I looked back at Dr. Puebla.

She smiled and silently clapped her hands. "Not all of that was visible to me, but I sensed it. Incredible. How do you feel?"

"It feels good to know that there is a way to be in control. I was worried it'd hurt someone who didn't deserve it. I'd certainly prefer it were more of a 'here's how to control your nahual in four steps' situation," I replied with a self-deprecating laugh.

I eased my nahual away, akin to closing a door and locking it away. My vision returned to normal, and I took a deep breath. There would need to be more practice, and while part of me knew using animals could be viewed as a scientific test, I wasn't too excited about it. The chances that I'd go too far as I learned were high.

"Do you mind if I take a couple of the books home? I want to get a closer look, and I know someone who might be able to help with translation."

Dr. Puebla looked shocked, but didn't push. "I have it on good authority that you know how to handle an ancient book?"

"My tía made sure," I laughed out, thinking back to the first time I touched an old text with crumbs on my fingers and she nearly chopped me in half. "There is something else I want to talk to you about before time ends."

She sat up straight and grabbed her tablet, her therapist's face replacing the inquisitive historian from the last few minutes. "Of course. What would you like to discuss?"

While we were still in the private garden, I didn't want to take any chances. I moved closer to her and set a silencing spell to cover both of us. "Honestly, I think every area of my life could use a good analysis, but I did want to talk about Wren."

"Yes, I remember. You gave him a chance and haven't said much about him since." Her nails clicked against her screen as she typed.

"I did, and it was going great. Then he lied about something...or omitted a truth thanks to a blood bond. He was doing some work for someone on the Cynod beyond security. From what it seems, he was sort of playing both sides."

There was too much nuance, too many things to add for context, but at the very least, I could say this.

"Okay. Did he put you in harm's way?" she asked.

"I'm not entirely sure. I think the accident was because he told them where we were."

It wasn't the only possibility, I knew this. In this era of technology, our lives are almost always being broadcast. There weren't many ways to ensure that people weren't constantly tracking you. Koa was better at this thanks to his extracurricular activities. However, it was always a possibility that our phones were tapped into, or someone saw us at the gas station and reported back.

Dr. Puebla considered this, her finger scrolling through something on her tablet. "He was also in the car, yes?"

"Yes."

That was the part I kept returning to. If he was doing all of this just to get me killed, why would he have been there next to me? Why would he have been the one to calm me down, to protect me with his own body? The relief in his eyes when he realized I was okay didn't feel false.

"Hm. Was it your parents on the other end of the blood bond?"

"No, it was...Dr. Aantaj."

"And that is someone you had a certain degree of trust with," she said, not a question, a recollection of a previous conversation. "And the creator of these pills."

A butterfly flitted between us, resting on my knee. The tips of its wings shimmered in the sun, a pink translucence contrasted by the deep orange pattern sprouting from its body. It wasn't clear what it was searching for, but it stayed still and peaceful as I looked back to Dr. Puebla.

"Exactly. He said they were interested in my grades at first, and that does sound like something Dr. Aantaj would ask. Apparently, it turned more in-depth after that, and the blood bond would have killed him if he told me."

"And he was already under the contract of the Cynod, so this wasn't completely out of the blue," Dr. Puebla added.

I nodded. "Right. I told him I'd hear him out after a bit of time to think. I just wish it had never happened. Things weren't simple, but they were...nice."

"If only we had control over that," she laughed warmly. "You can control how you move forward. You get to decide whether there is a boundary to be drawn or if there is a second chance to be given. We've all done...unsavory things with good intentions. He doesn't get to decide whether it was worth it, you do."

"If I forgive him, do you think that makes me weak, or, I don't know, stupid?" I asked with my gaze on my feet.

How many times did I forgive Forrest for doing 'unsavory' things? There were countless instances of my turning a blind eye or not reading into something deep enough. I was stupid then. There was no other word for it. So was I stupid now?

Dr. Puebla handed me a flower, bringing her back into my eyeline. "I think only you can truly answer that. But no, I don't think forgiving people makes you weak. Remember, you can also forgive without giving him another chance. It's all up to you. You hold every ounce of power."

The butterfly flapped its delicate wings and flew away.

"That's true. You know I like data. I want more information. It's hard to make a judgment call without knowing all the 'whys'. I was too angry before to listen."

Too many people were implicated by what he might have done. Sienna, my brother, and I. It wasn't only anger at the broken trust. It was that the people I cared for so deeply could have died.

"You'll make the right decision. Just like every other time you've been put into situations like this," she said as she stood. "Sorry for running over time, but I believe there is another reservation a bit after ours. Bring those books back to our next session."

I smiled and tapped them inside my bag. "I'll bring them back in tip-top shape. Thanks again."

As I disbanded the silencing spell and exited the garden, I couldn't tell if it was my gift that made things feel brighter or if things were just looking up.

24

MIRA

I remembered the last time I was sitting in my room waiting for Wren to pick me up. The last time I was *this* nervous to be around him. It wasn't even his presence that had me on edge. It was the conversation, what would come out of it. He wanted to go to his parents' home, not the estate I'd been to before in the city. To see who he was doing it all for, and I agreed. Like Dr. Puebla said, I didn't have to forgive him.

It wasn't the first time I'd have met Atlas and Zane, but it was the first time I'd see them in this light. Not the businessmen they were, just as Wren's brothers. I asked Sienna to make something for me to take, and she'd decided on a pastry with cream cheese and blueberry compote. They looked delicious, although I did worry that the gesture wasn't as grand since I didn't make them all by myself. I was there when she made them and took a couple of directions. At the end of the day, we both had our strengths. The delicate baking of perfectly crusted pastries with a balance of sweet and tart wasn't one of mine.

Too nervous to be cooped up, I decided to go ahead downstairs and wait in the lobby. I grabbed my bag, my phone, and the pastries and slammed the door shut with my hip. Sienna wasn't here right now, but I always made a habit of looking toward her dorm room when I left.

The galley was full and lively as it always was these days. Between the ones studying in the booths and the card game tournament that seemed to have no end, there were always bodies in here. Apparently, the tournament started as some

225

sort of drunken joke, and lots of students had taken it much more seriously than intended.

I pushed the elevator button, watching as the two opponents were coming to the end of their game. The tall girl with wire frames laid down her cards and immediately stood in victory, and the boy tossed his down, realizing he'd lost before even playing them. I chuckled to myself as the elevator doors opened and the students in the booths shushed their yelling.

It was nice seeing everyone in a groove here now. The first half of the semester was more of an awkward *how do we all fit together* game. But now, these were our homes...or as much of a home as they could be away from our families. We caught onto each other's routines and were all around a bit more comfortable.

That wasn't the case on some other floors; Bran had barely needed to come to ours, thanks to the fact that we typically got along. Rumor had it that there was a fight last week on the third floor, and that someone else lit something valuable on fire on the fifth. It ended with them being wrapped in some sheets and dangled out the window. I was just happy to not be under Bran's watchful eye...especially after what happened at the party.

The poor kid had taken a pretty bad beating from Wren, and I was only partially worried he'd take it out on me. Thankfully, it had made him extra scared of Wren and Koa.

I smiled at the door attendants. One piece of helpful advice from Bran was not getting on their bad side. Sienna and I had to bribe them one time with their choice of snacks when we'd gotten in too late, and we'd never messed up again after that.

I heard Wren's car before I saw it, the low but powerful hum of his engine drawing my attention to the entrance loop. Fuck, my heart was beating faster than it should. The problem was, I couldn't separate the nerves from the excitement. I was typically good at compartmentalizing my feelings. It seemed my body wasn't taking any of that today. Wren pulled to a stop and popped out of the car, his eyes finding mine immediately.

"Hey, lo—" He paused. "Hey."

I smiled, this unsure version of him a *little* bit funny. He took inventory of me from head to toe, taking note and filing away each section. My hair, clean and slicked down to my head, the curls in the ponytail fresh and bouncy. The outfit I was wearing, a lightweight brown sweater and slightly baggy jeans. Then his gaze rose back up to my face, searching for signs of distress or maybe nerves. But the dark smudges he'd seen the last time he'd spotted me across campus weren't there anymore. I was well-rested and moisturized now.

He quickly ran around the car, the amount of time he'd been looking at me more obvious as the doorman cleared his throat.

"Hey. I brought food. I probably should have asked if your family has any allergies. I didn't want to come empty-handed. My tía always said that was a no-no. Normally it would have been more of a meal and not only a couple—"

Wren grabbed the container as he bit back a smile. "I'm sure they'll love them. Thank you."

Shit, I was rambling. I was glad he cut me off. When I started a ramble, there was no way of knowing where it ended. For all I knew, I could have talked about the ingrown hair on Katia's ass. She'd sent a picture of it *right* before this. Thankfully, that picture was just for Sienna and me, not the one with Koa in it. He definitely would have left then.

"You going to get in the car, or...?" Wren held his hand out.

Oh, this is going so well. One of the doormen officially burst out laughing, and I shot him a glare. He tossed his hands up in surrender, but how quickly he pulled out his phone told me they might have been texting about us. I dropped down into his car quickly and buckled up before Wren even got to the driver's side.

"We've got a bit of a drive. You liked the last playlist we listened to, so I made another." Wren pushed a couple of buttons on the screen of his car, and a song from one of my most recent posts boomed through the speakers.

"This one feels familiar," I said with a small smirk.

We looked at each other again, Wren's face pinched slightly, and he pressed on the gas. I knew he was beating himself up about it all. Shit, he was willing to take a literal beating from Koa without fighting back. It didn't change the hurt I felt, and...a sick part of me was happy that he experienced some pain too. That he wasn't doing this all for shits and giggles—just to hurt me and laugh at the carnage.

"We should talk a little before we get there, huh?" I whispered, already afraid of what might come to light.

He responded as he brushed his hair out of his face, granting me a full view of him. "Probably a good idea, yeah."

"Are there things you still can't say?" I asked.

"I can't respond verbally for some, but my silence will be an answer enough," he offered.

I could work with that.

"How'd you even get blood-bonded in the first place? They've been forbidden for centuries."

Wren's body went tight. If I had to guess, he was trying to determine what he could and couldn't say without repercussion. "I do work for all the members. The contract my brothers and I have doesn't tie us to one member in particular. It just states we're at their disposal. We did a job for..."

"Let's call him The Doctor," I insisted.

Wren nodded once. "The Doctor. When my brothers left, he started asking questions about you. You'd mentioned before that you had some sort of mentor relationship, so I thought nothing of it. He wanted to know how you liked the school, how your grades were, and normal mentor things. I didn't ask how he knew we were acquainted; he just knew I'd have the answers. It got more and more...specific. I got concerned and told him to go fuck himself. That resulted in a forced blood bond."

"Forced?"

He switched lanes, checking his mirrors a couple of times as we approached the bridge. *The* bridge. I found myself doing the same, scanning for any fast-moving vehicles or indications of magic. This was my first time off the island. I knew Sienna and Koa ventured onto the mainland recently, but I hadn't yet.

Wren switched to driving with his left hand, his right cautiously moving to-ward me. I allowed it, letting him rest it atop my thigh in silence until we made it across. When my breath went back to an even pace, he brought his hand back to the wheel and spoke.

"Some language in the contract is left purposely ambiguous. Ensuring there are things we're under an obligation to accept. He used the clause to make me vulnerable. It was either bond to him and hope to the gods I could protect you, or leave the job open to someone else. I took the one I thought was best. The same choice my grandfather made."

I knew what it was like to be between two impossible decisions. Even more specific, ones that the Cynod was taking the lead on. But there were always ways around things, even when the odds seemed stacked against it all. No magic was infinite; everything had parameters, so there had to be a way around it.

"I'm not exactly surprised," I said, and looked at the bridge in the rearview mirror. "I get you couldn't tell me, I do, it just doesn't make it easier to accept."

He answered quickly, unable to wait another second. "I wanted to tell you. Every second of every day, I wanted to. They have too much power and too many resources. I even tried to figure out if Koa could help, but didn't want to implicate him either."

The whole reason I was here was to hear him out—to take the facts and make an informed decision. The fact was: he'd gone to great lengths, at great personal loss, to do what he thought was right, and he was nearly assassinated for it. He'd said before that when things like this were out of his control, he leaned into the fact that he could still protect his family. That even if it all went to shit, at least he did what he could to ensure their safety. *These* things with me had gone to exponential amounts of shit.

"When you took that last breath of air before drowning, when you almost lost your life for this lie, did you regret it? Or would you do it all again?"

He placed his hand on my knee. "I'd go to the grave for you, Mira. I could die and be resuscitated on a loop for three thousand years, and I'd welcome it if it meant you were safe."

I traced my gaze from his hand, up his muscled forearm, and to his perfectly sculpted face. That same blue aura flickered as before. Sienna said it meant honesty and trustworthiness. I wanted to believe it. It was hard not to believe it after that statement. Both my brother and I had done things to protect the other from the Cynod. Shit, I didn't even know the true reason I was sent to live with my tía until recently. Koa didn't know the number of times I tried to keep our father away from him when I still had the opportunity.

I understood the...drive. When you sensed their foul intentions rolling off them like poisoned smoke, it was hard not to do what you could to shield your loved ones.

His thumb brushed the skin through the hole of my jeans, a warmth unfurling akin to a blooming flower. My eyes went wide as it rushed through me the same as before, our nahuales engaging in some ancient dance I wasn't familiar with. The coolness of mine and the warmth of his twisted and blended until it nestled around my heart and fizzled out.

"Do you feel that?" I whispered, knowing that if he said he didn't, I'd be crushed.

"I do."

I rubbed my palm over my chest. "Have you felt it before? With anyone else?"

"No, never in my life."

This sort of...intimacy was new, the kind where magic was involved. Maybe this was how everyone felt. I didn't want to give breath to the ridiculous explanation—that we could be in the same boat as Sienna and Koa. For my brother and me to both receive the gift of that exponential connection after what we'd been through...and for mine to be here in this car. It was absurd, maybe even laughable, but for the first time, it wasn't impossible.

I had a lot less apprehension by the time we'd made it to his parents' house. I spotted at least one of his brothers' cars in the driveway, yet Wren held his foot firm on the brake without parking.

"Everything okay?" I asked.

He sighed. "I thought this was a good idea initially. I just hope they're on their best behavior."

I twisted the gear shift into park. "I've seen your brothers at the club. How much worse can they be?"

"So, so much worse," he said as he opened his door and came to open mine. "Remember, I'm showing you this side because I love them. Not because they are without faults."

"We're all flawed, Wren."

If I knew one thing to be true, it was that.

The house was quaint. On a busy street with cracked sidewalks and a flickering street lamp flashing onto their porch. It was obvious that his parents took a lot of care in maintaining the house. The grass was cut, white flowers lined the driveway, and an open window gave me a peek inside. Warm orange walls, an incredible smell wafting through the air, and an overall sense of comfort.

Even the way Wren walked felt different here. Where he normally moved like a predator on high alert, there was an obvious safety that fell over him. Relaxed shoulders, a leisurely gait, and a smile he didn't even seem aware of.

"Right here." Wren pointed to a crack in the beam on the porch. "This is the first time I bested Atlas. My dad kept it as a reminder."

I ran my finger over it as I imagined the two of them, young and tiny, beating the shit out of each other. "A reminder for you or him?"

"Both. For him, that I wasn't the weak little brother anymore, and to me, that I was more powerful than I thought. Wasn't my intention to break his nose, but it happened."

"How much time did you all spend with a healer as children?"

"We had our own little room. Healer called it the Ikari Lodge," he said as he pushed open the front door, and I wasn't sure if he was joking or not.

Before he even made it through the threshold, Zane ripped the door open the rest of the way. "Bout fucking time, I'm hungry and Mom won't let me have a bite until you get here."

"Ah, being the favorite has its perks." Wren smirked. "As you know, this is Zane, my oldest brother."

"Club lighting didn't do you justice," Zane said, but the way his gaze flickered over to his little brother told me it was bait. "Pretty girls like you get to call me whatever they want."

Wren's eyes glowed golden, a growl reverberating in his throat. Zane didn't flinch; the list of people not intimidated by that glare was short. His brother was more excited than anything. We moved into the living room, the smell of freshly made food causing my stomach to rumble. I didn't realize the brothers were still in a standoff.

"Touch her and I'll rip out your throat," Wren snapped.

"Still sore about the girls I've stolen from you growing up?" Zane mocked and rolled his shoulders in preparation for something that definitely wasn't necessary.

An older woman's voice came from where I assumed the kitchen was, distracting both of them.

"Get out of the kitchen." The snap of a kitchen towel hitting a body sounded—that body being Atlas. "We eat as a family."

He licked his fingers as he ran away and hid his laughter behind his hand. "Look, he's here! I'm getting abused for no reason."

"Abuse is a stretch," Zane retorted. "Look who else is here. Little brother's girlfriend."

Wren peered down at me with worry, but it was fine. They didn't need to know the complexities of our relationship, and it seemed like Wren might not have told them *everything*. Which was probably for the best.

"You remember Atlas," Wren said with a hint of that specific flavor of annoyance reserved for your loving family.

"Nice to see you again," I said warmly.

A small woman with features incredibly similar to Zane, Wren's oldest brother, joined us. "Oh, my baby!" she shrieked and ran over to Wren. His mother wrapped his arms around her, his height putting her head at his belly.

"Hey, Mom. This is who I've been telling you about," he said when she pulled back.

She turned to me with a contagious smile. "Hi, Mira! I'm Iseul. I'm so happy you're here. How's the temperature? Are you too hot, too cold? Do you want a blanket? Let me get you some slippers."

"I'm fine, I promise," I responded.

I was a little overtaken with the enthusiasm she exuded. Maybe it was rude to deny these things when she was offering them up.

"You sure? It's not a problem. Really, I can just—"

Wren interrupted Iseul with a gentle hand on her shoulder. "Food ready, Mom?"

"It is. Dad was just setting the plates. You ready to eat?" she asked.

All three of the Ikari brothers answered yes immediately, and we trailed behind her. It was adorable thinking of this woman raising these gigantic, unruly fae. I had to choke down a laugh as I imagined her pulling them by their ears as they bent at the hips and whined.

"So..." Zane put his arm over my shoulder, and I elbowed him in the side before knocking him in the jaw with my fist.

"Ohhhh!" Atlas yelled as he jumped up and down.

His mother turned around and looked over her shoulder. "Oh, honey, you'll do just fine around here. Good form."

"Okay, not like the others. Got it," Zane snickered as he rubbed his jaw. "I was only going to ask how you two met. But no touching, noted."

Wren was the picture of pure smugness as he tucked me into his side, dropping his arm over my shoulder the same way Zane tried. "Looks like I won't need to rip out your throats."

I felt a little bad, but Wren *just* warned him not to touch me. He had it coming, really. Not to mention, I had been on edge and ready to fight at any moment these days. Zane followed behind us, and we made it into the kitchen.

His father turned around, with a smile and a small bow of his head as he took me in. "Hello, Mira."

It wasn't lost on me that both of his parents already knew my name. His hair was longer than the other men in the house, pulled back into a neat ponytail at his nape.

"This is my dad, Kenzo," Wren introduced, and his father stuck his hand out for me to shake.

I hoped to the gods my hand wasn't sweaty and shook his. "I'm so happy to meet you."

Where both his brothers seemed to favor one parent, Wren was a pretty good mixture of both. It was fun to see what he might look like in a few decades…if I was around then. I realized that everyone was standing around waiting for something, but I just wasn't sure what.

"You're the guest. You can pick your seat," his mother, Iseul, advised.

Atlas and Zane were already standing beside the chairs that they wanted, so I chose one at the end of the table, and everyone shifted around me. An intricate fan was pinned to the wall to my left, a golden design painted onto the black paper, and a beautiful jade handle adorning the bottom.

"That is a family heirloom. It's been passed down generation to generation, going back to the time of the old gods," Iseul said with a wide smile.

"It's beautiful," I responded as I stared at each elaborate flower petal and vine.

"It is." Zane quipped. "Now, can we eat before I fucking die?"

The stark rise and fall of Wren's chest wasn't as subtle as I thought he meant it to be. But he took the top off one of the dishes in the middle of the table with minor annoyance. Everyone else did the same thing before scooping out their own portions.

Wren grabbed my plate, putting a little of everything onto it and passing it back. All foods I was familiar with, soba, yakitori, bibimbap, and kimchi. There was a restaurant near my tía's home that served these dishes. There was a pretty good chance this would be even better, since it was made with love and not quickly at rush hour as I picked up takeout.

"So, what have you been up to, Dad?" Wren asked.

"Same old, same old. Retirement is nice and quiet. Usually." He side-eyed two of his sons who were currently shoving each other to get to the last gyoza.

"You, Mom?" Wren followed up.

I forgot that so much of Wren's time was accounted for between school and his work. Atlas and Zane were most likely here as often as they could be between jobs, but Wren didn't have as much opportunity.

"Same as your father. I've got quite the garden growing out back. I need to find a *Kaban* to help with some of the plants less native to this area, though."

I jumped at the opportunity to get on her good side. "My best friend is a *Kaban*. I can have her come by when she's free?"

Iseul smiled widely. "Oh, yes! I'd love that. I've got some mugunghwa seeds from home that I've been trying to grow for years now. I'm down to my last couple, so I would love her help."

Wren's approval came in the soft caress of his thumb over mine. The moment was short lived.

Atlas cleared his throat. "I did have some...business to discuss." His gaze landed on me, and I wasn't sure if he was worried about who I was to Wren or who I was to society.

All of their eyes flickered over to where I sat, and for a second, I felt like I shouldn't have been here. Their looks weren't rude or mean, but I made a quick assumption that few people outside of the family had heard these updates. This was my first time here, and I understood the apprehension.

"Say what you need to," Wren said without flinching.

25

WREN

I knew at a young age I wouldn't have a life comparable to my friends. As my childhood companions grew and started to make decisions for themselves, I quickly realized there were things too far out of my control. They grew up wanting to be healers, teachers, fucking ballerinas, but I grew up knowing that my place wouldn't be with them. The reality that I'd be doing work they'd never imagine, that I'd have to adopt a different moral compass, was evident.

No, I wouldn't get to decide where my life ended. I wouldn't get the chance to decide what my profession was. There were no dreams for the Ikari boys. So, as a child, I decided I'd make the best out of whatever shitty situation I ended up in. If I had to be a killer, I'd be the best fucking killer the world had seen. If I had to do things that others would turn up their nose at, I'd do it with a smile on my face. Were there people I couldn't get too close to? Sure. Times that I wanted more than just a quick fuck and a rush of adrenaline? Definitely.

But it wasn't until the moment I was sitting across from my family and Mira that I thought maybe I *could* attain...more.

I was more than the Cynod's henchman. Not just a tool used and disposed of. I wasn't only capable of protecting the ones I loved and cared about. There was a life for me to enjoy. Right here at my fingertips was an opportunity for something greater. Probably bigger than I could even wrap my mind around. It wasn't only a physical thing between me and Mira; it was more, quite frankly, than I bargained for. I'd make that bargain again and again, though.

It was companionship and genuine affection mixed in with the desire, and fuck, was there a lot of desire. But atop all of that primal need for her were things I'd only seen in my parents. Empathy, kindness, understanding, and tru...well, there had been trust.

I trusted her—wholeheartedly. It was me who fucked up the other end of that. At the time, I thought I was doing what I was supposed to, what I'd done for my family from the very beginning. If someone you care about was threatened, you took action. You do everything in your power to put yourself between them and the danger, and fuck the consequences. But...it was more complicated than that.

Mira wasn't my family in that way; there weren't decades of this between us. It wasn't solely protection she needed from me, it was...love. Those things had been synonymous up until now, and I had to learn to separate them. If she allowed it.

I splashed some water on my face. I'd been in here too long. There was no doubt a 'shit joke' coming from one of my brothers. I just needed a minute. Atlas needed to talk business, and I needed to be in the right headspace for that. Slowly closing the door behind me to avoid my mother scolding for slamming doors, I exited the bathroom.

I understood Mira's desire to go back to her tía's after all the shit that went down before; this place was the same for me. We had the estate, which I loved, but this was where we were raised. You could feel the familial love in the walls, in the ground, even in the air.

Mira's laugh had goose bumps running up my neck, and like a creep, I stood in the hall for a minute to watch. Nobody had looked up or spotted me, which showed how comfortable we were here. All of us were on constant high alert outside of these walls. A footstep twenty yards away or the lingering of eyes would have been detected within seconds anywhere else. My mother was re-entering from the kitchen, a delicate teacup in one hand and a plate of wagashi in the other. This was actually a sign that things were going very well. My mother didn't allow just *anyone* to use these particular tea cups. Ikari men weren't even allowed to touch them.

My brothers pounced for the sweets, and my mother jutted out her fingers, a whip of water extending and snapping their hands. They groaned but allowed

Mira to choose her dessert first. My mother loved to match the wagashis to the season, and today's were flowers in orange and red hues. Mira took her time, hovering her hand over them for a bit longer than I expected, and when she flashed a grin up to my brothers, I laughed and distracted her.

With her gaze now locked in mine, my brothers grabbed theirs and stuffed them in their mouths. She closed her hand around the one closest to her fingertips, and I grimaced an apology with a hand on my chest.

"Leave the rest for Wren; he obviously has a lot of space in his stomach now," Zane said with a mouthful of food.

Knew that was coming. Mira tipped her head back and laughed, and I decided not to knock my brother in his temple as I passed by his chair. I'd observed Mira a lot. I liked to try to anticipate what she needed, learn things about her that I could remember for another day. Her orders for takeout, staying a step ahead of her routines, filling her vitamins before she knew they were low. There weren't a ton of environments I'd seen her *this* relaxed. Sure, when we were together, there was a certain comfort, but not always in this easy way.

She scooted forward for me to sit and brushed her fingers against mine. I had to stop myself from getting overly excited at the small gesture. It was the closest sign of intimacy she had initiated since before all the shit hit the fan. The tenderness in her eyes that told me she realized it at that moment, too. Instead of shying away from it or averting her gaze, she held mine. It was still contemplative, yet soft, open. Those golden flecks in her irises sparkled in the candlelight, and if we weren't where we were, I would have leaned closer to look at them. Count each glint, map them out in a constellation.

"Back to business," Atlas said, and we both jolted in surprise.

I wasn't sure if they'd seen any of that; my father and brothers still had their eyes on the plates in front of them. My mother, however, was smiling so wide she had to be watching.

"Yes, business," I said as I cleared my throat.

My phone buzzed, and I quickly looked beneath the table to see Mira's phone out too.

Mira:

I typed quickly.

Me:

Mira tipped her chin once in understanding, and we looked to Atlas to finish chewing so he could tell us what was going on.

"Last job we went on felt rushed. You know these people are typically meticulous and a few steps ahead. They were grasping at straws with this last one," he said with his fist over his mouth. "Not to mention Wren's last drop never made it. Something is going on."

"They had us looking for someone with damn near no information on him. Took us fucking forever. We got it done, but something was off," Zane added, his business mask now on.

"If you feel like something is off, it is. You all have your mother's intuition," my dad asserted.

There was a desire to keep them from this particular part until I knew what to do. Koa had effectively cut me out of the dealings with the rebels, and I didn't want to hide that from my family any longer.

"I have a lead on where my drop went. I think we're stuck in the middle of a brewing war." I blew air between my lips. "The rebels are real, and I've been in contact. They've been intercepting the drops."

"Fuck," Atlas groaned as Zane mirrored the sentiment.

"What does in contact mean?" my mother questioned.

I wasn't one to lie to my mother. In fact, I think there were times she wished I had lied to her growing up. Something about the way she raised us, our connection, made deceit feel impossible.

"The car that crashed into the ocean with Mira and Koa. The rebels pulled us out. They were the ones who took Sienna, Mira's best friend. It's all a bit confusing, figuring out what side we are supposed to be on," I admitted.

"My brother has been in contact since then. We've agreed to work with them after they met us in the middle on some of our demands. I don't think they're bad people; they share the same ideologies as we do. Albeit not in the best ways, but they want to help the people," Mira chimed in.

Atlas and Zane raised their brows. Most of us in our world were used to a fictitious version of Mira, the one where she was only Koa's untouchable sister. But we weren't the kind of family that would question what she said. If she was here with me, the fact I brought her into these walls meant they trusted her and her word.

"What is the Cynod's goal with the pills?" Atlas asked.

She hadn't told me that yet. Granted, we hadn't exactly had the chance while we were no contact.

"If I tell you, all of you are implicated," Mira said. "I don't want to be the reason something happens to...anymore of you."

All the Ikaris at the table raised their chins in understanding, and she looked down at her fingers. I wondered if they'd turned black with her gift again, if there was a struggle to contain it since the last time I'd seen her.

"They are planning on taking away our gifts. The reason we're even a remote threat right now is because we have power, take it away and..." Mira dropped her gaze to her hands again.

I clocked it and locked it in my mind to check in the moment we were alone. We all sat in silence for a few beats. This wasn't something fathomable to most fae. Our magic was what made us who we were. It wasn't disbelief that rang between the fae at this table. It was disgust at the audacity of the Cynod.

"I don't want you all involved in that," my mother said, barely more than a whisper.

The hard edge of Atlas' tone was missing as he asked, "What choice do we have?"

My father stood from the table abruptly, gathering himself before he kissed my mother's forehead and left. He'd never quite gotten over our status in life. The fact that it was his father's mistakes we were still trying to get from under was heavier on him than us. This was our life; we knew no differently. But he did. He remembered being a dreamer. He had flashes of what his life could have been, memories where, if things had played out differently, he'd be somewhere else. His children wouldn't be in this mess. That was the part that hurt him the most. No matter how many times we reassured him that we were perfectly fine, he knew what it was to be free and wanted that for us.

I sometimes thought it was worse to know freedom—what it smelled like and felt like, only to never have it grace your senses again. The estate was our attempt at carving out some sort of resemblance to a dream he once had. But the strings tied to it, those he wasn't a fan of.

My mother frowned and turned toward Mira. "He's..."

"I get it. Trust me," she responded with a hand atop my mother's.

"Atlas, Zane, you're on dishes," she said with a wink in my direction.

They groaned, but did as she said. Zane flicked me off before grabbing my plate. It was definitely my turn, and we all knew it.

"Mira, if you need anything, give me a shout. Or have Wren get you what you need," she said before she went in the direction of my father.

He was probably sitting in her garden. That was where he went when he was frustrated. She'd made him his own section, crafted specifically to relax him.

"So," Mira started with mischief written in her features. "You got to see my childhood room, do I get to see yours?"

Unlike Mira's room, which was full of things from her childhood, mine was...lackluster. There was, of course, my award-winning solar system.

"Is this a science fair trophy?" Mira gasped sarcastically.

"Won my middle school fair. What can I say? Maybe we both could have been scientists," I teased.

"Wait," she said as she spun the system my dad helped me create. They turned and rotated after the first planet gained momentum. "This is actually really cool."

There weren't too many things that brought me as much joy as, well...her joy. Watching as she tried to figure out how each piece of the system was turning with a smile on her face filled me with warmth. Some of it was a little too concentrated in one spot, and I adjusted myself in my pants.

She caught me staring and stopped toying with my science fair project. There wasn't really anything else to see here. A bed, a window, two dressers, and a safe. That particular safe was a gift from Atlas after my emerging.

"I'm not sure what I expected. This seems pretty on par." She plopped down on the bed.

I wanted to join her, but I leaned on my dresser instead. For more than one reason. One, because the need to pull her into my arms and press my lips against hers was too strong. Two, not that my mother was naïve in any way, but there was, a rule about girls in our rooms that I wasn't entirely sure had been lifted.

"I noticed you looking at your hands a few times. You having problems with your nahual?"

Mira sighed. "No, not necessarily problems. I don't know how to control it yet. I'm working on it with my therapist, actually. It's just that sometimes my hands feel like they don't belong to me? It's weird."

Other people had mentors to lean on who had already gone through this. Most of us were able to get guidance, know what to expect, and prepare. Not having any idea what would happen or what you were capable of was troubling.

"I think that's common when you emerge. Definitely took time for me to be comfortable in my shifted form." I rubbed my chin, not really sure how to transition into my next question, but I couldn't wait any longer. "How are you feeling about everything?"

'Everything' was a loaded word in that sentence. It was the only one I could think of to cover all of it.

"Hm," she sounded as she brushed her hand against the microfiber comforter. "I feel like I understand you better now. Your motives, the reasons you make the decisions you do. They aren't a hypothetical family you've fought tooth and nail to protect; they're real. I always *thought* I understood. We were both born into roles we didn't ask for. We both have had to maneuver in spaces we shouldn't have. Now I get that it's...different for you. This sense of protection and duty is imprinted on you—defines you in a way that's hard to fathom without seeing what shaped it."

It was why I wanted her to meet them. Mira was a facts and tangibility type of person. A scientist with a hypothesis, and without putting her hands and eyes on the variables being tested, my words were empty. Even with Atlas and Zane being assholes, with my dad storming off, and my mother being charming, yet maybe overbearing, she needed to see it all.

"I wish I could say that I'd make a different choice. I do wish I could change how things happened, but, Mira, if you are ever in danger, I'm always going to choose to protect you."

The blinds of my window were open, and the sun suddenly poured into the room. It lit a halo behind her, the dark curls tinting red with the light. I knew if she tilted her head slightly, the warm rays would bathe her skin and highlight her cheekbones. She wasn't concerned with the sun; every ounce of her attention was tunneling into me.

"That was also the hard part to wrap my mind around. Nobody has ever put themselves between me and the Cynod other than Koa and my tía, who felt obligated. Doing that without a hope of personal gain was...unlikely. Especially after just a few short weeks of knowing me, it wasn't that I doubted *you*, but I doubted the reality of the situation."

I'd never been able to fully understand what pulled me to her myself. Maybe part of it was seeing that she needed a shield from her life's storms. That would be the easy answer: a boy with a need to protect, and a girl in need of protection. I knew now it was more than that. I wished I had the words, had a better grasp on *this* reality.

Because even before I knew who she was or what plagued her, I was intrigued. It was the way she interacted with the world, like everything was a puzzle only she could solve. The way her eyes wandered and picked up pieces until she had the full picture. At the end of the day, that's what I was. A man in pieces, desperately in need of someone who could put me back together. Mira had the patience, the understanding, and the will to do so.

I pushed off the dresser smoothly, taking intentional steps toward her that she tracked attentively. She was on the corner of the mattress, and I kneeled before her, wrapping my arms around her thighs and hips. Mira relaxed, allowing me to pull her as close as I wanted—as close as I currently could. If it was up to me, there'd be not a molecule between us.

"And what about now, do you doubt me or the reality of our situation?" I asked, my voice low.

To her, she might have thought I was trying to be seductive. That wasn't it. I was afraid that if I asked that question too loudly, maybe her reply would change. If the gods heard it, they'd guide her away from me and to someone...better. Because I was prepared for her answer to be yes. That it was all too much, it was the answer I mostly expected. I didn't get these kinds of chances, and I understood if that was the case now.

Mira ran her fingers through my hair and tilted my chin up so I had to look her in the eyes. "It might take some time to rebuild that trust, but I want to try. Just...maybe one brick at a time."

One moment, I was on my knees, and the next, Mira was on her back atop my mattress with my body caging her in. She wrapped her legs around me, drawing my body closer, and I dipped into the crook of her neck, inhaling her scent. I kept my nose pressed against her skin, trailing up until I reached her ear, and finally pulled back to stare at her. There was no doubt in her gaze; it was void of regret and worry. I was only met with her beautiful features, relaxed and soft.

It was Mira who made the move, her chin tilting and her hand around my neck, pulling me in. Her lips, fuck, the sensation of her lips against mine after all of this time was enough to make me shudder. She pressed deeper, her tongue and the taste of her sweeping in. I could stay here forever, die in this position, and be perfectly fucking happy about it.

It wasn't the end of all our problems. It was a good start. Lucky for both of us, I had an endless amount of bricks to build that trust again.

26

KOA

Wednesdays were slow. The Vortex and The Underground, to no one's surprise, had days where incentives to frequent our establishments could be countered. Midweek crisis and all. Business deals continued without interruption, but the fucking around that happened every other day of the week came to a standstill. People were tired—or recovering. Or both.

I typically used the time to catch up on the books, see where we were in the red, and check in with my staff. New dancers and bartenders started on Wednesdays, which helped them ease into the rush of things, keep expectations where they could be met while testing them out on the crowd. Most of the dancers were *Xtabay*. It was where the money was. They were...natural talents. And if they weren't up to par, or were shy about their uniforms, or rather, lack thereof, Nola used the downtime to train them up on bottle service.

They practiced on the tabletops and served the business crowd under our supervision. We could see the entire floor from the corner bar, with the lack of bodies in here. Lights flashed between red and white, disorienting me from my notepad as I studied for finals. This was usually a place of peace for me. Instead, I found myself overstimulated from the lights, clashing music, constant chatter, and the feral grunting coming from the fighting ring in the center of the room. Too much going on—in life and here.

"Ikari, two o'clock," Nola said, sweeping her hands through her short, recently dyed auburn hair out of her face. She closed the little black book in front of her. Wren's *Ix* sight was better than 20/20, especially under the dim lighting.

We were taking hit after hit since cutting the Ikaris out. A surprise to no one but worth the pain if it meant any interactions we had from here on out were restricted to false pleasantries. It would take some time to bridge the gap. I wasn't stressing it, though. Between Nola and the Mercers gunning for the Ikaris' spot, outside of the drugs pushed here, it would only be a matter of time before we made it out of the red.

Fucking frankly, it wasn't even "red" in the usual business terms. It was only 'red' to me, as in, it ate into the stability of profits I was accustomed to. There was enough cash flowing in from this place and my other avenues to never know what true 'red' looked like for the rest of my life, and any kids Sienna and I had. Not to mention, with word of the Ikaris being on the outs spreading, the other Underworld patrons circled like vultures, seeing where they could steal an open spot.

Wren hadn't fought me on the contract being in breach. Eventually he would tire of playing to Mira's good side and I'd have to cough up the funds to either settle or buy him out.

I stared him down as he approached, and he stopped a healthy distance away. "The fuck are you doing here?"

"I came for business." He tossed his chin up in acknowledgment of Nola. "You can take my name off shit connected to the club, but you can't prevent me from conducting business as a patron. No rules, remember?"

"Get fucked, Ikari," I muttered, jaw clenched tight.

Wren glanced at Nola in that smug way that made my knuckles itch. She threw her hands up. "He's the one who signs my paycheck. Leave me out of the bullshit."

Coward. I couldn't blame her. It was an easy response. I did sign her paycheck, and she *was* loyal to me at the end of the day. That was an indisputable fact. But the truth of the matter was, they too had built a rapport over the years. They'd been around each other long enough.

"My appointment isn't for another thirty minutes," Wren said, casual as all hells.

"Then why are you standing in my face right now?"

His throat bobbed, eyes not as hard as they should appear when he spoke to someone he considered an enemy. "I wanted to speak with you."

I pushed off the bar, feeling the rumble under my boots as someone hit the floor in the ring—hard. The sound snapped through the haze of smoke, followed by a roar from the small crowd. Whoever it was just got laid the fuck out.

"I don't give a shit what you *want*."

Wren's smile curved with the kind of ease that pissed me off. "Fine. You wanted to fight," he said as he shrugged out of his jacket, letting it fall to the floor. He rolled his shoulders, loose and easy, as if he hadn't carried tension for days. "Let's fight. In the ring, you and me? I win, you hear me out. Maybe not today, but soon. You win, I pull out of the club completely, my brothers too. But *not* Mira's life."

"Mira is not part of this conversation." I didn't look at him when I spoke. Kept my eyes trained on the edge of the ring. The words came out even, steady. He knew she'd forgiven him. That didn't mean I had. It didn't erase the wreckage.

"You're right, she's not," Wren said. "That doesn't dismiss that I hurt you. So punch me in the face and get it the fuck over with, Canek. I know you want to."

The fucking gall of him, standing there, offering it like penance. An abrupt, hollow laugh pierced the air, and I recognized it as my own—disconnected as it may be, he was right. I *did* want to beat the shit out of him.

This time, I could do it without Mira's cracked voice begging me to stop when she deemed things went "too far". She wasn't here now. It was Ikari, me, and Nola for the feigned presence of a ref. The only time she'd step in is if I did, in fact, take it too far.

Others had killed inside this ring, but Ikari and I were to be the exceptions to that rule. Business partners and whatnot. This might have been a club for criminals, but that didn't negate the fact that there were examples to be set. Maintained.

There was no one here to hold me back. I wanted this. *Needed* this. So, I stepped into the ring.

I didn't need another reason to hate him. All the reasons in the world already existed.

Wren stood across from me, sleeves rolled and tattoos crawling under the red light in serpentine fashion. There was fire burning in his eyes. Nola leaned against the cage, arms crossed, unreadable, though I knew she was enjoying this. The crowd pressed in, feral and drunk, their fists slamming against the chain-link to the rhythm of the bass.

Forget a Friday night fight. An Ikari versus Canek—this was a main event. I was only sorry I couldn't profit from his inevitable loss.

He struck first. Fast enough to blur. *Ix* blood on full display. *Chikchan's* senses made us an unusually even match. The vibrations I picked up in the surrounding air had me shifting my weight, and I twisted, catching his ribs with a knee. Bone gave a little under the impact. He grunted, breath clipped, but didn't slow.

Wren darted back in, fists flying. I blocked one, absorbed the next to my forearm, and countered with a sharp elbow meant to break his teeth. We traded blow for blow. Only pure hatred on my end, and the desire for forgiveness on his.

Every sound echoed—the crack of cartilage, the wet slap of skin, the thunder of feet on a mat slick with blood and sweat. Vision narrowed. All I saw was him and the danger he had brought. His actions, as heroic as he made them seem to Mira, had almost killed her. Killed Sienna. For that, he needed to bleed.

The first offense was unforgivable; the second made me want to bring him a painful death. My mate was off-limits. Mate marks were funny little fuckers. Not only did I experience immense godsdamn pain and panic during my own drowning session—I'd felt every bit of Sienna's too. He thought he had been protecting Mira. His reckless actions had only brought danger to Sienna instead.

Magic rose between us.

Wren's eyes glowed with molten nightfire. I let venom rise. Fangs pressed lower, poison gathering on my tongue. I wanted to split him open and watch it drain. The brutality of my hits weakened his initial resolve. I felt the heat before I saw the flame. He ducked low, swept my leg, then surged forward with a burst of speed that had the crowd roaring.

I struck back with a hook aimed at his jaw, followed by a body shot designed to crack bones. His ribs, his sternum—who gave a shit? Not me. My *Chikchan* instincts itched beneath the surface. It wanted freedom and was desperate to unleash.

So I let go.

I dropped him into a vision. The ring dissolved for him alone, replaced with ash, ruin, his family's bodies motionless at his feet. Smoke curled from the corpses surrounding him in a prison of death. His breath hitched—hesitated—just enough.

I used it to my advantage. His pain fueled me.

Driving him to the mat with a shoulder, his skull cracked against the mat. I locked him there, teeth gritted. Flame died in his eyes for a heartbeat only to be replaced by guttural rage.

It pushed him to retaliate full force. Nightfire sparked again, a sudden burst of heat beneath my ribs as he twisted free. Claws raked across my torso, shredding skin.

I tasted blood. My own.

Good. Fucking good. I needed to feel something right now, and he was only feeding it. Pain sharpened me. I spat red.

We collided again. Faster. Sweat pooled on the floor, kicked up underfoot, heat clashing with the pulse of venom threading through my strikes. His hand caught my neck, and I slammed my forehead into his nose. Cartilage broke, blood spraying across my cheek.

He staggered back. I followed, caught his shoulder, spun him—until he struck again, this time aiming a low, brutal shot to my kidney. White-hot pain dropped me to a knee.

Nola shouted something. I heard nothing over the ringing in my ears. Maybe it was my name. It did nothing to lift my gaze. The roar in my ears drowned her out. Without the gift of healing, I'd be pissing blood for a week.

Wren grabbed me by the arm, chest heaving, voice raw. "Stay down."

I lunged.

He met me in the middle, rabid and unrelenting. This wasn't about winning. Not anymore. He wouldn't kill me, not if he still wanted Mira in his life, but it was clear that he would no longer be treating this as a friendly fight. Not after that vision. I sank my fangs into his wrist, venom flooding beneath his skin until it blistered black. He ripped free with a roar, flames spilling wildly enough to scorch the mat.

The crowd howled for more.

Three more moves later, I lay flat on my back, blood choking in my throat. He loomed above me—bruised, bloodied, and limping, but standing.

He didn't gloat. Didn't smirk. Simply offered me his hand.

"I had more to lose," he muttered.

I already knew what he meant. And I hated it. Despised the way the words made me feel. The pain it eased in my heart.

He meant me—whatever idea of friendship, solidarity, brotherhood—we'd come to understand.

Wren stepped out of the cage, blood still dripping from his knuckles. I clocked it immediately—the shift in his posture, the way he moved with pure predatory intent. He'd said he was expecting someone, and sure enough, two men stepped out from around the side of the cage. I recognized them: *Noctis Fraternitas* representatives from headquarters.

My attention followed as they moved toward a dark corner, Nola tossing him a clean towel to wipe off. *So that's why he was here tonight.* I didn't get the chance to watch the interaction unfold.

"Fiancé."

Her voice cut through the bullshit. A blade dipped in sugar. I didn't even have to turn. I felt her before I saw her—Alanna. All smug grace and carefully calculated confidence in a den full of wolves. Criminals.

She stuck out like a sore thumb. Completely out of place in her tailored mini skirt, strapped heels, and cashmere sweater. For once, she resembled nothing of the girl I loved. This was the real Alanna, finally presenting her true self.

I exhaled through my nose and glanced down at her from the cage. Alanna raised a glass of white wine. Scoffing at the inconvenience, I hopped down, ready to address yet another irritating stain on my night.

Alanna leaned in, far too close, pressing her lips to my cheek. When she pulled back, her thumb dragged across my jaw, wiping away a streak of blood with the same care one might use to brush away a smudge of food.

"You can stop pretending down here," I muttered, low enough only she could hear. "They're all under a blood-bound NDA that requires silence. But you know that already."

The consequence of the blood-bound NDA was tragic. First of its kind—an order I spent months hunting the right practitioner to craft. A blood bond, like the one Ikari carried, restrained and killed if broken. This bind could have been considered worse, depending on who you were. It broke the breaker—splintered their mind until nothing remained. Snitches didn't get stitches here. Too merciful. Mental torture was more my style.

Her glossy mauve lips turned into a saccharine grin as though I'd told her a secret she'd been waiting to hear. "Mmm. Never one to miss an opportunity to practice my acting. Some of us take our roles in society more seriously than others."

"*Some* of us don't care what others think about the perception of their relationship." I pulled my shirt over my head, the tightness of my already fucked-up jaw increasing in the scathing glare I sent her way. "If you've ever had a real one, you'd understand that the only thing that matters is what the two people inside are feeling."

"Well, that's quite romantic for someone of your...nature," she trailed after me, her hands up in a disgusted yet defensive position as she shrugged off the crowd.

"I'm capable of experiencing emotions other than anger and irritation."

She looped her arm through mine, and I tensed. "Then show me."

"Pass." I shook her off and went back to my spot at the bar.

"Koa."

"Alanna."

Her shove landed square in my chest. Hard enough to make it clear she had a point to make, but not nearly enough to move me in a direction I had no intention of going. Alanna turned on her heels and pushed the door open to my office, two fingers lustfully signaling me to follow in her stead.

"Move," she said.

I lingered for a second, mostly out of spite, then pushed past her and made my way inside.

"Invite me in," she demanded.

I rolled my eyes, tugging her through the wards. As the door swung closed behind us, I caught Wren's eyes—tight jaw, tight shoulders. He was in some shit, and it looked like he'd rather be anywhere else.

The click of the lock snapped me back.

"I understand this situation is the last thing you wanted," Alanna started, tone smoother than silk over glass. Practiced—ingrained in her through years of training. "I *also* am not stupid. You and that...girl—"

"Sienna," I snapped.

"*Sienna*," she echoed with faux sweetness. "You're still in a relationship. Secret as it may be, it's not impossible to figure out what with your lack of motivation to make this arrangement look the least bit believable."

I clenched my teeth, part of me ready to bark back, to shut this whole conversation down—but then I paused. There was a shift in her tone, something deeper layered beneath the smug exterior she typically displayed. It reminded me of the few seconds back in Professor Ugalde's class, where I thought she wanted to intervene on the student being escorted out for being verbal in their beliefs.

"Save the lies for someone moronic," she cut in before I could speak. "This isn't a threat. How do you feel about a little 'you scratch my back, I'll scratch yours' situation?"

I made my way to the bar cart in the corner, poured two glasses of whiskey, handed her one, then sat across from her.

I took a long drag of mine, washing down any remnants of venom and blood. "Talk."

"If this were real," she said, crossing one leg over the other, her skirt sliding higher, "I'd say the demand to be submissive was rather appealing to me." She winked, nails like tiny, coffin-shaped weapons resting on her knee. "I hinted at it during the engagement brunch. Now I'm ready to have a real conversation. As much as you resist, there is a very real possibility this facade becomes a permanent fixture—nuptials are not out of the question, Koa. We have little say and no control...as of *now*."

"No offense, but I'd rather fake my death and start over on another continent than let that happen."

"Offense taken," she replied smoothly, "and brushed off with my aspirations in mind."

"Aspirations such as? You're chatting without much to offer, and I've got shit to do. So get to the point, or fuck off until next time we're forced to pretend we're in love." I leaned back, letting my drink burn its way down. Pretty sure I lost a fucking tooth in the fight.

Alanna swirled the whiskey in her glass, unbothered. "You really lack the couth I expected, considering all the so-called training your parents made you suffer through. Anyhoo, my business plan. The one we briefly discussed. Have you had a chance to review it?"

"I have."

"And?"

"I'm waiting for you to convince me. If we did in fact make it to a ceremony—and that's a big fucking *if*—my money essentially becomes yours. Why are you so eager to jump on this now? A smart businesswoman would wait me out. Ask for forgiveness, not permission."

She straightened her posture. The coy mask slipped for a fraction of a second. "I'm not a businesswoman. I'm a fae with a cause and people relying on me to come through. A business plan caught your attention—now I've snared you in my trap."

That made me pause. I leaned forward, curiosity piqued. "You want me to pour ten million solits into rebuilding Bajío. Infrastructure, schools, and clean water for the very fae your grandfather displaced in the collapse of Mentiria's monarchy and the transition of power. A transition he himself helped facilitate. That's a lot of money for a woman whose stuck-up personality doesn't match the cause. Why?"

She dodged my question with a smirk. "I'd argue your entire lifestyle doesn't match yours."

I let out a laugh. "I don't know what you're talking about. The gyms are a facade. Charity to make an heir look like they give a shit about the world. We all have one, evidently."

"Mira doesn't."

"Mira doesn't have a foundation *yet*. It's in the works."

"Oh, really? What is it then? Because my people dug into your entire family, and there's nothing on her in that regard." She swept her curls over her shoulder.

I went quiet.

She took another sip, not breaking eye contact. "I know."

"Know what?"

"Everything and then some." Those sharp hazel eyes traced along the lines of my mate mark. I double-checked my glamour still in place. She leaned forward, reaching for the napkin beneath my inked up arm that rested on the end table next to me. I hid my sigh of relief.

"But for your sake, I won't go into the details. All I'm here to ask for today is a simple bargain."

I stared at her, maintaining my silence, fingers curling tight around my glass.

"My grandfather is hosting a gala this weekend at our estate," she continued. "I need your help. It's a sticky situation, but he won't be able to turn you down. Not without disrespecting the Cynod's generosity."

"If I were a betting man," I said, "and I am, I'd wager that your situation looks a lot like mine."

"And if I were a betting woman—which I'm not—I'd put everything I had on the fact that you're correct in that assumption."

I nodded slowly, reluctantly pleased in this unraveling. "I admit. There's more to you than I expected."

"That's what happens when you take the time to get to know someone, Koa Canek. Secrets emerge. Now, will you help me, or not?"

I looked her over. It *could* be a trap. Hells, maybe it was a trap inside of an already announced trap. But there was something in her eyes—more honesty now than I'd ever seen in her before. "What do you need?"

"Half of my request in funds donated to the Heart of Bajío Restoration Project. Publicly. During a toast. You'll claim it as a wedding gift to your betrothed in support of a cause that sits near and dear to her heart."

I huffed. "Win the people while spitting on your grandfather. Smart play."

"Shame," she mused, tipping her glass toward mine and meeting it with a *clink*. "Any offspring we may have had could've changed the world. Brains and empathy—as hidden as ours may be."

I didn't take it as an insult. Not now. Not with this new understanding taking shape between us.

"What do I have to gain from this?"

"I'll turn the other way when it comes to your relationship with your *mate*."

I shot to my feet, heartbeat hammering. "How do you—"

"As I said," she interrupted coolly, "I know everything. I see everything. I'm well-connected, Koa. If we are stuck with each other for an eternity, we'll produce an heir through IVF. I'll even allow you to blame me for why it can't happen the old-fashioned way. You and Sienna get to live your lives as though I don't exist—other than co-parenting duties, of course. That is, if she'll forgive you enough for not putting a stop to this and is okay with forever being a mistress."

Her words hit me like a sucker punch to the gut, and I was already going to be pissing blood from Wren's hit. Because what if I really *couldn't* stop this? It wasn't what either of us wanted—but it was something. A path forward.

"Deal."

27

MIRA

I loved that Professor Taran was old school. I hadn't seen a testing form like this in some time—one where you had to fill it out with a specific pencil. My other finals were all on the computer, so this was a nice break for my eyes. Taran packed every lecture with an abundant amount of information, and I realized he wasn't kidding when he said half of it wouldn't be on the test. The final was part of the curriculum, but we'd learned far more than just what he was 'supposed' to teach us.

It made the test a breeze. I appreciated the extra lessons in things we'd learn nowhere else. That wasn't the case for everyone. Nobody had dropped the class initially, but I had noticed that over the weeks, there were a few extra seats. Professor Taran had marked a few of the questions with an asterisk. Advising that we learned two versions of what the answer was, and a reminder to use the 'right' one for credit.

Which was the case for this one, the question was short with multiple-choice answers.

Who was Hagen Nob?

a) The second seat in the Cynod

b) Our savior and Solis' chosen

c) A warrior in the last battle

d) None of the above

The answer should have been d; however, the one that would be marked as accurate was b. Part of me wanted to fill in d on principle, but the need to ace this test won. The rest of it was a walk in the park. I double-checked, and then triple-checked that I had answered all the questions, and filled in a couple of bubbles that weren't quite as dark as the others. I wasn't the first one done, which was something the younger Mira always tried to achieve. The more mature Mira realized that just because something was done quickly, it didn't mean it was done well.

Katia was still working on her test, so I flipped mine over and waited. Professor Taran had a film playing with the sound off and subtitles on for those of us who finished early. Some professors let you leave when you were done, but he was one of the ones who thought that was disruptive.

The film was in black and white, and while it had a classic ambiance to it, there was a modern quality I couldn't quite pinpoint. He didn't tell us any additional details, just that it was an indie film he found enticing. It felt like one of those types of movies with multiple layers, the kind where one person could get one message, and someone else would sense a deeper meaning. My tía used to love these kind of movies. She'd go on and on about the uses of symbolism and the tiny little details that would pull it all together if you watched carefully.

A woman with two long braids trekked through a forest. The trees resembled a cage; everywhere she turned, there were more and more, with no exit in sight. I'd spotted a wolf following her a few scenes back, and she looked over her shoulder as if finally hearing it. Without the audio, it was hard to tell, but the lift of her brows and the whites in her eyes told me she was scared. She held a dagger tight and close to her chest, and her head whipped around toward the other direction. *Were there two wolves?*

The tips of antlers showed on the screen just as the bell rang and class ended. Professor Taran paused the movie and stood shouting, "Leave your tests by the door with our teacher's assistant. Scores should be up soon. For those I won't see in future semesters, it's been a pleasure teaching you all."

I let everyone else line up as I went over to his desk. "What's this movie called?"

"It's called *The Enemy Among Us*." He clicked play. "She's so worried about the wolf that she doesn't see the deer. The deer is so worried about a hunter that he doesn't see the wolf. Hunter kills her, wolf kills the deer. You can probably find it on one of those apps you kids love. I bought it at a film show."

"Hm, I might have to track it down," I said.

Even if I knew how it would end, I wanted to know the journey. As an anxious person, I related to the concept of it. Being so worried about one thing that you give every bit of your energy to defending yourself from it, just for a bigger, more dangerous thing to take you down.

Professor Taran beat his fingers against his desk. "Did you find anything of interest at the extracurricular fair?"

"Nothing I'm dying to join, but yeah, I might join the community service group."

He opened his mouth, then closed it, and I remembered how he watched me when I was speaking to Iris. It was hard to determine how he felt about it, as he always had a sort of analytical look about him.

He leaned forward. "Actually, I—"

"Mira, you coming?" Katia called from the doorway.

I glanced back, but he had already stood to pack up his things, and instead of whatever thought that originally came to mind, he just said, "Have a good break."

"You too," I offered, even though I wanted to know what he was about to say.

Katia stood in the doorway, a pencil clamped between her teeth as she pulled her dark hair into a ponytail. "You trying for extra credit or something?"

I laughed. "No, I emailed about that last week. Was interested in the movie. Did you get a chance to watch any of it?"

"No." She shook her head. "I went up until the last minute. I get test anxiety, had to make sure I didn't miss anything in the midst of my sweating and blurry vision."

"Definitely understand that. But yeah, I think I'll try to finish it later. It was interesting, and I liked the way it was filmed."

I rolled down my sweater sleeves as we stepped outside. The wind was blowing between the buildings, and the sun hadn't made it much warmer since we'd gone in. A banner reading, 'You did it, First Years!' hung between two trees. It was hard to believe our first semester was already done. Time moved fast when everything was on the verge of imploding.

"I don't think you've mentioned whether you're going home for break?" I asked Katia.

"No, I'm staying here. I worry that my parents won't let me leave if I'm there the *whole* entire break." She laughed.

"Well, you know we don't really have anywhere to go other than Koa's. You can hang with us." I bumped her shoulder.

"Good, because that was my plan already," Katia responded with a smack of her lips.

If there was one aspect of my life that was going right, it was this. Her, Sienna, and I, and how we all fit together seamlessly. No jealousy, no competition, just three young women existing and being perfectly happy together.

I stretched my arms wide. "I'm going to read, relax, and if Sienna is up to cooking, eat really fucking good."

"And now that you and Wren have made up, you can also get dicked down." She pulled out her phone. "I should let my dicks know I'll be staying as well."

I thought my groan was internal, but a bit must have slipped out because Katia raised a brow. There was a tiny, toxic part of me that was very much looking forward to that specific scenario, the apology through his body. Her phone buzzed with a melodic chime.

"Oh! Jed said we should go to their beach house for part of the break. Said we can all come and hang. Have Koa and Wren fought it out yet?"

"From what I'm told, they did fight it out, quite literally. I'll have to find out just how friendly they are now. I've been scared to talk to Koa," I admitted.

It honestly wasn't fear I felt in regard to the conversation; I was more nervous. Talking to Katia and Sienna about it was no biggie; having the actual conversation with Wren was one thing. My brother was another. Not only because he had a stake in things, but there was a certain level of...sensitivity when it came to him.

Sienna knew me best; she could practically narrate my life in real time. However, Koa had done so many things to protect me in the past, and I didn't want him to think I was careless with that fact. Or that I was the reason his business partnership had gotten to this place.

"Hurry up, I want to go to the beach!" We turned down the path toward the dorm. "Look at fate. There's your brother."

Koa seemed to have sensed me as he spotted us immediately, and I dragged my feet as I met up with him while Katia dramatically waved goodbye.

"Look who's done ducking and dodging. How was your last final?" Koa asked immediately.

Even with me avoiding him, there was no way he didn't know that was my main focus for the last couple of days.

"Good, I'm sure I killed it. You all done now, too?"

"Yeah, shit was easy." His eyes narrowed on me a *little* too intensely. "What's wrong?"

Well fuck, if there weren't approximately fifty-seven responses to that. Beating around the bush wouldn't serve me here, so I just needed to come right out and ask.

"Nothing is *wrong* per se. But, um, have you and Wren talked yet?"

Koa rolled his eyes. "Our version of it."

"Gods, you live by such a weird-ass code. You will need to actually speak, not just hit each other and call a truce."

We crossed a street, and Koa snarled at a student on an electric scooter that got a bit too close.

"Who says?" he pushed.

I motioned to myself. "Me, clearly."

"Sorry, this is starting to sound like an *'I forgave him'* conversation," Koa said in a way I was slightly scared to answer.

"Well..." I trailed off.

My brother didn't say anything. The look he was giving me said enough.

"Honestly? After hearing what he said and why he did it, it isn't anything different we wouldn't have done for each other. I don't like it, but I can't say I don't understand it." I peered down at my hands. "Not to mention, part of my gift is I can see...more about a person. Their true self and intentions, and I saw his."

"The thing about a lie is, it's never one. It's a domino effect, and I don't even know what dominoes were in play. He told me he had you, and he hurt you. Even if he didn't mean to, consequences are consequences."

If only things were that simple. I shuddered as the breeze picked up, pulling my jacket tighter to my body.

He slid me a side-eye, intent on figuring me out. "Is there a reason you're pushing this right now?"

Ah, shit. He's onto me.

"I'd like to be able to hang out with both of you over break. Plus, Katia said the Mercers invited us to their beach house."

"The house is Wolfe's. Are you sure they invited Wren, or just you?"

"She said all of us, so I assumed." Probably should have gotten more details before mentioning, now that I thought about it.

"They're the ones who brought all this shit up. You really think they're going to let him in their house?"

"If you've forgiven him, I think they will, too?"

Maybe we needed to set up a fight for them as well if that was how things were handled in this circle of trust-issues-and-ego-matches.

"You're doing a lot of assuming. Not very smart of you. There's more history there. It was a godsdamn miracle they managed to get along for those few weeks," Koa responded as he plopped down on a bench and motioned for me to join. "I've got to fly out to Mentiria for some bullshit with Alanna."

"You agreed to that?" I grimaced.

"We've come to somewhat of an understanding. No need to avoid her anymore."

"Does that agreement involve Sienna?" I asked.

"It does."

I was pretty damn sure she was not aware of this. Last I heard, she was considering Alanna as a test dummy for my gift.

"And she knows that?" I pushed.

He cleared his throat. "She will soon. I was planning to take her out after finals, but this shit got in the way. Now I'll have to do it over a phone call. Hopefully the three dozen roses, her own black card attached to my account, and tickets for that cooking show she likes waiting back at the condo will soften the blow."

"Ha, good luck." I kicked a rock. "When did we become adults with complicated relationships?"

"Was always going to be the case for us. I was a fool to think I could change that," he said, but where I said it more like a joke, there was a solemn tone in his voice.

"Just remember, none of us have to figure it out by ourselves. We've always known that we should lean on each other."

Koa nodded and pulled out his phone. "I've got to go, kid. You coming over with Sienna later?"

"Probably."

"Okay." He stood and clicked a button on his phone. "Don't forget to lock up and turn the security enchantment on, Venom."

Koa turned and walked away, his voice and steps going silent, telling me he must have used a silencing spell. I really hoped this break was good for us all, because, fuck, did we all need it.

28

KOA

Flying into Mentiria was always a slap in the face. Glossy skyline, marble towers, and a heat that clung to your skin like a second layer of sweat-slicked judgment. Alta Corona never rested, not even when the sun dipped below its platinum skyline. It made Inecha's capital appear dreadfully dull. Four seasons didn't touch this place, and that was saying something considering Kuxtal Isle never experienced more than a brief season of chill, maybe a little rain.

The plane touched down smoother than I expected, given it was commercial. First class on Tohil Skies was as comparable as I could get to the finer things. Fuck, if there were some luxuries I enjoyed in this life guilt-free, flying private was one of them. I couldn't excuse it this trip, however. As cozy as brushing elbows with civilians was, taking a private jet for a single night gala was equivalent to rubbing gold dust in the face of people already choking on ash.

There was more than the peace of a quiet flight to be missed. Ducking my head under the brim of a baseball cap, shoulders hunched as I pushed through the cameras flashing around Chichen's airports. It was migraine-inducing. Mentiria was easier. Fewer vultures. Less fae in my face, asking me to solve problems I had no chance of solving in the next two hundred years, minimum. Staying under the radar was easier when the people you walked among hadn't realized the exact value you had to offer them. That would all change by tonight.

Whatever, a deal was a deal.

A black car waited just past security, engine humming low, window tinted dark with the promise of privacy. No flag, no seal. Unmarked and efficient.

267

The driver didn't speak which was nice considering I wasn't in the mood for conversation. Being in Mentiria already required enough performance. I leaned back in the seat, watching the city blur into trees, gates, and estates that announced power without saying a word.

Alanna's house held millennia of stories awaiting to be told through its architecture—stone columns, shadowed windows, ivy strangling the facade in a way that was too perfectly curated to be natural. But I knew the Osorioses weren't old money. The land they occupied had roots deeper than theirs.

This estate had belonged to someone else long before the Osorioses moved in and slapped their name on it. A home to people whose legacy had been quietly overwritten by her grandfather when he helped their president reach power. *Colonizer*, I scoffed as I exited the vehicle with the slam of my door.

Staff moved across the lawn in a blur of pressed uniforms and purpose. Prepping for the night ahead that required nothing less than perfection if Alanna had anything to do with the planning. No one looked at me twice. Alanna stood at the top of the steps, hands in the front pocket of a gray hoodie, her tight coils twisted into a messy knot. For once, she wore no makeup nor held the glint of performance in her eyes.

"Hey."

I raised an eyebrow. "That's it?"

She shrugged. "Don't tell me you expected a red carpet."

"I expected words. You usually use too many."

"Solis," she chirped a laugh and turned on her heels. "I'm at home. No need to keep up the act. Come on, I'll show you to your room."

The door opened without a sound. We stepped into a hallway lined in marble and jade, air cooled beyond comfort. Niches in the wall held hand-carved obsidian jaguar heads and clay incense burners still faintly warm to the touch. Copal and burnt citrus lingered behind the smoke's wake. Sunlight streamed through geometric cutouts in the high ceiling.

"Not that I have any interest in sharing a bed with you, but the staff..."

"Answer to me," she cut in dismissively. "Not my grandfather."

I let the smirk pull at my mouth, attempting to bite down a snarky retort but failing in the end. "Did you buy their loyalty?"

"No. I earned it. They were...close to my mother before she passed. Many are from Bajío and have no home to go back to, so they stay on property. Helped raise me. They're family." Her hazel eyes burned with the power of an *Ajaw*.

The estate's interior screamed of wealth as we walked through. Careful curation of every piece of decoration was an understatement. Every artifact and display piece was arranged with surgical precision. More museum than home. It appeared to be a place built to impress, not live in—something I was all too familiar with. She stopped outside a door.

"My room's across the hall. Grandfather's in the west wing. Staff is in between. My dad, step mom, and brothers won't arrive until later tonight, and even then, they don't tend to stay the night."

I studied her expression, then glanced at the hall behind her. "Always been like this?" There weren't many times in the past month and some change that I'd interacted with her family, but each time the awkwardness rivaled my own relationship with my parents.

Her brow creased. "Define 'this.'"

"Playing politics inside your own home."

She held my gaze, and something inside her shifted. Sorrow, maybe. Definitely despair—it hardened as quickly as it wavered. "No. Not that that's any of your business. And since you prefer to keep things transactional, you won't get more than that."

Fair enough. Her eyes flicked down to my hand and up my arm, tracing along the invisible lines of the mate mark. I did a double take, making sure I hadn't screwed up somehow and lost my glamour. It remained intact.

She recovered, gesturing to the door behind me. "Your suit's inside. Freshly steamed. Your mother was oddly insistent."

"She would be."

"Speech ready?"

"With a signed check."

That earned a faint huff. Not a laugh.

"Seven sharp." She turned and disappeared into the corridor.

I stood in the center of my room for a moment, rolling my shoulders as I took it all in. It was bigger than I expected—vaulted ceiling, obsidian-tiled floors, and walls the color of sandstone. Everything had weight. History.

The bed could have belonged to some long-dead emperor, pillars carved with jaguar heads at each corner, sheets crisp and white as bleached bone. Whoever designed the place went out of their way to make it look effortless, but you could practically hear the generational wealth creaking in the walls. Wealth that I had to remind myself—yet again—did not inherently belong to this family.

Stolen and brought on the backs of suffering. It may not have been Inecha, but history repeated itself in every corner of Herta.

They hadn't spared detail either. Dark mahogany beams crossed the ceiling, and at the far end, a sliding glass door opened out to a private courtyard filled with succulents, papaya trees, and a serpentine fountain. I caught the faintest scent of copal smoke still lingering in the air, and it reminded me of Sienna. Someone had tried to cleanse the room before I got here.

It was four hours until the gala. No assignments. No Mercer mess to clean up—Nola was on it, and with Ikari working his way back into the club, my role was paused for now.

Peeling off my travel clothes, I tossed them in a heap by the chair. The plane was still clinging to my skin. Recycled air, a light sweat from the crowd at the Chichen terminal, the grime of being touched, watched, followed, *gross*. Even flying first class, people found a way to test boundaries. Some holopad in your face, some whisper barely concealed. I hated the way it stuck to me. Like static.

The shower was its own sanctuary—floor to ceiling stone with copper fixtures and steam that built fast. I stood under the water until my shoulders relaxed and the heat chased out the last of the airport.

When I stepped out, I toweled off and glanced over at the suitcase someone had already unpacked for me as I stole away at the hot water. My suit was hung and steamed as Alanna had advised, my cufflinks placed in a velvet tray at my bedside. My mother's touch, no doubt.

I grabbed my phone and sent a quick check-in text to Sienna.

No reply, *still*.

Probably elbows deep in paint, or more likely, charging up another splurge on my card just to make a point about how *thrilled* she was about Alanna's deal. We'd fought over it, but she'd come around. She always did. She saw it for what it was—leverage. A backup in case things didn't fall our way. A safety net with sharp edges.

Still, her silence gnawed at me.

I slid on a loose linen shirt Sienna had packed for me and rolled the sleeves to my elbows, stepping into the hall in search of a meal. This side of the estate had a different air to it. Quieter. No staff hovering or bowing. Just long, echoing halls lined with carved reliefs and quiet judgment.

This wing wasn't curated for guests. It felt claimed.

I followed the faintest trace of food—beans, maybe some rice, and grilled fruit—down a narrower corridor when something caught my eye. A display case tucked into the corner, subtle, but too deliberate for my nosey ass to ignore. I slowed.

A tattered piece of paper with delicately placed inscriptions into the frayed sheet—clearly aged and stained. The significance to history damn near seeped out of it. Glyphs carved into stone were placed around it. Though *I* couldn't make out what any of it said. I knew someone who could...a woman who read the word of the old gods so well, it was as if they spoke to her. Symbols framed the case.

They pulsed with recognition. Like it knew me. My skin prickled.

I stepped closer, unable to resist.

There was power behind the glass. Old, patient magic that responded to my touch. Though I could not understand it, it clearly called to me.

"You lost?"

I don't scare easily, and I certainly don't jump. But, I admit, in that moment of distraction, Alanna's grandfather scared the shit out of me. He stood at the end of the corridor. His silk loungewear was sharp, no creases. I could easily be convinced the man ironed his socks.

"Looking for the kitchen," I said, attempting to maintain the confidence I was known for.

He studied me like I'd peeled paint off his walls. "Two lefts. Then follow the noise and chaos." His gaze flicked to the case and lingered. "That portion of the wing is closed to guests."

I nodded once, not bothering to smile, turned, and walked away without protest. I'd be back when the house was sleeping.

The gala was all velvet edges and polished stone. Light pooled from the high chandeliers—honey, warm and completely artificial. The music was string-heavy and elegant. My dark suit was tailored to perfection once put on and cut from something expensive yet understated. Alanna matched in color scheme, her dress more conservative than anything she'd worn in Inecha. It highlighted the local culture, silk and woven threads in deep earthy tones, delicate gold along the color.

She smiled only when she had to. And I didn't miss the tick of her jaw every time her grandfather directed her toward another one of his handpicked allies. The fakeness dripped off her like perfume now that I'd seen her multifaceted ways. Alanna lacked her usual insufferable attitude, which made the night easy to slide through instead of dragging along as I'd expected.

The ballroom hummed with forced laughter and clinking glasses, expensive cologne threaded through the air. My jacket itched against my collarbone. Across the room, her grandfather held court—the leeches in attendance pretending not to orbit him while doing exactly that.

After hours of boring fucking conversations, the two of us had tucked near the marble bar, behind a row of thick-set columns that kept the worst of the spotlight off us. She loosened in demeanor if only slightly. Tension leaked off her, the first honest breath of the night.

Her back wasn't ramrod straight anymore. One heel popped slightly off the floor as she leaned into the barstool. Alanna's fingers traced over the rim of her glass, her drink barely touched as the condensation dripped in lazy trails down the side.

She caught me staring. Not at her, exactly. Just...trying to read her. She was different here, in her home—less combative, more reserved. Even her dress was toned-down. Alanna blended into Mentiria as though she was born of it...and I guess, she was.

"You okay?" she asked, and her tone held no malice.

"Yeah."

It came out flat. True enough, though. She smiled. Not the smirk she typically bore as a weapon, but a smaller, unguarded one. Another glimpse of someone I hadn't quite become accustomed to being in proximity to.

"Okay." She shrugged.

My defensive shield slid back up, no longer interested in a relaxed conversation with someone who I needed to remember was the enemy, as easy as this evening had been. "What's funny?"

"I don't hate you right now."

That made me pause. "Well, I couldn't tell you hated me before." The sarcasm fell off my tone naturally. Back and forth was where any levels of comfort between us began and ended.

She obliged my jest. "Oh, I very much did," she said. "I'm just good at my job."

I offered a low breath of something reminiscent of amusement. "No need to put on a persona around me. I much prefer people who are who they say they are."

"It wouldn't have made a difference winning you over." Her eyes fell to her glass, and she swirled the white wine inside, her grandfather's choice. He'd curled a lip at her cup full of robust red and ensured the bar served her something that wouldn't stain if spilled.

"No. It wouldn't have."

There was no point in lying. She knew the truth now. There was never going to be anyone for me besides Sienna. The gods had deemed it true, and now the only focus I had was figuring out how to make that reality. Torn between my mate and the duty I was born into.

Inecha and its people, or the woman that I loved.

Those were my choices. And as easy as I wanted it to be to say fuck the world, a chance presented itself with the rebels to make the difference I'd always dreamed of enacting. It also put Sienna and me on opposite sides...again.

"But it mattered around your parents. And my *grandfather*," she added, scanning the crowd once more. "So the show had to go on."

I nodded, quiet. I wanted to ask—*What do you really want from me? From Inecha?* But the words didn't come out. Too many people nearby. Too many risks. It would only lead to larger questions that bit at my tongue...*How do you know all that you do? Who are you connected to? What do you truly stand for?* Alanna and her complexities had only added to the list of shit to sift through in my life.

She beat me to the next one.

"What's she like?"

"Who?"

She stared me up, then down, with an agitated yet amused expression. "Sienna."

My jaw tensed. This wasn't a conversation I'd prepared to be on the docket for the night. While it made me uncomfortable in the slightest of ways, speaking of her, painting her as something other than what the media attempted to depict of her...felt right.

"She is everything I wish I was. Inecha would be a better place if someone like *her* had a seat at the table."

The shift was immediate. I didn't need to look up to sense the way her spine straightened back up. The soft edges vanished. The air cooled like glass, fogging over. I cleared my throat, instinct kicking in to smooth it over. I was not comparing the two of them; it was merely a general statement, though it probably seemed a slight to her.

"I know what you meant," she cut me off. "Unfortunately, that's not how the world works. And now you're stuck with me."

She turned toward the center of the room, leaving me in her wake as she called over her shoulder. "Ready for the toast? Nights winding down."

I swallowed whatever the hells I thought I was about to say and followed her back into the performance.

The crowd parted with polite expectancy, every gaze sticky with interest as her hand closed around my wrist, then slid to intertwine our fingers. She tapped her glass with the back of a fork once we reached the mic near the orchestra in the center of the room. Her polished smile clicked back in place more weighted than armor.

"Good evening," she said, voice sweet as sugar. "My fiancé and I would love to thank you all for coming out tonight. Grandfather, it's always an honor to attend one of your events. The company you keep is truly...inspiring. I always leave feeling as though there is a greater impact to be served in the world. Around Mentiria, and now, Inecha."

Her grandfather gave a smug, approving nod from his place near the oversized fireplace. Alanna continued with more of the expected platitudes. "It's the time spent here that reminds one of how grateful we are for community, for unity, and for the legacy we carry forward..."

Her words blurred in my head. I could see the exact moment she wanted me to step in. Her grip tightened briefly on my arm. I lifted my glass and began a speech my parents had spent countless solits ensuring I could deliver with grace throughout my life.

"In just a few hours, I've spoken with brilliant minds, passionate leaders, and kind hosts. Your generosity and vision are humbling." I paused for dramatic effect, letting my eyes sweep over the guests. "Mentiria feels...strangely like home." *Truer words had never been spoken...fake ass...* "And I'm honored to begin building a future with you all."

I saw the way a few heads tilted. Interest. Curiosity. I leaned into it.

"To that end, I've made a twelve million solit donation to the Heart of Bajío Restoration Project. Their work rebuilding the schools, streets, and libraries honors those lost—including Alanna's dear mother. It reminds us that the past should never be buried. Only remembered. And rebuilt with integrity, care."

The silence hit first. A beat too long. I fought to keep the smugness off my face. I knew what I'd done. What I'd said. Then came the applause—tentative, then roaring, fed by cameras and champagne.

Alanna's fingers twitched against mine. She looked at me, *really* looked. Pride I hadn't asked for nor cared to receive hung there. The surprise on her face wasn't performative. It cracked through her mask with something like real emotion. Soft and startled. Fae.

She leaned in and kissed my cheek. It wasn't for me. It was for the press, the room, and her grandfather. But part of it felt real anyway—a silent thank you of two fae on opposing sides coming to an understanding.

The cameras ate it up, anyway. A perfect image of unity. We smiled. We toasted. And to my utmost pleasure, we withstood the fiery glare her grandfather sent our way for the rest of the night.

After what had dragged on for an eternity of handshakes and posed farewells, the ballroom finally cleared. Staff moved in to sweep up shattered crystal and discarded programs. Alanna and I walked side by side down the long, tiled corridor, her heels clicking a metronome between us. We hadn't spoken directly since the toast.

"Thank you," she said.

"For?"

She kept walking without bothering to spare me a glance. "The deal was half up-front, half at a later date. You exceeded such."

"The money does no good rotting in my bank account. It can't follow me to the grave. You have your reasons," I shrugged and loosened the knot of my tie. "I have mine."

What I didn't say: that I'd had the Mercers dig into Heart of Bajío and Alanna before coming. That I'd watched footage of her at groundbreakings, talking to kids in dust-filled neighborhoods littered with destruction from war. No cameras that she knew of. No handlers. Just her and a cause. And that tonight, when she spoke on the topics she cared deeply for, the mask didn't slip because it wasn't on.

At least that part of her was real. That was enough.

"Sure," she said, giving a small, knowing smile, her eyes flickering back down to my mark.

"Can you see it?" I asked, grabbing her arm and stopping her from disappearing behind her door.

Her brows furrowed, hazel eyes trained on mine, a slight glimmer behind them. "Goodnight, Koa."

"Goodnight, Alanna."

Hours passed. The estate had gone still, the hush of the deep night the only thing ringing in my ears. When I was sure the staff had retired and the corridors were empty, I slipped back out, barefoot against the tile.

The hallway was darker now, lit only by wall sconces. I made my way to the wing that was apparently forbidden, to the alcove I'd clocked earlier—a glass case buried into the corner like an afterthought.

I stood there for a long time. Just...feeling it.

Magic buzzed faintly along the glass. It was ancient, I knew it in the depths of my bones. They remembered what I could not. What I was certain my ancestors did. The very essence of my being fought to remember this simple artifact as though it once mattered.

I took photos from every angle—close up, wide, the surrounding floor tiles, even the faint symbols etched into the base. My fingers tingled the entire time.

I knew better than to send the pictures in the group chat. Instead, I drafted a single message.

[The Detectives + Wren]

Me:

> **Found something. Might be nothing. Might be everything we didn't even know to search for.**

I hit send and stared at the screen as I lay in bed. Inecha was in a different time zone—three hours ahead. They'd all be asleep. No point in waiting.

Even as I lay back in the dark, the buzz of that old magic lingered as if it hadn't finished speaking yet.

29

WREN

Sitting outside of Aantaj Labs was the last place I wanted to be. For a multitude of reasons. It was break, and I'd be spending it with Mira…and the rest of our new 'friend group.' Never in a million years would I have guessed that I'd be referring to Jed and Adler as friends. Koa was one thing. We didn't have the decades of feuding. For the Mercers, our grandfathers, all those years ago, had been the ones to spark the hatred, and we'd done nothing but continue it.

The hate seemed to be diluted with each son born; it was hard to maintain hate for someone in an identical circumstance. There were too many other worthy people to reserve that disdain. We'd had jobs together, thanks to both of us being tied to the Cynod involuntarily, but we did our parts and got the fuck out. It wasn't until recently that I'd even really seen them as people. Them helping find Sienna, us going to the same school, having mutuals, especially the fact that they were dating Mira's friend. It all made them more real.

I wasn't sure how they felt, but I was ready to focus all of my violent energy on the true enemy. Either way, going to the beach house was going to be interesting to say the least. Couldn't get there without dealing with this first.

With my darkest pair of shades on, I got out of my car and walked toward the entrance. This building was where all the secret shit went on. With The Doctor's office being here, and all the initiatives he kept close. Security spotted me and waved me through, pointing me toward the side stairwell that put me right at Dr. Aantaj's office. They did it every time I came, as if I'd forget where to go. I felt their eyes on me until the door closed. Even if I wanted to be a threat to the man, I couldn't be. Not while I was under this blood bond.

It rushed through my veins as I got closer to him. There were stories I'd heard from the time of the gods that they would have their most loyal subjects bond to them in this way. Sovereign leaders would do the same. For some, it was seen as a privilege; for others, it was their demise. These were deemed forbidden a very long time ago, and it became clear to me why once I was under one myself. It fought against everything in me, like my will was water, and his was oil. A sticky reminder that I was tied to him. If I went against our agreement, my blood would turn solid, and I'd be dead in seconds.

Very few were permitted in this section of the building, and when I noticed his office entrance was ajar, I ensured the stairwell door didn't slam. There was a gallery into the labs to the right of me, so I couldn't stay here long without someone potentially seeing me. I moved as slowly and precisely as I could, trying to hear anything in the room.

A woman's voice reached me first. "It's not working."

Then Dr. Aantaj. "Failure is not an option. Keep testing and refining."

"I've done every test I can think of!" The woman responded, the shuffle of a chair following behind it.

"Go back over her notes. There has to be something you're missing. I'll overlook this outburst once, not again."

A clear dismissal, and I picked up my pace so I looked like I was just now reaching this floor. The woman rushed by me, dark hair hanging in front of her face. Something about her felt familiar, and when I glanced back, she was also staring at me over her shoulder.

It was Iris.

I knew she worked in the labs, but I'd never seen her in this building. She huffed as if I were merely another inconvenience in her day and turned away.

"You're early," Dr. Aantaj said as I filled the doorway.

"By five minutes," I responded and sat across from him.

I'd met a lot of authoritative men. They all had certain ways of going about things. Some of them were all force, making sure we remembered our place. Some tried an odd camaraderie, where they pretended to understand and relate to us. The latter were typically men who fought their way to the top. The former were the ones born into power.

Dr. Aantaj was an odd combination of the two. It was hard to predict what version of him you'd get. One day he'd be positive and smiles, the other, hard lines and stern.

He sat forward. "I'd rather you be early than late."

I didn't know why I was here. He didn't tell me the purpose of the meeting, only asked—commanded that I'd show up. Most of our contact was done over the phone, and there wasn't anything I owed him right now. Not to mention, there hadn't been nearly as much interaction between us after the car crash. Minutes passed, but he broke first.

"How is your progress going with Mira?"

"Good."

His nose twitched, and my blood boiled. "More than that."

Fuck, I hated this. My mind and body fought against the magic, trying to find the right thing to say.

"I think she trusts me," I said. Not a lie, but not in the way he assumed I meant it either.

"Excellent. That will be pertinent soon."

"What does that mean?"

"Nothing as of yet. You'll be made aware when it's time. I wanted to make sure you were still on track before you went on break." He tugged on the bond, my blood stopping cold in my veins as he grinned at my pain. "Use this time to get as close as you can."

That was all this was. The blood bond was always there, but only when we were in person could he give me a physical reminder. The lack of contact didn't mean I was off the hook; it only meant I wasn't useful to him at the time. I shook it off and straightened, trying to grasp at any strings of dignity that remained.

"If I knew what I was preparing her for, it might be more helpful," I said with caution.

His eyes narrowed on me, but he had no reason to believe I'd turned on him. I was still alive, my blood still flowed, so I hoped he took the bait.

"Mira has been a test subject in my labs for quite some time. She has been the consistent variable in her aunt's work, and it seems her blood will be needed again. Iris thought she could recreate what Celeste did, but she's having...difficulty. If she doesn't work through this, you will either have to draw it yourself or bring her to us for a." He paused. "Larger sample."

Bet you're fucking happy the crash didn't do what it was meant to, now. I steadied my heartbeat and nodded. "Understood."

"Enjoy your break. By the time it's over, we should have made headway in the next phase." He flicked his gaze toward the door, and his desktop monitor flashed.

"Alright," I said as I got up I made for the door, but turned around before leaving. "Once this is done, will I be released from the bond?"

"I don't see why that would be necessary."

"You have me on a contract, I've proven myself. Why would this still be needed?"

He continued reading his computer monitor. "I prefer a guarantee. Without one, you can go slink into the shadows and do as you please. This way, that promise flows through your body."

"That wasn't said at the time I agreed. Voluntarily, might I add."

"You were eager to protect; you should have stopped to think about what you were doing." He lifted his phone to his ear, not allowing me to respond.

Eager to save my girlfriend from whatever the fuck he was planning. I took the long way out of the building, following the path I saw Iris take. Looking over the gallery, I located the lab she'd been working in. If Mira were here, she could probably tell me exactly what it was she was doing, but from this spot, all I saw was her writing on a whiteboard. Vials of blood were lined up on a metal table, and another young man in a lab coat was bringing a case of something else in.

Security turned the corner, and I dipped my chin as I passed him. Iris flipped the whiteboard and pushed it across the space, her assistant clutching a clipboard with wide eyes. The staircase turned away from Iris' office, so I didn't see what happened next, but I pulled out my phone to text Mira.

Mira was already inside when I pulled up to her tía's house. I liked that I didn't need to park down the street. The only upside to this situation with Aantaj was that I no longer needed to ensure we weren't seen. Discretion wasn't a requirement. I didn't ask if her parents knew of the predicament. Mostly because I was too afraid of what the answer would do to her. She didn't hold much affection or hope for them, but if we could avoid adding to that plate, I would.

With the news of our crash being blasted across headlines it was almost a certainty they were privy to our relationship. Gods knew what would happen the next time we were captured in public together. ChismeChak would pay a pretty solit for a solid incriminating pic.

Being back here brought back the memory of that night. That night, the genuine connection we'd had, the way she let me see all of her...that made the decision to do the blood bond simple. Mira wasn't someone just anyone could read easily. The world had made her that way, but that night, I saw the vulnerability and emotions she kept close.

Something about seeing her in this place she grew up, no mask on, open and comfortable in my presence, made me want to keep her like that. I'd do whatever was necessary to let that be her reality. Not only in these walls, but anywhere. I didn't want her afraid to face a damn thing, because she knew I'd be there facing it with her.

Knocking once, I turned the knob and walked through the door. Mira said she might be in the attic, and to let myself in. As expected, she was still up there, trying to carry some large floaty down the ladder.

"Might have been easier if you deflated it," I said as I rushed over to grab it from her.

She laughed, a smile stretching across her face that made my heart jump. "That's what my tía said. Do you know how much breath it took to inflate that?"

"Well, now you have magic." I snatched her down from the ladder by her hips.

Swiping a rogue curl from in front of her eyes, she leaned closer to me. "You know, I keep forgetting that."

I stood still as a rock, letting her be the one to determine how this would go. Had it been a few weeks ago, I would have swooped in for a kiss without a second thought. Now, I didn't want to rush her or make her think that I expected that already. She wrapped her arms around me, nuzzling her face into my chest, which, honest to the gods, was as good as a kiss.

"You smell amazing," she said as she took a deep inhale.

I winked. "I know how much you like that."

Mira picked up the floaty and tossed it into a pile of things she gathered. That was the downside to living in the dorms, with limited storage, there wasn't room for anything outside of the necessities. One thing that I could always expect was for Mira to be prepared for literally everything. There were cards and board games, beach towels and chairs, an assortment of children's toys, and I pointed to one of the buckets.

"You going to build a sandcastle?" I teased.

"Yeah," she responded, no humor in her tone. "Why else go to the beach?"

We laughed at the same time, and fuck did it feel good. Mira gestured for me to follow her into the kitchen and handed me a cold water bottle.

"Okay, what did you need to tell me?"

This was the hard part. I couldn't directly say what Dr. Aantaj was up to. There were specific parameters: I couldn't tell anyone who bonded me, I couldn't advise of his plan, and I couldn't interfere against Dr. Aantaj's wishes.

There was a fuck ton of gray in there, but the consequence of going too far was irreversible.

"Let's play SketchGuess."

30

MIRA

Lucky for Wren, we had a large SketchGuess pad and easel. Sienna, of course, won almost every time we played. At this moment, I really wished she were here to interpret, because I had no idea what the fuck Wren was trying to say.

"I'm trying to work around this as much as I can. I don't know which parts will fuck with the bond," Wren mumbled under his breath as he scribbled more lines. "But this is not my strong suit."

Every time I'd been in this house since my tía's death had been a little bit easier. I still felt the weight of memories, but they weren't as heavy as before. The blanket in my lap right now was her favorite, the one she'd snuggle up with every evening. My fingers ran over the soft fabric as Wren took an unsure step back.

"That much is clear." I narrowed my eyes. "A flower."

"What *kind* of flower?"

There were ruffles at the perimeter of the petals, three darker, bigger ones bracketing the stem.

"An...iris flower? Oh! Iris?" I asked eagerly.

"Boom," Wren said, tapping the word 'yes' he'd written in the top left corner.

I clapped, excited that I was right, but the excitement waned as I realized this wasn't good. The next one was easy to decipher: a syringe and blood drops. He drew an arrow from the blood to another stick figure drawing with curly hair and a flat smile.

"Is that supposed to be me?" I gasped, offended.

He sketched a smile and added boobs and ass, and I shook my head with a chuckle.

"Okay, it's me. She wants my blood? It wouldn't be the first time. I've been part of the trial for this drug for years."

He circled 'yes.'

I understood why that would be an immediate concern to him. Not everyone grew up giving a couple vials of blood to their relative every few weeks. It was odd that they needed it now after all this time.

"Why now is the question. I haven't participated in anything for months." I bit my nail and sat back on the couch.

"Problems," Wren said with a bead of sweat gathering on his brow.

"Don't push it too hard," I said, and he relaxed his shoulders with a deep breath.

I wasn't sure if I could save him if the blood bond moved too quickly. Anything involving magic on magic wasn't the most uncomplicated process.

"Whatever hypothesis they made previously must have been negated with someone else's blood. Iris is the only one who can answer these questions." I pulled out my phone.

"Whoa, what are you doing?" Wren rushed over to me.

"We need to talk. She said I could reach out to her if I needed to when I saw her on campus. Later that day, she sent me a burner phone number," I explained.

I was almost certain this place, between these four walls, would be a safe place. A neutral location she wouldn't dare sully. At least that's what I hoped.

Wren stared down at my phone before flicking his gaze up to my eyes. "I still don't like it."

"Well—" I dialed, "—you should have been better at SketchGuess."

Wren tapped his body—hips, ankle, and belt line. The places he normally kept weapons. He sat beside me, watching the door as if she'd manifest. One thing about Wren, particularly these days, was that he never tried to change my mind. He'd let me know how he felt, and then would get right behind whatever decision I made.

"Hey, Iris. It's Mira. I think it's time for that chat."

Against his better judgment, Wren decided to stay in my old bedroom while Iris was here. He said he'd be monitoring and would come out if it was needed. If Iris hurt me here, she truly wasn't the person I thought she was.

"She's pulling up," I said in the doorway of my bedroom.

Wren had a gun in one hand and a knife resting on his lap as he sat in my desk chair. I could feel the desire to protect me beating against the parameters of what he was able to do in this particular situation.

"It's going to be okay," I reassured, thinking that this specific scenario would be much more fun without his shirt and the person standing on my porch.

Iris knocked on the door, forcing me to leave Wren behind. The last time she was here, I was sure she let herself in. So much had changed since then. I turned the knob and found her still in her work clothes minus her lab coat.

"Come on in." I gestured for her to enter the living room.

Her hands were in fists, shaking as she wrapped her arms around her body and whispered, "I haven't been back here."

"It feels wrong without her," I offered, but I wasn't in that place of my grief anymore. Not after I'd spoken to my tía, since I'd moved forward.

Iris nodded, and I watched as she decided between sitting in her normal spot or somewhere else. Instead, she chose to stand awkwardly in the middle of the room.

"So what did you want to talk to me about?" Iris asked.

I could practically sense Wren in the room. Iris didn't walk around or check for anyone, and I wondered if it was her comfort here or if she wasn't quite used to being the bad guy yet.

"You knew that Dr. Aantaj was the one who ordered the crash, yes?"

Iris' eyes narrowed, a coldness falling over her. "Perhaps."

Off to a great start.

"What else do you know?" I pushed.

"You're going to have to be more specific."

"Am I a factor in your current work?"

Iris bit her cheek, the angle of her jaw changing sharply. "As much as I tried to change that, yes."

That meant she failed. Whatever attempt she made with the drugs didn't pan out, and she was back to square one. *I* happened to be square one.

"What are you trying to do with the drugs?" I said as I took a step forward.

"Mira..." she trailed off.

I didn't let up. "Tell me. I'm tired of everything *happening* to me. I want to know. You owe me that."

"There are big players here. You saw what happened to Celeste, what almost happened to you," she said, and the battle between who she was before, and who she was now raged behind her eyes.

"You're still alive, so there has to be a reason. I could ask why you weren't found with my tía, but I'm not. What is Aantaj after?"

Her eyes lined with tears for just a second before she blinked them away. "She hid some things from me, you know. I knew why she wanted to make sure you were protected, I thought it was the same reasons as me. In some ways, it was, but there was another level. One I think you are familiar with now."

"Perhaps," I said, mocking.

"I started on this project because I wanted to slow the effects of diseases directly impacted by our nahuales. Arcanoma was the first thing I wanted to cure. We realized the drug could act as a barrier in some cases. We wanted it to cure disease. Aantaj saw another opportunity."

"What she did with me...He knows the effects it had on my nahual?" I responded.

"No. Not that it blocked you from emerging. He knows the parts we tested on anxiety, but your blood, for whatever reason, has been the most receptive to every test we've run."

It was likely that she hid it. Shit, I didn't even know what it did to me until after I stopped taking them. It did help with my anxiety, but the more I thought about it, I had a feeling it was numbing my senses to a certain degree. Yes, our nahuales didn't emerge until this age, but they were with us the moment we were born. Mine experienced everything on a level beyond the average fae. Sensed things unseen to the naked eye. I wondered if all these years, every time things got to be too much, part of me was experiencing things my body didn't know what to do with. A healthy mixture of that and general anxiety, I was sure.

"My blood won't be used to hurt people," I stated firmly.

"I don't want it to either. I need to figure out how to focus him back on the disease. Until then, I'm playing along with whatever it is I need for that to happen. At the end of the day, he owns the research. He can do whatever he wants with it."

"That doesn't seem worth the risk."

"Hundreds of thousands of people *die* because of what I'm trying to cure. I'm not taking part in stripping people of their magic. If he takes my work and does that, it's on him."

My nahual took over my vision for a moment, showing me that she was serious—her version of genuine honesty. The blue radiated, pulsing before evening out and mixing with the yellow and the orange. It wasn't the bright yellow I'd seen in others; it was dark, like it had been blended with a teaspoon of black. Iris felt it, even if she couldn't see it, she sensed that something was happening in the air around her.

"She would never make that compromise. That's why she's dead and you aren't," I whispered, and just as I thought I was through my grief, it came rushing back. My world spun, and I stumbled back into a floor lamp. "Did you know what was going to happen to her?"

"Mira..." Iris stepped toward me, but Wren emerged from the bedroom with his gaze on the broken ceramic lamp.

Iris barked a laugh, whatever comfort she was ready to give me, vanishing. "You are an *idiot*," she spat at Wren. "There is no way whatever you think you're doing is going to work."

Wren stepped between us. "Step away from her."

"I broke the lamp, not her," I reassured. It wasn't a physical blow that hurt me. "Iris, what happened to you? How did you turn into a person who could do that? Tía would be ashamed."

It was clear that Wren wasn't playing the part assigned by Aantaj. Between him hiding in the first place, and the genuine concern for me all over his face, Iris clocked it immediately.

"She was ashamed. She died mortified at what I was willing to do for our research. For her, I won't tell Dr. Aantaj whatever it is that's going on here. I'll make a mistake right now, but it won't happen again. I'm going to save lives, Mira. You watch."

"You won't be getting a drop of my blood," I snapped.

She looked at Wren. "If it comes to that, it won't be me who makes that happen."

Without another word, she left the house. We sat in the thick air of the words she left behind.

"Can he do that? Force you to bring me in?" I asked, quiet.

"He hasn't used it in that way yet. Just as a contingency that I'd listen to him. I don't *think* he can control me, but I really don't know."

I peered back at the stack of old books my tía had collected, and the one I'd taken from Dr. Puebla. It wasn't the type of beach reading I planned on, but it'd do.

"Well, I'm going to figure it out."

31

KOA

Sienna hopped off my lap and rushed over to Mira, Katia already scrambling toward her with a gelatin shot, demanding she catch up. The Mercers exchanged a glance, the tension in the room stifling as Wren lingered in the doorway with their bags. We had damn near a week here—without true peace established, things could get dicey.

I hadn't exaggerated when I'd cautioned Mira about the fragility of the relationship between clans. Outside of their generational feud, trust had been violated. As far as the Mercers were concerned, a slight to me was a slight to us all. *I* was the closest to Wren besides Mira, so if he'd betrayed me—betrayed us—what other shady shit was he capable of? The only thing we were really worth was the integrity of our word.

There was only one way to control how this little gathering went. I'd promised Mira I'd "lead by example". If I could forgive him or whatever, then the Mercers could work through their shit. Maybe. Fuck if I knew. I wasn't used to this—the whole friendship and feelings thing. Might as well finish the night braiding each other's hair and reading *human smut*. I cringed at the thought.

Sienna tipped her chin at me. *'Be nice.'*

'If you told me four months ago, I'd—'

'Then what?' Her brow lifted, and Mira glanced between us, chewing on the inside of her cheeks from being left out of the conversation.

"Ikari," I said, moving toward the glass sliding doors. The roar of the ocean rushed in as the tide gnawed at the sand. "Come grab a smoke."

Jed cut for the front door, ripping the bags from Wren's hands with a growl. "Don't need to worry about any wires or trackers, do I, Ikari?"

"Stay out of my shit," Wren snapped. His eyes slid to the offending Mercer. A simple glance, but enough to set off his instincts. His canines bared low in defense at the knowledge he was on enemy territory with the wrong numbers.

To my disappointment, my sister interrupted the show, her hand pressed against Jed's chest in hopes of pushing him backward. He side-eyed me and backed away. I may have wanted to see the show, but anything other than obliging my sister would piss me off, their home or not.

"Katia said it was an open invitation, didn't you, Katia?" Mira glanced over her shoulder at her amused friend.

Katia lounged behind them like a bored goddess, eating an apple slice and dipping it into a jar of peanut butter Adler was holding with an arched brow and smile. "I did."

"Are you calling your girlfriend a liar?" Mira asked, her tone all innocent poison.

"Oh, I'm not—"

"You're *not*?" Jed stumbled at Katia's words, clearly caught off guard.

It came at the same time as Adler's nervous cough behind him, Katia's finger now frozen inside the jar of peanut butter.

She removed it slowly and turned her amused gaze on both of them. "You know, I'm starting to think maybe I should've extended the invitation directly through me instead of Mira. Then maybe my charming, almost-boyfriends wouldn't be so rude to my guests."

Jed opened his mouth, shut it, and looked to Adler like he was searching for a script.

"You're not rude," Katia went on, tilting her head to wink at my sister. "Do this for me, then maybe I'd be inclined to say yes to your incessant demands to put a title on things."

Adler sighed, resigned. "What do you want?"

She perked up from the couch and took the jar of peanut butter from him to free his hands. "Hmm. A drink, for starters. Something cold. Then maybe pay the pizza spot extra to get some food here within the next ten minutes. I have been so gracious with my time. Let's not forget about the plane ride over here."

Jed was already halfway to the kitchen.

"What happened on the plane ride here?" Sienna asked with naïve curiosity.

"Too much," Wolfe said, his first words since Wren arrived and pushed to his feet to refill his drink. "Way too fucking much to have their cousin on board and only one bathroom to hide in."

"We took their smaller jet," Katia explained behind a performative hand meant to block out her loud whisper. "Apparently, it's solar-powered or whatever. Guess money really can buy the impossible."

"Anything else?" Adler asked through a tight smile, joining his brother in the kitchen.

"Yeah, a chair for Wren and for all the Mercers on the property to stop looking like you're about to piss on the rug."

"Focus." Mira snapped her fingers to drag Adler's attention back to her. "We're guests in your home, and a good host doesn't check their guests' belongings." She set her sights on Wolfe, who ultimately had the final say, being it was his house in name and title. "I wouldn't disrespect you by bringing anything that could break your trust, and neither would Wren. Let's just have a good time, okay?"

Two sharp, ear-piercing whistles sang through the air in my impatience. Wren's eyes snapped to mine, and he crossed the room full of Mercers with nothing short of confident swagger. He slid the glass door closed behind us. I kept my back to him, lighting my first smoke of the night. There were bound to be plenty...I mean, what could go wrong when you mix drinking games, drugs, and two hardly amicable clans? *Yeah, the whole trip is probably fucked.* And by *probably*, I meant the clock was ticking.

"What are your regrets?" I said, blowing smoke into Wren's face, and leaned against the deck railing.

"Pardon?"

There was a bite in his tone that, quite frankly, didn't sit right with my temper. His hands remained in his pockets, a slight shrug of his shoulder, all so...relaxed. Casual. I decided to find the calm that Sienna swore I could attain through deep breaths to understand his position. He was up in arms after being cornered by the Mercers. *Sure. Yeah. I'll leave it at that.*

'His reality is not the same as your perception, Snake.' Sienna stood against the glass doors, drink in her hand, back to us as she engaged in conversation with the others.

We'd found that with the bond and practice, I could keep my mental walls down for her to engage first whenever she pleased—within a reasonable distance, of course. I'd never tried before being mated. Never had a reason to. She'd hidden it well, but Mira was a bit frustrated with that development, feeling slightly left out. Nearly an entire night of attempt after attempt, and the second I eased off that thin tendril of our mental bridge, all communication between us came to a halt.

"There was no hesitation in my words or a stutter from my tongue, Ikari," I tried again, attempting a patient smile through gritted teeth. Ashing the butt of the cigarette, I took another pull, studying him over narrowed eyes. "I don't give a shit about apologies. I want to know what ate your soul the most. That's the tax on my forgiveness."

To my complete and utter surprise, Wren godsdamn Ikari listed them without hesitation. "Mira. My greatest regret is how my actions hurt Mira."

"How poetic." I rolled my eyes.

"I mean it. I had her trust, and I broke it. I don't take that shit lightly. I have...strong feel—"

"Yeah." I held out the cigarette with a grimace and cut him off. He took it with a grin. "I got that. Refrain from telling me more."

"No, let's do this, *brother*. You want to get sentimental." He spread his arms out wide, opening up his chest. "I'm an open book within reason."

"Within blood bonds," I snarled in reflex.

'Don't start, Venom,' I snapped before she could cut in. *'This is me being civil.'*

The light whisper of her laughter echoed through my mind. *'No one said a thing.'*

"Yes. Within blood bonds. Which is the *only* reason I did not bring you in once I suspected the true intentions. You're her protector. I know that no matter what, you'll be the last thing standing between her and even a hint of danger. You can't do that if you're dead for playing hero and breaking a damn blood bond at the first opportunity that arises."

"Hero," I scoffed. A humorous thought.

"For those girls in there, yes."

Despite the retort that rose in my throat at such a claim, I could hardly say he was wrong. For Sienna and Mira, I would do anything, including give my life—and I guess since Katia would probably do the same for them, she fell under my umbrella of protection. The handle of said umbrella, but nevertheless, she fell under it.

"I don't use the term *brother* with you lightly. I've said it a few times," Wren said, holding my stare and passing the cigarette back to me. "I mean it each time."

The sincerity of the moment made me feel weird. Normal, maybe. A genuine relationship, friendship, not based on any other exchange other than the mutual desire to not want to fucking kill each other six times per interaction. With Wren, it was more like two. When he started a sentence and when he finished it. Never the in-between.

Naturally, I gave him my back and turned toward the water. "I regret beating the shit out of you."

"That's not how I recall it," a sharp, clipped laugh filtered in from my right side as Wren leaned against the spot next to me on the railing. "And no, you don't."

A smile dared to crack across my face. "You're right, I don't. I eat my cereal while replaying that shit in my head every morning. Run to it. Shower to it. Fucking frankly, I close my eyes and fall asleep to it."

"No one's forcing us to talk this out," he said, slapping a hand down on my shoulder and nodding at the party clearly ramping up inside. Mira and Sienna danced on the island in the kitchen as Katia tossed ones at them. She reached back with the snap of her fingers every so often as Jed and Adler shuffled her more. "I'm good if you are. The fight at the club was enough, if I'm being completely honest."

I tossed the butt of the cig into the sand and jerked back in mock disbelief. "Ikari, shut the fuck up and go inside before you make me mad. This conversation was obviously sponsored by my little sister, and if you're wise, you'll continue to attempt her good graces."

"Lesson learned, trust me."

"A little soon for that, no?" I snarked, glad he found the humor in it as we made our way back inside.

32

MIRA

I slid down to sit on the island as Wren came in from talking to my brother. It was hard to see through the glass how it went. There weren't any bloody noses or bruised knuckles, so I assumed it went as well as it could have. Adler hadn't taken his eyes off Wren; in that light, this was going to be a long trip.

I understood where they were coming from. It was their house, but who else did they think I'd bring when given a plus one? Wren either didn't notice or pretended not to. Probably the latter, he didn't miss much. Sienna continued her dancing as Katia clapped to the beat of her ass shaking.

Wren put both of his hands on either side of my body, caging me in and leaning close to my ear.

"Go ahead and ask," he said.

"Are we going to have problems this week?" I asked quickly.

"Nah. Koa and I are cool. Mercers will be fine. Can't say we'll be playing card games or anything tonight, but fine."

Maybe not a card game...

I pulled back, looking over my shoulder. "Let's play truth or dare!"

Sienna and Katia cheered, moving out of the kitchen and into the living room area.

"Mira." Wren dragged me closer, his arm around my back.

"It'll be fun. Call it an icebreaker. I want us all to have a good time. Fighting each other isn't going to get us anywhere anymore." I brought my lips to his ear. "I'll make it worth it."

He let out an exhale, his arm flexing before he gripped my hips and stood me on my feet. "Fine."

Koa sat at the end of the couch with his arms crossed. "Feel like it's worth noting this may not be the best idea, Meems."

"I think everything that could have gone wrong has already. Might be a little tense at first, but embrace the fun, bro." I slapped the back of his neck as I passed him, and he grunted.

Thankfully, this house was gigantic, and the living room alone had enough space for all the machismo and egos filling the air. Three couches sat in a U shape, with a marble coffee table in the middle. A knock on the door had all the men standing to their feet with weapons raised. So much for easing the tension.

"Who else are we expecting?" Jed asked.

Wolfe flicked a switch, and a series of monitors lowered from the ceiling. Surveillance covered every inch of the beach house, it seemed. Atlas, Wren's brother, walked in with two large duffel bags. It was clear that they weren't full of clothes as he dropped them to the ground, looking surprised to see us all.

"What are you doing here? Thought you had a job?" Wren asked.

"Owed Wolfe some shit. What the fuck kind of party is this?" Atlas responded.

"Wasn't my idea." Wolfe stood and opened one of the bags. "This is everything?"

"Everything you asked for. Two more in my trunk," Atlas said.

"Help me put it in the safe," Wolfe said, the two of them walking away as if we all weren't watching the encounter.

I leaned closer to Wren. "Are they...friends?"

"Would be the first time I'm hearing of it," he said, his gaze still on the hallway they walked down.

I prayed to the gods this shit wouldn't go sideways. Who knew what Atlas brought here or why Wolfe needed it?

"Anyway!" Katia stood and clapped. "How do you all play? I think Jundi has its own unique way."

Right, the game.

"Go around the circle, pick truth or dare. Draw names from a bowl for who gets to come up with what you do. Drink if you can't do it," I said.

"Perfect. Very similar to our way," she responded.

"Well, what's the difference?" Sienna asked.

"Ours involves knives…"

"Yup, we're going to avoid that. Not with this crowd," I said as I grabbed a notebook and wrote our names.

Wolfe hadn't come back, so I didn't write his. Everyone else went into the decorative bowl already on the coffee table. I really, really hoped this wasn't a terrible idea. It could go either way.

"Atlas is staying," Wolfe said as he returned to the room.

Wren's eyes narrowed on his brother, who didn't make eye contact but sat beside me. I quickly added them into the bowl.

"Alright, since it's my idea, I'll go first," I said. "Everyone has their drinks?"

The group of criminals, plus Sienna and Katia, nodded, lifting their cups.

I swirled my hand in the bowl dramatically, grabbing out a paper and unfolding it. "Ha, Sienna."

"Cosmically connected," Sienna said as she sat forward. "Truth or dare?"

She probably expected me to tell the truth, but I figured I'd do the unexpected today.

"Dare."

"Oh shit, okay…" Sienna looked around the room. "Koa, you might want to close your eyes."

Koa grumbled and pulled the strings of his hood tight enough to cover his whole face. "Fucking great."

"Remember that music video we were super obsessed with last summer?"

"Sienna…"

"Do the move." My best friend got up—knowing I'm not nearly intoxicated enough for this—and pulled Wren into the open space. "You can stay right here, bud."

I stood and chugged some of my drink. "He is far too tall for it."

Sienna had already thought through it, placing a sturdy footrest a couple of feet in front of him with a smile.

Well, here goes nothing. Wren watched me cautiously, both excitement and confusion etched on his features as I stretched my arms. Sienna and I had practiced this move on each other approximately 100 times until we got it. When my tía walked in during it, I think she had more questions than anything, but she just left us to our foolery.

I glared at Sienna with my tongue out before I turned back to Wren, placed my hands on the footrest, and popped into a handstand. Thankfully, the stool was the perfect height, and the back of my knees lined up with his shoulders. I used my core muscles to pull myself up into a sitting position, Wren's mouth lined up with my...other core.

Katia and Sienna cheered, and when Wren looked around my body, all the boys averted their gazes quickly.

"Is my sister done being a harlot yet?" Koa asked, still covered by his hood. "Truce or not, I'm not above beating your face in, Ikari."

I dismounted, doing the whole move backward and ending in a curtsy. "All done, Mr. Puritan."

Wren's hand found my side as we sat down, pulling me closer as he whispered. "We'll be coming back to that."

"I'm sitting right fucking here," Koa grumbled as he downed his drink and snapped for the pitcher of party punch.

My best friend mock-cheered me with her drink like that was her plan all along, and I nudged Wren to pick a name out of the bowl. He picked one out, unraveling it and chuckling sarcastically as he flipped it around for us to see.

"Adler."

There were more people who weren't fond of each other in this room than there were the opposite, so the chances of this happening were pretty high.

Adler ran his hand down his goatee and sat forward. "Truth or dare."

Wren held his gaze. "Truth."

Jed looked to his twin, and if I didn't know better, I'd think they had some sort of telepathy like Koa. There were endless questions to be asked between them.

Years of built-up resentment, even if there was a short stint of working together recently. They weren't at the center of that; Sienna was, and everyone in this room would drop what they needed to help her.

"Why did your grandfather do it?" Adler asked.

"Party foul," Sienna muttered, slouching in her seat.

'It' was loaded. When their grandfathers—the Mercer's and Ikari's—were set up by the Cynod, it turned them all against each other. I'd heard the Ikari side, their grandfather agreeing that they would work with the Cynod to protect their more vulnerable family members.

"Do what? He agreed for the same reasons yours did," Wren responded.

"Why did he rat us out?" Adler followed up.

"You think my grandfather is the one who set them up?"

Accusations weren't taken lightly with this group, so Adler didn't say yes, but you could tell it was what he meant.

"And what do you think he got out of it? I'm right there with you, working for them against my will."

"They said it was him. He got a better deal than we did," Jed added.

Atlas looked at his brother, both of them more than confused.

"Our contracts are identical. I've seen them," Atlas explained.

"They are indeed. Down to the final dot," Wolfe chimed in.

Jed and Adler turned to Wolfe with surprise as they spoke at the exact same time, "Why would you not tell us that?"

Wolfe raised a shoulder. "Found out this year. Didn't seem worth a mention after this long. People believe what they want."

"If you are fighting each other, you can't fight them. Never believe anything they say," I said.

The fun and exciting atmosphere officially fizzled out as they sat in silence, looking down at their hands.

"Well, this was a buzzkill," Katia mumbled. "Everyone drink!"

Koa watched the Mercers and Ikaris in the room with caution, like this might have blown up the delicate balance they had. Katia's exclamation was actually a demand, and she took it upon herself to lift cups to mouths until everyone was back to their previous state of buzz.

"My turn." She pulled out a name. "Mira. Give me a dare."

"I dare you to put an apple on Jed's head and roast it with your dragon fire," I said, tapping my fingers together.

"How the hells did I get pulled into this?" Jed stood, clinging to his locs as if his life depended on it.

"Oh, hush. I won't burn your hair. I like it too much." Katia grabbed Jed and lined his body against the wall.

She put a cup on his head, then the apple atop the cup. It was sort of cheating, but whatever. They'd been practicing in the junior military classes her use of dragon fire outside of her fully shifted form. She whistled, smoke rolling out from between her lips before a stream of lava-like fire darted like an arrow from her mouth. The apple caught on fire, melting in on itself until Jed swatted at the cup and took a deep breath.

"I'm not going to lie. I wasn't sure how that was going to end," Jed said, laughing into his cup.

Of course, Jed and Adler both picked dares, and I was sure Katia slipped her name into the bowl a couple more times because both of them pulled her. She had one of them strip down naked and run around the house, and the other had to remove all of their weapons and put them in the other room. That one lasted about five minutes, and he had to drink.

It was Koa's turn, and I could already see how much he was dreading it. He drew a paper, sighing as he looked across the room at us. "Wren."

"Good thing you guys are okay now, right?" I said awkwardly.

"Truth," Koa said.

"True or false, you love having me as a business partner." Wren grinned.

My brother groaned, took a shot, and stared back at him, but in Koa language, that was pretty much an astounding yes. I took it as a win.

Sienna whacked him in the back of the head and pulled. "Mira, my love. Dare."

Rubbing my hands together, I thought up exactly how I should get her back for my dare.

Thankfully, spirits stayed high for the rest of the game. Atlas and Wolfe only stayed for about half the time, whatever was in those duffel bags needing their attention. Now, Katia had taken the twins on a ride over the ocean, which was hilarious to witness. Sienna and Koa had slipped away to the beach as well, though I wasn't entirely sure which part.

I was just happy for some time alone with Wren. We were always surrounded by people, some of whom we loved more than anything, but the quiet was nice too. Who knew that truth or dare would have been so hilarious while simultaneously deep?

I passed Wren a cup, but found him already looking at me with mischief in his eyes.

"What?" I asked.

"Truth or dare," he said.

I debated. "Truth."

"What is one regret you have?"

"A regret? Um…" I thought back at the many things I might have done differently, and chose one that wasn't too heavy. "There was this girl at my prep school I used to talk to a lot. We flirted and hung out a couple of times, but it was around the same time I met Forrest. I ended up dating him, and she ended up dating someone else. I wish I had explored more with her."

"You mean sexually?"

"Um, yeah," I said.

"Do you still want to?" Wren asked.

It wasn't embarrassment I felt, but something close to it. There was no reason to be embarrassed; I knew that. I didn't want him to think saying yes to that meant I didn't want him. Satisfaction was not a problem. When I'd hinted at it with Forrest, it made him jealous. He thought people like me were just insatiable. He'd said to pick a lane, be with a man or a woman, and leave the rest for everyone else. I knew Wren wouldn't react that way, but it was still in the back of my mind.

"Not a trick question, love. I wouldn't want you to live with any regrets, that's all," he added as my mind spun.

"Yeah, I'd still want to," I said quietly, staring back into the dishwasher.

Wren twisted me to look at him. "I mean it. If there's anything in this world you desire, I'd never hold you back, only encourage and help you attain it. I don't think it's a reflection of how you feel about me, if that's what got you going quiet."

"Would you be interested in exploring it...together?" I asked.

"Only if that's how you prefer," he responded.

He held my eye contact and let his genuineness shine through. Not that suggesting we explore this particular thing together was such a hassle for him.

I smiled, nodding. "Yeah, I'd like that."

"Then I'd love to."

I passed Wren the last dish to dry and switched the subject before I got awkward again. "What do you think of the game?"

Wren grabbed the plate, wiping it down with the rag before putting it into the open cabinet. "I'm just happy to have kept my underwear on."

"Fair," I laughed. "Have you and the twins never talked about your families' history?"

"There's been little conversation around it. Jabs here and there, but up until recently, we weren't ones to sit around and talk about anything. I suppose we can thank you all for that."

We sat back down on the couch, the room now free of almost any indication we'd all been here. I really wanted to explore more of the property the next day. Everything was crafted with intention, even the setup of the living room was made for conversation and connection.

"Didn't mean to come in and crush all of your fabricated rivalries," I responded.

Wren didn't run with my sarcasm, his tone only serious. "I wondered how true a lot of it was. My grandfather was a great man, but we don't always make the best choices when we're cornered. There'd been times the Mercers seemed to feel the same way, but I'm glad it's out there now."

"Sometimes it's easy for me to forget who you all are. I get this version of you, and they get another."

He shook his head once. "Version isn't the right word. I'm the same person here with you and out there with them. I do what I have to do, but who I am at my core remains the same."

I understood his reaction. Version held a flavor of deceit. As if it was an intentional decision to be one way with me and another with everyone else.

"I didn't mean it like that..."

Wren scooped his hand underneath my ass and flipped me to straddle his lap. His warm hands sparked as they caressed my arms. "I don't want to leave room for misinterpretation anymore. There's no part of me I want to keep hidden from you."

"I appreciate that." I smiled.

This time, Wren was the one who leaned in to kiss me. As if he could put his words into physical form, he exposed every part of himself in this kiss. The stone-cold killer, the vulnerable mama's boy, the kid with a dream. I held each piece of him in my heart, ensuring every portion was admired and embraced. Then, I poured myself into him. Wanted him to sense my fears, my desires, my own dreams.

His lips never left mine, never let any of the things I gave to him go unseen. It felt good—*really* fucking good. Neither of us was walking on eggshells, afraid of what might be exposed. There was no hesitation on account of the past; there was only forward.

He pulled me closer, and I dragged my hips against him as his hands slipped up the back of my shirt. In one smooth move, it was removed, and his mouth left mine for just a second before finding his way to my nipples.

I moaned, picking up the speed of my hips, but my foot hit something on the arm of the couch.

"What's that noise?" I said, Wren not seeming to register it at all.

The monitors unfolded from the ceiling again, and I fumbled to undo whatever it was I had done.

"What the fuck," Wren uttered with his gaze on the screen.

"Sorry, I'm—"

My words were quickly cut off. Atlas and Wolfe were in the garage, but many of their clothes were now missing. Wren's brother gripped Wolfe by the back of his neck and slammed his lips into the Mercer. It felt...angry, but also very, *very* hot.

"Guess the family feud was already over, we just weren't caught up." Wren scratched his head with a small smile.

I flipped the switch, but after the second crash from the garage, we decided it was probably best to give them some privacy.

33

KOA

As much as it pained my soul to say it, tonight was pretty fucking fun. It had to be well into the early morning at this point. By the barely decipherable cresting of the sun on the ocean horizon, we were riding the edges of dawn.

Salty sea air kissed the sweat on my skin. A chill licked down my spine, and my lids lowered, heavy from everything I'd indulged in tonight and what I hoped to indulge in shortly. Sienna shoved my shoulder as if reading my thoughts. She was humming to herself. An upbeat tune that had her shifting on the tips of her toes.

I held out a hand, and she took it with a mocking curtsy. The Cheshire grin on her face turned sinister, and I knew she'd take it too far. I also knew I'd go along with whatever made her happy, made her smile. It was a rarity in my presence these days.

Our relationship wasn't perfect; that was fucking obvious. At times, I wondered if she was coming to regret accepting the bond. Which, the more I thought about it, was odd. We'd moved past the whole Alanna thing...sort of. But something lingered unspoken between us.

If we'd had the amount of time around each other that we'd taken for granted the first half of the semester, I'd probably be able to guess what it was. At least be in lukewarm territory. Right now, I was at a total loss. All I knew about her day these days was what she and Mira opted to share...and whatever else popped up during Nola's daily debriefs.

So when she tugged me toward the beach at sunrise, I followed. If it made her laugh, I'd make a fool of myself a thousand times over. Sacrifices. Isn't that what they said love was?

I thumbed my phone and pressed play on the first track that loaded. Heavy metal exploded through my speakers, setting a completely different vibe than I'd been going for. Heat flushed my cheeks in embarrassment for what was likely the third time in my life. It did not typically occur to me to bother with such a waste of energy.

Sienna cupped my face and pulled me in for a kiss with a giggle. She slid my phone from my hands and locked the screen, pushing the device back into my pocket and replacing her hand within mine.

Watching in admiration, I took in her soft beauty as she spun in circles, over and over, screeching when the water lapped at her ankles. She rested her head on my chest, rocking side to side with me, and the world faded to simply the two of us. The air didn't lose its chill, nor did the ocean lose its rage, but in that moment, I cut all that shit out. My only focus was on the two of us.

We'd come so far in so little time. It wasn't fair. Then again, that was the game called life. None of that shit was fair for anyone but the person running the show. And I, for one, could proudly claim I'd made life a little sucky for some of the fae in question since the moment I was born.

She twirled again, slower this time, until she lost her balance and tumbled to her knees in the sand with a surprised yelp. I was already there. Sienna burst into laughter as I caught her by the elbow. It was the breathless kind—a sound that could only come from pure joy, not humor. Her head dropped against my shoulder, and she moved to straddle me, pushing my ass onto the ground. Minutes passed, and we sat there, tide creeping in and lapping at our clothes with each roll of foam.

"I forgot how absolutely fantastic it is to just...be," she said, voice muffled against my shirt.

"Same," I murmured, pressing my chin to the top of her head. "Well, actually, not really. This is all I know. A constant state of being on guard, wary of people in every corner of my life, in every role that I play. But not with you, it's different.

You make it tolerable. So yeah, I forgot how good *this* feels. I forgot what it feels like to forget."

"I have to tell you something."

That sobered me up. It was the equivalent of 'we need to talk,' but whatever she would reveal would place the ball in my court. Humor was absent from her tone, and the expression on her face put me on edge. She nibbled on her bottom lip, her gaze falling down to my lap. Sienna's hands melted into the sand as she made way to put distance between us. I wrapped my hands around her wrists, holding her steady. I refused to let her run from me again. If there was a problem, we could solve it. *Together*.

"I'm listening," I said, tempering my tone.

She shifted her weight, still refusing to meet my gaze. "Remember how I said the rebels creeped me out? That even being within ten miles of them was too close and made my skin crawl?"

"Vividly."

She made sure Mira and I knew *exactly* how she felt about working with the rebels on the way to the meeting at the gym and on our way back. At this point, I just assumed it was one thing the two of us would never see eye to eye on. We needed the rebels. There was no changing my mind on that. It was a promise I'd made to myself a long time ago.

Going into the Cynod with my 'big ideas'—as my father put it, disappointment in his tone—wouldn't go over well with the others. They enjoyed their power and had no intentions of leveling the playing field. Even if Mira ever took her seat, the two of us would never make a difference as long as the others remained. I didn't take the breaking of promises lightly. Now there was an opportunity, and luckily, I was blessed with a mate who understood my choice. One who would not stop me, although she may not agree.

"Great," she said dryly, rubbing her bare arms. "So then it's probably going to come as a shock that I reached out to one of them."

Actually, it wasn't. I noticed everything. Very little surprised me, especially these days. "Let me guess. Silver?" I asked, my brow lifting in expectation.

She blinked. Brown eyes met mine for the first time since she began her little 'confession'. "Huh? Who's—wait. You mean *Strider*?"

I nodded slowly. "Are you sure?"

I could have fucking sworn it was something cool. Who names their kid *Strider*?

"So positive," she said. Sienna's eyes raked over me, processing, then jerking back as something clicked. "I thought I told you to take that damn tracker app off my phone, snake."

"I did."

I also didn't need a tracker to stay in the know where Sienna was concerned. I had people for that. What was the point of having a staff full of those who worked the shadows of Inecha if not for my own personal gain? Shit, well, I guessed it was always my personal gain. But this was more of a favor than business.

"Then how did you—" She paused, then her expression flattened into a grimace that I'd seen precede reluctant truth time and time again.

"Venom…" I started, and she held up a hand to silence me.

"Oh, come on. I mean, coincidences happen all the time, contrary to the world you all seem to exist in."

I shrugged, unapologetic. She pushed to her feet with a sigh and started toward the dark edge of the water. The hem of her skirt dragged through the sand, ebbing and flowing with the waves from the glossy, cold sea.

I leaned back, freeing my sealed cigarette case and pulling out a pre-rolled feyfog joint. Putting it to my lips, I flicked my lighter and inhaled. A few hits in, I stood and wandered over, letting the smoke swirl between my fingers before offering it to her. Her eyes remained on the horizon as she reached back to grab it.

"I'm going to say this," I said, stepping behind her, hands on her waist, and lips tickling her ear. "And then we can pretend this conversation never happened. Because, quite frankly, I had a very different idea of where this was headed when you lured me out here."

Her body went rigid, and she turned ever so slightly. I tugged her in gently, and Sienna blinked up at me. I leaned in and caught the smoke from her lips, exhaling slowly before going back in for a kiss.

"You are above existing in a state of denial," I said against her mouth. "He resembles the man listed as your father in Celeste's flash drive. You know next to nothing about your father. Someone—not related to your mom—set her up in that house. At dinner, she hinted about once being attached to some powerful asshole with empty promises. The math is there, even if we don't have the full equation. Now tell me, Venom, then we move on, why did you make contact?"

Sienna drew back, passing the feyfog as she looked at me through lowered lids. I tossed it into the sand—my full focus solely on her. "There are answers I want before I can commit to working with the rebels in good faith. Which I do, by the way, intend to work with them. If it's important to you, then it's damn sure important to me. We're a team, Koa. Mated for life. What you take on, I'm your support."

Her hands fell to my biceps, and she gave them a light, absentminded squeeze. "I guess he just...I'm not sure. Something about Strider felt familiar. Like there's been this sense that I can trust him from the moment I saw him. I wasn't sure how to define it before, but now...I suppose it all makes sense."

The word cut between us. Familiar. Her voice snagged on it. The way her eyes darted off toward the water, the tiny shift of her jaw like she was biting back a bigger thought. She tried to cover it with that stubborn tilt of her chin, but the air had already shifted.

I swallowed down the rattling in my chest at that word. Familiar. It was too loaded, too dangerous, and I hated how naturally it rolled off her tongue. I knew she didn't mean it the way my gut twisted it. The idea of her soul recognizing another's aside from mine released a more primal response than I'd intended. I'd had my suspicions for a while now. But old habits died hard, and I had a lot of those.

"I want to meet up with him," she continued. "If we really are...related in some way, he's safe. Probably. He said he would be willing to talk when I'm ready."

"You think you are?"

"Fuck no."

We laughed, because if we didn't, we'd have to admit how fucked all of this really was.

"But I'm going to do it anyway," she said. "I'm always telling Mira to face the things that scare her the most. What kind of friend would I be if I didn't live the same way?"

"Shit, with your impulsive track record, an *alive* one, probably. Which is how I prefer it. You're an agent of chaos."

She elbowed me. The tension eased. That was how she did things. Never staying in the deep too long. Didn't let grief make a home. The weight of anything heavy—she carried sideways, turned into movement. A pastry. Meditation. The noise of music. A joke. A meal. A dare.

I knew the truth. Sienna had no fear. Not of grief. Not one question came from revelations. Sienna simply knew better than to sit still in the dark. It was how she'd kept herself afloat all the years she'd been left to deal on her own. Stillness made space for pain. And pain—she'd had enough of that for ten lives.

I refused to attempt to pull her back. This was not for me to fix. To get involved with. If she wanted answers, she had every right to search for them, no matter the source. Preventing her from getting them wasn't love. Not for someone like her. So when she was ready to come to me, to sift through all she found, I'd be here. Waiting.

Sienna stared up at me, her rose-shaded lips puckered into a pout. The overwhelming desire to touch her won out. Cupping her chin, I grinned. Satisfied by the ego-stroking fact that the palm of my hand took up the better portion of her face. Her lips parted. A slight gasp escaped her to my greatest pleasure. Tilting to meet her halfway, I offered her the softest of kisses, leaving her desperate for more. She lost her balance on the tips of her toes.

I chuckled. The teasing was cruel. But I would never feel bad about drawing out her pleasure. I caught the tip of her chin again, this time taking a moment to admire her beauty. The brown of her skin had reddened from our time on the beach yesterday. A radiant orange and pink in the morning sky did nothing but accentuate the soft lines of her face. Sienna's smile brought my mouth back to hers, and I tugged at her bottom lip, begging her to open up for me. She obliged my desire, kissing me back with that same rhythm. Muscle memory.

When her mouth met mine, she moved like she knew me. Not just now, but always. As though kissing her was something I'd done in another life, and our bodies never forgot how. That soft whisper of a moan left her mouth and weakened my knees. I *needed* to please her. Even though it pained me, I broke away from our kiss, directing my energy toward her pleasure. Her favorite spots. The ones that made her soaked for me.

I kissed the sweet space between her jaw and collarbone, right at the cusp of her neck. She tilted her head further to grant me access. Taking my time, I dragged my tongue down the side of her neck, nipping and sucking when I felt her pulse spike.

"Bite me, snake."

What she asks for—Sienna could take, snatch, *demand* anything she wanted of me, and I would only drop to my knees to thank her. I lowered my fangs, the bitter tang of venom shocked my tongue as I swept it over them and tugged Sienna tight to my body. My hand brushed along her jaw, angling her neck to the perfect position. I sank into her. She gasped at the venom pushing into her bloodstream, going weak in my arms, momentarily paralyzed.

I took advantage of the moment, removing one hand from her body only to replace it moments later at her core. Her wetness soaked through her panties, and I found myself too impatient to waste time teasing her from on top. Sienna's pussy clenched around my fingers the second I thrust them in. She dropped her head back. The movement removed my fangs from her neck, leaving behind two swollen dots dribbled with blood. I cleaned up my mess, licking the wound, enjoying the moan loud enough to drown out the sound of the lapping waves.

Her body jerked in response to the curve of my finger, hitting that spot I knew brought her close to the edge. But I couldn't push Sienna over. Not yet. I'd just started my fun.

'Take your panties off,' I said, thrusting a third finger inside her.

She didn't respond. At least not verbally. How could she when I pressed my lips against hers? Desperate to be as close to her as possible. Sienna shimmied out of her panties.

Eyes sharper than daggers met mine as I untangled our bodies. Her mouth and pussy now free of my touch. With a smile, I lifted her skirt and dropped to my knees. She stared back at me. A grin as lethal as my own. I tore from our locked gaze, setting my attention on her pretty little cunt.

Evidence of her arousal glimmered at her entrance. I had to check myself. I could have sworn I was fucking drooling. She turned her head, distracted by something. I followed her line of sight and chuckled as her panties washed away into the ocean.

"Those were my favorite," she whimpered, biting down on her bottom lip.

'Focus. Eyes on me, Venom.'

That snapped her right back to where I wanted her. Sienna's eyes reflected nothing but the most sinful mix of love and lust. Even on both knees, the height difference wasn't ideal. I tugged on her leg, pulling it over my shoulder, lining her up with my mouth that watered at the thought of tasting her.

Sienna shivered when my stubble brushed against her inner thigh. Goose-bumps prickled underneath the firm grip I had on her. I dragged my tongue against her entrance, maintaining eye contact as I pushed it inside. She squirmed, and I held my ground. The icy water splashing against my knees was the only thing keeping me from coming, tempering my lust.

I kissed her clit, then opened my mouth, fangs still lowered, brushing against her most sensitive spot. Sienna jolted, knees buckling. The chuckle rumbling from my throat against her core only intensified the wave of satisfaction flowing through her body. Small hands gripped the top of my head as she rolled her hips. She was close. I could tell.

Flicking my tongue in synchrony with her swaying, Sienna's movements slowed with the release of her orgasm. She pulled me up with one little pointed nail beneath my chin. I gripped her hips, smiling with her arousal still coating my chin.

Her fingernails traced down my arms, clawing, leaving reddened scratch marks. Sparkled mischief shone in her pretty, almond eyes. Sienna's hand fell to my dick, and she gripped it. She licked her lips, smirking as she unbuttoned my slacks with ease, dropping one knee, then the other into the sand—her skirt still raised over her hips, forcing me to watch the waves touch her in places I wished I still were.

Brisk morning air hit me where I usually preferred it didn't. Sienna's mouth made me forget why. Her lips wrapped around the tip of my dick, swirling, lapping up any hint of pre-cum. The flick of her tongue taunted me. She took me down the back of her throat. Short, sweet, gasps of air ebbed and flowed. I dropped my head, taking my hand and wrapping it around her curls. Her free hand thanked me for freeing it, molding, gently squeezing the base of my balls.

'Fuck, Venom. You're gonna be the godsdamn death of me.'

The latter sentence, she took problem with. And she punished me for it. Teasing me, bringing me right to the edge, then backing off. Slowing down or by removing her mouth—it didn't matter her method of cruelty. She reveled in the power.

It became a game. Me trying to find that sweet, sweet, release and her forbidding me from achieving it. I tightened my grip against her curls and eased myself against her tongue. Sliding back and forth, holding position in her throat.

She moved back in quick motion, but it was too late. My cum dripped down her throat, and instead of backing away, she pushed forward. Taking it all. Tears fell from her eyes, her pretty face turning red until she pulled free with a gasp. I moaned at the change of temperature, looking down at her still on her knees, hands in her lap—staring up at me like such a good girl.

I held out my hand, and she took it. Kissing the top of her head, I pulled down her skirt, then intertwined our fingers. We moved through the sand at the same pace. Both eager to make it back to our room to...well, do unspeakable fucking things that a sunrise on a beach backed by an all windows mansion made impossible to do. Not without traumatizing my sister.

Though I pretended not to, Sienna's stolen stares did not go beyond my notice. She kept glancing up, then away, like she was scared she would look over and I would no longer be there. Shit. I couldn't blame her. The only reason I noticed was because I'd been attempting to steal my own damn stares.

The bottom floor of the house was spotless and quiet. Yeah. I could take one guess and know who was behind that. *Wren, you poor motherfucker.*

A thought that quickly switched to—*Wren, you motherfucker*—at the loud thud that came from Mira's room down the hall. Tossing up a silencing spell wrapped *tightly* around my fucking body, I did my best not to think about what that meant. Sienna chuckled, releasing my hand and skipping her way down to our room on the other side of the mansion. It was tastefully decorated for a Mercer, I had to say. They were flashy. No way around that. I didn't expect the inside of this place to look like Incecha's Architectural Digest.

Sienna laughed again. This time, she placed a finger over her lips and then pointed at the door across from ours. She disappeared into the darkness of the room. I briefly dropped my spell. The moaning coming from that room was absolutely diabolical. They weren't even trying to hide what was happening over there. I scratched my head. *Wolfe must have a local he fucks when in town. Good for him.*

I backed into our room, closing the door behind me, taking extra precaution to both lock it and expand my silencing spell to the entire room. Someone had to have some godsdamn decorum around here.

Breathing was, apparently, a privilege. One that Sienna could revoke at the whim.

The curve of her naked body was outlined by the light of the bathroom in the doorway behind her. I trailed over every inch of her. Marking with my eyes where I wanted to touch. Kiss. Suck.

Bite.

I fell onto the bed. My knees no longer capable of maintaining my weight. She tsked at me, shaking her head and crossing the room with a long stride. The saunter of her hips made her scold fall onto deaf ears.

"No outside germs on the bed," she said, pulling me up.

One glance around the room and I could probably list about ten places I would happily bend her over and fuck her on. At least six more if I got creative, and this room was nothing but minimalist-inspired decor at its core.

"So," Sienna teased, her tongue slipping between her teeth. "We'll have to shower before making our way to the bed."

My clothes were on the ground by the time the first drop of water splashed against the ashen gray floors. Sienna's back was pressed against the glass shower door overlooking the beach by the second. The sun had finally crested the horizon. It was a beautiful background to lose myself in as I buried myself in my mate. She let out a gasp, and I pressed a hand to the tempered glass. Wolfe had made sure to mention that it was the kind you could see out, but not in, on the tour when I'd casually mentioned security concerns.

She balanced between my hips and the wall, wrapping her legs around me, and her arms looped behind my neck. She kissed me, slowly. This time with less need. It was intoxicating. Like I could *feel* everything she did. Every word she wanted to say. I pumped myself in and out of her, the rush from my own movements gone as well. Our climax was slower. More intentional. Sienna came up for air, her lips a mere whisper over mine as we came together.

The tips of her toes found the ground again, but instead of breaking our connection, Sienna rested her head against my chest, the hot water hitting her directly. Her curls were plastered against her face. I reached behind her and grabbed her shampoo. Lathering it in my hands, I worked it through her hair, gently massaging her scalp.

"I love the feel of your curls," I said, bending to kiss her neck, the spice of dripping shampoo not enough to ward me off. I pressed another to her cheek and then her nose.

Sienna said nothing, her eyes remained closed, but the pure, simple smile creeping across her face let me know she heard me. I dunked her under the second stream of water from a smaller extension connected to the wall with a laugh. She cackled, tossing her bottle of shampoo at me in defense. I caught it with ease.

I appreciated the view from behind as she turned around to allow me easier access to rub it in. My eyes remained on the plump swelling of her ass the entire time, not breaking my trance to switch from conditioner to body wash. Selfishly, I made sure to pay that part of her body extra attention when rubbing it across her soft skin. She grabbed it from me and circled soapy patterns across my body. Her focus as sex driven as mine—on my cock.

Turning the knob behind me, the other four showerheads came to life on the ceiling, pelting us with perfectly tempered water and rinsing us off. Going back to Kuxtal Isle was going to suck. Facing reality was going to fucking suck. I wanted to live this life with Sienna every day. I refused to believe I was a fool for holding out hope. Sienna gravitated to me as if our thoughts were aligned. I kissed her. Once. Twice. Three times.

I didn't want to stop, but the fucking water getting in the way of her taste was pissing me off. I turned the water off and tossed her a towel from the warmer in the corner.

'I'm not done with you.'

She arched her brow in a dare, taking her time, drying off at a slow, torturous pace. I scoffed, not bothering with a towel. Water dripped over the floors, but it wouldn't matter in a few seconds. One press of the illuminated buttons on the mirror and magic was released from the ceiling. Warm wind rotated in gentle, yet oddly efficient, movements, drying both of us off in under a minute.

"Rich people." Sienna rolled her eyes.

I closed in on her, grabbing her ass with a certain possessiveness to my grip. "I'm growing a bit impatient here, let's wrap up the chit chat, yeah?"

"You mean my unsolicited discourse of ethical consumption under extreme capitalism isn't a turn on?"

"Oh yeah," I coughed a laugh, guiding her through the door and giving her a push. "Talk dirty to me, Venom."

Sienna landed ass over the mattress. She looked back at me, finger hanging out of her mouth with a giggle. It was a delicious sight. I was on her immediately. No mystery, no second attempts to find her entrance. I pushed into her, no longer holding back.

She cried out, and my hand found her mouth. There was no need. Not with the silencing spell, but I knew she'd need something to bite. Sienna pleaded in the pockets of air behind my palm. Harder. Faster. The cries repeated over and over as I drilled into her.

Her pussy clenched around my shaft. I grabbed her arm, holding her against my body and removing my hand from Sienna's mouth. She whimpered, and I lost it. I moaned, falling over her as I filled deep inside. I flipped her over. Brown eyes stared back at me, begging, but mostly furious for cutting her orgasm short.

I simply wasn't done.

The sight of her swollen pussy was a gift from the gods. An altar I wished to worship at. I lowered my head, challenging her to look away as I cleaned up what leaked from her. I used my tongue, pushing my salty cum back inside where it belonged, using it to pleasure her until she squirmed to a finish.

I let her catch her breath, then picked her up, tossing her up further on the bed. She laughed, a final, genuine one—for tonight at least. There were still four days left on this trip. I had time to bring more. I joined her on the bed, pulling the covers over us and bringing her onto my chest. It wasn't long before sleep found her. But not me.

Instead, I was tortured with the knowledge that this trip would end and we wouldn't be able to cut the world out anymore.

34

SIENNA

I could really get used to this. I mean, from the outside, I was a hater. I admit it. But from the inside? Cosplaying rich was a pretty sweet deal. *No. Bad Sienna. That's a dirty, traitorous thought.* Oh, who am I kidding?

Free from the constraints of inequality—in a perfect world, everyone could get a taste of this. Seriously, the view from the lounge chair along the side of the pool was stellar. Forgetting my painting supplies was such a rookie mistake.

It wasn't like I'd traveled often and was accustomed to packing for a vacation. Sure, Mira had provided me with a packing checklist. Printed and laminated. Which I would have used if I didn't accidentally throw it out in the middle of my stress cleaning. And I was far too proud to ask Mira for another copy. Then she would have asked me how I lost it, followed by questions on why I was stress cleaning, and then it would've been a whole thing.

Sipping the delicious latte that Wolfe's private chef offered this morning, I pulled out my phone to check for any local arts and crafts supply stores in the area. Apparently, there was one along the boardwalk. I loved it when the stars aligned. That was precisely where Koa and I were heading the second he wrapped up catching up with Nola on how the weekend went at the club. It would be a total sin to leave this place without capturing the beauty of the ocean.

Kuxtal Island had an absolutely gorgeous beach, don't get me wrong, but the colors here in Chan were incredibly vivid. I'd never seen this many hues of blue. It was almost as if Kukulkan himself had blessed the place.

A tall figure crept from around the rocks, and I nearly choked on my coffee. The property was pretty remote for security purposes. No one should have had such easy access to...*Oh.*

Atlas glanced around, not spotting me from this angle courtesy of the hedges separating the pool area from the beach. He tucked his silky, patterned shirt into his black trousers, fixing the buttons to realign and leaving it open to expose his completely inked chest. Visually, he was a less threatening Wren. Skinnier but still muscular. Tall yet not quite his younger brother's height. His face was just as sharp, though his eyes were softer, kinder.

It was all a farce. If the rumors I'd heard were true, he was the most unhinged of them all. Atlas was smart, but his...habits kept him jumpy and chronically short fused. A little paranoid. If he no longer trusted you, that was your life. Which was what made his relationship with Wolfe all the more interesting.

Business was business to them, I supposed. If *I* were a criminal mastermind who made a ton of money, I would probably put centuries-old grudges aside for the sake of a solit or two.

"Morning, sunshine." I grinned up at him, still reclined in my seat.

Atlas damn near jumped out of his skin. For an *Ok*, you'd think he'd be more aware of his surroundings. "Fucking hells."

"You look like you've had better nights."

"Yeah, well, sweetheart, most nights I average ten to twelve hours of sleep," he chuckled more to himself than me as he ran his hand over his sanded face. "At least."

I took another sip of my honey oat latte, twirling the paper straw to mix in the melted ice. People complained about these far too much. Saying they made your drink tasted like cardboard was an outdated stance. Plus, the turtles.

"You know this is a vacation house, right? You're not on a job. No one's forcing you to be awake right now." I tossed a lazy hand back toward the house. "And Wolfe has a million rooms in this little villa of his. No need to sleep on the beach."

His brows bunched at the center a bit, and he tilted his head with a smirk. "Right. Yeah. The beach. Can't get any closer to the sound of the waves than sleeping outside."

"You eating with us later?" I pivoted the conversation away from whatever had that uneasy gleam shining in his eyes as he spoke.

His confused face was significantly less creepy. Sure, we were in a house full of criminals. Yes, I happened to be dating a notorious one. And so were my best friends. I suppose we all kind of overlooked that and excused it for their pretty faces. Atlas failed to have that effect on me. I wouldn't show it, though. He was definitely the type to pounce on someone's discomfort.

"The fancy chef Wolfe hired challenged me to a cook-off for dinner. Everyone's gonna judge us for all five courses. Not to be a bitch—kidding, I totally mean to be one—I think the fanciness of culinary school takes the seasoning out of things," I finished the latter in a whisper.

Atlas scratched his head and glanced behind him. He turned back my way and said nothing, simply stood there, semi-menacingly.

I blinked at him with a polite smile. "You're so chatty. Everyone but Wolfe is heading down to the boardwalk at some point today. We're going soon, I think Mira is going later. You're welcome to join."

"Nah, I'm good." Atlas gave me a final glance over, ending with a wink, and made his way inside. He paused at the door. "Thanks for the invite, but I could really use the Zs."

Left to my lonesome, I resumed the position of relaxation and finished off my latte. Picking up my phone, I opened my favorite app, FableForum. Mira always teased me and Celeste for the amount of screen time we spent there. She said everything couldn't be a conspiracy, but I begged to differ. Shit, the one about Solis and the old golds was already proven to be at least partially correct. The anonymity of the app didn't make the thoughts shared any less valid. In fact, I'd argue quite the opposite.

Minutes passed, and motion caught my eye once more. Wolfe came jogging down the beach from the same direction Atlas emerged from. There must be a crazy view there or something. I honestly didn't think anyone besides me and Koa would be awake. We hadn't even woken super early, but being that neither of us ever really slept in, we were both up by ten after only a few hours of sleep.

Wolfe spotted me about the same time Atlas did. It was kind of cute, the way they all were so comfortable here—letting their guards down. He offered a timid grin, frozen in place as if I'd caught him sticking his hand in the cookie jar.

It was easy to forget about the past that the two of us shared. That was a…chaotic time in my life. A girl just wanted to have some fun. Dangerous fun. If someone asked me, I'd tell them it was a lifetime ago, because honestly, it felt like it. He'd been a major help in the others finding me after I was so rudely kidnapped. Then there was everything he did to pull the flash drive—though that was a paid endeavor—maybe extending me a place in his home was a step too far.

"This isn't weird, right?"

"Huh?" Wolfe said, lifting his cap off his head and exposing his tapered fade—crisp lines, as always. "What? No. Why would you say that? What would be weird?"

I snapped my fingers, rising to my knees with a laugh. "Exactly! Glad we're on the same page. You know, we had a fun run, but it was just that—fun."

"Yeah, it's whatever." He brushed me off and walked away, still talking. "You found your mate. I found…"

I watched him with an arched brow, waiting. "Yeah?"

"Peace. I found peace." He shot me a look over his shoulder with something close to a smile. "It's cool, darling, don't even sweat it."

I turned back to the pool and the stretch of ocean beyond it, took a slow sip of my drink, and leaned back. "Oh yeah. This is gonna be a *long* ass week."

Koa, for whatever reason, was taking his sweet, precious time to make it out here to me. Luckily, I'd already meditated for the day, and my patience well was relatively full. For about another twenty minutes. Turning on some tunes, I decided to vibe out for a bit—until my thoughts caught back up to me. The conversation I'd had with Koa last night replayed in my mind like a broken record.

I needed to act now. Preferably, before I had the chance to chicken out. Pausing the music, I scrolled to my message thread with Strider and tapped the number he'd added a few minutes after his message telling me we could talk. Closing my eyes, I hit 'call.'

It rang once. Twice. Three times. And I panicked. Hanging up, I tossed my phone to the edge of the lounger with a tight scream. It immediately started to ring. The R&B ringtone that usually brought me excitement brought a chill to my bones. *Strider*. With a video call. I stared at it for a few seconds, then answered it.

Passing, ironically comfortable seconds of silence stretched out to what was probably the better of a full minute. I didn't know what to say. Strider was a poster child of the word calm as he peered back at me with a patient smile.

"Hi."

I fought for my words and settled for one. "Hi."

"You called?" he asked, the world passed by him in the windows of what seemed to be an SUV, but it was clear he wasn't the one driving.

The tint of the windows was so dark, I couldn't tell if it was day or night wherever he was. It was still the afternoon in Inecha, it couldn't have been home.

"I called."

His laugh was rich and genuine. It threw me. I cringed inwardly, realizing I was merely echoing him.

I shook my head, remembering the visage of confidence I preferred to display. "Is it...safe to chat for a minute?"

"As safe as it will be for a while. What's up?"

That was, quite frankly, the least comforting thing he could have said. Instant regret flashed over his face as he seemed to come to the same conclusion. A woman's voice trailed over the roar of the engine in the background.

"I mean, you could probably take this call any other time *but* now. Given we're a little busy at the moment."

Flag on the freaking play, I recognized the voice. I shook it off, not able to put my finger on who. Probably Zélia or Vitória—except the inflection of their words weren't the same as what I recalled.

Strider rolled his eyes into the camera. "Sorry about that, my assigned partner for today is...less than pleasant. I take it you're ready to have our little chat?"

"Yeah. Yeah, I think I am."

"I'm out of town for the week," he said. "But when I get back? Sunday?"

"Seriously, Strider. You're the map of this operation. You heard Zélia, this is time sensitive. So put your little family reunion to the side and focus."

My breath caught. Strider glanced sideways, then back at me, apology softening his features. His head tilted—enough to say a thousand things at once—instead, all he gave me was, "I have to go. I'll call you tomorrow."

A photo of Koa and I the night of the masquerade replaced the caller ID screen when Strider hung up. But not before I heard him speak a name. The chill hit instantly. A sharp contrast to the hot, humid day. Weight anchored in my chest. My heart pounded. Hard enough to drown out reason.

"Did he just say—"

I whipped around to find Koa standing behind me for gods knows how long. "Alanna," I finished his thought.

His eyes narrowed, studying me like he was seeing a ghost. Then he gave a slight shake of his head. "Nah."

"Oh, please, spare me. We both know you could pick her voice out from a giant ass crowd."

"Is there something you intend to insinuate, Sienna?" Koa challenged, a less-than-pleased scowl pointed right at me.

I closed my eyes and took a deep breath. I was on edge. Koa had given me no reason to not trust him when it came to Alanna. Besides, that troubled part of our relationship was a thing of the past...ish. We weren't totally ignoring reality; we simply understood where we stood with each other. And for now, that was the only thing that mattered.

"Nothing."

Pushing from the lounger, I paced along the edge of the pool. His eyes followed me, but Koa remained dangerously still. He was processing. Thinking.

"How do they even know each other?" I tossed my hands in the air. "Am I the only one freaked out by that?"

"Her business proposal," Koa mumbled, still thinking things through.

"You mean your little wedding gift?" I folded my arms, then rolled my eyes with a sigh. "Sorry. I'm snippy."

"Clearly. But not without reason."

"What does her organization have to do with anything?"

"After last weekend," he released a weighted breath. "I'd gather—everything. The cynic in me is silent when it comes to her involvement with the Heart of Bajío Restoration Project. There are personal ties there. Her mother. She even has a decent relationship with her staff."

"Excuse me while I find it extremely hard to imagine her as anything more than a bitch," I said.

"You don't have to be kind to care."

Not Alanna. Him. The correction was a gentle reminder of who I was speaking to. Koa was proof to not judge a fae by what they presented to the public. You never really knew someone's values and core beliefs until you had a chance to speak with them on a deeper level. Even then, some things would always be held close to the heart. Only to be shared in the intimacy of privacy with the person you care for the most. Or no one at all aside from oneself.

"I still don't think we should trust her," I concluded, "not with this."

"Agreed. That doesn't negate the fact that Strider and the rest of the rebels find her trustworthy. We need to find out if it's innate or bought."

"Bought?"

"Yeah," Koa shoved his hands into the pockets of his linen pants. Vacation looked *very* good on the man. "Some sort of reciprocal relationship. They both have something the other needs to succeed—like us. We need their numbers, they need our relatedness to the Cynod, and your ability to decipher the old tongue. Our causes are aligned and closely related, but not entirely the same. And when we get down to it, I doubt we envision this ending the same way."

"Or she's *with them* with them."

It made sense. Just took me by surprise, is all. I'd yet to meet her face-to-face, but the glares she sent my way from across campus were the subtlest of actions she'd taken to make me feel uncomfortable in spaces I belonged. For gods' sake, she followed several fan accounts that constantly made posts comparing the two of us, daily, always in her favor. If that weren't insensitive enough, she *liked* them. Every post.

So yeah, my hesitancy to work with a group who also worked with her only increased tenfold by the end of that call—regardless of the reasoning.

"Right, Venom. You catch on quick." He strode to me and leaned down to kiss my temple, pulling me into his chest. "It is possible that she's actually with them, and our engagement just happens to be as convenient for her work with the rebels and her grandfather. Let me pause there and be clear that the two of them have two extremely different goals. That much was evident."

"You learned a lot in twenty-four hours."

"I'm observant," Koa said, tilting my chin up to look him in the most soulful eyes I've ever seen. Love was such an understatement when it came to how I felt about him. It went so much further—deeper—than the roots love could reach.

His confidence soothed my concerns if only slightly, "Urgh. This is exhausting. I don't know how you do all this scheming and conniving all the time."

"Drinks and drugs, Venom. Drinks and drugs."

I gave him a slight shove, palm flat against his chest. Koa grabbed onto my arms, and we fell into comfortable silence. But silence wasn't the same as stillness—not when my mind kept circling back to Alanna's slip. Family. The word wouldn't leave. It pressed against the inside of my skull like it was trying to carve out space it didn't deserve.

My hand lingered against Koa's chest longer than it should've, probably because I needed the steady rhythm of his heartbeat to remind me mine hadn't stopped. He tilted his head, studying me, sharp enough to notice the edge in me I hadn't managed to hide.

"You're rattled," he said simply.

I forced a breath, then tossed my head back with a groan. "All I wanted to do was enjoy my first rich person vacation."

"Well, it won't be your last, and what Wolfe Mercer provides, I can offer you in abundance. So remove this expectation and picture something suited for my mate."

Heat stormed to my cheeks. We had ironically and obnoxiously been referring to each other as such in private. The concept still felt surreal.

"And the week is still young. As is the day," Koa whispered into my ear. "Let's go."

"To where? I'm pretty sure this Alanna thing is hot-pressed news."

"The best course of action here is to ask Strider. You can't do that until he calls you back tomorrow. There's nothing we can change about the situation that's worth pausing our day." That lazy, maniacal grin spread across his face. He leaned in, his lips hovered over mine. "Fuck everyone else. It's me and you."

He took my hand, guiding me toward the shoreline as I giggled. I sent a quick text to the group chat:

Me:

> We'll meet you back at the house for dinner. Some...developments. Don't worry, though. Enjoy your day! Don't forget to meditate!

35

MIRA

After Wren went to sleep last night, I stayed up studying the book Dr. Puebla let me borrow. I probably shouldn't have brought it across state lines to a house full of sand and water, but we were here now. Just as I thought, there was a section about blood bonds. Along with some other spells and things lost to time that I certainly wouldn't be fucking with. Even if I was a seasoned magic user, I wasn't sure I'd try. The *Eb* were able to quickly analyze these things, but I was not a magically gifted genius.

I didn't want to tell Wren that there was a possibility I could break the bond until I absolutely knew I could. He already had such little hope, I didn't want to crush it completely out of existence.

So, yes, our trip to the boardwalk was to spend time together, but it was also because I was looking for something. Coincidentally, it was something that Chan was known for—cacao. Not just any cacao, but beans from a rainforest along Lake Balacar. In our ancient days, cacao was something of a currency, and this type was as expensive as it got. This was a gift from the gods, with spiritual and transformative effects not to be taken lightly when mixed with magic. It was said that one of the greatest kings of that time stayed powerful by having three cacao drinks a day made from these specific beans. I only needed a small amount, and I hoped one of the markets set up would have it.

"I know you're up to something," Wren drawled, placing a straw hat atop my head. "But I won't push."

"Thanks, because I really want it to work. Can't get too ahead of myself."

"What to wor—"

I put my finger on his mouth. "Nope. You just said you weren't pushing!"

"You're right," he laughed and put the hat back on the table.

There were so many handmade and unique pieces on this boardwalk that I wanted to buy every single one. Wood carvings, pottery, fabrics, and pretty much everything else you could think of. I remembered my tía taking a trip out here before and coming back with a basket full of things. It was hard not to wonder if she'd been in this exact spot before. It was unlikely. There were thousands of places to visit here, dozens of boardwalks.

The sun warmed my cheeks as we turned to the ocean at our backs, the crashing of waves barely covering the low thrum of voices along the boardwalk. Eyes followed us, whispers curling through the crowd.

"*She's* with *him*—"

A hand clamped over the mouth of the speaker, but not before the click of a phone camera cut through the air. Wren stiffened. His eyes reflected every bit of the boy who grew up having to defend himself and his family. Or maybe, it was for how it would impact me.

I slid my hand into his. "Ignore it," I murmured, letting my thumb brush over the back of his hand. "Koa's been in the press every week for years. There's always another scandal waiting in line. They'll move on and we'll eventually be old news."

The tension in his chest eased and his grip tightened around mine.

"I'm done hiding. Let them whisper and stare. I don't care what my parents have to say about it. What's the worst they can do, order another hit?" I teased with a smile.

If they really wanted him gone, he would have been gone. On the long list of shit they were dealing with, I wasn't on the top. Last thing I heard regarding my relationship with Wren was at the cafe on campus. Before recent events, and my first return to being in the spotlight, they were worried. Now, there was a full-fledged rebellion.

Sticking out like a sore thumb was a building under construction, marked with the Cynod logo.

"It's impossible to escape them," I sighed.

They didn't try to match the architecture already here, which was absolutely beautiful. Natural stone, tiered stairs, cobblestone pathways. They might as well have picked up the massive glass building from the city and dropped it here.

"They're calling it an outreach center," an elderly woman said, her gaze following ours. "Haven't told us what services yet, but people are nervous about the impact on our shops."

"Think they'll drive away business?" I asked.

"I hope not, but a government building isn't exactly welcoming."

The breeze blew, a mixture of sea salt, coffee, and cacao dancing between us.

"Do you have a shop here?"

She nodded. "I do. Herbal beverages and the like."

"Oh, that's actually what I'm looking for. Do you sell cacao?"

She brushed her hands down her apron and pointed a couple of stores down. "It's one of my best sellers, come on, I'll take you. I'm Yolotli, by the way. I was just coming from lending my friend a hand at her jewelry store. You should take a gander at her shop when you're done with mine. The most beautiful clay jewelry you'll ever see."

"Oh, you really want us to spend our money out here today, don't you, Yolotli?" I joked.

"Well, what do you say, Mr. Quiet and Mysterious? You going to buy your girl some jewelry?"

"I'll buy her the whole store," Wren answered, no hint of a jest.

"Buy her mine first." She winked. "Here we are. I have some samples you two can try. A new tea I'm trying with anise leaves."

She pulled out two of the tiniest glass tea cups I'd ever seen and poured a taste of the tea into both.

I took a whiff. "Smells sweet."

"It is, tell me if it's too sweet, will ya?"

Wren and I clinked our cups together gently and sipped the tea. The perfect balance of sweet and spiced coated my tongue, and I was actually sad that more didn't fit in these adorable little cups.

"My mother would love that," Wren said, scanning the bags behind Yolotli. "I'll take a couple."

"Excellent, and you, sweetie? You were looking for cacao, yes?"

I toyed with my fingers. "Yes, uh, not already prepared. Beans if you have them."

Yolotli's eyes narrowed on me. "Fermented and dried?"

"Yup," I answered in an attempt to play it cool.

"Interesting. You stay here, you're too big for the backroom. You come with me, mija." She turned without seeing if I'd follow her.

Wren snapped into bodyguard mode, scanning the shop, but Yolotli had unlocked the building when we came in, and nobody else was here. She guided me down a hall and into a much smaller room. Wren was too big; she was right.

"Now, what are you performing?" Yolotli said, running her finger down the shelves.

"Performing? I just want to make a xocolatl," I responded, my eyes everywhere but on her.

"If that was what you wanted, you'd want them roasted and ground. Now, I can help you, but I need to know what you're performing."

"I, uh... I'm..."

Come on, Mira. You know how to lie.

"In my many years, I've become pretty good at reading people. So have my wards. If they let you in, I know you're here for the right reasons. I have a strict 'what happens in my shop doesn't leave' policy."

There was no easy way to explain this to a stranger. One who looked like she'd been around the block when it came to magic and spellwork, judging from the content of her shelves. I focused on her, easing my nahual open in my chest. It didn't always do this on command, so many times it seemed to show me something I needed to see before I even tried. This time my vision eased instead of a harsh switch. A trustworthy aura emanated from her just a moment before my nahual went to rest again.

"I'm looking for Balacar cacao," I said quietly.

"Oh." She bit her lip. "What have you gotten yourself into, mija?"

"Not me, I'm trying to break something placed on someone else."

She rubbed her chin, eyes flicking to the door. "That boy out there?"

"Yes."

"Well, I won't ask any more questions. Lucky for you, I got some in last week."

She located a box on the top shelf, three cloth draw-string bags inside. Testing the weight of each, she picked the one in the back and held it out for me, but paused before I could grab it.

"You're aware how careful you need to be, yes?"

"I read about it. I know not to mix it with anything but natural ingredients, and to make sure I'm intentional about the spell."

Yolotli puckered her lips with worry, moving a few of the boxes around and straightening them up. She rubbed her hands together like she was trying to remember something else.

"This isn't just a spell. If you're doing what I think you are, you're performing a ritual. Not just a verbal formula, this is much bigger. You'll need this bark paper, too." She pulled out a few sheets of natural parchment and tucked them into the bag.

"Yes, I understand. Thank you."

I wasn't used to the verbiage yet, but I did know that it was more than a simple spell.

"I hope that boy loves you as much." She waved at the door, and it opened, letting us into the regular portion of the shop.

He did. Wren would travel through all nine levels of hell for me. I could do this for him.

"He doesn't kno—"

She swatted at me. "I figured as much. I won't say anything."

"Thank you," I whispered as we made it to where Wren was still watching the front door.

"Got what I need." I shook the bag. "You ready?"

"Yeah, how much for whatever she got and the anise tea?" Wren asked.

The wooden counter appeared to have been carved centuries ago. Little scratches and marks left behind from happy patrons. Clouds outside parted, and the stained glass windows behind her had the whole store sparkling with colors. I hoped she'd be in business for another century or two. Mostly, I hoped that the Cynod building wouldn't impact her negatively.

"Hers is free, yours is seventy solits." Yolotli pushed a couple of buttons on her register, and Wren slid his card through the reader.

She handed us our bags with a smile. "Thank you very much. You've got a good one here, I hope you keep her happy."

"I hope so, too." Wren smiled, his gaze conveying that he was wondering what had happened in the backroom.

"Don't forget to check out my friend's jewelry store!" Yolotli yelled as the door shut behind us.

"I think she might come after me if I don't buy you *something* from her friend's shop," Wren chuckled.

"Don't see me arguing." I flipped my hair off my shoulder. "Wait, the sun is pretty here. Let's take a picture."

We turned to face toward the sun, and Wren bent down so that he'd actually be in frame.

"You know, Sienna told me about this hack where you take a video and grab stills from it. She said it's a foolproof way to get a good shot." I fumbled with my phone, sliding it to video and hitting record.

We moved through a couple of positions, him kissing my cheek, me kissing his, one smiling, and one very serious model-esque shot that was hard to do without laughing. I lifted my finger to stop the recording, but the ground rumbled. Not in the way an earthquake did, wide and elongated. This was central, one big impact. Then another, and another, and another, until the force of it nearly shook me off my feet.

Wren grabbed my arm, and we turned toward the sound as the loudest and most vigorous boom reverberated through the air. The remaining windows burst as the Cynod outreach center crumbled from the outside in. Wall by wall, it reduced to rubble, shards of glass and concrete spraying like lava from a volcano. People on the boardwalk screamed, and shop owners ran inside and locked their doors.

We didn't move, only scanned for the possible threats. Wolfe's place wasn't directly nearby, but it was close enough for whatever the fuck this was to make its way there.

"Those are rebels," Wren said, taking out one of his guns, handing it to me, and grabbing another off his hip.

Soldiers in all-black combat gear came running through the streets. A couple of them jumped into the river, but IDCC was already on the scene. They were probably already stationed within the building, so however the rebels took it down had to be calculated.

Smoke bombs erupted all around us, but there was no damage done to the boardwalk outside of the Cynod building. Wren led us through the smoke, toward the water, and atop some large boulders.

IDCC officers had a couple of rebels pinned down, giving them one hell of a run for their money. They were all split up and engaged with rebels, all but three that chased two soldiers coming right toward us. My vision flickered, my nahual coming to the surface and showing me...something I wasn't quite sure about. Auras, but I recognized them. I focused on the bodies, their faces covered with masks, making it impossible to identify.

"That's Alanna," I said. "Fuck, that's Strider. We need to help them."

Wren didn't ask questions; he moved into action, night fire erupting from his fingers, and sparkling like stars through the smoke. I realized he was using it to lead them toward us, and they finally caught on. Once they got closer, I could tell who was who. Their souls were like fingerprints, the aura so specific now that I could analyze.

"What are you two doing here?" Strider's muffled voice carried through his mask.

"That's the question you're going to ask right now?" I shot back, gesturing to everything around us. "You can come with us. We have somewhere safe."

"Safe is relative," Alanna said, her accent thick.

"We can let the IDCC officers behind you take you somewhere safe instead?" Wren retorted.

Alanna huffed, out of breath from the dash over. "Fine."

"Too late," I said as two soldiers cut through the smoke and emerged from behind them.

"Get on the ground!" One yelled.

Wren raised his gun in response. "You get on the ground."

"Who the fuc—"

Before I even realized what I was doing, my hands were raised, and my magic pulled tight against their souls. Their bodies went rigid, their eyes frantically flitting back and forth. It was the only thing I left them in control of. I made them drop their weapons and fall to their knees.

"Alanna," I said, holding steady. "You want to erase the last ten minutes from their minds?"

Her eyes were wide, fear warring with confusion. But one thing Koa made clear about her was that she was going to do what she needed to save herself. She stepped up, placing a finger on both of their foreheads, and pushed.

I'd seen my mother do it before; coercion could be used in many ways—a favorite being time manipulation. It wasn't the same as mind manipulation from the *Eb*, where a memory could be removed completely. For the *Ajaw*, they were able to jumble up time in a person's head, turn it back, and make them forget a few minutes. Or remove the couple of seconds they saw a face or something they shouldn't have.

Both the soldiers fell backward, their eyes rolling as they thudded hard to the ground.

"Let's move," Wren said with a hand on my shoulder.

"How safe is this house?" Strider asked.

Before we could answer, his hands sparked, creating more smoke to cover us. So he was a *Kib*, I wondered if he was the one to spark whatever bombs they had placed.

"Completely off the grid." Wren led us through the haze. "Forty-five-minute walk through the woods, unmarked, to the other side of the beach."

Alanna's boots scuffed on the stone as she kept pace. "How do we know you aren't setting us up, too?"

"Oh, no more future sister-in-law talk?" I quipped.

I sent a quick text to Koa, no specifics, just advising we'd be coming with unlikely visitors.

"We agreed to work with the rebels; we take that seriously," Wren said.

Strider's gaze snapped to him, sharp beneath the mask. "I don't remember you being at the meeting."

Well, Koa and I agreed. I'd caught up with Wren on what happened, and he quickly got on board with it.

"Koa and I are partners, and so are Mira and I. Whatever they agreed to involves me," Wren stated.

Strider raised a brow and looked at me. "Is Sienna there?"

"And Koa?" Alanna added.

This was going to make an already rocky situation exponentially rockier. Koa would absolutely despise the fact she was there. Sienna might have had questions for Strider, but dealing with that on what was supposed to be vacation wasn't going to be preferred.

"They are." Wren directed his gaze at Alanna. "And so are a lot of other people who won't hesitate to act should you try anything stupid."

He'd agreed to the rebels, not Alanna. I wasn't sure how much he knew about her, but something about the way he said it led me to believe he knew more than I thought. Whether through Koa or something else, I made a mental note to ask once we were alone again.

Strider pressed his finger on an earpiece. "Everyone made it out."

"My brothers?" Alanna asked in hushed tones, but it was too quiet in this forest for us not to hear.

"Everyone," Strider repeated.

The walk back to the beach house was eerie, all of us looking over our shoulders at every sound. When we made it to the property, Koa and the Mercers were already standing outside with their weapons. Wolfe's surveillance left little unseen. They'd been watching us for a while.

Koa crossed his arms. "What the fuck do we have here?"

36

KOA

The woman of my dreams brushed against my side as the woman I was forcibly attached to walked down the beach. Mira and Wren approached from the northern path that cut through the jungle, Alanna and Strider in tow.

It was hard to sneak up on this house. Crazy motherfuckers with honed senses aside, security was airtight. The front of the property was gated at the end of a private road that took twenty minutes to reach from the highway. Only way through was getting past armed security. The back of the property lined up to the ocean with a small pinch point between land and sea that gave way to a jungle. Wolfe had cameras and sensors everywhere one would think to place and at least ten in spots one would not.

We knew they were coming the second they were two breaths away from stepping a toe on his land.

"My betrothed." Alanna smirked. "No invitation to your lovely vacation?"

The Alanna from Mentiria was gone—what stood here was the mask she wore for the world. Fine. I didn't have time to wrestle with her whiplash.

Sienna froze beside me, every muscle wound tight. This was their first face-to-face, and clearly, Alanna wanted to set the tone, agreement or not.

Strider broke the tension, eyes shifting between the two of them, probably trying to figure out who would pounce first. "All this for the two of us?"

The Mercer twins blocked opposite paths, making sure any exit the two could flee from was impossible. Katia made sure of that as she crossed her arms under the doorway leading into the house.

"You just blew up a government building." Mira moved to Sienna's left, her eyes raking over them with hesitant suspicion.

Wren stayed put at their backs. If their hackles weren't raised by now, they were thicker-headed than I'd given them credit for.

"Oh," Alanna said, the tips of her greased-up hand covering her forced yawn. "Yeah. That."

"I have so many questions right now." Sienna kept her focus on Strider.

'You okay, Venom?'

This was undoubtedly hard for her. It had to be. She didn't want to work with the rebels in the first place. Then—for me—she'd decided to give them a chance. Hear them out. Attempt to speak with the one person she felt trustworthy. That same person who showed up with the source of her suffering over the last few weeks.

The optics weren't fucking fantastic.

'Okay?' Her tone dripped with sarcasm. *'This is the best day of my life. If I could relive the last few minutes forever, I'd die happy.'*

Alanna set her sights on Sienna, extending her hand with a tilt of her head. A malicious smile teased the sides of her mouth. "You must be the mate. Pleasure."

Sienna—my fucking venomous girl—didn't move. She stared at Alanna's outstretched hand as if it were poison. Not a blink. Not a flinch. Just ice, blistering and still. Strider's head snapped toward Alanna, a flash of disbelief cutting through his usual calm. The glare of betrayal shone in his eyes.

He didn't know.

Which meant she'd kept it from him on purpose.

My pulse ticked. *What the fuck are you playing at?*

Power probably. Control over the revelation without a doubt.

The rebels had been clawing through every whisper and scrap of the prophecy like addicts hunting their next hit. Yet Alanna sat on this. She knew it mattered. Knew it meant something. Still, she'd kept it to herself.

This was beyond manipulation. It was war-level strategy. And it answered the question we'd been circling since the second they stepped on the property. Same sides, different goals.

"Did I forget to mention that minor detail?" Alanna pinched her fingers in front of her narrowed eyes.

Wren cleared his throat. "I believe we have more important topics to discuss in exchange for your current safety."

I flicked him a quick nod. Grateful.

"They're not setting foot inside my house until it's clear they can be trusted. Earpieces in the pool. Now." Wolfe growled from his perched position on the lower tier of the roof.

"This one we can trust." Wren motioned toward Strider, yanked out his earpiece, crushed it under his boot, then sent the shards skipping into the water.

"And this one." I tipped my chin at Alanna. "Depends on the day. Her attitude and general disposition leave plenty to be desired."

"The longer we stand out in the open, the more at risk we are. *All* of us," Strider added, quiet but firm.

Silence settled. Even the ocean fell victim to the tension within the group, the tide easing in its pull.

Atlas crossed his arms. "His house, his rules."

"At risk from whom?" Mira frowned, sunburn tightening across her cheeks.

"You just saw us blow up a building," Alanna said, deadpan. "Who do you think?"

Jed let out a humorless chuckle, breaking character at the prospective threat. "This place is off the grid. Privacy isn't a concern."

"No place is private from the Cynod. Not truly." Strider didn't bother to look at him; his attention stayed on one person the entire conversation—Sienna.

Katia shifted to a defensive position. "You're quite eager to find your way into our space."

"It's suspicious," Adler spoke for the first time. He ran a thumb along the edge of his belt knife before flicking his gaze toward Alanna.

Brave or recklessly confident, I wasn't sure at times when it came to her; she simply rolled her eyes. "Oh, *please*. We don't have time for this stupidity. Air patrols are already sweeping the coast. Move."

She walked past me. Past Sienna. Mira.

We all let her.

Because we'd seen Katia on a pitz field—dropping men twice her size without breaking stride. No point in stopping her when we could watch the fallout.

Alanna tried. Foolishly. She squared her shoulders, ready to bulldoze through. Katia stepped forward, solid as concrete, and knocked Alanna back with her own momentum. A hit not forceful enough to injure, but a message all the same.

Alanna's eyes cut sharp, and she reacted with lightning speed. Grabbing Katia by the arm, she twisted *hard* slamming her into the glass doors—hands pinned with her forearm pressing across Katia's collarbone.

It was a shock to me as much as it was to everyone else. Only then did it occur to me how many secrets my '*fiancée*' harbored and just how little my files upon files of research had revealed.

"Don't touch me without permission," she said through her teeth.

Katia growled low and shoved off the glass with her full weight, forcing Alanna back a step. She turned, getting in her face, close enough to bite. "*You* touched *me* first," she snapped. "Do it again, and see what happens."

Energy coiled between them. A fuse about to burn. Mira moved first, stepping into Katia's orbit. Then Sienna, surgically taking position at Katia's side, her silence as lethal as her stare.

The display of mortification on Strider's face created an automatic read of the rift now between the two so-called allies. Her actions had silenced any possible defense he cared to give—unable to excuse yet another case of unnecessary force from people he claimed needed to work together.

Sienna exhaled slowly and took a step forward. "I'm going to touch you now," she said, voice tempered. Even. "No, I won't ask for permission. You're on our property, and no one but Koa can tolerate your presence, let alone trust you. Now stop being difficult and tell us why you're really here."

She placed her palm against Alanna's sternum. Purple light pulsed under her skin—faint but steady. My stomach tightened. Sienna was using it.

Her persuasion.

She never advertised when she practiced. Hated admitting it was inconsistent. But right now, it was working. Alanna's body locked up, her posture rigid as Sienna placed her hand over the fastest avenue to the truth. The heart.

Because evidently even Alanna had one of those.

"I was assigned to this mission with Strider," she said, tone flat. "Drew the short end of the stick."

 Sienna tilted her head in annoyance. "Obviously. But *why* are you here blowing up buildings?"

"I don't know. I do as I'm told."

"By whom?"

Alanna hesitated, the words fighting on the tip of her tongue. Her muscles tensed. Jaw locking. She was fighting it.

Strider moved half a step forward before taking a look at the company around him and thinking better of it. "Is this really necessary?"

"Shut up," I silenced him.

"Ask her again."

Sienna rolled her eyes at Wren's request. "Duh."

"Who assigned you to this mission?"

Alanna's lips parted. "Zélia."

The breath caught in Sienna's chest. I moved closer on instinct. Mira caught my eye and gave a sharp shake of her head—*not yet*.

Sienna steadied herself. "Why are you working with the rebels?"

Alanna's eyes clouded over—the same dead, trapped look Wren wore when we first cornered him and he couldn't figure out how to explain himself. "I can't say."

Every person around me adjusted their stance. We knew what it meant. If she was fighting this hard through the power of persuasion, there was something worth shielding.

Wolfe dropped from the roof with a solid thud. "Fuck no. Get her out."

"If she goes, I go." Strider's eyes and tone held a mild panic. "We can't separate."

Atlas shrugged. "Okay, and who the fuck are you to us?"

"Someone that we need," Sienna said.

I nodded once. "Both of them, unfortunately."

"Appreciate the warm welcome." Strider raised a brow.

Sienna turned to me, and I met her stare. She shifted her focus to Alanna after a few beats. "Can we trust you?"

The world waited.

Then, "Yes."

Sienna let go. Green eyes churning with thick fury glared back at her. The *Ajaw* didn't take well to being bent. Alanna's lips curled.

"We've got time," she said. "Plenty of it—for me to return the favor. *Mistress.*"

"Shut up and get inside." My chest rattled in warning as I grabbed Sienna's hand. A threat to her was a threat to me. Her fingers curled into mine, following my lead through the door.

Mira and Wren entered next. Then Alanna, Strider, Katia, and Atlas. The Mercers swept in last—Jed checking corners, Adler watching windows, Wolfe locking the door behind us all.

I blew a sarcastic chuckle through my nostrils at the sight of Alanna making herself at home as if she hadn't been two seconds from a brawl. She sank into the couch, posture perfect, legs crossed, one arm slung over the back like she owned the place.

Tapping on the cushion next to her, I grinned at Strider. "Sit. Now."

He sat. Mouth off. Smart choice if I ever saw one.

The girls sat opposite them. Katia was perched purposefully, her eyes never still. Junior military training presumably kicked into gear here. I couldn't imagine this was how she operated growing up or on a day-to-day basis. She was from Jundi, for gods' sake. It wasn't as if her parents were under constant threat the way the Cynod and their heirs were.

Sienna's body was taut, but her gaze slid toward Strider with a flicker of softness. A thread of sympathy in the storm. Maybe comfort too. She wasn't offering it openly—still, it was there.

Something I knew it cost her to give.

Strider caught it. His shoulders loosened, if just barely. He was in over his head. And she could see it, same as me. The sympathy offered by Sienna was a gift. He wisely, once again, chose to shut his fucking mouth.

Mira rolled in a whiteboard from the garage, markers rattling in the tray. Her grin was too bright for the tension still clinging to the room. The elevated heartbeat vibrating from Wren to the left of me as he took in my sister made me borderline violent.

I stared at her blankly. "Where the hells did you get that from?"

Wolfe didn't look up from sharpening a knife he didn't need. "She ordered it. Poor delivery guy showed up at the gate at dawn. Had to call off the dogs."

Katia's brow twitched. "What dogs?"

"Exactly." Wolfe winked.

Adler blinked at the board. "You ordered a whiteboard on vacation?"

Mira frowned, genuinely confused about why anyone here was confused. "How else am I to organize my thoughts?"

"So why is it rolled out in the center of my professionally staged living room right now?" Wolfe criticized, still sharpening his knife.

"To get to the bottom of whatever *this* is." She gestured to Strider and Alanna like they were in a research study. "If they're going to sit around trying to wait out the government, we might as well be productive."

'Good thinking, Meems.'

She straightened up a little taller at the compliment. Pride looked good on her.

Strider shook his head. "Uh-uh. We're not doing this."

"You don't really have a choice," Wren said, voice calm, eyes anything but.

Strider's voice held strong. "Orders are given. We follow them. That's how this works. It's for our benefit as much as it is theirs."

"Not a single question regarding them? Color me shocked." Sienna's distaste remained unhidden.

The front door unlocked, and the room went up in arms. Groceries clattered against the ground at the sight of nearly a dozen weapons pointed in the private chef's face. Pretty sure he pissed his pants.

"Out. Have the night off. Be here first thing in the morning," Wolfe said, sheathing his knife. "Any breakfast requests?"

"Oh, pancakes sound great," Jed said, licking his lips, his brother nodding at his side.

"That frittata from yesterday was surprisingly pretty good," Wren added.

"Eh," Atlas disagreed, "was feeling more of an omelet kind of situation."

"Whatever's served, make sure it has a side of alcohol for the headache we're about to clean up," I grumbled.

Wolfe nodded, weighing the options. "Pancakes, ham & cheese omelets, side of red onion, right?" he looked at Atlas, snapping his fingers.

What the fuck?

Atlas nodded.

"And mimosas, with that honey latte Sienna had this morning." He waved his hand, dismissing the chef. "Oh. And send a text when you're headed to the property, I thought we went over this already. I don't fancy repetition. We may not wait to see who it is next time."

The chef fought back his uncontrollable trembling and scurried out the door. Mira and Sienna passed a disbelieving glance between each other. It, if nothing else, was a not-so-gentle reminder that this was the world I'd desperately fought to keep her away from. Even at the expense of our relationship. Not for nothing. Mira had her sacred formative years away from it. Yet here she stood, in the midst of probably the biggest mess of shit I'd gotten into thus far. So maybe it was for nothing after all.

Strider passed Sienna a sympathetic glare, bringing us back to the conversation at hand. "We don't ask questions. It's meant to protect us."

"From what?" Katia folded her arms.

Alanna yawned, grabbing a cherry from the fruit bowl at the center of the glass coffee table. "Plausible deniability when caught. Who cares?"

"You should," Sienna snapped. "Because if you don't ask questions, how do you know if you're on the right side?"

"Trust," Strider answered, quieter now.

I huffed a dry laugh. "Blind trust is pathetically unintelligent. It's how corpses get made."

Wren tapped the side of his head. "Critical thinking never killed anyone."

"Well-timed questions have." Atlas stepped into the circle forming around the board, dragging a finger along the edge of the couch like he was already bored.

Wren smirked, eyes flickering to his brother. "I suppose you're not wrong."

"He's not," Wolfe added. "But we're already in this mess. And now you're here, in *my* house. So we ask the questions, and you're going to kindly help us answer them."

"Let me guess," Alanna plopped another cherry in her mouth. "If we don't, you'll torture us?"

"Yes," Atlas said flatly.

Strider stiffened. A slow tension rose through his spine. Alanna masked it well, but I saw the twitch in her eyebrow. The Ikaris were well-known for a few things, but Atlas had made his own reputation around that subject.

Jed cleared his throat. "He's kidding. I think."

"He's really not." Wren glanced toward the ground with a chuckle.

Alanna tossed her hands up. "Whatever."

Mira uncapped a marker and turned to the board like she'd been waiting her whole life for this. She stood back, hands on her hips. "Strider. Walk me through your assignments. Let's find the overlap."

Alanna opened her mouth. I leveled a stare at her—cool, flat, final. She shut it. Progress.

"We've been bouncing from state to state every two weeks. A couple of weeks ago was Kuello, then Balamku, uh...after that was—"

"Jundi," Katia mumbled, cutting off Strider. "Last time I talked to my dad, he said they weren't sure if it was a terrorist attack from a group or just some random trying to prove a point. The Cynod sent the IDCC to assist in the investigation."

Strider nodded slowly, eyes dark. "Yeah. That one was ugly."

"I was assigned to Jayna and Yaxumi prior to this...I received orders this morning for the next. Chichen." Alanna tapped her fingers against the armrest.

Mira's gaze flicked to me. Eyes so similar to my mother's yet so vastly different in the depth of their softness looked to me for guidance. I gave her a nod. She turned back to the board and drew overlapping circles, labeling them *Site One* through *Site Six*.

It all started to click.

One by one, the pieces fell into place—communication hubs, black sites rumored to hold stolen Abysmi prisoners, archive facilities...their next and final act, propaganda distribution hubs, a.k.a., government buildings. Another circle was added. A commonality found.

All empty.

"All of them?" I asked.

Strider leaned forward. "Yeah. Seven straight. Communication hubs were cold. Power rerouted before we even got there."

"The black sites?" Wren asked.

"Cleaned. No prisoners. No furniture. Explosives were already placed before we even touched the grid."

"They wanted it gone," Wolfe said. "No trace."

"The archive missions were considerably worse," Strider went on. "We were told to secure any intel or torch it. But there was *nothing*. Shelves gutted. Building stripped. And we were sent in with gear that couldn't crack a safe, let alone survive a firefight. It was uncharacteristically ill-planned for our efforts."

"And the propaganda hub?" Sienna asked.

"No flyers. No Cynod insignia. I'd say it was dead air, but there were Cynod guards on standby."

Alanna spoke again, the toned-down, Mentiria version of her slipping through briefly. "That's technically seven in a row—guards aside. Six definitive ghost buildings. Either the Cynod are ten steps ahead or someone's sending us after shadows."

Atlas tilted his head. "You seeing what I'm seeing, little brother?"

Wren nodded once, his dark hair falling in front of his forehead. "Yeah. I see it," he concurred.

Wolfe's arms dropped from his chest. "Shit. So do I."

I turned back to the board. Then it hit me—hard. "Fuck."

The girls looked at me, confused. A unified "What?" escaped them.

Wolfe was already halfway across the room, booking it past the stairs. We waited. Footsteps. Drawers opening. Rummaging. He came back with two rolled-up maps. He unrolled both and placed them side by side on the kitchen island.

We crowded around it, Strider and Alanna staying on the opposite end of the rest of us. One map was basic—the kind we grew up learning in grade school. Posted around classrooms and shit. The other...not so much. Only a select few had those.

And only half of the people in this room had ever seen it.

Red marker in hand, Wolfe circled each of Alanna and Strider's mission sites, one after the other. My stomach fell to my ass at the confirmation.

"What are the markings for?" Katia asked slowly. "Jed and Addy have those symbols tattooed on their chests."

"The Brotherhood," Sienna mumbled.

Katia's brow furrowed. "*The* Brotherhood?"

"One and only," I said.

Mira stepped back, placing the cap back on her whiteboard marker and resting it against her lip. "Maybe...maybe it's a coincidence."

I met her eyes. "Coincidences don't exist, Meems."

"*Noctis Fraternitas* has state headquarters within five miles of every single site," Wren said. "That's not a coincidence, love. That's strategy."

Sienna's face twisted as she did the math in real time. "Why would the Brotherhood—" She stopped herself. "Never mind. That answers itself. Of course, the anti-government, pseudo-spiritual underground cult of criminals would want to start shit between the people and the state."

"The rebellion's just the easiest route," Strider agreed. "Fewer questions. More chaos."

Katia raised a hand like she was asking to speak. "Cool, cool. So how's everyone feeling with that little bombshell? Because *I* have questions."

"You and the rest of us," Jed said, slipping an arm around her waist as he stepped in behind her.

Strider's jaw ticked. "Only two people could answer them."

Every head turned.

He hesitated—shooting a glance at Sienna. "Zélia...and my tio. Your father."

The silence that followed was bone-fucking-deep. Of all the moments for a world-shattering revelation, the dumbass thought *now* was the time. Sienna wobbled a bit, placing her palms on the edge of the counter to steady herself. I pulled her into my side, rubbing a palm on her lower back for reassurance.

There would be a time to discuss this, and it wasn't now. Not in front of everyone. But the truth would have been revealed once Wolfe raised his palm, pulled up a holographic screen from his tech panel, and ran a search. Strider understood this. It was better to come from his mouth than the two profiles that flickered to life. Both were stored in his database from the flash drive.

Katia surged forward and stopped hard in front of one of the images. She pointed. "Who—who is that?"

Alanna snorted. "Well, the screen says Zélia, so I'm gonna take a wild guess and say...Zélia. And before you ask, she's who I report to, therefore, it is...in fact, *Zélia*."

All the blood drained from Katia's face. Her hand dropped.

Mira stepped toward her. "Katia?"

"You okay, babe?" Sienna's eyes narrowed as she inched closer to her friend.

"I'm gonna pass out," she whispered.

The girls moved fast, guiding her to the couch. Jed ran for ice water. Adler snatched a cold compress from the freezer.

Tears rimmed Katia's lashes. She blinked up at Sienna. "That's who had you tortured?"

"Again," Strider said, pinching the bridge of his nose. "It was a misunderstanding."

"Semantics." Sienna shrugged, brushing Katia's arm gently, putting her own shock aside for the sake of being there for someone who clearly needed it. "I'm sure she...meant well. For the cause or something."

Mira crouched next to Katia. "Do you know her?"

Katia offered a shaky nod. "Know her? That's Kiania. My sister."

A pin dropped somewhere on each level of hell.

"Pardon?" Adler choked.

Sienna cleared her throat. "Wait...the, uh..."

"The dead one," Katia said, distant. "Yep."

Wolfe let out a sharp whistle and shoved his hands in his pockets. "This group. Shit. You people live inside a telenovela."

"Would be nice if the gods gave them a season break or two," Atlas muttered.

Wren and the Mercers shot them synchronized glares. They raised their hands in surrender without saying a word.

I stared at Katia. "I'm not following."

"Well I guess she's going by Zélia now," Katia said slowly. "But her real name is Kiania. She died four years ago. At least...we thought she did."

I leaned against the edge of the kitchen island, the heel of my palm digging into the wood. My head swam with timelines and names—lines that weren't supposed to cross. The air inside Wolfe's house wasn't exactly breathable anymore. Too many bodies. Too much truth.

Feyfog wasn't strong enough to stave off this mess of shit.

"That tracks," Strider said. "Leadership must disappear from society in order to operate under the radar the way that we do. It's essential to operations. Without the secrecy and the shadows, we wouldn't have had the opportunity to grow this big. To get to this point. As you know, Thaddeus followed the same protocol. Established it."

"*I* don't know shit." Sienna hissed.

"They're both here. Somewhere." Alanna rested against the couch, uninterested in the emotions running rampant.

"We were all separated in the blast," Strider's voice raised a notch to accommodate her coldness. "We're all to touch base tomorrow, sixteen-hundred sharp at the rendezvous point over on the mainland."

"Then I guess you'll have company," Mira concluded.

Strider glanced at Alanna. A silent conversation passed between them, but neither of them argued.

37

MIRA

Water lapped over our toes as the tide rose and fell. Our fingers had long been buried under the sand, but we kept them linked. Katia had barely spoken a word—barely blinked—since we came out here. She sat between Sienna and me, staring out at the starry horizon. Tears had been sporadically rolling down her cheeks, and I felt her move between anger and grief, sadness and confusion. To now, where her body had settled on just existing.

I was sure one or two of the boys were somewhere behind us on watch, but they were quiet. Katia's lips parted, a steady, long breath pushing between them before she spoke.

"I tried to contact her once, you know," she whispered. "Went to the local medium. She wasn't very respected; people said she didn't truly have the gift. Necromancy hadn't been seen in so long, but I wanted to believe she could speak to Kiania. She couldn't, said my sister didn't want to talk to me. I told her she was a liar...turns out that wasn't necessarily true."

I'd been on her side of this sort of hurt, and I knew she didn't want a response. She simply needed to release the pressure pushing against her skin. Her body tensed, and I knew it was only the beginning. Katia ripped her hands out of ours and stood, her arms opening wide as she tilted her head up to the moon.

"Why'd you do it? Was I not enough?" she yelled as she walked into the water shin-deep. "You left me to pick up the pieces, blasted a hole in my heart, just to go play a hero from a folktale?"

The last words came out on a choke, as that rage once again waned into sorrow. Sienna and I stood, wading into the water with her until we were waist-deep, still clothed.

Katia finally looked at us. "I'm the one who cleaned her room out, who organized her funeral. *I'm* the one who knew before our parents. How do I face her? What would you do, Mira, if your aunt were really alive?"

"Uh..." I trailed off, not sure how to answer. "I think I'd need the facts. I'd need to know why she did it, and why she thought the need for it outweighed the pain she'd bring me."

It wasn't that simple, I knew that. She did have a unique opportunity to confront her sister for what she'd done. Katia nodded, that wild mix of emotions once again calming. Jed stepped onto the shore holding one of his guns at his side. Adler was still in the trees, but he watched us three in the water.

"I'll go with you to the rendezvous. You're right, I need to talk to her," Katia said. "Thank you both for this. I'd better go let them know I'm okay."

"Anytime, babe. We mean it," Sienna replied with a smile. "We'll all go together, you won't have to face her alone."

Katia pulled us into a wet, salty hug. An embrace not only meant to show how much she appreciated this but also how much love there was between all three of us. We'd all come from somewhere broken—a home, a past, a family. Sisters in pain and heartbreak, and there for every waking moment of it.

When Katia made it to Jed, he put his gun into the holster and picked her up. Sienna and I trailed behind them as Katia laid her head on Jed's shoulder, and Adler rubbed her back. Their steps were slow and patient, careful with her. If I was honest, it wasn't because they thought she was delicate or fragile. It was because she was one wrong move away from detonating. Sienna slowed down by the pool, and I stopped right behind her.

As soon as the twins stepped into the house, Koa and Wren stepped out. They didn't come straight to us, but respected our privacy and hung out by the door.

"So you decided to go?" I asked.

Sienna shrugged. "Decided as I said it I guess."

"She'll understand if you change your mind. I can go with her. I don't have any stakes in the game, but you have a really fucking big one," I said.

Sienna fiddled with something in her hand, and as she turned it over, I realized it was a flower. She turned her palm up, blooming it to life, then closed her hands, withering it. She did that on repeat as if she was drawing strength from the bud.

"What you said back there to Katia, I think it applies to me, too. I need to know why. I grew up with so much love, but I'd like to know why he thought I didn't need...his," she said.

"Yeah, I think it's a must. It was different when he was just this fictional character. Now he has a name, a face, and other family members tied to him. He owes you that and more," I replied.

My best friend sighed and leaned onto me, her body going completely loose and forcing me to catch her. She laughed, and I heard the sudden stop of feet behind us. Probably Koa thinking she passed out or something. But she did this often. Our sort of weird version of a trust fall when things got too serious and overwhelming.

"Keep your soul eating on tap, might need to get rid of him if I don't like his answers," she said as she stood and looped her arm in mine.

We walked to the house, Wren and Koa still standing guard, and I whispered, "Done. That's if Koa doesn't bite off his head first."

Tomorrow was going to be a long, long day. Katia had to deal with her sister. Sienna needed to face her father. The rest of us needed to figure out what the rebels were doing and how we fit into the picture. There'd be no shortage of drama, but right now, I just wanted to relax.

Wren opened the door and caught me by the waist as we walked in. He bent down to bring his lips to my ear and muttered, "I have a bath ready for you in our room, extra lavender salt and incense burning."

Oh, fuck yes.

The rendezvous point wasn't exactly close. Not entirely far either, but we had a couple of hours to drive. Which we were doing in a not-so-subtle tactical van. Of course, Wolfe had a fully stocked vehicle with gadgets, weapons, and a bunch of other shit I wasn't even familiar with. I'd made the argument that it seemed like a threat, but Wren and Koa said it was necessary.

Jed and Adler went to the demolished Cynod building to see if they could learn anything. Professional secret finders and what not. They'd tried to come, but Katia was pretty firm in the fact that she didn't want her sister to meet them yet. Whether that was because she was afraid of what Zélia might do, or because she was afraid of what she'd do herself, I wasn't sure. We'd reassured the twins that we'd take care of her, and even Strider mentioned that he was certain Zélia wouldn't hurt her.

I understood where Katia was coming from. There were some things that had to be done on your own two feet, no romantic partners to hold you up. Wren drove, and I sat in the passenger seat, Alanna and Strider in the row between the rest of the gang—Koa, Sienna, and Katia.

My brother didn't give them an option but to sit between us all. He was particularly cautious around Strider. Alanna he'd dealt with, but Strider was still a wild card. Koa *hated* wild cards. Especially when they weren't in his favor.

But I'd read Strider's aura, and I saw nothing but good intent and love in him. I wondered if Sienna was his only remaining family outside of her father, his uncle. Part of me really wondered if maybe he knew her as a kid. He was a few years older than us, not much, but enough for him to remember Sienna, and her not to remember him.

"We're fifteen minutes out," Wren shouted for everyone to hear.

"Run me through it again, Sterling," Koa said with his hand on Strider's shoulders, and not in a fun, playful way.

"His name is Strider," Alanna drawled.

"Whatever," Koa snorted. "Run me through it."

Strider cleared his throat. "It's another warehouse."

"You people love your warehouses, don't you?" Sienna mumbled.

"They have the space we need," Strider said. "And this one in particular is still operative, just by us."

"What are you moving?" Wren asked, looking at him through the rearview.

Alanna's nose scrunched. "This one's moving fish, and it smells just how you think."

"It's an easy cover-up, and fish are used all over the nation. There are maybe four other fish warehouses we run. We get in and out of places easily; nobody is stopping the people delivering this kind of food," Strider said. "It's our newest location, but it's proven valuable. However, downstairs there are rooms, not on the blueprints, and very secure."

They'd really thought through all of this, which was a good sign. We had no interest in joining any half-assed movements.

"And in those rooms are…?" Koa asked.

"Zélia and Thaddeus, for one. They run the show, but leaders from a couple of other states are supposed to be there as well. We have to discuss the impact of our last hit and what we'll do next."

"What other hits have there been?" I asked.

"You're in our future plans," Alanna chided. "but I'm not sure we should discuss the past."

Strider nodded. "Zélia will need to clear you for that."

"Look forward to it," Katia said under her breath.

Wren reached out his hand, squeezing mine in a way I thought was purely habit, but when our tires hitched over the first panel of a bridge, I realized why. I was okay, though. The warmth of his magic spread between us, and I couldn't help the smile pulling at my lips. No, I wasn't going to have an anxiety attack. Didn't mean I wouldn't enjoy the feel of him.

"There it is," I said, pointing to the most stereotypical-looking fish warehouse ever.

The sound of gun clips sliding and magazines being jammed into place filled the car, and even Wren was somehow driving with a knee as he checked his weapons.

I turned in my seat. "Sienna, Katia, you ready?"

Their heads moved up and down but they didn't exactly look ready. What does ready look like to meet a once-dead relative and a relative you'd never met but sired you? Who knew.

Two workers waved Wren into a loading dock, and he glanced at Strider through the rearview as he let go of my hand.

"They're taking you in the right direction, we're here for frozen Amberjack fish," he reassured.

Wren slowed, taking the time to scan the area before putting the van in park. A man walked up to his window, and he rolled it down with his left hand, his right tight around the grip of his gun.

"What ya here for?" the man asked.

"Frozen Amberjack," Wren replied flatly.

The man tipped his head toward the tunnel to the left. "Park in there, someone will help you with that order."

Wren did that weird grunt thing men did in recognition of each other and pulled into the tunnel. It was dark, but lights illuminated ring by ring as we moved through. Someone was waiting at the end, holding up a hand for us to stop.

"He's going to drop us down," Strider said when Koa leaned forward.

Wren's fingers released their tight grip on the steering wheel. "Better hope you're telling the truth."

The land beneath us shook, the walls going from the light blue hue to black as we were dropped down a level with the assistance of a *Kaban's* earth magic. A bright overhead light beamed on us, probably meant to scare the people in the car, but Wolfe's windows were so damn tinted it barely did anything.

"Bodies," Wren said, and Koa shuffled to the front, his back bent as he looked out the windshield.

"Three," Koa added.

"It's just the ones who let us in." Strider said as he went to open the door. "You two are worse than the rebels, damn."

Koa shuffled ahead of him, getting his hand on the handle before Strider and hopping out of the vehicle. His boots hit the ground hard, and Wren joined him.

The two of them strolled, visibly unbothered, to the front of the van, and the light turned off.

The woman who'd come with Zélia to Koa's gym, Asha, stood before them, two other rebel soldiers with machine guns bracketed her. I couldn't hear what they were saying, but they both looked back at us at the same time and motioned for us to get out.

Alanna practically pounced out of the car, and I *may* have shoulder bumped her as I got out. From what I remembered, Asha didn't speak, and she let her gun hang on the strap to sign something to Strider.

"Mira and Wren saved us at the building bombing. Took us back to their house until things died down. Zélia should be expecting us," Strider said while signing.

Asha nodded and let the steel door open, exposing a very well-lit, clean corridor. Surely wouldn't have guessed this was beneath the rundown warehouse above us. Asha led us in, and we made it halfway to the end before Katia suddenly stopped and turned around.

"I feel you," Katia said with her chin raised. "Come out, sister."

Zélia manifested out of the shadows, an uncharacteristic hesitation taking over her body. Gone was the bravado and confidence she'd faced us with; now the vulnerable parts were exposed. Even leaders of rebellions had them. Which was why, I assumed, they had to die and become new, leaving those vulnerabilities behind them.

"Katia, you look—"

Zélia was cut off as her sister swung her hand back and smacked her across the face. The rebels all shifted forward, but Zélia lifted her hand to stop them.

Her free hand fell gently to her cheek. "I deserve that," she whispered.

"How could you do this?" Katia pleaded.

"Leave us," Zélia commanded, but we didn't move.

"My people will stay behind me, because that's what you do for the people you love. You stay with them," Katia responded.

There was a new hurt in Zélia's eyes now. One of being replaced, but she had done this to herself. Katia was right; if she wanted us here, we wouldn't move a muscle.

"Do you remember Luiz?" Zélia asked her sister, jumping straight into it.

"Yes, he was your boyfriend before the crash; we didn't see him again after the funeral."

"He was the one who recruited me. I'd started small get-togethers in Jundi to fight the Cynod, to wake them all up. A couple of rebels attended, and they saw something in me. They told me I could make the world better. They could give me the resources I needed."

Katia only nodded, no understanding falling from her lips.

"The Cynod is out of control, you know this. I'm sure it's only been confirmed further with your new...friends. They had been trying to get a stronger foothold in Jundi, and I couldn't do it anymore. They needed to be stopped. I wanted a better world for you," Zélia explained.

My friend's body was rigid, as if afraid to let her sister see anything going on in her mind.

"I have no problem with what you're doing here," Katia's voice shook for the first time. "As a matter of fact, I would commend anyone else in this position. But you knew what it was like for me there, you left me behind, discarded me."

Zélia moved closer to her sister, and I shuffled a step closer just in case. But she rested both of her hands on either side of Katia's face. "I never discarded you. You were young, and I knew you'd end up at Kuxtal. That you'd see how much bigger the world was than Jundi. I couldn't help you from there, but I can now. They will not make you another soldier in their war, not another cog in their weapon of destruction. You should be able to decide what you do, where you go, who you go with."

The last bit of Katia's resolve withered away, and she pulled her sister into a hug. She was nowhere near forgiven, but fuck, what I would give for a hug from my tía. Even if I was angry, I'd take that time and time again.

Someone cleared their throat, and we all turned back in the direction we were heading originally. A man with deep brown skin, kind eyes, and cropped hair stood with his hands behind his back.

"Hello, my daughter."

38

SIENNA

Part of me wanted to refuse him the decency of turning around. To deprive him of the opportunity of speaking to me after twenty-three years of silence. That option would inevitably result in some mild regret come morning meditation. I'd come here for answers after all.

Then came the real issue at hand. I actually wasn't quite sure what questions I had for the man. What was I supposed to say? *Hey, pops. So nice to meet you. Where the hells have you been the last two decades, and why'd you say 'fuck my entire family'?*

I mean, I guessed I could. But was I really ready to hear the answer to those questions? I didn't think there was enough soul-searching in the world that could help me come to a definitive answer for that.

Thaddeus Collins' image had lived in my head day in and day out since we pulled his file on the flash drive. I'd be able to spot the man by his pinky a block away at this point.

That line of thinking still left me ill-prepared to face him as I met brown eyes that mirrored mine. He was remarkably unremarkable. Handsome, but not in the way that sets you back a step. Tall, yet Koa and Wren were taller. His athletic figure lacked the posture that posed a threat. I supposed that was the point, though. Every aspect of him served as a benefit for his role in a rebellion.

"You don't get to call me that." There was a lack of bite in my voice that triggered what I imagined others considered embarrassment.

"Perhaps we should allow these reunions some privacy?" Strider intervened, attempting to usher Koa, Mira, and Wren out the metal doors we'd emerged from what felt like an eternity ago.

"Sienna stays within my eyesight at all times," Koa cautioned, his glare lethal. "That's a nonnegotiable."

Thaddeus remained focused on me. His back was to Koa, wrongly assuming his words were mere warnings when really, they were a threat. Next would come action.

"I pose no threat to Sienna," he said. My name did not flow freely from him. The pursing of his lips was a dead giveaway to the two words he was refraining from uttering—as if honoring my wishes would mean anything to me.

"Good." I crossed my arms. The posture gave me a false sense of control, even if my hands were shaking slightly beneath it. "Then you can answer my questions with or without an audience."

"I know what you want to ask," he said.

"Do you?" I tilted my head. "Because I'm not even sure what the hells I want to hear right now. I mean, what's the script for this? 'Sorry I missed every milestone of your life, sweetie, but I was off playing revolutionary.'"

"I didn't fake my death to play anything," he hissed, thumb hammering against his chest. "I did it because I had to disappear to *build* something. For you. For all of us."

I never thought he was dead. Actually, I wasn't ever certain what I thought. Gone was all Momma said. *He* was a topic I knew not to bring up. It sent her into a spiral she didn't need in her rare moments of free time.

"Oh, so it was for me? That's funny. Because I don't remember benefiting from your little vanishing act."

"The house—"

"Fuck the house," I spat. "I was only ever alone in it, anyway."

Everything in the room went hush. Not quiet. Hush. The kind that creeps under your skin and presses a finger to your mouth. Zélia grabbed onto Katia, dragging them into the shadows. Given the fact that she didn't scream for help, I assumed she chose to go freely with her sister, back through the doors we'd entered through. Mira touched my arm on her way out. Gentle. Her version of *don't fall apart yet*. The others followed her. No one asked me if I was ready for that. Spoiler: I wasn't.

'Afraid I'm not enough?' Koa teased.

I sensed him behind me and glanced over my shoulder. He stood there—apocalypse eyes, radiating that brand of danger that would send everyone else running, but me crawling. His possession of me was masked as concern. It pinned me in place, peeled back every layer I'd glued on to get through the last few minutes of my life.

'Thank you,' I said, realizing Koa had likely cleared the room himself. I was simply talking back before. Alanna, Asha, Strider...they were the last people I wanted to lay witness to me falling apart. Which, at this point, was only a matter of time.

His presence almost helped. Except my stomach was upside down and my ribs were made of bees, and I was close to screaming into the void or maybe laughing so hard I cried.

A muscle in Thaddeus's chiseled jaw twitched. "I stayed away because I had no choice. I had to become someone else. Someone who could survive long enough to make a difference. That means no ties to familial lines or anyone that could be used against you by the enemy."

"And did it ever occur to you that *I* might've needed someone too?" My tone wavered before I could stop it. "You think I care that the movement needed some leader? You were my *father*, and you left."

I hated how he stood there. All poised and relaxed as if he'd rehearsed this and it was going exactly as planned.

"Leaving behind Marlie was the hardest thing I have ever had to do. There is not a day that goes by that I don't consider the 'what if.' But this is bigger than the life that could be. While there's...more to the story that is not my right to share, *this* was the best outcome that could be. You see, Sienna, there was no movement when I left. When none of this had a name, I saw what the Cynod were becoming long before others of our time did. I tried to sound the alarm from within...we are of Hagen's line, you and I. There should have always been a seat at the table for you and me. No one listened to my warnings. Though that didn't stop certain Cynod lines from noticing...keeping an eye on me. They killed Kaheim, my brother, as a repercussion for my lack of silence. When Marlie told me she was pregnant, I knew I had to disappear. For the world to think I was gone—because I had work to do. Work that could not be done with a family. Or a name. I *am* the movement. The movement is reborn through me."

The worst part was...I got it.

Somewhere between his b.s. and his conviction, I could feel the shape of the truth. Not the pretty kind. A truth that hurts to hold. The kind that fits too well inside the ache I've carried since I was old enough to ask where he went.

And gods help me, I hated him more than ever for making me understand. There was nothing I hated coming across more in the wild than a logical man who knew they weren't fucking stupid. Why should I even care? I *had* a father. Ethan raised me. Ethan taught me to fight, to listen, to never back down, to build something out of broken things.

He held my hair when I was sick, carried my secrets when I couldn't hold them, and feared what Momma would say. Ethan was the one who taught me what love was supposed to *do*—not say.

But still.

There was a part of me—the stupid, aching part that wanted this man to have *tried*. And it was *that* part, the soft part, that I hated most of all.

Koa hadn't moved. I could feel his energy humming in the background, tethering me to the floor. A living wall between me and the swell of pain that left permanent marks. Thaddeus's eyes flicked to him, calculating. Then he took a step forward.

My body reacted before my brain did—a half-step back, breath catching, shoulders twitching like they wanted to fold in. My instincts didn't trust him.

"Another step in her direction and it will be the last fucking step you'll ever take," Koa warned.

Thaddeus had the audacity to question me. "Your mother approves of this...arrangement?"

"You could've sent something," I said. "A message. A sign. Anything. I grew up thinking I wasn't worth fighting for. Did you know? Do you have the trait too?"

Thaddeus licked his lips. "I did not. No. I thought it died with your grandfather." He swallowed hard, and I hated the guilt in his eyes.

"I watched from afar. I knew you were at Kuxtal. I knew you were safe."

"Oh, good. You were stalking me. That really fills the emotional void. So then you also probably knew I was being tortured, right?" I snarled.

He reached for me then thought better of it, profusely shaking his head. "No. *No*. That was never supposed to happen, as I'm sure your cousin explained. I never liked Vitória, but Zélia has the authority to form her own team. Though I wish she'd tighten the leash now and then. They were punished appropriately, believe me."

Silence stretched between us.

"I joined with Zélia five years ago. She had a smaller movement buzzing out in Jundi, and it felt appropriate to join forces. Publicly, we were dead. Privately, we were useful. Together, we rebuilt the rebellion's core in order to protect the people from what comes next."

"And what now? What's next?"

"That's what I was hoping to get to soon. Though you coming here brought that day sooner than plans had allowed. I'd like to explain why we need you now."

39

KOA

"I would like the others to join us for this, if that's okay," Thaddeus continued, his voice smooth but heavy with implication, his eyes locked onto mine. "We can continue this conversation in a more...private location."

"Over my dead fucking body," I said.

Thaddeus offered me the smallest of grins that said 'that could be arranged.' Typically, I respected the overstated confidence. A smart fae doesn't tempt a fight they feel they could lose. And Thaddeus didn't spark me as a dim bulb. Right now, I was itching to have a lethal reaction. That was the wrong fucking answer, given he donated the sperm to create the love of my life.

His real punishment wasn't a fist to the jaw or a knife through the jugular. It was knowing the best parts of him—if any existed—had bloomed inside someone he'd never know. Entirely because that beautiful gem of a woman would never trust him to. Not the way the people she was closest to did. Not the way *I* did.

With an exasperated sigh, Thaddeus rapped the doorframe twice. It swung open instantly.

Katia walked in first, arm brushing her sister's. The others followed behind. Vitória. Strider. Asha. Alanna. Mira. Wren.

Vitória clicked her tongue and scanned the room as if we were all beneath her. Which was ironic, truly, when reflecting on the reason we were packed into this fish-smelling shit hole. "Gangs all here. This should be fun." Her attention landed on Sienna, who hadn't moved since the door opened. Just locked up. Breathing steady.

Ah shit. She was meditating, which was not a great indicator of how this was about to go down.

Zélia stepped forward, silencing Vitória with a stare. "This was not how we intended your first meeting to go. However, as the situation presents itself, all important parties are present. We may as well begin."

"Begin what?" Mira asked.

Asha signed something, not caring to hide that she was clearly talking about my sister. Which I wouldn't have let fly regardless, except the gods had clearly decided someone else would end their day with bruised fists. Vitória read it, laughed under her breath with the briefest of nods toward Sienna before signing something back. That was all it took.

A vine ripped from the floor and yanked their legs clean from beneath them. Asha hit the ground with a dull thud. Unfortunately for the second party of interest, Vitória recovered midair, twisted, and lunged at Sienna as if she'd been waiting for an excuse.

I moved first to intervene. Didn't make it far before complete admiration swept over. Sienna took her down in two moves. Sharp pivot. Shoulder throw. Then she was on top of her, raining down hits that made it clear she remembered everything Vitória ever did to her and wouldn't be forgiving her.

Half the room started toward them. Mira and I were aligned the second our eyes locked. We turned and blocked their path.

"I think she deserves a few licks given their last interaction," I said, arms crossed.

Strider sprang forward with the intention of breaking it up. I side-stepped in front of him without a word. He stopped short. Besides, we both knew Sienna wasn't the one who needed saving at this very moment. Shit, the way that girl has been training since her kidnapping, probably never again.

Glancing behind me, I watched as Vitória tried to roll her hips and buck her off. Rookie fucking mistake. Sienna shifted fast, brutal, driving her knee into Vitória's ribs. The air left her lungs in a harsh whoosh. If she drove it home as I taught her, a hairline fracture would be a sweet surprise when Vitória's adrenaline wore off.

The grunt that escaped her went beyond pain—it was a surprise. Sienna used that second of slack to slam her elbow down across Vitória's jaw. Her head bounced off the floor with a crack.

Another hit. This time with her fist. Full weight behind it. I sighed, tilting my head with fascination and caution alike. Had I created a monster? *Ha*. Shit. Maybe.

Vitória's hand flailed, caught nothing. Blood spattered the floor as Sienna's knuckles smashed her nose. Mira winced on Vitória's behalf with widened eyes and an accompanying prideful smirk. The sound was loud. Wet. You could *feel* the cartilage give.

Part of me knew I should've stepped in by now. That is what the greater fae would do. But that was Sienna's job, not mine, and right now, the 'greater fae' was relieving some of that trauma on its source. Even Strider had backed off. Not out of fear—but recognition. This was a release. And she deserved every second of it.

Thaddeus and Zélia hadn't moved from their spot, though Thaddeus kept sneaking glances at his daughter. If I didn't know any better and already assume the absolute worst of the man, I'd say he resembled a proud father. Alanna, however, couldn't appear more bored.

Vitória twitched on the ground, blood streaking her face from what was probably a broken nose. Sienna straddled her, chest rising fast, curls sticking to her cheeks.

"Press up on me again," Mira warned, stepping toward Asha with a poisonous drawl. "And I'll make *Sienna's* ass-whooping look like foreplay."

My eyes crinkled with amusement, glancing at Wren—who was practically vibrating from attempting to contain his laughter. I burst first, a deep howl of laughter echoing down the open bond between our minds.

'Our taste in women is impeccable.' Wren said down the bridge.

"Oh, Thaddeus," Zélia murmured, a touch too pleased, her accent as thick as Katia's. "Your daughter, she is..."

That pulled Sienna's attention. She gave Vitória one last shove into the floor and stood. It was adorable. "I am the daughter of Ethan and Marlie Hayes.

Now." She brushed blood from her knuckles sheepishly, returning to her usual disposition. "I think I'm ready to hear what you all have to say."

'That was hot,' I said, closing the bridge off to Wren and opening it for my mate.

'I know I said I was working on my anger since coming to Kuxtal, but fuck,' Sienna replied with a euphoric whoop. *'That was a greater rush than that time I set Forrest's car into neutral and down a cliff.'*

I side-eyed her. *'Yeah. We're coming back to that one, Venom.'*

"Let's hurry whatever this is along," I said aloud, stepping forward with a sharp grin that promised violence wrapped in velvet. "Before I get bored and start turning people into stone until you get to the point."

Thaddeus didn't so much as flinch. "This movement is far greater than you could conceive."

Wren's voice cut in. "Then enlighten us."

"Resourcing is no longer a problem." Zélia crossed her arms over her sleek black jacket, hugging her muscular frame. "The support of the people is behind us, and so is the backing of powerful people in high places."

"Doubtful," I said flatly.

Thaddeus tilted his head, his sharp cheekbones reflecting the aggressive overhead lighting. "What reason would we have to lie?"

My sister was unconvinced. Her lips fell into a tight frown. "We came to you, not the other way around. Offering up this information now feels...manipulative."

A quick glance at Sienna beside me showed a calm and composed facade. But that's all it was. That narrowed, hardened look in her eyes gave it away. She was coiled like a blade back in its sheath. Thaddeus had painted her as the linchpin of the revolution they were orchestrating. So yeah—it *was* manipulative. They needed her. They would've come eventually when it benefited them, damn whatever Sienna would have going on in her life. No options were intended to be presented to her when the time came, and the irony in that wasn't lost.

I turned back to them. "We want everything you know. No fragments. No cryptic bullshit. Lay it all out. Right now. Even footing, or this ends here."

Zélia's smile did not meet her eyes, and something told me it probably hadn't since she faked her death. Too bad I didn't give a damn.

"That simply isn't possible." Wren opened his mouth to speak, but Zélia raised a hand, cutting him off with infuriating ease. "But," she said, already walking, "we'll show what we can. Something I think you'll find interest in. Follow me."

She moved to the far wall where a door shimmered into view as the shadows peeled back. Katia was already moving after her sister before the rest of us exchanged a look. We stepped inside a large lift. Vitória—wisely—maintained her distance from Sienna, who shot her a smug little grin that made me proud as all hells. Thaddeus pressed his palm to a sensor embedded in the wall, revealing a holographic display in the air. His fingers moved in an unfamiliar sequence, and the lift descended.

Inside the lift was quiet, and so was the outside world surrounding it. Too quiet. Wren's eyes met mine. Both our fingers drifted toward our weapons.

"You really think they'd allow you to keep your weapons if they felt you were truly a threat?" Alanna drawled. "Gods, the male brain. Such simple thoughts."

She had a point. I hated that she had a point. I released a sharp breath through my nose, irritation tightening in my chest. The lift slowed and the doors parted with a hiss. Obsidian walls with gold-flecked sconces lit the corridor in ceremonial procession. Between each flame, the symbol of the rebellion burned in pain that shimmered faintly with magic.

"Welcome," Zélia's voice was full of warm pride. "*La Última Resistencia.*"

"The last resistance of the people..." Sienna murmured, the words rolling off her tongue naturally—a cradle-born echo of the mother tongue, guttural and unpolished. Real. Filled with culture and experiences, life lessons.

Not the true mother tongue, but a splinter of it, a language born in protest. A patchwork dialect, the first fae stitched together to distance themselves from what came before. *Civilization,* they called it. Gods forbid they simply carry the weight of their ancestors without rewriting the story.

The language spoken now came later. Polished and approved by the Cynod, sold as unity and bred for obedience. It was sanitized and stale. This was what was taught in schools. Our real mother tongue nearly died when the Veil dropped.

Only the wealthy—or the willful and brave—kept it alive. Households like Celeste's, which is where Sienna picked it up.

And now the rebellion was using it. Owning it. Twisting it back into something sharp. That power made something in me sit up and listen. Reluctant respect.

We moved down a winding corridor that seemed to shift the longer we walked. When we stopped, the door in front of us was wedged between many forgettable designs. One by one, we slipped through.

The second I stepped across, magic slithered down my body: the ward latched onto me akin to a second skin, humming through every bone. It was layered. No signal could penetrate it—no recording, transmission, nothing. Anything electronic died the second it crossed the line. But more than that, it read intention.

And I bet it cost them a fuck ton to have done. That or their connections *were* far greater than they were willing to admit. This was not a mainstream, one-size-fits-all kind of thing. It was conjured. Old, heavy magic.

Alanna strolled through and didn't immediately turn to ash. I stared. She caught the shock on my face and smirked, flicking me off without breaking stride. *Right, of course she passed. Maybe the ward doesn't read sarcasm.*

The room was circular with lime green walls that reminded me of the Astral-Codex. It had that same strange stillness—like it existed out of time. We formed a loose ring around the center. Thaddeus was the first to break the silence. "What's shared here today cannot be repeated outside this room."

I let out a sharp exhale. "I'm sitting on the edge of my seat."

"The background work on this *revolution* has been fulfilled," Zélia announced with forced annunciation of her vowels. "It's time we enter the next phase—the final phase before rebuilding can begin."

The door behind her opened. None of the rebels bothered to turn around and face the intruder. Their face was blocked by an oversized white machine that they pushed into the room with what appeared to be great effort.

"Fucking hells," Wren said with a half-laugh as Mira froze at his side.

I blinked once, twice—and then all the pieces clicked into place. "Of course," I muttered.

Professor Taran's eyes landed on me first. "I always knew you were worthy of the truth," he said, then turned to Mira. "Glad to see there are two Caneks with fully functioning brains."

He rubbed his hands together with the same diabolical grin he used before passing out final exams. "Prepare yourselves." With the press of three buttons in a specific sequence, the machine came to life.

And the floor dropped out.

Metaphorically speaking, but that's how it felt. My stomach flipped once, then again, and the edges of the world melted into something else entirely. Old stone and sunlight, blood in the dirt, the smell of salt and smoke, and something sweeter—jasmine crushed underfoot.

We were back.

That thing, whatever it was, had to be a more powerful version of the Astral-Codex machines on campus. Those were best described as an experience. *This*, this was living. If my memory of the world I'd left behind was not intact, I would assume I was teleported here and starting a new life.

Right now, we were right in the middle of the same nightmare of history. The air was tighter...heavier.

"We've seen this before," Mira said, tensing beside me.

"Yes," Taran answered, "but not through this lens and not in its entirety."

Because that didn't sound ominous at all.

The same ancient city, carved from limestone and jade, stretched before us—familiar and devastating. Ixchel sprinted through the smoke-thickened air, cradling that tiny life, its heartbeat echoing through time. I hadn't noticed it before. Or maybe I had, and never really processed it.

Neither had I acknowledged what sat next to *the* arch. The one currently smack in the middle of Kuxtal Academy, tied to stupid school lore. Had it been there before? Or was this intended to show us what we did not have access to on campus? Ixchel darted under the arch into the forest, one arm briefly leaving the baby's back to toss out a stream of light-sparked magic at the structure.

The group descended on it, curious. Thaddeus, Zélia, and Taran hung back, clearly having seen this particular bit several times. At first glance, the center of the structure appeared nothing more than a circular stone. It was wide as a burial pit and carved in tight, interlocking spirals that looked more like time than art. The outer ring held markings so precise, they made my eyes itch.

Alanna flicked her eyes to me. There was slight tension in her jaw that read as recognition. The connection.

A pulse of understanding ran through me. Professor Ortega's midterm, the replicated fragment of a tablet, his mention on how history was fractured and knowledge surviving in pieces. The symbols repeated in a similar fashion. It still wasn't clear what exactly *it* was.

I snapped my gaze to Taran, who held his chin up high under my gaze. *Son of a bitch*. He smirked, a *shh* quietly forming on his lips. Our finals. The etchings were too similar to the monument in front of me to disregard. Visually, this thing was ancient, even within the time and context in which it existed.

"Something catch your eye, Sienna?" Zélia asked, her voice closer than expected.

I glanced sideways. Sienna was already inching forward, eyes locked on the artifact. Her stare was sharp, near ravenous, though her body language screamed controlled curiosity and dripped with focus. *Too* focused. Entranced.

Thaddeus and Zélia watched her, and I watched them.

She tilted her head slightly, curls falling, fingers twitching at her side. Whatever it was, she understood it—or she was trying really fucking hard not to. Then Sienna smiled. A lie dressed in sweetness.

"It's simply beautiful, is all," she said smoothly. "I enjoy history."

'Liar,' I teased.

Sienna didn't look at me. Something in her voice had set me off. Not the words. The restraint behind them. Whatever that thing was, Sienna recognized it. And she wasn't saying a damn thing. Now was not the time to press her or Taran, and as if agreeing, the Codex warped again, the scene shifting.

This one wasn't familiar. We weren't watching a war or a massacre, or seeing religion form—we were watching gods.

Chaac leaned against a pillar in the furthest corner of a long, straight hallway, his weapon balanced casually on one shoulder. He swung it down, breaking the monument that once sat next to the arch into pieces. Ixchel sat beside an unfazed Kukulkan, who was hunched over a long piece of parchment, scribbling fiercely. The baby—*the* baby—was cradled against Ixchel's bare chest, wailing softly as she whispered something low and rhythmic, fighting to get strands of her hair back from its grip.

The hallway was arched and impossibly wide, broken up by what appeared to be...windows. Except none of them matched. Each pane was its own world: desert storms, jungle cities, a burning sky, a walled-up compound of a small city, frozen mountains, grassy hills filled with flowers. None of it made sense.

Kan scratched more symbols onto the page while Ixchel peered over his shoulder. I didn't know what it was about the writing, but it hooked something in my chest. The pull was magnetic. I couldn't look away. I didn't understand the symbols the messenger god was drawing. They weren't letters. Not the way I knew them. But they pulsed with something ancient. A language buried too deep for speech. And yet, somehow, I knew them. Or they knew *me*. The pull hit hard—a hook behind my ribs, reeling me forward.

My subconscious led me to take a step.

Chaac sat slouched in the far corner like this was all a waste of his time, but I caught the way his gaze tracked everything. He wasn't bored—he was calculating. Watching the room like it was a battlefield he hadn't decided how to win yet.

He lifted his axe and pointed it at one of the windows. "That one."

Ixchel turned her head. "If you are certain."

"I make no mistakes," Chaac replied with a smirk that almost qualified as charm, he passed her half of the circular artifact. "There is much to be learned in this world."

"The record nears completion," Kan murmured without looking up.

He scratched the final mark, held the parchment up to inspect it—without fanfare, Kan ripped it down the middle.

We watched on. He strode toward the second window Chaac had motioned to—a land choppy in rocky beaches and jungles, like Inecha's coast—and tossed the other artifact half in.

Ixchel stood and stepped through the first window Chaac had pointed to. A land so similar to ours before modernization. My heart kicked. She was only gone for a breath. Ixchel reappeared with no child in her arms.

"I apologize for the delay." She pulled the strands of her hair forward, fully covering her chest. "That took quite a bit of convincing. I have forgotten what it's like to bargain with other gods."

"Great," Chaac grumbled, then vanished into smoke.

Kan faced Ixchel with a slow exhale. "What must be known has been pre-served—for those with the will to remember."

"In time, they will come to understand what was broken and what must be found," Ixchel concluded. "The rest will depend on whether they are worthy of knowing it. Of finding that world."

"The pieces are scattered. As was always foreseen." The two halves of the ever familiar papers burned in the palm of his hand. "They will appear where they must. In time, they will reveal themselves to those meant to wield them."

With that, the world around us faded and returned to the sickly lime green. I blinked hard, adjusting to the harsh glow of the room. My head was pounding.

"What's your role in this, Taran?" I asked.

"How else could one know the true history to program?" he replied, as if it should've been obvious. "I'm just shy of a prophet, but I possess the ability to receive messages from the gods."

"*The* gods?" Sienna echoed, brows drawn.

"As do you," Taran said, looking directly at her. "Though admittedly, we achieve the same goal in different ways."

"Meaning...?" she pressed.

Taran didn't answer right away.

"Sienna, there are certain lineages blessed by the gods with the gift of their blood." Thaddeus stepped in instead. "Ours is one of them. The Tarans. A few other families aside from the Cynod. Each of us possesses the ability to speak to—or for—the gods, the memory of the old tongue, our mother tongue, per-manently ingrained within the fiber of our being."

"My line, for example, obtains visions of the past to protect its integrity and lessons. Someone has to speak the truth," Taran added with a wink.

"Our family," Thaddeus continued, "has the ability to *read* the word of the gods—in *their* tongue, not ours."

I'd never heard that the gods had their own language before. But the more I thought about it, the more it made sense. They were ancient. Our languages—all of them—were fae-made. I tried to tamp down the excitement crawling up my spine and act like it wasn't a big deal, but I was fucking hooked.

"The Canul's are bound to the living code," Thaddeus went on. "They can interpret sacred signs in Herta—weather, movement, growth. The earth speaks through them with the words of our gods. Tun's, as you know, are gifted scribes, though they are not to be trusted with pertinent information. Their family was called to serve the Cynod as the official scribes for as far as history tells. They've chosen to side with the movement as, wisely, they understand their true calling. But in caution of potential *Ajaw* intervention, it's best they assume plausible deniability."

We were sucked back into the world of the Codex. Snapshots of history flashed like memories, showing the lines throughout generations. The chosen ones were interacting with the gods whose blood ran through their very veins. Most felt closer to the god that blessed their line. My eyes immediately flicked to Sienna. She was already staring at me, wide-eyed. She'd arrived at the same conclusion I had.

'*Kan,*' she said.

Sure enough, the scene shifted again. Same god, same eyes—but the people around him changed. Different clothes. Different cities. Decades passed in seconds. Through it all, one thing became obvious: her line went generations without the gift appearing.

"Can all dyslexics communicate with him? Or, them, I guess." Sienna asked.

Thaddeus released a laugh fueled by genuine humor. "No. As far as I'm aware, just us. While I'm never going to understand the severity of what you experience, based on my father's account, your dyslexia is different from others. You had trouble through the testing process when it came to diagnosis, yes?"

Sienna nodded. Too stunned to speak. It was a side to her I had not yet seen—when quick wit and sweetly nasty retorts abandoned.

"It's not a flaw, Sienna. It's a filter," Thaddeus said. "The symbols—the prophecy, the artifacts—weren't written for linear minds. They're meant to be read in layers. Spatially. Like...memory, not logic. You see, the way Kan *intended*." He studied her cautiously, trying to gauge how much was too much information. "Your dyslexia was not diagnosable because your brain processes glyphs, symbols, and language like a three-dimensional map. Not a line of text."

"So let me get this straight," Mira said, working through the theory the same way she tackled everything—methodically and sharp. "There are inheritable traits that only activate in those touched by a god? Or should I say, with godsblood?"

Strider offered a single nod.

Mira tapped her foot as she thought. "So if either of them has a child, they'll carry the gene, even if it doesn't manifest? And it won't show, unless tapped."

"You just said that last part, but, correct," Strider replied.

"Okay." Mira tilted her head side to side. "Cool."

Sienna narrowed her eyes at my sister. Mira mouthed *sorry*, backing down, though the fascination still held a gleam in her eyes.

"The Codex focused on being able to speak with the gods." I cut in. "And we were guided to scenes that had some sort of magic draw to...what? What are we missing? Why show us this now?"

"We aren't sure either," Taran said. "But after watching it well over two hundred and eighty times, I've concluded that obtaining these three artifacts will bring us closer to an answer. Closer to our goal."

He swiped his hand, and three images appeared midair.

The crumbled stone artifacts we already had. The torn paper, and the arch.

"You've got two of the three located," Katia pointed out. "What do you need them for?"

"I'm the only one who can read what Kan wrote," Sienna spoke in a flat tone, as if it were just a matter of fact.

"And I know where the paper is," I reluctantly added, watching the room still as everyone turned to me, "At least half of it."

"Where?" Zélia asked, far too eager.

I turned my sights on Alanna. "Mentiria."

She did her best not to waver, but her mask slipped for half a beautiful second. "The hallway?"

"There's a million halls in that place, but yeah," I said. "West wing."

"I always thought it had a creepy little tug to it." She peered up like the gods were listening. For all we knew, shit, they probably were. Nosy fucks. "May the gods not strike me down."

"That's perfect then," Zélia said. "Because we know where the other half is. Jundi."

Katia's surprise was unfiltered. "Oh my gods. Mom's office?"

Zélia nodded. "It was recently moved to be displayed during the grand opening of the Jundi National History Museum. Anonymous donation."

"Which was to be secured during transport by hired help," Thaddeus added, his stare pointed directly at Wren. I did a double take. "*Trusted* hired help—we needed to keep our hands clean with this one, given the sensitivity of the parties involved."

Smart. If anything went sideways, the Cynod might've launched a full investigation into what Katia's family had hidden in their damn house.

"He was murdered before he had the chance," Vitória said, spitting the words like a wounded lover. *Ah.* They were fucking. "Soren Oberon."

She said the name as if it was supposed to mean anything to me—

Oh, *shit.* I did my best to keep a grin off my face, turning to Wren, who was biting down his own smirk after we made eye contact. He tossed his hands up with a shrug.

"Nothing? No excuse, no defense? You murdered a man in cold blood."

"I was called to fulfill my responsibilities to the Brotherhood," Wren said, not the least bit sorry. "It was him or me. My family relies on me. So here I stand."

'Asshole,' I chuckled.

'He was a prick anyway,' Wren responded, dead serious in tone, *'and not really a loss to society much like his girlfriend. Sienna is family, too. No one hurts my family.'*

Zélia shot Vitória a visible warning. She backed down. Inching to Asha.

"With that out in the open, your relationship with *Noctis Fraternitas* is now fair game," I said. "Talk."

"There are far more important topics to discuss at the moment," Thaddeus interjected. "And time is limited."

"Speak with your contacts," Zélia concluded. "It's not our responsibility to divulge their interests."

Thaddeus apparently considered that the end of the conversation. For now. "Let us discuss the logistics."

40

Mira

It was almost time for us to go back home. While it wasn't exactly a relaxing trip, it was nice to live in a different reality for a few days. I hadn't told Wren about my plan yet, especially after the last couple of days of drama with the rebels. There hadn't been a minute to think about it. Now, the fact that we had to return to Kuxtal, back to the place that held us in fifty types of binds, it was time to snip at least one. Or try.

"Hey, love," Wren said as he opened the sliding glass door off our bedroom. "Uh...what's going on here?"

It was a fair question. Last time he was out here there were only two chairs and a small table on a slightly raised platform. Now, I had candles, matches, a firepit, a mug, a dagger, stones, a book, a molcajete, the cacao beans, and extra ingredients I'd pulled from the kitchen.

"Okay." I took a deep breath. "I've figured out a way to break the blood bond."

Wren's eyes widened, then settled, his hands flexing and relaxing like his hope was being contained by spiderwebs.

"This is why we went to the market?" he asked.

I nodded.

Wren stepped forward and removed his jacket. "What do you need me to do?"

"No questions, concerns, overall nerves?"

"It's you, Mira. I know you researched, researched some more, and then triple-checked before you even thought to bring it up. I trust you."

He had a point. He also knew me very well.

397

"Part of me hoped you had questions so I could run through it again," I mumbled.

The side of Wren's mouth ticked up. "Feel free to ask yourself questions."

"I'll just talk as I go," I responded and gestured him over.

Roasting was the first step. I grabbed the three stones, all the same size and shape. Thankfully, smooth flat stones were in ample supply at the beach.

"Okay, the individual stones represent the sun, the moon, and Herta—the earth. The three sources that bind us. To break a blood bond, you have to roast the cacao beans under the moon."

I lit the fire pit and let the heat spread evenly. The stones needed to be connected on either side, forming a triangle. Once they were situated and balanced, I carefully placed the light brown beans on the stones, equally spaced out. My book was open to the page detailing the ritual, and I ran my finger down the parchment until I found the step I was on.

"They need to roast until they're a deeper brown. We should hear a couple of cracks, and they'll be ready for the next part," I told Wren.

He was still sitting patiently beside me. I really hoped this fucking worked. Not only would it be extremely embarrassing if I failed, but I didn't think there was any other way to break it. Success was the only option.

"This isn't going to be easy," I started, biting my cheek. "We're both going to need to be entirely present. Pure intentions, pure focus. It isn't like a spell, it's going to require our entire being. I put a sign on the door so nobody comes in, too."

Wren moved closer to me, his eyes scanning the pages. "Is it dangerous for you?" he asked.

"Maybe, but I'm okay with that."

"Well, maybe I'm not." Wren's gaze continued trailing over the text.

I put my hand on his face and turned him back to me. "You keeping this bond is more dangerous to me. The benefits outweigh the risks here, and I'm confident."

We never came back to it after leaving my tía's house. The possibility that Dr. Aantaj could escalate the use of the bond. It wasn't just an insurance policy like Wren had thought. Sure, it would still notify Dr. Aantaj if he broke the rules, but if he could actually control him...that was far worse. Wren was already a weapon; it was why the Cynod wanted him. He was good at what he did, and that happened to be killing—hurting their opponents. Which I was in Aantaj's eyes.

The first crack of the bean shook me out of my thoughts, and Wren seemed to be on the same wavelength as me. The bond had to go, or the repercussions could be catastrophic. Especially if Koa found out that there was a chance Wren could be forced to hurt me. We were already all walking a tightrope of trust, and even if it wouldn't be truly Wren to make that choice, the possibility was enough.

The cacao bean shells darkened by the second, now a rich dark chocolate brown, cracking and roasted. It was time to remove them and move to the next step, and the weight of this ritual doubled. This was where it got complicated.

Using the dagger, I scraped all the beans off the stones and onto a stone that wasn't being heated. The book said that anything hard would work to remove the beans, so the dagger handle would do. I whacked the beans, just hard enough to crack the rest of the fragile shell until the nibs were fully exposed. They were a little lighter than the shell, but still a toasty brown.

"They look like almonds," Wren whispered.

"Well, almonds can't do what we're about to do," I joked.

The smell was heavenly, and if I wasn't about to mix it with blood, I might have suggested Sienna use it for some dessert. A breeze swept over our patio, and damn if it didn't feel like some sort of divine acceptance as all the shells dispersed. It was the *exact* thing I was about to do. Being outside was important, the connection to all four elements. The fire in the pit, the stones from the earth, the water we would mix the nibs with, and the air that blew in this moment.

Now that the shells were out of the way and the nibs were cooled slightly, I gathered them all into the molcajete. This one was as genuine as they came, the bowl made of volcanic rock from the region. The texture made it perfect for grinding down just about anything. With the help of the pestle, I pulverized each nib down to powder.

"Do you trust me?"

I knew he did, but I needed verbal reassurance in this particular moment.

"With everything I am," Wren answered.

Holding out one hand and gripping the dagger in the other, Wren seemed to realize exactly why I was asking. I needed his blood. He didn't hesitate, but placed his calloused hand in mine and let me cut a gash through it.

"I don't need a lot," I reassured, letting four drops cascade into the bowl, and another couple onto the bark paper at my side.

"Blood isn't just a bodily fluid; it's a conduit to the divine. Or at least it was seen as one when the gods walked the land. It was used as a way of connecting us to them. A blood bond melds with that connection, and it becomes spiritual, not only physical. Beyond a simple spell."

It was my turn, and I cut my hand with ease and without delay. The same amount of blood to maintain balance. Carefully, I retrieved the water pot located on the other side of the fire. It should have been warm, but not too hot to drink. Our blood and the nibs mixed together, swirling as the water filled up the molcajete.

I shook a couple of drops of all-natural vanilla into the mixture. "This is just to make it taste better."

"Can't say that's too much of a concern right now," Wren said with a chuckle.

Shrugging a shoulder, I stood and dragged Wren over to the center of the candles. "You stand here and I'll join you in a second."

The ingredients needed to be properly combined, so I took my time lighting each candle and pouring the mixture into the mug. When I came back to Wren, sweat sparkled on his brow, the fire casting orange over his skin.

"These cacao beans aren't regular beans, they're from the rainforest on Lake Balacar. That forest was blessed by the gods, and consuming the beans is going to have a couple of different effects on us."

"Like?"

"Well, it's going to take us to a spiritual place within ourselves first. The burning of our blood together on the bark paper and the candles will assist in getting us there, along with the consumption. We'll be able to see the foreign object in your blood, and we'll have to get it out. After that, our serotonin levels will be at an unnatural high, so..."

"So I'll want to fuck you even more than I already do?" Wren asked.

"To put it lightly."

"Sounds like the perfect place to end this. Let's get to it."

Unable to hide my smile, I shook my head. Unfortunately, the first half of this probably wasn't going to be nearly as enjoyable. We had that to look forward to after, I supposed. I used the candle fire to burn the bark paper, the smoke wrapping around us and removing our ability to see anything but each other. This was said to create something like a portal, to thin the Veil between the physical world and the spiritual.

"Time to drink," I said, lifting the mug to his lips, and then bringing it to mine.

"We taste good together," Wren teased.

Before I could respond, everything around us flickered. The laws of physics I'd come to know in this plane zapped away. Every single cell in my body felt as if I was being stretched and compacted, held under water, and lifted to the surface just to be pulled down again.

"What the fuck," Wren's deep voice came from somewhere, but I had no idea where.

I swore my eyes were open. Then I realized a different kind of vision was used here. Tapping into my nahual, into my spirit and its connection to the world, the eyes I needed here opened. It wasn't the gods' realm that Sienna described. This was something else entirely. This was bright lights, colors I couldn't describe, a…weightlessness, I couldn't quite figure out. My feet were on the ground, but my body's weight was nonexistent.

Wren. I turned, finding the man I knew, yet, more than that. He felt bigger here, not in a physical way, but his presence was unrelenting. His chest expanded as a sound of pain tore from his throat, and his nahual emerged from him. The massive jaguar encompassed him, a thin translucent second body. It moved with him, his fae jaw and jaguar maw tightening and loosening. His fae hands turning over with his clawed paws.

It was my turn for my nahual to make itself known, and unlike Wren, where it jumped out of his chest, mine seeped from my bones.

Wren's eyes went wide. "Mira."

I lifted my hands, seeing that my second body was my skeleton. An x-ray come to life. My finger bones moved as I made a fist, and let it go. As if this realm knew I needed to see, the ground became reflective. My skull was the most jarring of everything. It was adorned in jade embellishments, creating a pattern of flowers on my forehead and beneath my eyes.

"Death," I said as I grazed my finger over the jade.

"You're...devastating," Wren said genuinely. "If anyone could make even death an art, it's you."

As he got closer, his nahual and mine combined, that same sensation I'd had in our intimate moments taking over. Except here, it was overwhelming. The warmth and comfort I'd only *felt* before was tangible, visible as my bones emanated light from within. Wren's jaguar spots glowed golden, a call and response bouncing between us.

"You know they say that the jaguar was the only being that could walk through death and come back," I whispered.

"I do."

We stayed there, nahuales and souls combined, and in the next moment, I sensed the foreign substance in his blood. Like an alarm going off. It was wrong and misplaced—a violation.

"You see it too?" Wren asked.

This...thing pulsed as it rushed through his nahual. An ugly formation of magic stretching his veins from his heart, to his limbs.

"Yeah." I bit my lip. "And I've got to get it out."

"Can I help?"

"Just stay relaxed, and remember to keep the intention of removal at the forefront of your mind."

The tips of my fingers—the fae ones—turned onyx black. The way that my nahual presented itself in the physical world. I wondered if it was a way of protecting me from the disease that was this bond. After all, nothing stood against Death.

As I got closer, I realized it was connected, a web within his veins. It wasn't just pulsing and flowing. It had become entirely entwined. Like a dark and disgusting blood clot.

"This might hurt," I warned as I wrapped my finger around the substance and pulled.

It barely budged. The black of my nahual spread down to my wrist, and I wrapped my entire fist this time. Still, it only moved about an inch.

"Wren," I said. "You've got to let it go."

"I don't understand. I have, I want it gone," he replied frantically.

I took a step back and looked into his eyes. Not into them, through them. They said eyes were the windows to the soul, and it was validated as I focused. Pain, rage, desperation. He battled against it all with force, but it wasn't his own pain he focused on. It was everyone else's. A shield to his loved ones, without concern for what beat against his side.

Willing my nahual to caress against his, I held his stare. "Your purpose isn't only what you can do for others. It isn't just to protect. You, in your mind, might want it gone, but you have to remind your body and soul that you're more than that. This bond was a result of you diving into that ideology, and you've got to vanish it."

"What am I if not a protector?" he said, barely above a whisper.

When you're told who you are by external voices for so long, it's hard to believe anything else. It takes work, self-reflection, and support to find your true self. I was his support, and I'd tell him exactly who he was.

"You're the night sun. A symbol of light and power in the darkest of times. You're a protector, yes, you fight for the ones you care for. But that shouldn't be at the detriment of your being. The weight of everyone else's bad decisions shouldn't be on your shoulders alone. You're part of something greater now. We're going to make this world a better place. Let us...let *me* take some of it away so you can shine again."

A tear ran down his cheek, and I brushed it away. His body relaxed in a way I hadn't even seen in his sleep, and he nodded his head. This time, when I pulled at the blood bond, there was no tension. I wrapped it around my hand like yarn until there wasn't anything left. Without a host, it shriveled second by second until it was nothing but dust.

Wren took a deep inhale, and his eyes shot back up to mine. "I can breathe. He's not...it's not..."

He wrapped his body around mine with such speed I didn't realize my feet were off the ground until he spun us in a circle.

"I'll never be able to thank you," he said into my neck.

"Eh," I teased. "I feel pretty good just being successful."

My feet met the ground again, his hands still in mine, our gazes still locked. There was relief behind his eyes. The bright colors of this realm began to fade, and simultaneously we leaned deeper into each other. Our souls truly connected one last time until we were back on the patio of the beach house.

The gravity of this realm took a second to adjust to, then the cool breeze of the air helped ground me. And then the other effects of the cacao pulsed through my veins.

Our breaths turned heavy, eyes dilated, and chests practically heaving. Wren moved first, picking me up and slamming me against the sliding glass door. I wrapped my legs around him as tight as I possibly could, still not close enough after what we'd experienced. Our kiss was bruising, and my fingers tousled through his hair, neither of us inclined to breathe.

His canines were exposed as he finally pulled back to drag the sharp tips down my neck and tugged down the straps of my shirt. I was intoxicated with lust and overall *need.* It didn't matter where he touched me; I just needed any and all contact. Wren kissed across my clavicle, taking his time to return to my lips.

I wrapped my arms around his neck, and he took the opportunity to pull me from the glass door and slide it open. He left it ajar, letting the night air blow in and cool our overheating bodies. With the wall of windows, it was as if we were still out there under the stars.

My back met plush velvety soft blankets as he lay me down at the edge of the bed and flipped me over onto my stomach. He took his time removing every article of clothing, sliding my already wet panties down my body with his teeth. Wren started at my ankle as he made his way back up my body with kisses, bites, and tongue swipes. A trail of barely controlled desire until he reached my shoulder blade and I turned back to catch the next kiss on my lips.

His fingers lightly ran all over my body as the kiss deepened, one more barrier between us gone, and fuck did I feel it. I shouldn't have been surprised when his fingers grazed my inner thighs, but I was so focused on where our lips were connected. I twisted to give him full access, our chests lined up and already dewy with sweat.

Taking my hand and placing it atop his head, I pushed him down to my breasts. His warm, hot mouth wrapped around my nipple immediately, teeth coming into play and squeezing tight. I pushed him further, but it wasn't much of a push, because he was already heading to where I wanted him on his own accord.

He placed gentle kisses, getting me used to a soft, tender touch before he ravaged me whole. There was no warning for when he unleashed himself, just passionate laps of his tongue against my clit. I bucked my hips to the rhythm and pace he set, a finger and then another filling me up. The pressure from the inside and the outside combined, and I let out a moan as it overwhelmed me.

I put my hand over my mouth and felt a silencing spell settle over us. Which I was thankful for, because the next finger he inserted forced an even louder sound as he stretched me out. It sent me over the edge I was teetering, bliss unlike I'd ever experienced pulsing with my orgasm. The cacao multiplied everything by one hundred—one thousand. As if I was back in that spiritual realm, weightless and vibrant.

Wren didn't allow me to sit up and repay him. He lifted my still tingling leg to his shoulder and ran the tip of his dick from my entrance to my throbbing clit. His eyes were on fire, not figuratively; they glowed with night fire as if his desire had materialized. That golden molten gaze snagged with mine, and he pushed himself deep inside.

He never missed that first face I made when I took him in fully. It was like he lived for it, survived off my pleasure alone. I could tell he felt the entire impact of the cacao now as his eyes went wide and he groaned, no, whimpered, unmoving as he adjusted to it.

Ever so slowly, he pulled back and spread my legs even further. His next thrust went deeper, his pace picking up to an unrelenting tempo. I lifted my hips and fucked him back, every slam of our bodies together building to a crescendo I wanted to live in forever.

I wrapped my legs around his back to bring him close, needing his lips. My taste was still on him, and I made sure none was left, tugging at his bottom lip, exploring the inside of his mouth. Sex between us had always been otherworldly, but this was another level of raw and intimate.

His hips undulated, and he moaned into my mouth, "Fuck, Mira."

He felt it too, whether it was the aphrodisiac elements of our evening, or the trip to a spiritual world, it was all overwhelmingly sensational. I flipped us over and I retreated, his dick slipping out of me as I moved to stand. He chased me, his hands reaching for my body in a frantic frenzy of need and confusion.

"Come here," I said with my knee on the edge of the bed.

Wren listened, coming to a sitting position with his feet firm on the ground. Wrapping my arms around his neck, I tossed my leg over his lap to straddle. I rocked a couple times, letting him feel me slide over his dick before he got impatient and thrust back inside.

"Somebody's greedy," I whispered in his ear.

He palmed my ass cheeks. "With you, always. It will never be enough."

"Hm," I sounded and interlaced my fingers behind his neck.

I pulled back my hips, hanging off the edge and keeping my feet on the mattress until I got to his tip. His nails dug into me, almost painful, as I thrust, pulled back, and thrust again, using the momentum of every drive of my hips to keep going. It granted me full control, and him full access. My head fell back as I felt my orgasm swelling. I bit my lip, so close I could practically taste it.

"That's my girl. Chase it, come for me, baby. I can feel it," Wren said, his voice all smoke and gravel.

And I did. I came, holding him deep inside as it thrummed through me. Wren stood, the only change in position being the altitude. The coolness of the glass wall of windows bit into my back, ending this how we started.

Wren fucked me so hard the lamp beside us rattled and crashed to the ground. He was assiduous in his need to get me there one more time before him. His body warmed to an unnatural temperature, sure to form steam had we been under water.

I scratched my nails down his back, into his hair, and over his bulging biceps. The silencing spell was put to the test as I screamed, somewhere inside me hit like a button of culmination. His head fell into the crook of my neck as he came, a feline-like roar escaping him as his nahual fought to be released too.

He stumbled us back to the bed, both of us falling to the mattress in a mess of limbs and sweat. Another breeze blew through the room, raising goosebumps across all of my exposed skin.

Wren's hand found my face, and he turned my chin toward him, his thumb running over my bottom lip. "Thank you."

"I feel like I should be thanking you." I smiled.

"Not for that. Thank you for believing in me, even when you shouldn't have. For going to another realm to save me. I..." He trailed off, his brows drawing together. "I love you. I've never loved someone in this way, so altruistically and without bounds. It feels fucking phenomenal."

"It does." I scooted closer to him, basking in every drop of truth in the statement.

41

KOA

"Doesn't flying private negate your public persona?" Alanna asked, arching one perfectly sculpted brow as we leveled out at cruising altitude.

I lounged back, letting the leather seat cradle me as I glanced at her over the rim of my glass filled to the brim with whiskey and ice. "Being engaged to *your* public persona has already damaged my less-than-shimmering reputation."

As if I had one of those. Alanna's image and cold demeanor had slightly tarnished some of the weight I had around the gyms. Sometimes it felt as though they assumed they were just another charity case for the rich to dip their funds into, but that couldn't be further from the truth. In time, they'd see that, though. Patience.

"That's not what the polls show…" Alanna clicked her tongue.

I offered her the remnants of a low chuckle. "Don't be naïve," I said, voice dry. "Those are bought and paid for. Common knowledge."

"Hmph," she muttered, eyes narrowing slightly. "Tell that to the people of Mentiria."

Alanna's dark hair was braided in one curly, long braid down her back. Between blowing up buildings and meeting ten stories underground, she hadn't had a chance to maintain her typically perfect image. The mention of Mentiria's constituents grabbed my attention. The desire to ask her what she meant briefly swept over me, but I dropped it. It was a wasted effort trying to drag information out of Alanna that she was not ready to provide. And at the moment, I didn't have the energy for a half-assed attempt.

"The Mercers have three planes with the ability to drop radar," I said, setting my glass down on the table separating our seats. "You want to do this the public way or the easy way?"

"I'd love to see how you plan to get away with this little heist, *fiancé*."

"Me?" I barked out a laugh, placing my hand to my chest in mock surprise. "I think you mean us, *my betrothed*. The two of us are in this together—for life, if you have any say in it. My consequences are yours. Surely you didn't think otherwise."

That shut her up for a beat. Just one. But the reward of gagging her with her own game was enough to get me through the rest of the flight.

"Obviously." She blinked as though she were rebooting. "Let me think."

Her deep brown hand waved down the stewardess with the effortless grace of someone born into power, requesting a fresh mimosa. She sipped it slowly—a wicked smile tugged at her lips.

"Actually." Her voice was syrupy and sly. "I think this is my brothers' department."

"Dinner was absolutely riveting," I muttered, letting the sarcasm drip slowly and poisonously.

"Grandfather's home, grandfather controls the conversation," Alanna shot back, her tone as dry as the martinis they kept forcing down our throats. She kicked off her heels as we stepped into the upstairs hall, the click of leather against tile snapping through the silence.

Evidently, dinners here weren't meals—they were performances. Us, her brothers—Daniel, Manuelo, and Fernando—and an uncomfortable three-to-one ratio of staff.

I cleared my throat, breaking the heavy hush as we wound toward our wing of the estate. "Ten-thirty?"

"Make it eleven," she corrected smoothly, running a hand through her sleek, freshly straightened hair. "He's in bed every night by nine, but sometimes he paces the halls if sleep escapes him."

"And if that happens?" I pressed, already mapping exits in my head.

"Don't worry about that." She gave a wink that didn't quite reach the detachment in her eyes. "Staff has it under control."

I slipped into my room without another word. My door shut behind me with a heavy click, sealing me in a silence that wasn't silence at all. This house hummed. Lurked. A quiet so artificial it set my shoulders tight, as if the walls themselves leaned in to listen.

Three hours to kill.

I dropped onto the edge of the bed, exhaling as I dug my phone out of my pocket. My thumbs hovered over the screen, ready to text Sienna—but she'd already beaten me to it.

Venom :

You alive or in a coma from how thrilling that dinner sounded?

I smirked, some of the tension bleeding out of me. No one could make me feel more grounded with a single message.

Miss you.

The typing bubbles appeared right away, and my stupidly enamored heart pattered against my chest. When it came to her, I was ruined.

Venom :

I'll see you soon, snake.

I leaned back against the headboard, staring at the ornate ceiling. This place was a trap disguised in silk, gold, and jade. Wards shimmered on the windows and doors if you knew how to look. Display cases reeked of protective magic. Guards prowled the halls, waiting for a single misstep. Cameras tracked everything, even the shadows. Our job was essentially to rob a national museum in broad daylight. Easier in movies than in practice.

Everything had to fall into place. No skipped beats. No second chances. We only had one shot before the cage snapped shut.

It was draining. The acting, the smiling. Playing along. Pretending I gave a damn about their legacy...*'our'* legacy.

The screen lit up again.

Me:

Venom :

Sienna sat on the edge of a massive bed with white sheets. Her curls spilled to one side of her tilted head, catching the light. Red lace panties clung to her hips, shaped in a heart that pointed to the place I ached to taste. Her bare chest gleamed smooth and warm, skin the color of earth kissed by fire, and a lustful glimmer in her eyes that unmade me every time.

A sharp breath caught in my throat.

Godsdamn.

My belt came loose with one practiced tug. I slipped my hand down my boxers, gripping the base of my already hard cock, blood surging hot down my stomach. She knew exactly what she was doing. She *always* knew. I bit back the moan building in my chest, teeth sharp on my tongue.

Venom :

Her words hit me in her voice, and my cock twitched in my palm. Heat crawled up my neck as I pushed off the bed, already tearing at the starched trousers.

Me:

Another photo was her only response. Closer this time—her thighs pressed together, lace stretched taut, one finger teasing the waistband like an invitation. The angle gave me an unrelenting view of the art hugged around her body. Nature took over, the *Chikchan* pride in me overwhelming at the sight of me circling her legs and wrapped around Sienna's torso. My grip tightened. A curse burned the back of my throat as I adjusted against the mattress.

> **You gonna beg for more or what?**

My lip twitched. Her mouth would be the death of me.

Me:

> **I'd buy you the fucking world just to feel your lips around my cock right now.**

Her messages slowed, but the anticipation rising in me only climbed higher. I stroked, closing my eyes and imagining her beside me—how her skin would feel under my hands, riding my dick, how her mouth would taste. The way she whispered my name when she came apart.

It wasn't just the sex with Sienna. It never had been.

The woman made me feel tethered. Grounded. As if someone had finally carved out a space where I didn't have to second-guess every move. Every motive.

My phone vibrated again.

> **I know you're touching yourself. I want a picture.**

I would never deny her anything. I leaned back against the pillows, angling the camera in order to do her one better. A video. I stroked slowly at first, imagining her whispering my name again. What I'd do to her when I finally had her in front of me again, under me, around me.

One thought of my tongue sliding into her pussy sent me over the edge. Release hit with a muted hiss. My body jolted, breath ragged, sweat cooling on my skin. White stars tainted my typically clear vision. I lay there for a moment, phone now flat against the sheets like it had witnessed something sacred. I picked it up and pressed send on the video.

A minute later, my breath returned to me, and my phone buzzed again.

I'm obsessed with you, you know.

My reply was easy. Simple. But more importantly, true.

Venom, obsessed doesn't begin to cover how I feel about you.

After twiddling my fucking toes for hours, my phone buzzed once at 10:45—Alanna's confirmation text lighting up the screen faster than a starter pistol. *Go time.*

Staff had double-confirmed that her grandfather was in bed. Predictable, just as she'd said—man's in bed by nine unless the ghosts of his past keep him up and wandering. I pressed my ear to the door, waiting. The walls were thicker than the secrets held within. Still, I could catch the soft pad of her steps leaving her room.

I waited a full minute, long enough to count out my breathing and suppress the quiet buzz of anxiety weaving up my spine. If I were caught, there was no telling how my parental figures would respond, let alone the Cynod. I slipped out after her, finding her already waiting at the manicured overgrowth near the south corridor of the garden. Staff had gone all out.

An overly eager aide had thrown together a whole scene: pillows on the grass, a star-gazing blanket, and an obnoxious amount of candles in hurricane jars. Not to mention at least four different bottles of wine arranged like in those stupid romantic comedy movies Meems and Sienna forced me to watch. Not bothering to speak, I grabbed a bottle by the neck and sat beside her on the velvet throw, chugging half of it.

"Must you chug in such a barbaric way?" she said, nose crinkled in a dramatic way that screamed I offended her entire lineage with my actions.

"To get through the rest of this night? Shit. Probably."

"You act as if I'm so hard to digest."

I wiped my mouth on the back of my hand, releasing a burp. "No comment."

Her responding laugh was unamused and lacked surprise. "You know," she said, plucking at the edge of her coat sleeve. "Your first trip here, the gala, for a second, I thought it was possible for us to be friends if nothing else."

"I don't have friends."

Alanna offered a level stare, pushing a strand of her long hair behind her ear. "Wren is not a friend? The Mercers?"

"Wren is complicated. The Mercers are…" I paused. What the hells were the Mercers to me? Never really stopped to consider it as of late. "As close as I get. We're business partners. Acquaintances. Men who find ourselves aligned because of timing, power, and our women. That's not exactly friendship. It's survival in our world."

"How sad," she said, more statement than pity. Alanna and pity didn't belong in the same sentence.

I snorted. "Speaking from experience? Not really."

"Speaking from experience," she echoed. "Yes, really."

The breeze carried through the already chill air as the sky darkened. Daylight hung around longer here in the winter than on the island. I turned my head, studying her now. This wasn't the mask she wore. No teasing smile or snarky response. Just…a person under the glass.

"It was, admittedly, lonely before Mira and Sienna showed up." I offered up, surprising myself as much as her. "We have a family now, our own family, separate from our parents. Mira's always had that. Me? Not so much. It takes some adjusting, but if I had to call anyone a friend, it would be them."

Alanna sighed—long, slow, a release of my shit she had no intention of carrying.

"I thought the same, by the way," I added. "But with my mate, I'm afraid you've crossed one too many lines."

Her eyes flicked to the bottle of white wine I'd chugged from. Fingers tightened around its neck, then she tilted it back and downed the rest. Alanna scowled, wiping her mouth at the burn going down.

"Understandable. I suppose there is no starting over for us, huh? What we got as first impressions is the life we're destined to."

"I'm not the one who offers forgiveness," I told her, and it was true. Forgiveness had never been part of my vocabulary. Meems and Sienna brought that into my life, and I wouldn't exactly say it was something I was fond of practicing. "*She* is, and these days, it's a hard sell for her."

Alanna didn't blink. "Strider's telling the truth. Vitória and the others went rogue. Thaddeus's orders were clear; if we could not get Celeste, Mira or Sienna were to be brought in unharmed."

I waited. Words not laced with sarcasm or false charm appeared to be flowing freely from her. Wrongly, I assumed she'd reveal more about her involvement with the rebels. Something shifted on her face. One of those silences that said more than words could. Alanna swallowed whatever was on her tongue and checked her phone instead.

"Ready?" she asked, all polished indifference.

"As I'll ever be."

She stood first and reached for my hand like we'd done this a thousand times. Ever the performer. Born to play royalty. Her laugh came easily—high and flirtatious. Her palm pressed to my chest, she tilted up, lips grazing the line of my jaw. I tensed on instinct. Every nerve screamed *wrong, not Sienna.*

"Easy. For the cameras," she whispered against my skin. "We mess this up, they'll come for her. Get it together."

The simple reminder sobered me. No fucking pressure. I dropped a kiss that burned to the top of her head and wrapped my arm around her waist as we moved down the hall. Lovers who couldn't wait for a room. All part of the plan. The world was simply our stage. If staff were watching—and they were—it was all champagne lust and whispered nonsense. Her estate. Her future husband. She was good at this. The scene outside and the evidence left behind needed to appear real in every aspect. It would be our only alibi when the time came.

Of course, we didn't hear a robbery; we would have been too busy fucking. And now, there were witnesses leading up to the act.

We entered the corridor near the garden, stepping into the blissfully heated hallways of the property.

"I'll be punished for this regardless," she muttered, pulling a silver stick from her pocket. "Might as well make it the real thing."

Our initial discussion had been about using the diluted shit sold at shops and made in a lab for medicinal purposes to keep our wits about us. But shit, my tolerance was high, and I was always down for a hit. Besides, tangible proof that we'd been here partying, clearly not stealing, would never hurt. She lit the feyfog and blew a plume of scented smoke into the air. It rolled violet, floral, and bitter at once—lavender with the edge of licorice. She handed it to me and let her fingers linger a second longer than necessary.

I took a drag, let out a rookie cough for effect, and hauled her closer. We laughed like idiots at absolutely fuckshit, stumbling into each other, flirting far too loudly. If I did say so myself, it was the performance of a lifetime. Shit, you couldn't write in a script. And it was easy when I let my mind pretend it was Sienna at my side, and not a woman whom I wished I would never have to see again.

"Almost there," she murmured near my ear. "Going to need you to not over-react when I do this."

"I don't overrea—"

She shoved me.

To be clear, it was not rough enough to hurt, yet just enough to be believable. I staggered back into the wall. Alanna tossed her hair to the side, cutting off the view of the camera so they could not see that our lips were not touching. She leaned in, whispering against my neck. "Now pretend I'm not repulsive to you and push me into the other room near the case."

Got it.

I slipped my hands around her waist, spun her fast, and shoved her down yet another hallway. *The* hallway. We stumbled through it until my back hit the wall nearest the case. She slipped off her coat and tossed it behind her. It landed where expected—draped over the case.

Clever.

She'd told me to layer up after dinner. I assumed it was to fend off the Mentirian air, not stage a fucking striptease. It clicked now.

We shed our clothes. Fast. Frenzied. A sleeve here, a belt there. No real contact. No real heat. But the illusion of it? Perfect.

From the outside, it looked like we were seconds from the floor.

We weren't.

We stood close—bare enough to convince, far enough not to flinch. Her eyes met mine. Neither of us wanted this show. But we'd put on worse for less. Alanna and I were here to play our roles and keep moving. I only wished I knew exactly what she was playing at in the rebellion and why. Though it was clear that it was information she had no intention of ever offering up.

"Camouflage," she whispered. "In and out."

I phased, reappearing across the room like it was all a part of our ruse. Foreplay. She smirked as if she were humored. Enjoying the show. I phased again. Alanna chased. And again. Flashing between walls, around shelves, layering a full, believable blur of movement. By the time I landed behind the case, the illusion was solid. No one would question it.

The wards sparked as I reached in. Panic sparked as it bit at my skin. I hissed a slew of profanities. Alanna did her best to keep her glance away from the camera and her mask up. I inched forward again, meeting no resistance this time.

"Fernando," she breathed a sigh of relief. Her brothers had succeeded, taking over the security booth through force or farce, I wasn't sure. "You have thirty seconds."

I didn't waste one.

Without much effort, the glamour appeared as real as what I held in my hand. I slipped the real paper under the illusion she'd already placed. Then I phased back to her side, my hand curving around the base of her neck. "Let's go."

She snatched up her shed clothes. I grabbed my shirt, the torn paper camouflaged at my side, its magic tugging at something in my soul. We ran half-dressed, grinning like thieves. Genuine laughter at having pulled it off spilled between us. The hallway blurred past in flashes of shadow and light. We turned the corner and slammed right into him.

"Ouch, fu—" Alanna choked, "Grandfather."

She bowed her head, eyes docile. He stood there staring down at her—disapproving, expression carved from judgment. "It's nearing midnight, Alanna. Quiet hours have passed."

His gaze slid past us. Down the corridor. Toward the nook we'd left.

I moved fast, stepped into his line of sight, and threw on my best half-drunk accent. "Are all the bottles around here this fucking delicious?"

Her grandfather remained unfazed, his lip curving up, nose scrunched as he took me in. "Sad you couldn't be more like your parents. In time, I suppose."

He moved to step past me again, still scanning, still certain he was the smartest person in the room. I didn't let him get further. I turned him to stone—clean, fast, efficient. The shift in his body was instant, every muscle arrested mid-motion, mouth still twisted in a half-smirk that didn't match the weight in the room anymore.

Alanna inhaled sharply behind me. "What the fuck did you just do?"

Panic isn't something I liked to admit I was capable of. It's not useful. Not efficient. But in this case, it sliced through me before I could stop it. I didn't have time to weigh the choices. I reacted the way anyone does when the world narrows and survival instincts take the reins.

"Control the situation, which was *your* singular responsibility. I thought you had staff watching over him."

"I did," she snapped, peering down at her phone. "The staff texted a warning, missed it in the middle of," Alanna gestured between us, expression full of irritation.

"Doesn't matter. What do we do about the situation now? If he goes over to that case, we're fucked."

"Well, we can't exactly leave him this way," she hissed, taking a calming breath. "Walk him through one of his night terrors—he gets stuck in them sometimes. Thinks he's back in the coup. Sees me as my grandmother."

The coup. That, I knew. Or at least, the sanitized version of it—Mentiria's revolution, the rise of Alanna's family, the presidency they backed, and the blood that made this estate theirs. I'd watched the footage of her in the aftermath, smoke-stained and shell-shocked, speaking to a crowd like her spine had never cracked under fire. I'd studied their history because I had to—but also because something about it always felt unfinished.

She touched his arm tentatively. "Un-stone him or whatever. Keep us in the vision and escort us to his room. Two lefts and then one right, fourth door over. I can get the staff to convince him it was another terror."

It was evident she was not 100 percent certain the plan would work. Given we had no other option, I slid into his mind carefully, tugging on the threads of whatever trauma kept him so haunted. Channeling what I knew of the coup and the footage I'd seen of Alanna in the aftermath, I pushed them deeper into the vision. The scent of burning stone filled my nose—the same smoke he must've smelled when the city burned under siege.

The floor cracked beneath our feet in the illusion, and somewhere in the distance, a child screamed. I pulled him toward the memory, and as we moved through it together, he didn't resist. It was difficult to multitask this way, and I didn't use my gifts like this often. *Chikchan* had to essentially split their brain, focusing one side on the real world, and the other lost inside another mind. With the ambassador of Mentiria and his entire family, *Ajaw*, things were complicated. Alanna could not compel him, which meant that this had no choice but to work.

If everything went according to plan, by this time tomorrow, her brothers would have staged a clean robbery. One that left no fingerprints, no surveillance trail, no indication that anyone from inside the estate had anything to do with it. No cameras would catch them. No guards would remember a thing. The wards would stay untouched. And any suspicion would drift toward faceless outsiders with enough motive and recklessness to pull something of this magnitude off.

Alanna and I would be the portrait of lustful innocence.

At the last door, two staff members were already waiting. They opened it without asking questions. I passed him off, and Alanna slipped in after him. She turned at the threshold, looked back, and nodded once.

I walked back to my room, shut the door hard enough to rattle the hinges, and leaned into it like it could anchor me. My hands were shaking. The artifact was still warm against my side, magic calling. Beckoning. A second heartbeat. I didn't know if I was wired or furious or about to burn the whole estate down just to breathe again. Maybe all three.

"Gods," I muttered under my breath, then reached for my phone.

I opened the encrypted thread—Mercers, Alanna, Sienna, Katia, Mira, Strider, Thaddeus, Zélia.

Me:

Package received. Situation may be unstable. Stay on standby for extraction.

42

MIRA

I wished we could have stayed here forever. The beach, the views, the forest, it was all so relaxing. Made me feel small, but not in a negative way. In the way that I loved having all of these greater, more powerful things surrounding me. Trees that had stood for centuries, the force of the waves crashing, the mountains that touched the clouds. My problems weren't so big here.

But it was time to go. Alanna and Koa had already left yesterday. They had a much longer trip than we did, outside of the nation and into Mentiria. Jundi wasn't too far from here, it would have been a much longer trip from Chichen. Sienna wasn't exactly happy about the arrangement, but she couldn't show up to Alanna's home without causing suspicion.

So, Katia, Sienna, and I gathered the last of our things. Wren lugged the bags out into the truck, and the twins had gone to speak to Wolfe before they left, too. I doubted Wolfe would ever invite us over again. We'd brought uninvited guests, smashed a couple of items, and dragged him into a literal rebellion. Not the best houseguests.

"Alright." Wren slammed the trunk. "Everything is in, love."

That little nickname seemed to hold more weight than before. His smile grew, and I knew he was thinking the same thing as I was.

"Thank you." I wrapped my arms around his neck. "Where are you going next?"

"I've got to deal with some *Noctis* shit. Don't actually know where I'm going yet. I'll let you know when I can," he said before pressing his lips to my forehead.

423

"Don't *love* it, but I understand," I responded. "You still feel okay after last night?"

"The sex, the ritual, or after I said I loved you?" he teased, rubbing his nose on my hair line.

I smiled, cheeks heating. "Um, all of it? But ritual first."

"I don't feel the weight of him anymore, which is fucking wonderful. I've got to say I am worried about seeing him again. Will he know it's gone?"

"From what I understand, these blood bonds are used as contingencies. A sort of one-way street to ensure that if you directly disobeyed, you'd pay for it with your blood. He wouldn't know that it's gone right now, but he might if you see him in person. If he tried to tug on his side, he could notice it was missing. I'm not really sure," I said truthfully.

I hated that it was unknown. But what he could have done under Aantaj's influence was worse. Especially when they decided it was time to bring me in.

"I'll avoid it the best I can. I know his tells when he pulls on it. I can pretend." He scratched the back of his neck. "As for the other stuff..."

My eyes widened with panic, and he chuckled.

"You know I could eat your soul, right?" I pulled back, arching a brow and pointing my finger at him.

"I'm just kidding." Wren kissed my hand. "If you weren't here to remind me of what happened, I might have thought it was a dream. This, holding you so freely right now, doesn't feel real. I don't take back any of it."

"Me neither."

I rose to my tiptoes to press my lips to his—a kiss that held only a fraction of the passion from last night. One that would leave his lips tingling for at least a little bit after I left.

"Get a room," Katia said behind me, and I whirled around.

"If I swab your lips right now, will I find some Mercer DNA?" I asked.

"Oh, for sure. 100 percent chance," she responded with a laugh.

I tilted my head playfully. "Exactly, so leave me alone."

She threw her hands up in surrender before tossing a bag she hadn't left by the door into the trunk. It was damn near packed to the brim, a week's worth of shit for all of us. The driver was going to take it back to Koa's since we were heading to Jundi right away. He'd most likely be getting a pretty hefty tip.

My friends waved at Wren as they got into the car, and I sighed. "I'd better go."

"Be careful, okay? Jundi is peaceful, but so was this place before last week," he warned.

"I will, I promise. You be careful too. Don't forget to check in when you can."

Wren's gaze wandered all over my face, as if he was committing it all to memory. That's where we were now. Every turn was dangerous, and we never knew what the next day held for us. I knew one thing, though.

"I love you, too," I whispered.

Wren damn near purred, his hands glowing and warming the spot they rested on my back. He squeezed me tighter before he pushed a curl away from my face.

"Earning your love is my greatest achievement," he said, tone graveled.

Sienna's voice carried from the cracked window of the car. "If you don't get your ass in here, we're going to miss our flight."

Wren opened the backseat door, unable to hide his smile, which had both of my friends looking at me a little too closely.

"Watch each other's backs," Wren said as he closed the door behind me.

I buckled my seatbelt and pretended that they weren't burning holes in the side of my skull. The driver put up the discretion wall, but these people were bought by Wolfe, and he didn't play around with this kind of stuff.

"You going to tell us why you two were cheesing so hard?" Sienna asked.

"Oh, he just told me he loved me last night after some pretty world-shattering sex." I took my phone out and scrolled through PhotoPhantom, feeling them vibrate with excitement as I played nonchalantly. "And I broke his blood bond."

"What the fuck." Katia shook my shoulder. "How did you do all of that in one night?"

"Can we get back to the fact that he said he loves you?" Sienna added.

"And the blood bond," Katia chimed in.

"Yes, it was a pretty eventful night," I laughed. "I was just happy to solve one of our problems. The rest feels like finally closing the chapter on the stuff that happened before, you know?"

A new, blank page in the book of us. One without the stains of the past, where *we* got to write what was next. Of course we still had tons of things to deal with, but this, our feelings for each other, we had control over that.

"Yeah," Sienna said, smiling just about as wide as Wren had. "I'm really happy for you, Mir. A few months ago I wouldn't have imagined we'd be where we are."

Katia nodded, knowing a good bit of what I'd endured, but Sienna knew it all. Every last ugly detail. She was there for every tear I shed, every disappointment. None of it mattered now. Sienna's lips twitched downward, and I leaned closer. Something was off, and we gave her the moment she needed to gather her thoughts.

"I've got to tell y'all something," she said.

"What is it?" I pressed, trying my best to keep my nerves calm, but I was sure I was doing a terrible job.

"I saw something in the vision the rebels shared. It's not something I really understand, but it felt like it wanted *me* to see it," Sienna explained. "It was this...circle with all of our nahuales on it. I'm not sure what the purpose was, but it was important."

"Have you seen it anywhere else?" Katia asked.

"At first I didn't think so, but I remember Koa doing some sort of homework for Ortega's class. I saw a picture of something that looked very similar, but if Taran hadn't figured it out yet, maybe he doesn't know what Ortega has?"

"You think we should tell everyone?" I asked.

"No." Sienna shook her head. "I think we should keep this between us for now. I don't want Koa trying to turn either of them into stone right after they shared the important stuff."

Katia and I nodded in agreement. I'd stand by Sienna for any decision she makes, but I hoped it was the right one. Not to mention, with all these great powers at play, maybe being one step ahead wouldn't hurt.

The airport came into view, but the driver pulled around back.

"Where are we going?" I asked.

"I thought we'd try something different." Katia smiled a dually terrifying and invigorating grin.

"It'll be fine." Katia swatted her hand dismissively.

"Have you ever flown that far?" I asked.

I didn't mean to doubt her...mostly, I just didn't want to die. Not after there were a couple bright lights in my life. Maybe a few months ago when waking up was too much I would have said to hells with it. *There goes your dark humor, Mira. Inside thoughts.*

Katia shrugged. "No, but I need to practice. What better way than with you two?"

"If you can't go that far, we'll be stranded...where?" Sienna added.

"Guys, we're in Chan. It's not *that* far. It'll be okay. If something happens, feel free to hold it over me for the rest of our lives." Katia stretched her arms.

"Funny thing to say when our lives might end," I mumbled, and Sienna raised her brows in agreement.

This was a pretty common thing for airports. Dragons that worked for delivery services or for the military often took off from places like this. They had decked out saddles, dragon-sized food, and lots of water. It was a good place to touch down when going a long distance. My father had come to check on the military side of the airports often. So it wasn't that I was surprised at the suggestion, just...nervous.

Katia winked at us one last time before jogging out to the field. This was the space specifically for them to shift, big enough for even the biggest of dragons like my father. She took a deep breath, her skin melting into red scales and her body growing in a flash. Much like Koa and the basilisks, there was always an element of their fae body that identified them. The shape of their eyes, a birthmark, the way they smiled. Katia's eyes were the same, the hazel irises slitted, but I could point her out in a crowd of dragons.

The ground shook as she walked over to us on all fours, stretching her neck and wings. If she could speak, I knew some sort of cocky comment about how badass she was in this form would be falling from her lips.

"We don't get to see you like this that often," I said as I swiped my hand down her scales.

A couple of the airport workers brought over a double saddle and tossed it onto her back with the help of some air magic. Four large buckles fastened across her chest and stomach, big pockets with locks on either side for our things. We wouldn't have to bring the saddle back here, as long as we left it at one of the state airports, we'd be fine.

"Well, here goes nothing," Sienna said.

They'd brought out a ladder to get up onto her back, and she climbed it first, settling in the rear seat. I followed and sat in the front. Sienna probably knew I'd want to see what was happening the entire time.

The spikes on Katia's head looked lethal from this angle, jutting around her crown and down her jaws like a lion's mane. She stretched her neck out far and let out a screech that had every fae turning back to find her.

An airport employee directed her toward the path to Jundi, and we fastened our seatbelts extra tight. She had to learn the flight path, but it was something she'd already been studying in junior military training. Dragons had to know all the flight paths from each major city within Inecha.

Katia's steps quickened as she went from a jog to a full-on sprint down the runway. The air picked up around us, and a curved windshield lifted from the saddle to take away the brunt of it. Her wings extended, and the altitude change settled in my stomach as we lifted into the air.

My knuckles were damn near white as I squeezed the saddle handles and my eyes even tighter. People did this every day; it wouldn't be permitted if it weren't reasonably safe. Wish I knew the statistics of deaths on dragonback. There was no reason to freak out. If I fell out, Katia would probably catch me before my head cracked open like an egg.

I opened my eyes one at a time, astonished at the fact that we were already so high. The saddle warmed the cooler it got, maintaining a comfortable temperature in our little bubble. Sienna held her hands out at her sides as her fingers delicately cut through the clouds, her smile easing some of the anxiety in my stomach.

Gods, this country was beautiful. I'd spent all of my life in the city and in the suburbs, I forgot how these places untouched by the fae looked. No homes, no roads, no Cynod buildings. Just trees, hills, grass, rivers, and lakes. Deer galloped in a field, wolves chasing each other in the distance. It was almost too much to behold at once. *This* was how we were meant to live. Where the gods intended for us to be. We'd taken so much of our technology and advancements for granted. Not to say I wasn't grateful for modern medicine and science, because I really, truly was, but there was something healing about being a witness to this, too.

Katia cut above the clouds, surrounding us in the fluffy white substance. The sun illuminated beyond, and when the clouds finally faded away, the mountains separating Kuello and Jundi came into view. These mountains were one of In-echa's treasures. One of our wonders that we put on postcards, the backgrounds of our laptops, and a location people around the world knew us for.

The range is what bracketed the Sacred Lands, and if you asked me, some of that magic had seeped through the border. Some people, the ones who believed in the old gods and studied forbidden texts, knew it as Ixchel's necklace.

Each mountain gleamed, the sun reflecting off the ribbons of bright green jade. The range curved into the Sacred Lands, the other end into Jundi, just like a necklace. The sun seemed to make the jade pulse from within, Kinich was giving life to each and every mountain. The many lives beneath me caressed my nahual, an entire ecosystem existing peacefully.

Sparkling water caught my attention. Waterfalls poured from between the mountains and into a lake, the reflection a perfect untouched mirror to the beauty above.

"Oh my god," I said as I pulled out my phone.

Two jaguars emerged from the trees, a cub and what I felt was a mother. We never saw them. I actually didn't think one had been recorded in the last half-century or so. They were symbols of power from the gods, and fuck if I wasn't going to bask in this moment. Katia seemed to notice, staying high but looping back around so we could fully take them in.

The mother dipped its snout down to the water, carefully lapping it up. The cub followed her lead, but miscalculated and immersed its entire face in the water. The mother rubbed her cheek against him, and when he was ready, tried again. This time, the little guy was successful. It pounced around with what I could only assume was feline excitement. Too big paws disrupted the shore line and spraying water with every step.

I wanted to take a picture, but when the mother looked up, eyes locking with mine, where I was nearly hanging out of the saddle, I tucked my phone away. Some things were meant to only be experienced, and the memory would last with me forever.

43

MIRA

Katia pulled into Jundi's state airport, a replica of the one we'd left from. She landed on a runway marked for arrivals, her thick claws scratching against the asphalt. Once she got to the end, two people came out to help remove the saddle. Instead of waiting for them to reach her, she shifted back to her fae form.

"Katia!" I shrieked as the saddle enveloped her body, and Sienna and I were added weight atop her.

"You're supposed to wait until it's off," Sienna said as we hopped off.

Katia crawled from beneath the saddle with a nervous smile. "Yup. Haven't gotten that far in training yet. Makes sense now."

The airport employees laughed as they handed us our items from inside the pockets and dragged the saddle away. Katia stretched her arms out, her legs a little wobbly, and we offered her support until she righted herself.

"You know when you get off a treadmill and the ground feels like it's moving as you walk? That's how I feel right now," she laughed and took out her phone. "Let me check my mom's location. I didn't tell her we were coming. Oh, good, she's at work, you guys can see the Jundi senate office building."

"Oh, my mom will love that. It'll look like I'm taking on that responsibility she wanted me to take so bad," I responded.

As we walked through the airport, there was a noticeably different air here. It was fresher, lighter, and the people seemed...happy. Everyone wore a smile; nobody was sneering or trying to snap pictures. Nobody was in a rush or pushing people to get out of the way.

433

Katia once said that Jundi was a slow place, and I saw it now. Maybe growing up here would have you yearning for a faster city, but for me, this was paradise.

"Texted my mom's driver," Katia said as she scanned the pickup lane. "Ah, there he is."

An SUV similar to the one Wolfe had called for us sat in the lane. A cheery older man with hair only on the sides of his head waved at Katia. His brown skin was full of freckles and smile lines, and they only got more pronounced as he pulled Katia in for a hug.

"This is Felipe. Known him my whole life. Felipe, this is Mira and Sienna," Katia introduced us.

He opened the door for us and nodded his head, pointing to refreshments in a basket. "Any friends of Katia are friends of mine. Enjoy some snacks."

"Okay, do you feel like we're in another universe?" Sienna whispered to me as she got in the backseat.

"Um, yes," I replied and slid in beside her.

Katia got in the front and started updating Felipe on everything that had happened to her at Kuxtal so far. Leaving out the parts about rebellion and kidnapping, of course. He encouraged her along, excitement flaring each time she mentioned something positive. Katia didn't stop talking until we pulled in front of what I assumed was her mother's building.

"Will you be at dinner tonight?" Katia asked Felipe.

He shook his head. "Not tonight. Isabella isn't feeling too well."

"Oh no, I'll send her healing wishes. Thanks for driving us!" She gave him one more hug and hopped out of the vehicle.

I handed Sienna my phone as I stood next to the sign that read 'Jundi Senate' and she knew exactly what I was asking for. She snapped a couple pictures, and I threw it up on my PhotoPhantom story. The one my mother could actually see.

We followed, more smiling faces meeting us in the lobby. Everyone perked up around Katia, some trying to stop and talk to her, and she politely let them know we were off to see her mother. This building wasn't set up to intimidate or to force the constituents to gawk at the wealth of the Cynod; it was welcoming and open, almost warm.

Katia's mother's office was on the top level, and the elevator zoomed to a stop right into her waiting area. The walls were a soft green with the words, Miciela Carvalho, Senator of Jundi, painted in black. An admin sat at a desk, eyes going wide with shock as she saw us, and Katia lifted her finger to her lips to shush her. The woman nodded, falling in behind us as Katia opened the door.

"Surprise." She held her arms out as if performing a magic trick.

Her mother rose from her desk with her hand on her chest. "Oh my, I had no idea you were coming! You nearly gave me a heart attack, filha."

Katia and her mother resembled each other, but I had a feeling she took more after her father. Where my friend was tall and muscular with soft features, her mother was short and petite, all harsh lines. She had a stance about her that I knew both commanded a room and put them at ease.

"You two must be Mira and Sienna," she said as she turned to us.

"Hi," Sienna offered.

"That's us," I replied with a smile.

"I've heard so much of you two! Katia goes on and on about her new friends who have become family. Consider me your mãe too." Her mother pulled us both into a hug.

"That means mother," Katia responded with a thumbs up behind her mom.

Between the shock and the weird patting I was doing, I was sure it was extremely evident that I didn't come from a hugging family. She didn't seem to mind. Once she released us, she sat back at her desk and rang the admin back in.

"Clear my schedule for the rest of the day," she said before turning to us. "What brings you to Jundi? How'd you get here?"

Katia wiggled her eyebrows. "I flew."

"Oh, you'll fly us home! I have to see!" She clapped with excitement.

Katia bowed as if she just earned some award. "I'd love to, and...we came because I need something from your home office."

Her mother gathered things from atop her desk, tossing them in a large purse and slinging it over her shoulder. "Of course, anything you need."

"That easy?" I said before I could stop the words coming out of my mouth. "I'm sorry, Mrs. Carvalho, I didn't mean any offense."

I expected us to have to trick her, or bargain, or offer something in return. Honestly, straight-up stealing it was what I fully expected. The corners of Katia's lips turned down in a frown.

"You poor thing. I've heard stories. Anything I can do to help any of you three, I will gladly do. Call me Miciela."

We rode bareback to Katia's home, which, thank the gods, was not that far. I much preferred the safety of a saddle and restraints. Her home radiated everything else we'd experienced in Jundi. Exactly the sort of place I would have expected her to be raised.

After explaining the item we needed from her office, Miciela ran up to get it as we ate hummus and pretzels.

"How much does she know?" I whispered.

"I've explained that we've had some new friends with a strong sense of justice. I'm pretty sure she knows everything except about 'Z', but keeping it all above board," Katia responded before crunching down on her pretzel.

"She's so eager to help," Sienna said.

Sienna, unlike me, did have a loving mother. However, her mother worked so hard and long that Sienna often felt like certain things were a burden. We always tried to solve things ourselves before bringing her in, even when we were children. Like the time someone was bullying us at school, and instead of telling our parents, we set up a trap of sorts to humiliate them. Couple cameras and a bucket of fish guts went far.

Sienna's mother would have helped if we had asked. The problem was, she would have had to get off work to come to the school. My tía could have done something, but she was also busy trying to literally save people. So for the two of us, seeing a mother having the ability to drop everything *and* the desire to help was...different.

"I was lucky when it came to parents. Didn't appreciate it as much as I should have until I went to school," Katia said.

"You've shown your appreciation in many ways," Miciela said as she entered the room and cleared her throat. "Jundi as a whole has been the home to ample things that might be used with malice in the rest of Inecha. Our family, in particular, has been the protector of multiple artifacts. This being one of them."

Katia's mother joined us at the breakfast bar and laid the torn paper down before us. Alanna was right; there was a certain tug in the air around it. It wanted all of our eyes to be focused on it, but at the same time, this type of magic had a repulsive quality. It was so potent that, if the books I'd read were correct, the ink Kan used was the culprit. A mixture of carbon and wood brought from whatever land they hail from.

"Do you know what it is?" Katia asked.

"My grandfather believed it was the gods' tongue. Back then, there were still some artifacts from the Sacred Lands floating around, and the language was identical. We don't know what it says, though. Even if we did, half is missing, and we know how one or two words can completely change something," Miciela said.

Katia and I both looked at Sienna, and Miciela tracked our movement. Going to need to work on that in the future.

"I was going to wait until you came home for summer, but I think having all three of you here might be better. Let's go on a little trip." Miciela stood. "Bring all of your things."

We'd been walking for about an hour. Katia's home was on the outskirts of the city, backed up to huge mesas. Miciela led the way, even though there were no paths or markings that I saw to identify where we were going. This was the true wild, long grass and unruly flowers tangled around each other. Almost felt wrong to be walking through it. I tried to be as conscious as possible with each step, but after this long, there was something beautiful at every turn and I couldn't avoid it all.

"Almost there," Miciela sang over the wind.

I noticed that Katia had taken her shoes off at some point, fully grounded to the land she'd come from. Her hair flung in the wind, pure contentment radiating from every part of her. I imagined her dragging the Mercer twins out here without all their technology and weapons. Sienna looked over at me as I chuckled, but I swatted my hand out.

Miciela got to the base of a mesa. Instead of going around, she ran her fingers over a groove and stepped right through the rock.

She stuck her head back out. "Each of you must do the same, and it will let you in."

One by one, we did as she asked, a small prick on her hand, and a tug toward the mesa. We walked into a cave so similar to the one on campus that I had to do a double take. This one didn't have names engraved on the walls, but there were tons of icons, lines, and symbols that created pictures. Other items were scattered around, all appearing intentionally placed. Weapons that looked ancient, bowls, books, scrolls.

"Certain things I've kept at home and close, but many items I have stored here," Katia's mother said. "The spell wouldn't allow you in until your magic was activated in your blood, Katia."

"I remember when we'd come and hike the mesas, you'd sometimes disappear for a little bit on your own path. This is where you came?" she asked.

"It is. I am one of three people alive who know about this place. Now six, I suppose," she responded.

Tunnels behind me caught my attention, and I inspected the opening. "These go across the country, don't they?" I asked.

"You found the one on campus?" Miciela asked.

"Sienna and I did. Ours only allows..." I trailed off for a moment, but realized that I could trust her. "It only allows descendants of the gods."

Miciela nodded with a smile.

"You all are descendants?" Sienna asked.

"Many of us in positions of power are. This lineage was seen as a powerful thing at first, and we were sworn into these roles that stay within our families, generation after generation. My grandfather said that at a certain point, they removed this knowledge from everywhere. Even straight from the minds of the people. The Cynod wanted to be seen as the only ones greater than the *common folk*. My grandfather slipped through the cracks and was able to keep the knowledge."

"What about the senators in other states?" I asked.

"I know of at least two. One in Chan and one Kuello," she responded. "However, I am not sure they are aware."

It made sense why the Cynod didn't want anyone to know. That would make people feel powerful, it would force them to validate the true gods. Easier for them to get rid of it, pretend it was a folktale. How many of us were walking around with the blood of gods, unaware of what flowed through our veins? Endless cycles of generations—*cycles*. Like the prophecy.

"Taran is, too. He had extra gifts because of it. Do you?" I asked.

"According to our records, we did have the ability to sing songs of the gods. Nothing I've seen for myself. You are from two great families, what about the Tecuns and Caneks?"

I needed to know if Taran had always had the gift, or if this was another part of the prophecy. If the cycle was spinning, and these things would start being seen in the families with gods' blood. It could bode well for us, or it could be to our detriment depending on who's side they were on.

"My parents would never willingly give me the knowledge. If something manifests, that is how I'll find out."

Maybe there was something in the old books from Dr. Puebla. We'd had a virtual check-in while I was at the beach house, just to make sure that things were going okay. I planned on seeing her again for a full session once break was over, and I wondered if she had more books I could research.

"Well, you do have a special gift already," Katia suggested.

"Your nahual has emerged?" Miciela asked.

My heart thumped in my ears. "Yes, *Kimi*."

Miciela rushed toward me and grabbed my hand. "You must not tell anyone you don't trust. That is...things are changing. I can't tell if this is for the better or the worse."

She scanned the room like there was an answer somewhere between the artifacts, but seemed to come up short.

"Shit, me either," I joked.

"You three found each other for a reason. Remember that knowledge is the most powerful thing you can attain, and it should not be given freely."

Sienna had left the conversation a few minutes ago, and I didn't realize where she'd gone until she came back holding something in her sleeves.

"What is this?" she asked. "I've seen it before."

It was made of stone, but so much of it was destroyed. Some markings were unmarred by time, though not enough to make out what they meant.

"We don't know. A piece of something touched by the gods, we can feel the signature, but can't determine from when or where."

"Hm." Sienna sat it back down.

These days, it wasn't something to ignore. If she thought it meant more, it most likely did.

Miciela didn't push her for information, but did analyze her. "What is your father's surname?"

"Biological father is Collins."

"Mm, yes. Colinao was your family's original last name. These things tend to change over the years."

Katia nodded. "Ours originally was spelled with a 'z' instead of an 'h.'"

"Colinao," Sienna said, testing the name on her tongue and turning to me. "Was that name on the walls in Kuxtal?"

"I don't remember," I responded.

"Well, you can find out." Miciela walked over to a tunnel. "This one takes you straight back to the academy."

"Aw, I was going to try to stay for dinner," Katia said.

Her mother's mouth turned down into a frown. "I think whatever you all are doing is more important. You come back when you have these things straightened out, my dear."

"You're right." Katia pulled her mother into a hug. "Give Papai my love."

"It was always going to be us, the children of the gods, that took back their land. You all be careful and watch out for each other. I'm but a tunnel away now. For all three of you," Miciela said, eye contact strong and shining with truth.

She handed Katia the paper we'd come for in a case that sparkled with magic. Some people were meant to be mothers. Miciela Carvalho was one of them.

"We will, we promise," Sienna responded with a smile.

"Always," I added.

Katia's mother took a deep breath and watched as we trailed through the tunnel and disappeared.

44

WREN

While there weren't a lot of lines in the sand when it came to *Noctis Fraternitas*, there were a couple to be mindful of. Disloyalty, disobedience, and lying among the few. The thing I needed to determine was how close to lying was walking into this building with the knowledge that rebels were among us, and not mentioning it.

Every single person in the Brotherhood was a rebel of sorts. None of us conformed or supported the current regime—or any regimes, really. We thrived away from the rules and authority. With that said, the rebellion might have been considered their own sort of government. That was how these things went. How history played out. A rebellion would overthrow one regime and replace it with their own. Could be better than the last in many ways, but they all brought along their own bullshit.

So knowing that there were rebels here, plotting on what they might turn us into was...unsettling. I'd do whatever I needed to do to protect my loved ones, but that little bit of uncertainty, I was not a fan of.

Loved ones. A category Mira fell into now. One she'd fallen in for some time, but it was out there now. It hung in the air. My knowing how I felt and her knowing were different things. This was dangerous, but I wasn't the one in danger. The love I held for her was lethal—a weapon locked and fucking loaded. *Anyone* who got between us would be quickly ushered into whatever afterlife they believed in.

443

She was fully aware of who I was, the things I was capable of, and she loved me back. Mira knew what she was awakening by saying those three words. If I knew my girl, she didn't take the proclamation lightly. She would have thought through every piece before putting it into the universe. Made it that much sweeter. It wasn't like she hadn't seen the lengths I'd gone to for my family. That extended to her now, tenfold.

I lowered my eye in front of the retinal scanner. The infrared light beam scanned across my retina, and the door unlocked.

"Ikari," a deep voice sounded the moment I stepped through the threshold.

Someone was always directly on the other side of the door. No matter what. Nobody had ever successfully breached one of these buildings...but we were a paranoid bunch.

"Pritchett," I responded.

He was one of the usuals on security here. Fucker was the size of a truck. Anyone in their right mind wouldn't even attempt to try him.

"Got called in by Hamish. Going to the tenth floor," I added.

No matter how many times he saw me, he always gave me a hard time. He inspected me as if someone else could be wearing my skin, as if I didn't just scan my fucking eyeball. Eventually, he selected the tenth floor, and the elevator dinged.

"Don't get into any trouble," he said.

"Me? Never." I winked as the door closed.

I'd been a part of the Brotherhood since freshman year. A younger, more reckless version of myself. I liked the idea of not having rules or repercussions after being tied to the Cynod. Which I still was, but that frustration was let out inside these walls a couple of times. Thankfully, not against anyone who could do permanent damage. Everyone was a little fucked in the head here, so it wasn't unusual that people died on *Noctis* ground. You had to keep the *not fucked* parts of your head on straight, or all of it would kill you. You'd get too big for your britches and fuck with the wrong person. Especially when all of us were together.

This wasn't a chapter meeting; those happened once a month and were mandatory. I'd just gotten a call and was told to show up. That wasn't uncommon. I had access to certain areas that not everybody did. My brothers and I were favorites here. Many members didn't go above the third level. Certainly didn't have one-on-ones with Hamish.

I knocked once, opening the door and finding the *Noctis* Vice President at the table, studying something in front of him. Hamish Elrod was an unassuming guy. Walking down the street, you'd never guess what sort of power he had. He was just a level below the head honcho and was the main person I worked with. The one I preferred to work with. He didn't do bullshit, but also didn't have an ego to battle like some of the others.

Actually, he was the one who ordered Soren Oberon's death. He could have been working for the rebels and getting rid of a bad apple. After all, Soren was Vitória's boyfriend. He could be opposing them with his own angles. I found it hard to believe that Hamish didn't know about the rebels using this building. He knew everything that went on in here, and if there was someone they would have cleared it with, it would have been him. I decided to wait it out and see if he gave any tells. Giving up the knowledge I had around the rebels, or not giving it up, could both be seen as breaking the Brotherhood rules.

"Wren," Hamish said and gestured for me to sit beside him. "Thank you for coming in on short notice."

I always had to remind myself that this put-together version of him wasn't his only side. There was only one time that I tried to puff my chest to him, and I never did it again. Man was as much a killer as I was. A Chikchan that rivaled Koa. Two of them were like fucking peacocks when in proximity to each other. Chests rattling and slitted eyes every fourteen seconds.

"Not a problem. What's going on?" I said as I sat down.

Hamish folded his hands in front of him and pinned me with his stare. Getting comfortable in this sort of silence took time, but I was more than okay with it now. It was exhilarating because the person using it as a power move expected you to squirm, but I sat like a rock.

"I've been made aware of a new alliance of yours," he said and waited.

I didn't respond, only waited for him to continue.

"You knowing about that side of things actually makes my life easier," he followed up.

Good, it wasn't a test.

"I could imagine," I responded, relieved.

"Lines are getting blurry here. I don't like blurry lines." Hamish took a deep breath. "What is your take on them? The rebels."

"Sir?" I probed.

I wasn't asked these sorts of questions. They called me in, gave me a job, and didn't ask for my opinion. That question caught me off guard, and I was almost embarrassed by my reaction.

"Fair," Hamish laughed. "I've always liked you, you know that? When Zélia advised me that you all had been introduced, I was relieved."

No, I didn't know he liked me. Never said so. As a matter of fact, I didn't know he liked people in general.

"Just thought you enjoyed how fast and efficiently I could take care of what you need," I responded.

"That too. Part of why I like you." He cleared his throat. "We got into business with the rebels because we had similar interests. But as you know, there always needs to be someone on top. That hasn't been made clear yet."

It was going to be a fucking problem. The Brotherhood didn't bow to anyone outside of our own, that was our whole deal. So unless the rebels decided that they were going to hand shit over to us in the end—the lawless society—things weren't going to end well. I'd be the one cleaning up the godsdamn mess. Already was, apparently.

I scratched my chin and sat forward. "What was the deal with Soren?"

"Soren thought he was you. Believed he could float between these spaces and be valuable. People who didn't grow up the way you did aren't capable of doing that easily."

"So he got too committed to one side?"

Hamish ran his tongue over his teeth like speaking of Soren pissed him off. "Found out he was calling himself a rebel and ignoring his duties here. Ambitious. A victim of his own desires. The men I supply still report to me. That was the deal. He was mine to take care of."

"Makes sense." I shrugged a shoulder.

He watched me as if there was more to be said. I didn't speak without a reason here. Not when it could be used against me.

"So," he pushed. "Your thoughts?"

"Thaddeus seems stable enough. As does Zélia, but I did already get into a shoot-out with her, so, not my favorite. I believe in what they're trying to do, I just hope it can be pulled off."

"I agree. Zélia does appear to be focused on her goal," he responded.

"Yeah, sounds like her."

I knew what was coming. Really didn't want to be right, but I could see it on his face. Felt it in the air.

"If anything comes up that raises concern, I'd like you to let me know," he said.

"In regard to the Brotherhood," I led. "Or you specifically?"

"Both, I suppose."

There it was. Played out the same way every fucking time. I wouldn't agree to shit anymore that didn't serve me or Mira. At least, things I could easily avoid.

"Is that an order, sir?"

He straightened. "Does it need to be?"

"If I can be transparent?" I waited, and he nodded for me to continue. "I'm being torn in fifty different directions on the regular. I love the Brotherhood, and I'll always keep our interests at the forefront. I believe in what the rebels are doing, but I don't want to end up another Soren. If there is ever anything I think will impact the Brotherhood, I'll advise."

Hamish bit the inside of his cheek and tilted his head to the side. "I can respect that. After all, who would I send after you?"

I laughed, hoping he really meant it as a joke.

"Next rebellion meeting will be here in a couple of weeks. I'd like you to be here. Some of them get rowdy, and we need some support. Not everyone has been brought in on the...partnership."

These are the details I was looking for.

"Will there be a time they are?"

Hamish unfolded his hands with a shrug. "Not sure. I don't think everyone will align."

"I agree."

Another break in conversation. This time, it didn't feel like he was building up to ask me something. More so, he felt unsure if he wanted to say whatever was on his mind.

"Have you thought of what you're going to do after you graduate next year?" Hamish asked.

A life with Mira, hopefully.

"Not much. As you've witnessed, I've got a few paths set out for me already."

"You should consider joining the upper levels of the Brotherhood. Pay is good, as you know. Less field work. You remind me a lot of myself at that age. You could end up like me at mine."

I'd never really thought about it. Didn't think a lot about my future in general. At the end of the day, when it was all said and done, I was still owned by the Cynod. My brothers included.

"I'd consider it," I said, hopefully truthfully enough.

Hamish nodded and stood. "While you're here, a job did just come in."

How many times did you have to kill the same sort of person before you were considered a serial killer? There had to be a number. If it were up to Hamish, I'd soon be known as the Traitor Slayer or some shit.

This was exactly what I was worried about when it came to the *Noctis* and Rebellion partnership. Someone always had to be on top. People would always lean more toward one side. It was our nature to determine who was the most powerful, who gave the greatest chance at survival, and to go all in on that party. Unless you were like me, as Hamish pointed out.

In some ways, so was Mira. We were both born into worlds we never wanted to inherit. You learned that the only side to take was your own, but let everyone else think you were on theirs. Mira put on a mask when she needed to be the Cynod daughter and heir, and I did when I needed to be all the things I was outside of hers. A lackey for the Cynod, a *Noctis* member, protector of my family, and now, apparently, a fucking rebel.

According to my brief, Malin Callahan had been offering up *Noctis'* secrets to someone in the rebellion. Not to Zélia or Thaddeus, or anyone on that level. But loose lips got you killed, and he'd run his mouth to so many people that it had gotten back to Hamish.

The information on what he'd said specifically to get *me* sent wasn't given. I preferred it that way. The less information, the better. Treating them like a thing to cross off my list was best. Got harder when you remembered they were people.

Malin frequented this shitty dive bar downtown. Thankfully, it was one that worked with the club. We had quite a few that did business with us, whether it was supplying alcohol, using our facility for meetings, or requesting some sort of muscle. I tipped my chin to the bouncer who was always here, and he let me in.

It wasn't quite late enough for regular people to be here, just the ones who were trying to escape from their everyday lives for a couple more hours. Quite a few middle-aged men with briefcases, staring off into the distance with absolutely nothing behind their eyes.

The bartender tilted his head toward the backroom. That was where the slot machines were. Someone was subtly clearing the people out, but Malin was in the back corner, his forehead pressed against the machine as the reel spun, and the machine blinked. He didn't notice as I locked the door or as I pulled down the blinds into the bar.

He did jump when I pushed the machine from under his nose. His eyes were glassy, and he smelled of liquor, but he didn't sway on his feet or slur as he shouted, "What the fuck, bro?"

Sometimes, Hamish made requests on how things were handled. Gun, claws, dropped in a river with a cement block around their ankles. Traitors were always slow, and with knives. Every time. While I wasn't an expert carver like Atlas, I wasn't nothing to sneeze at.

"Should have kept your mouth shut. Bro."

I retrieved my knife from under my jacket and slashed it across his leg. He grabbed at the wound, and then I could see the decision not to go down easy falling over him. Fine by me.

He charged, tackling me around my waist and bringing me down. I dug my knife into his lower back, and he realized his miscalculation pretty quickly. His back arched as he rolled off me, and I stood up, straightening my jacket.

"Who sent you?" he shrieked.

Eh, a dead man can have that knowledge.

"*Noctis.*"

He nodded, his jaw ticking as he raised his fists. Man was bold, I'd give him that. I didn't leave the house without a couple of weapons, but coming *here* without a weapon felt exponentially stupid. Air flowed around him, an *Ik*, but from what I'd seen, not a very strong wielder.

The ends of his shoulder-length hair shifted, his brow pinched as he focused. Fucker was trying to conjure an airball to knock me into the wall. Unfortunately for him, he was too slow.

I launched my knife at him, aiming to the right of his body so the wind shifted it directly into his stomach. Hit exactly where I wanted it to. Directly in the left gastric artery. *Ha, call me a fucking scientist.*

His magic sputtered out at the shock, and blood poured out. This time, he did sway on his feet as he yanked the knife out and turned it toward me. The blood had already pooled at his feet, and he slipped through and onto his back.

"Sorry, bud. Nothing personal," I said, taking back my knife and skewering his heart.

Probably a quicker death than Hamish preferred, but it'd do. I grabbed his phone and slipped it into my pocket. They'd want to run diagnostics and see if he let anything else slip.

Banging on the wall twice, I let the cleanup crew know the job was done. They should have already had the van ready for me to dump the body in. Two small fae in hazmat suits rushed in. They didn't bother to look at me as one of them used their water magic to clean the blood, and the other inspected the scene.

I realized Malin was heavier than he appeared as I picked him up and put him on my shoulder. The hallway was clear, the door to the bar was closed, and no mingling bodies in the alley where the van was parked. I dropped him onto the metal floor, closed the van doors, and knocked on the side to let the drivers know they were good to go.

I wiped the blood off my phone and opened my text thread with Mira.

Me:

Miss you.

45

SIENNA

We parked in the narrow alley across the way from The Underworld, my new coupe purring in a way that didn't belong in this part of town. A beautiful blue that was sleek, gleaming, and far too pleased with itself.

Katia unfolded from the backseat with a groan, hand cupping her lower back, the cropped hem of her hoodie riding up enough to show the waistband of her leggings. "If I didn't know any better, I'd say you got this car to spite me."

"It's cute." I twirled the keys around my finger, the gold of my rings flashing in the sunlight.

We'd returned to Kuxtal Isle late yesterday, and with our little piece of contraband, it was straight to rebel business. Koa had vanished before sunrise to play Big Important Man with the boys, 'setting things in motion for the next quarter' before school started next week. Which, in my observation, meant over-caffeinated meetings no one wanted and crossing off meaningless tasks. But whatever made them feel productive.

Mir and I had swung by the Mercers' to collect Katia on the way. Mira leaned toward the coupe's window, fluffing her curls in the glass and straightening out her matching sweater set. "I totally thought you'd have gone with the off-roader."

"Who said I didn't?" My grin carried the energy of someone holding a winning hand but pretending it was nothing. The keys had been waiting on Koa's nightstand, neatly placed on my side of the bed. He was dead asleep when we got home last night and woke up to the sound of me squealing.

"He did *not*," Katia said, disbelief threading through her voice.

"It's my brother," Mira sighed, rolling her eyes. "Of course, he overcompensated."

I shrugged, the loose sleeves of my oversized hoodie falling past my wrists. "If I get a reward every time he has to play husband to that discount villain, I'm happy to turn the other cheek."

"You don't mean that, Si." Mira's hand brushed over my back, catching me before I could dig the hole of lies and hidden emotions deeper.

"I don't," I admitted. "But it's whatever. I know he's not trying to buy my heart or anything, I think he...feels bad about literally breathing at this point." My platform sneakers scuffed the curb as we headed for the side entrance.

Katia filled the silence again, apparently determined to keep our group therapy session alive. "In my experience, straightforward communication on how you feel is the best way forward. Dealing with two brothers? Overcommunication is the *only* way it works."

"Except when it comes to your sister?" I teased, desperate to redirect the conversation to take the heat off me.

"*Especially* when it comes to my shady, not-so-dead sister," Katia snarked. "This is going to be a blast."

We slipped in through the side camouflaged door, the one designed to fool anyone who didn't belong here, nodding at the bouncers who stepped aside—creating distance from their bosses' 'most prized possessions.'

The club in daylight felt stripped down—no bass thumping through the floors, no crush of bodies. Scattered patrons lingered in booths, voices low, papers and glasses sharing space on the tables. The air still carried a faint trace of last night's liquor.

Nola spotted us and approached with that small, tight smile, saving me from having to continue on with this conversation. I already had enough on my mind as is. "They're back in Serpent's Hollow. You're the last to arrive." She handed out our drinks without ceremony—mine cold and sweet, Mira's dark and bitter, Katia's fizzing pink. "Feyfog? Cigar?"

We shook our heads, and she waved us toward the back hallway. The sharp edge of her voice trickled down in echoes, issuing orders to the staff without breaking stride. Our pace slowed the deeper we went. I'd never been inside Serpent's Hollow, but we'd all heard a softened story from the boys about the conversations that typically took place there. At this point, I was almost certain I could hear Mira and Katia's pulses, as well as my own.

"Here goes nothing," Mira said, her hand hovering over the handle.

A chuckle escaped me. "Here goes my integrity," I muttered.

They gave me matching stares. I lifted my hands. "What? The papers are already in there. Koa dropped them off this morning."

Serpent's Hollow didn't welcome you. It appraised you, decided whether you were worth the trouble, then shut the door behind you so you couldn't leave. The black stone archway gleamed faintly in the dim light, silver veins catching the glow of a low-burning chandelier. Inside, the air was cool and dense, steeped in secrets, sharpened by the metallic tang of old grudges. It smelled the way betrayal would if it wore perfume.

The table stretched the length of the room, a slab of dark wood polished to a near-mirror shine. Rebel leadership was already assembled. Zélia sat with an ease that suggested she'd been running this table long before anyone here realized it existed. Across from her, my long-lost, deadbeat of a father sat in calculated stillness, assessing me from head to toe. I scanned over him with indifference, noticing Vitória sat further down, profile sharp against the candlelight, and it hit me then—three women, three faces carrying echoes of the same place. The same ancestry. Zélia's eyes, Katia's jawline, Vitória's cheekbones...they were all carved from the same stone as the Jundi bloodlines.

The boys had claimed their territory, naturally. Koa and Wren parked at opposite ends of the long table, Mercers smack in the middle across from each other. It left Asha, Alanna, and Strider sprinkled between them in a way that screamed *deliberate*. A seating chart disguised as chaos.

We slid into the gaps—Mira by Wren, Katia next to Adler, and me slotting in beside Koa. The scrape of my chair legs on the stone was loud enough to turn a few heads. Mira caught my eye, then her mask fell into place. Neutral, pleasant, and in that famous Tecun-Canek way, unreadable.

Koa's hand moved, sliding the papers my way without breaking whatever invisible staring contest he had going with Thaddeus. The two halves were still warm from the press of his hands and the magic begging to be freed.

'Every eye in this room is on those papers,' Koa cautioned, and there was something in his tone that filled me with confidence. *'Which means every ounce of power is yours.'*

I glanced up at him and nearly folded under the prize hidden in his gaze. He'd never ask me to act against my best interest, but the flex of his jaw said enough—pride on the surface, something closer to *please don't burn the world down* underneath. Mira's slow nod across the table tipped the scale.

They'd get what mattered—the pages, the artifacts for the arch, the prophecy.

The rest stayed in my pocket, locked down and untouchable. That circular artifact and everything I suspected about it would rot with me and my girls before it saw daylight in this room.

I pressed the papers together, and they shone with a faint pulse. The symbols flared, their glowing spreading like wildfire beneath my fingertips. I cleared my throat and began, fighting off the shake in my voice.

"A Manik will spark the flame of rebellion. For death is the beginning and death is the end—its touch will ignite a new cycle. When two halves of the same soul unite, balance shall return to the land. Two branches from the same tree take root for the first of their kind." I glanced up at the tension-filled room. All eyes locked on me. "We knew that already, thanks."

The latter more so muttered to *Kan*, who at this point, I was freaking certain was listening, then continued, eyes on the paper, chest tightening. *"To walk the paths of many worlds, you must divide, for the gates open but twice in the turning of the year—when day and night hold equal measure."*

"Spring equinox," Mira mumbled.

Asha signed something, rolling her eyes and grunting when Zélia's foot found her shin. Vitória didn't bother hiding her distaste. Her slow, appraising glance said she'd already written us off. Asha matched it with narrowed eyes. It was obvious neither of them were fond of having to work with people they probably consider Cynod adjacent. I could respect that if they weren't so bitchy about it.

"The shards shall be bound, and the reading must rise beneath the highest throne, where shadows fall long and silent. The way will now be shown, the prize unnamed; only those who learn can see what must be claimed. Relics stand as trials—proof of worthiness to restore the fractured balance. Fail, and the gates shall not open again for generations untold. When all the pieces converge, the next trial shall begin."

I dropped the papers with care, the room swallowing the prophecy whole.

First time in history this had ever been done and I was the one stuck doing it because; fate. Because a few millennia ago the gods decided to determine the path of my life. It was never really mine to steer. To choose. Everything had been set for me before I was even born. Conceptualized. None of this felt like an honor. Not with Thaddeus sitting straight-backed in his seat, proud disposition over his *daughter* reading the direct words of Kan before the rebellion.

Except, I didn't trust them, not any more than half of them trusted me.

"One of two days a year." Koa broke the silence, leaning back in his chair, arm resting behind me. "When day and night are equal. An old astronomical marker for *Kabal* farmers—saw it on the Codex. When The Veil dropped, they had to learn to grow their own food instead of stealing or trading for it from the humans. Miss the moment, and hunger is the harvest. We have two chances. When the shadows are the largest in the sky. Noon and midnight."

"Day time's a no." Adler shook his head, running a hand over his waves. "Too many eyes on campus to pull it off."

"Wouldn't just be risky." Jed's arms crossed, the leather of his jacket creaking. "It'd be suicide."

Zélia leaned forward, gaze sharp enough to pin anyone who thought to argue. "Midnight."

No room for debate.

"That doesn't mean we won't get caught in the fallout," Thaddeus rumbled, the warning thick in his voice.

Koa's eyes flicked toward Alanna. She tilted her head at him, a slow smile unfurling. It sent a pang of pain through my heart. Made me feel like the two of them were in on something I was not.

"Never met a ruse that didn't get me out of bullshit." She sounded almost bored.

Thaddeus spoke again, nodding as he took it all in. "We'll need somewhere to keep the artifacts until the plan moves forward. Anywhere on us or tied to us inherently poses a risk."

Mira didn't look up from the table, but her voice was steady. "We have a place."

Zélia's eyes narrowed. "Where?"

"It's safe," I said before Mira could offer more. "And accessible to anyone who needs it—when the time comes." I didn't add that 'anyone' was a handpicked few. Katia's mother had warned us to keep it to ourselves.

"Safe for who?" Vitória's voice had an edge.

"Safe for the people who matter," I said, meeting her stare without blinking.

Mira's heel tapped under the table—our silent agreement. The caves were ours, not theirs, and I wasn't about to hand them over to people who might decide one day that our usefulness had expired. The rebels didn't hide their distaste. Thaddeus's jaw worked. Zélia's fingers curled against the tabletop.

Katia leaned forward, eyes flicking between me and Mira, settling on her sister. "I'll have access."

That seemed to please Zélia enough to lay off our case, if only for the moment.

Thaddeus wasn't nodding. He was staring at me. "I'd like to speak with you."

"No." My gaze stayed on the papers. "You waited twenty-three years for the first conversation. We'll speak when I say we do."

I didn't want his explanations dressed as apologies. I'd work with them because restoring balance—whatever that really meant—might actually be worth it. Because the people of Inecha deserved better than they'd had. Because saving Herta was apparently my gods given destiny.

Ethan was my dad. It all started and stopped there.

Thaddeus's mouth pressed into a line, but he didn't push it. The silence between us was a taut rope that he knew better than to pull.

Koa cleared his throat, drawing attention back to the table. "Then it's settled. Midnight. We gather the pieces, keep them hidden, and wait for the equinox."

Vitória slouched back, arms crossed, her gaze drifting to the high, shadow-soaked beams of the ceiling. "Midnight or not, eyes will be on us. On you, or any suspected sympathizers to our cause."

"That's where we make them see what we want them to," Alanna said, propping her chin in her hand with a sly grin. "Give me a stage and I'll write an unforgettable performance. Can't be two places at once."

Jed muttered something under his breath about Alanna's overconfidence getting them all killed. She only smiled at him like she was cataloging which of his weaknesses to exploit first.

"We'll touch point every week via a secure source," Zélia said, her voice flat with authority. "Our plan needs to be airtight before we step out of this room. Thaddeus and I keep moving, never in one place too long. The Cynod's tightening the noose since the last attack. Coordination this close will raise questions if we slip up. I trust that with the same end goal in mind, this alliance is—"

"If you break this alliance, I'll send Ikari to kill you all. Slowly. With Atlas in tow," Koa said, his voice tight.

Across from me, Asha signed something brisk to Vitória, her hands quick and precise, the flick of her fingers punctuated by a sharp look toward Zélia. Vitória's reply came with a tight shrug, but she was already fishing a folded scrap of paper from her pocket—lists, contacts, something to keep them moving. Strider studied the notes over her shoulder, tapping once on a name before making a small correction with a piece of charcoal. The three of them were set to head north, reviving an old smuggling chain that could move people and information without drawing Cynod suspicion.

Koa cleared his throat, cutting through the low chatter. "We need to pull masses of civilians to one spot. Somewhere we can control the mess."

Alanna's fingers drummed the table, a smirk tugging at her lips. "Mentiria worked because we owned the spotlight. People assume fools don't pose a threat. We use that. We control the noise, the distraction."

Wren's nod was quick and sure. "The Vortex. Big crowd, loud enough, packed tight. We keep them busy for hours."

Alanna's grin sharpened. "Civilians will see everything, flooding the place, too many eyes to ignore. When the Cynod looks for someone to blame, they'll find hundreds who saw us—though no one will be allowed to speak from the NDAs—unless under the influence of the *Ajaw*. Testimony in which will be nothing other than the truth as the patrons understand."

Koa's eyes locked on me. "You and I go first to set the stage. Make a damn scene. Alanna is pissed off, we're stirring trouble—people will talk for days. Wren and Mira keep the party going until we say when."

Katia's voice cut in, steady and clear. "Where do I fit?"

Koa's answer was sharp. "You and the Mercers hold ground, ready to move. No one suspects you. No reason to."

Zélia gave a slow nod, unreadable but clear enough.

MIRA

It had been quiet for weeks. Quiet was never good, not around here. The rebels were doing their routine check-ins, nothing more. Dr. Aantaj hadn't called Wren into his office, only spoken to him over the phone. Nobody had come for my blood. Yet. I was concerned that it meant Iris had found another way. Relief should have been what I felt, but in reality, not needing me could have been worse.

Wren also should have been relieved that Dr. Aantaj hadn't been outright suspicious. But alas, we were both on edge. My phone vibrated, a text from him popping up on my phone.

Wren:

> **Look, I put up a painting. [picture]**

I laughed, typing out a response.

Me:

> **Did you steal that from Sienna's room?**

Wren:

> **I'll have you know she gave it to me. Said it gave 'killer cat vibes'**

Me:

> **Well, it looks good. Less like an insane asylum.**

Wren had shown me his apartment once we got back. I'd seen both of his family homes before, but not the place he stayed on campus. Once I walked in, I realized why he'd never taken me there. There was absolutely nothing in it but a bed, a couch, and a dining room table. The walls were all white. There wasn't even a plant, dead or alive.

He'd said that he was never here long, that he always ended up at one of the other homes or in his room at the club. It was just a place to be when he wasn't on a job or when he had an early class the next day.

Still, I thought it needed some sprucing up. I bought a plant that didn't need much of anything, a new comforter, and a centerpiece for his table. All on his card, but that wasn't the point.

School had picked right back up for all of us. This wasn't the type of place that eased into the kickoff of a semester. We were already elbow-deep in homework, reading assignments, and projects. I only had one class with Sienna and one with Katia, unfortunately. With their nahuales emerging this semester, they were guided toward classes specific to their path.

I hadn't determined what I was going to do yet. An email from admin had already been sent to me advising that I hadn't logged a nahual yet. They said I still had a few months, and if I needed assistance they could help. For now, I was still in these more generic and wide classes, which I was okay with. I liked having a variety of knowledge. Like this next class.

This professor was new to me, but so far I really liked her. It was a literature class, but with a focus on symbolism. We'd been assigned a reading last night, and I was excited about the discussion we'd have today.

"Good morning, Mira," Professor Mendoza said as I walked through the door.

"Hi," I responded, thankful my preferred seat was open.

This was a smaller class, meant to encourage lots of discussion and more comprehensive learning. Our desks were set up in a curve, allowing us to see each person as they spoke. I double-checked that my phone was on silent, not that it ever was on sound, but she'd chewed into a student last week for their phone going off.

The class filled up, nobody missing today's lecture. It was the type of class you needed to be present for. The discussions weren't recorded, so if you missed, you were behind.

"I trust everyone found the short story interesting," Professor Mendoza said, clicking away until the screen flashed onto the wall.

Everyone nodded, including me, because it truly was interesting. *The Legend of the Makech* was an enticing story about just how far we'd go for the ones we love. A princess was shipped off to marry the king from another kingdom, but she fell in love with a warrior from her own. They met under a great ceiba tree in secret, finding comfort in each other.

Once her father found out, he said he would have him killed. She pleaded, begging to spare his life, and in return, she'd go through with the original marriage. The king let him live but had him turned into a beetle by his mage.

The princess took her former lover and adorned him with jewels. She then wore him like a brooch, close to her heart forever. Keeping true to her word, she still married the neighboring kingdom's king, but never removed the beetle from her chest. She performed the duties she had to as queen, and when she was buried, it was with her former lover still pinned to her chest.

"Anyone have starting thoughts?" she asked.

"I found the choice of a beetle interesting," the girl beside me said.

Professor Mendoza nodded. "How so?"

"The king agrees to keep her forbidden lover alive, but has him transformed into a beetle. Something he probably finds: one, unlovable, and two, easy to get rid of if needed," the student said, waving her hand like it was obvious.

The more I thought about it, the more the story started to parallel my real life. Honestly, it was a shock my parents hadn't turned Wren into a beetle at this point. They'd mostly been pretending I didn't exist, again. Even the rare check-in calls from Linda had stopped. I could only hope my own arranged marriage wasn't around the corner... and that they needed the Ikaris too much to kill Wren.

"Mhm, so do we think that it was truly meant as mercy, or as a way to continue her punishment?" the professor asked.

Could be both, but from my time with a bit of a crazy monarch-type parent, it was probably punishment.

"Don't you think the decision was born of his love for his daughter?" a boy, of course, asked.

"Wouldn't genuine love for her mean letting her marry who she loves?" I asked.

He looked at me as if I were the last person who could chime in. "When you're in a position of power, sometimes you don't get those choices. I'd assume out of all people you're aware of that."

I had to keep my cool. Especially as my nahual reminded me that I could eat his soul if I wanted to. I really needed to ask Wren and Koa if theirs felt so...alive.

"Maybe that's why I'm adamant about it being wrong," I responded. "But beyond that, there's something to be said that the princess turned him into something beautiful."

A few of the students nodded, and I was glad not to be alone in the thinking. To take such an atrocious thing and find beauty in it was admirable.

"Do you think her father expected that?" Professor Mendoza inquired.

"No, I think he imagined she would find him appalling and run away. I'd think he either felt intense shame for what he'd done, or he was upset his ploy didn't work."

Or, he could be a soulless monster. That was probably the case.

Professor Mendoza crossed her legs. "So what symbolism did we find?"

"Eternal love," someone said.

"That's the main one, yes. Any others?" she asked.

It took a couple of beats as everyone picked a different symbol. Eternal love was the most obvious one. Professor Mendoza tapped a pencil against her knee, watching as the cogs in our minds started moving.

"Sacrifice," someone finally said.

Another raised her hand. "Dedication."

"Disguising greed as duty," I said, barely more than a whisper.

"Why do you say that, Mira?"

Oop, didn't mean to say that one out loud.

Leaning forward, I rested my chin on the palm of my hand and committed to the thought. "There was no indication in the text that the marriage was necessary. Just that the king wanted access to their resources. It was greed at the root of the forced marriage and at the transformation into a beetle. Framing it as something a princess *had* to do was manipulative."

"Would you feel differently if it *were* necessary?" the boy beside me asked.

"Don't people deserve to be happy?" I asked.

Today's symbolism for me might as well have been a fucking mirror. Thankfully, not everyone in this room was aware of how on the nose this story was for the Canek siblings' lives.

"Should one person's happiness have more weight than, I don't know, children in her village eating?" he challenged.

Professor Mendoza stood from her chair. "The purpose of this discussion is to analyze the text and find the symbolism. Not hypotheticals, Oliver."

He huffed, but didn't say anything else.

"Symbolism can be found everywhere, but many of these old texts and stories are riddled with it. Serpents can represent duality, trees represent life, fire can be seen as death, and that in turn can mean a new beginning. In this case, the beetle represents their eternal, undeniable love. Not many of these discussions have identified the symbolism in her father, so props to you, Mira."

I smiled softly, trying not to be *that* girl, but one hundred percent eating that shit up in my mind.

"Today's text won't be as easy to identify. There are many layers in this story; it is a bit longer, but I promise every bit of context is needed, so don't skim. It is a translation from a lost language, therefore parts may be difficult. You can start now; the file is on the class forum."

I opened my laptop and made my way to the folder she spoke of, finding the title, 'A Promise from the Messenger.'

Sienna's marker squeaked as she filled in a flower in the adult coloring book they'd given out at the mental health seminar. Dr. Puebla suggested we go, and there was honestly a lot of great information given.

These coloring books in the goodie bags were actually very relaxing. She'd already finished more than half of hers, thanks to her father, and to, well, my brother.

"Pass me the coquelicot," she said.

I scanned the markers in front of me with no idea what the fuck that meant.

"The one that looks like a poppy," she followed up.

"Mhm, mhm, obviously...it's...this one?" I held up a purple.

"The red-orange color all the way to the right, Mir."

"I was testing your knowledge of colors." I picked it up. "Here."

"We all have our strengths," she teased.

It was between classes, and the one we had next was the only class we had together this semester: Combat. Which was barely a class if you asked me, but it was fun at the very least. We still had two hours, as it appeared Combat was exclusively an evening class.

I didn't mind that. Having a nice place to channel some of this violent energy was nice. This semester's Combat was more focused on actually attacking, taking down opponents with or without the help of our gifts.

While my magic was brutal, it was important to keep the non-magical fighting polished up. There were people trying to tamper with that ability. If, for some reason, I ended up on the other end of a dose of that drug, I wanted to be prepared. Part of me wanted to call Iris, ask her why they hadn't come for my blood yet. Maybe it would put this worried thought away that the drug was already being produced.

"What's eating at you?" Sienna asked, her eyes on my fingers tapping together.

"What if they've already made the drug and it's being distributed as we speak? What if thousands of people are being stripped of their magic right now? What if—"

Sienna cut off my spiraling. "I think the rebels would notify us."

"Did you notify them of everything you knew?" I pressed.

We all kept secrets. There was no way of knowing one way or the other.

Sienna shrugged a shoulder. "Point made. I *did* tell them what I thought they should know. What was needed. A power-stealing drug on the loose would be something, in my opinion, they'd think we needed."

I was thankful Sienna understood my question was purely a result of my thought process, and not a shot at her. All of us had a common end goal, but how we got there—*if* all of us got there—worried me.

"I'm so tired of doom and gloom," I sighed and stood up, grabbing the book I'd gotten from my therapist that spoke of my nahual.

There wasn't as much information as I would have preferred, but something was better than nothing. Apparently, my nahual was used for a few different reasons in those times. One being warriors, but the other was as shamans of sorts. The way we were able to read and see things was leveraged by leaders in the villages. We performed ceremonies on the dying, to heal the sick.

They would take the power of the soul as someone died, and gave...something akin to a boost to someone who needed it. Like popping out the battery from the smoke detector and putting it in your new gadget. It was beautiful and really solidified the idea that death wasn't the end.

Practicing had been a little bit more difficult lately, but I had gone to the garden with Dr. Puebla one more time. We were testing out a session every other month this semester. I'd pretty much mastered the overwhelming feeling that I'd experienced when my nahual first emerged. I still had a very long way to go to master it completely. At the moments I needed it most, it worked, and I was thankful for that at least.

I was in a good place with my anxiety. After dealing with it for, well, my whole life, I knew that it didn't mean I would always be. I wasn't...fixed. With the tools I had now from Dr. Puebla, having people I trusted around me, and especially my nahual, I felt good. Didn't mean I wouldn't hit a rough patch and take ten steps backward, but I was living in the now. Being present.

Love had helped, too. Someone I knew was solely focused on me and my well-being. Wren was so patient and understanding, and would go far out of his way to make sure I was comfortable. Not that I never had love. I always had Sienna and Koa, even Katia. But they all had other things and people to worry about, as they should. Not to mention, Katia was mending fences with her sister while *also* juggling two relationships. She seemed happy, though. I was ecstatic to know that they'd found something like what I had. It was nice knowing that Wren was all mine, and I was all his.

I'd turn him into a brooch if he were ever transformed into a beetle.

"Are you in the *Symbolism in Literacy* class?" I asked Sienna.

Thankfully, my best friend was more than used to my random outbursts and changes in topics.

"No, not one my counselor said was required for *Kabans*," she responded, carefully shading in a flower with spots.

"Well, there was a new reading assigned today that I found interesting. Much of it seems to have been altered, names switched out, et cetera. But I think it was once a story about Kukulkan."

Sienna's head tilted in interest, and she put the marker down. "What makes you say that?"

"It's all about this message, promising that things will be turned around, but the character is speaking in metaphors and symbols."

"Sounds like Kan to me," she agreed.

We all would have loved it if he had been a little more straightforward. Alas, here we were.

"It just made me think, anyone who didn't know of him would have no idea that there was a connection. How many things have we been taught that were half-truths? They say the arch itself is cursed and never to touch it. Who started that rumor? Someone who knew it was dangerous?"

Her eyes squinted, a sign she was piecing together my antics. "Someone who didn't want people to get close to it," she said.

"Exactly. These things have spanned generations. The Cynod didn't have enough information to know what it was capable of, but they had enough to keep people away."

"Right. Where's that big brain of yours going with this?"

"I wonder what else is out there that they're trying to hide. I mean, that's a portal to another fucking universe in the middle of a park. Not to mention we might have extra...godblood gifts," I said as I tapped my chin.

There were tons of historical sites kept untouched. They'd said it was to keep the integrity of whatever it was, which was surely the case for some of them. However, maybe that's not the case for others. There could be a staircase to every level of hell in Katia's backyard. We wouldn't know unless an old book turned up, or if a fae with godsblood developed a gift.

"I'd hope that's the biggest secret, but you're right. Could be tons more."

I slammed my hand down. "Exactly! And then that begs the question, are we the only ones who know?"

Awh, fuck. That's the *look.* I didn't have to see a mirror to know what I looked like in Sienna's eyes. A mad scientist, the ones with the eye twitching and hair going every which way. Sometimes she'd entertain me for a few more off-the-wall questions, and other times...

"Mhm, yeah." Sienna fished something out of her pocket. "Why don't we light this?"

I grabbed the joint and a lighter and took a big drag. "And then you have the other nations. What about Mentiria? Why was part of Kan's paper there? Koa said they have tons of shit." I glanced down at the joint. "Oh, that's good."

Sienna took it from my fingers and hit it. "You can spiral about this for days, babe. We can only do what's in our power."

"I know." I sighed, the effects of the feyfog already calming me. "I'm just imagining all the shit that had to happen for *us* to be the ones to be here *now* with this knowledge and this task. I'll relax."

Sienna went back to coloring, and I lay down on my bed, hoping the gods had chosen right.

47

Koa

The Mentiria job hadn't blown back on us—yet. The paper we'd lifted was too important to go unmissed, and I knew searches were happening behind closed doors. My parents had been dragged into at least thirty meetings regarding the issue since we'd returned. Not that they'd ever tell us that, but the Mercers hacked Linda's email and calendar. From everything Alanna and I could tell, no one was pointing fingers our way. A miracle, considering the circumstances. Business carried on as usual. Now it was all a waiting game.

Voltan Complex was designed to fuck with your head. Light filtered in weirdly here, hazy through an enchanted glass dome. We were spread across five large circular patches of concrete in the center of a lake, bordered by acres of dense forestry. Underneath us was a confusing jumble of an underwater network of caves. As above, so below. There were levels to hell after all.

Halfway through the semester, and we were already moving on from the 'Stealth' portion of *Advanced Stealth and Tracking*. Most of us had mastered the art of blending in with our surroundings while working with our *nahuales* groups freshman year after we emerged. It was basic shit given on principle our nahual magic heavily relied on honing skills for reconnaissance, hunting, and evasion—shifters or not. I had the ability to camouflage with my surroundings, which made *stealth* easier than if an idiot like Rowan Rainwater tried to cover his scent or steps with a storm.

We'd received no further instruction upon arriving in class today other than to put on our training gear and cluster into previously assigned groups listed on the bulletin board. Professor Torres was what I liked to call an obnoxious fan of surprises—you never really knew what to expect when walking into her arena.

She clapped her hands with a wide grin at the center of the lake, her voice amplified over the current lapping through the water. Torres was a water *Imix*, though one would never guess she was once a high-ranking general in my father's army when face-to-face with the enthusiastic redhead. "I've hidden five magically entranced artifacts around the arena."

If she was waiting for a reaction, this wasn't the class to give her anything other than annoyed eye rolls and slouched stances. I wasn't sure if it was luck of the draw or we'd all just procrastinated taking this course until there was no other option, but none of us ever fell for her 'positive energy' shit. It was far too early in the morning for that.

"You may have already noticed," she announced, recovering as if the smile hadn't wavered from her tanned, freckled face. "There are five groups. Each artifact has been bound to your magical imprint and can only be found by the group as a whole. It will not reveal itself unless you are working together."

"We haven't even covered this in our readings," Tara complained at my side.

Despite the drama at the party last semester, our situation as combat partners had remained relatively unaffected. Everything between us had been casual anyway. We'd made it in years prior as partners for the worst classes on the schedule as a way to get through without wanting to fucking die. I was glad to have her on my team, given we were paired up with two magically illiterate fae when it came to tracing *or* stealth, plus Rowan.

"I heard that," Professor Torres chimed in. "There's no better way to learn than through experience! This exercise is to help you discover what sparks your *nahuales'* interest. Tracing a magical pull is an intimate affair, and one must be in tune with the body to do so. I cannot teach what is otherwise recognized as fae nature."

She paused, allowing the groans and moans to echo around her before silencing them with more claps and a gentle spray of water, her smile still intact. "Grades will be dispersed in the order of artifacts found. First place receives an 'A' for the exercise; last place fails. Well, you can figure out where all the middle goes. Okay, off you go."

With that, she shifted in the span of a blink. Her iridescent scales disappeared with a splash under the surface. Torres, as painfully cheerful as she was, was as hard as any other professor at Kuxtal. There were no easy answers, and questions were for those who did not care to understand the basics through learning themselves.

We all stared at each other—across circles and within. That explained the wetsuits for today. It was at least a mile to shore. Even once we made it, we could soon discover our artifact might actually be underneath.

"Flip a coin?" Tara asked, looking up at me, not interested in the others. We had a system, and it worked. Got us out of having to stay for the entire block of bullshit assignments

"What coin?" I scoffed, motioning to skin-tight apparel, absent of pockets. "Rock, paper, scissors."

We tapped our palms three times. I tossed out paper, and she mirrored my movements.

"This is ridiculous," Rowan complained, one hand on his hip, the other above his eyes, blocking out the artificial sun.

I glared at him, then over at the others, daring them to protest. They tossed their hands up, taking a simultaneous step back.

"Did you just growl at— Never mind." He gestured, running a palm through his hair and glancing toward the other teams as they made their decisions. "Go ahead."

Tara elbowed me to continue. Her rock beat my scissors. "I say land first."

"That was going to be my suggestion."

I dove into the water, falling into an easy stroke as Tara splashed in after me. Three more followed at our backs until a default pace brought us into an arrowed formation. The closer we got to land, the clearer the water became.

If there was one thing I appreciated about Voltan Complex, it was the lengths the academy had gone through to make each terrain we interacted with as real as possible. Talk about being dedicated to higher education. A school of fish dove deeper into the coral, the constant splashing on the surface from our class sent them for cover. The few sharks scattered about weren't too far behind. It was evident by the time my toes touched the sand that whatever we were looking for wasn't in the water. It was on land.

There was a natural tug flowing from the depths of the jungle that didn't exist in the mock sea. Similar to how the torn paper formed by the words of Kan had prickled at my every being—my body simply desired to get me close to the source. All I had to do was follow my gut. There was no way to explain it other than listening to that quiet voice in the back of your mind. The one we'd evolved not to need on a day-to-day basis. Not when everything was handed to us or easily accessible. I got it now, why Professor Torres said it could not be taught. You had to be secure within yourself to actually *know* you were being called on.

Tara and Rowan felt it. I could tell how our bodies pivoted at the same points on the path. Our hands lifted to redirect when we missed the mark, somehow, and had to double-back. Unfortunately for the other two, they would have been dead in the wild a few hundred millennia ago.

They drifted off at a split above, too lost in their heads to notice they were going the wrong way. Tara huffed in annoyance. "I'll go get them. You two keep going. We'll catch up."

Being left alone with Rowan was not high on my very small list of desires in this lifetime. Matter of fact, it wasn't on the list at all. I made sure to spend the least amount of time with Cynod cucks as possible. I was already tied to them for a lifetime; no need to force the situation before it was time for it to begin. He didn't try to break the silence.

I stepped with my left. So did he. I pivoted right. He was right on my fucking heel. We kept to the same infuriating dance. My patience expired three minutes in.

"A little space, please, Rainwater." I came to an abrupt stop, whirling on him.

He wasn't much shorter than I was, but his muscles appeared in different areas—different fighting classes. But Rowan wasn't a fighter. That wasn't his style. So why he stood so damn close with his chest fucking puffed was beyond me.

Rowan Rainwater had a death wish.

Had to or was clearly losing his fucking mind. He grabbed hold of my wrist as if protecting himself from getting hit before I had the opportunity to act. His brown hair was plastered to his forehead, a mix of sweat and water from our swim. Rowan's eyes darted over my shoulders. Checking for someone. Something...privacy.

"Talk," I snapped.

"They're on to you."

I chuckled at that. A lot of people could be on to me for a lot of different things. I was involved in a lot of shit. That was the nature of running a club and everything I pushed through it. Drugs, weapons, favors that never stayed clean—it all circled back, eventually. "You'll need to be more specific."

"The Cynod. My uncle," Rowan dared to take a step closer, his voice falling to a whisper, eyes bouncing around the area. "All of them. *They're* watching."

I tilted my head, assessing him. He stood tall under my gaze. I had him pinned against the closest tree with his next breath, peering behind me. I could hear Tara and the others bickering about which way to go, but they were still out of earshot with our hushed tones. "And why would they be doing that?"

The blank stare back made me want to punch him. It was his lucky day. I didn't have enough time to clean up that mess.

"I think we both know why," he snarked, a smile and a touch of confidence appearing at the sight of the other's approach.

He knows. There was no doubt in my mind. He'd practically proclaimed himself a civilian sympathizer in *Magical Ethics and Responsibility* lecture last semester. I whistled to the others, getting their attention, and they upped their pace. I used their presence to buy myself some time. Rowan had attempted to corner me. I didn't like that. Though I supposed I did respect it.

Unfortunately for him, I took cornering as an opportunity for a new path toward manipulation. He had to show his cards now. He'd left himself vulnerable.

All I had to do was set the trap. Make him useful. What was the Cynod going to do? Dispose of all the heirs close to coming of age to hold their seat?

I let the others fall ahead and take the lead, nodding off toward the direction the pulse was damn near tugging me toward. Now that I knew what it felt like, had identified and homed in on that magical signature, it was easy not to be distracted. Torres had carefully placed scraps of magic throughout to throw us off the scent.

Rowan caught the hint, dropping back from his conversation with Tara, who glanced back at me with concern. I nodded at her in dismissal, and she scoffed, throwing me a finger. We could have been done by now if I hadn't been toying around with Rowan, and she knew it.

"My sister thinks that you are trustworthy." It was a blanket statement, no real emotion or lure behind it. "I trust her judgment. What is it that you want?"

"What?"

"You want something, right?" I was losing what little patience I'd regained. He wore confusion in an irritating way. "That's why you're bringing it up. Name your price."

He shook his head, eyes glancing toward the part of the trail that caught my attention as well. "I have no price. I want to help."

Tara snapped at the others, and they followed after her like puppies as she course-corrected them back on track.

I considered Rowan's words. He seemed genuine. But a lot of shit appeared as rainbows and butterflies until you ended up walking into a pile of shit. His offer scraped against the portion of my brain that disliked all things that were too easy.

"You have two minutes to convince me you're not snaking us before I make your death look like an accident of Voltan."

"We're on the same side, Canek," Rowan risked a punch to the throat for the second time today, clamping a hand down on my shoulder. "No need for threats. I'm an open book."

I let a rattle free from my chest, and he wisely removed his hand. "Look," Rowan continued. "Why I want to help doesn't really matter at the end of the day, does it?"

"I can assure you that the reasoning will determine whether you live or die."

"Okayy," he drawled. "I didn't grow up thinking I was going to be the heir. Not the way you or Mira did. That only happened once my parents were dead and my uncle was past one-fifty. Childbearing wasn't an option anymore. I remember what life was like before power was promised. Even from my privileged seat, I could see it wasn't fair. A decent fae wouldn't turn their cheek to the opportunity to make a change. The three of us taking our seats in a hundred years won't change anything—not substantially. You know that. Mira knows that. I know that."

His words gave me pause because I'd once said the same thing—and I know Mira shared the sentiment. "What are you offering?"

"To help in whatever way I can," he said, exasperated as we closed in on the object. We were right on top of it; we could sense it.

We located the object after a few minutes of silence from the group. Rowan didn't push, but I could feel him watching me, waiting for an answer I had no intention of giving without making him sweat for it.

The rusted dagger was half-buried under the roots of a weeping willow, immersed in an inland swamp. I was too irritated with Rowan Rainwater in my fucking business to be annoyed at the fact that we'd finished second. A 'B.' Not bad, not good. Tara was sure to show her displeasure. If anyone was more of a perfectionist about her grades than Mira, it was her. There goes that easy partnership I spent three years building in order to avoid being grouped exclusively with idiots.

I lingered near the locker room exit. Rowan emerged a minute later, hair still damp from the showers, adjusting the strap on his bag.

"You're dating that girl," I snapped my fingers—her name just out of reach. "Gabby."

"Geri," he corrected, brows pulling tight. "And no. We broke up last semester. My uncle didn't approve."

"Yeah," I cut him off. "I didn't ask for your entire life story. Her mom runs ChismeChak, right?"

His glare was all the confirmation I needed.

"Great. This ex situation—" I draped an arm over his shoulders and steered him down the hall. He went rigid upon contact. "Is it 'I hate you' territory? And what are you doing on the spring equinox?"

"Do you have to choose the bougiest fucking restaurant every time?" I asked, leaning back in my chair and eyeing the crystal chandelier overhead. The damn thing looked like it cost more than my car. And my car wasn't cheap. Not with that suspension.

"On your dime? Yes." Alanna's smile was pure mischief as she unfolded her napkin, lowering her voice. "They're strategic, darling. We've gone over this the last three times."

"I wasn't listening," I said, reaching for the bread basket and popping a dry roll with far too much yeast in my mouth. I knew the difference now—thanks to Sienna, my taste buds were permanently altered.

"Oh. We know." She took a sip of her wine.

Around us, the low buzz of conversation mixed with the occasional flash from someone's phone. Alanna always picked places like this: where the lighting was flattering, the crowd high-profile, and the odds of being photographed hovered somewhere between inevitable and guaranteed.

It had become our little routine: one public date a month, staged enough to keep the press talking but painless enough that neither of us had to work too hard. On campus, it was easy to pretend. We'd fallen into the habit of walking together between our shared classes and were able to write off other public appearances due to focusing on our education and respective studies.

Kept our handlers happy and off our case for the most part. My mother had even reached out a few times to see if I'd "found a liking" to my fiancée and sounded mildly relieved when I'd answered with a simple "sure".

While the situation wasn't ideal, it worked. Sienna stayed at the condo when she could, though it wasn't what we preferred. Naturally, the academy had eased up on restrictions, but there was still a curfew for all first years. Bran was already rich as fuck from his daddy's money, so unfortunately, there was no buying Sienna or Mira's freedom out. Wren had already tried. Last semester, they'd practically lived at the condo; now it was a few nights a week.

Alanna set her glass down, her tone shifting to something softer. "Xumi and Ash wanted to check in about that vacation we had planned this spring." The code names rolled off her tongue like nothing was unusual. "We're all set, right? Visa paperwork handled? They said if we need help, they'll step in."

"Same answer as last time, babe." The word came out heavy, given that it was not part of my vocabulary. It was so...bland. An unthoughtful term of endearment. "We'll see them when we get back. Souvenirs in hand."

She nodded, poking at her entrée.

"Not hungry?" I asked. Usually, she was the first to clean her plate at these things. Even if it were a public appearance, they were always spots she was excited to try.

She rolled her eyes. "Grandfather said my eating habits weren't fit for the wife of the Cynod. Too many eyes and cameras around for it to be considered polite."

I shrugged. "Fuck him. Eat your food."

"Koa," she hissed, scandal dripping from my name.

I made a face that mocked her fear, forgetting where we were and that joking wasn't something we did. "What?" I tossed my napkin on my empty plate. "Mentirians believe a wife belongs to her husband, right?"

She gave me a wary nod.

"How...traditional." I kept my tone even. My mother would have a fit if my father even attempted to treat her as anything but an equal. The idea was laughable, truly, even for the wickedest of them all. "If that's the case, your grandfather doesn't get a vote on what or when you do or don't eat. I do. So eat."

She stared at me like she was trying to read the fine print, then straightened in her chair and started eating her pasta. I let her have the win without comment. Though I couldn't help thinking that the more I learned about her family, the easier it was to understand why she'd taken the side she had in all of this.

I cleared my throat, changing the subject. "Oh. Almost forgot." I took the last sip of my whiskey on the rocks. "I booked a private photographer for our vacation. Make sure we capture the moment."

"Someone I know?" Alanna didn't do nerves, but her tone reeked of unsettledness.

I nodded. "He's popular. Knows all the right people. Gets tipped off about the perfect shot."

She tapped her glass against mine. "Fabulous."

We lingered long enough to be noticed, then made our exit. Outside, the cameras caught us smiling, holding hands like it was instinct, sliding into the car together. I dropped her off at her car in the parking garage of the condo.

"Same time next month?" she snarked, unfastening her seatbelt and opening the door of my truck.

"Yes." The word was caught in my throat at the sight of Sienna standing frozen in the lot, yoga mat over her shoulder.

Alanna walked past her without so much as a glance and slid into her car. The silence left between Sienna and me felt heavier than it had in a long time.

48

KOA

End-of-the-month reporting was arguably the most painful aspect of being a business owner. I sat staring down at the stack of bullshit on my desk. Running numbers, shuffling through shipment invoices, and checking inventory in the hours prior to fight night really hitting its stride. It was the quiet before the storm—the hum of the bass from The Underworld was muffled through the door and the scratch of my pen.

My phone lit up with a text. Nola.

NOLA:

> **You need to get out here. Now. It's bleeding into The Vortex.**

Given she didn't bother with providing details as to what the *it* was, I knew it was bad. Nola could handle almost anything on her own. Pick the biggest, baddest motherfucker out of the crowd, and my money would be on her. If she was texting me, it meant the situation needed force—my kind of force.

I'd missed this. Being good all the time was a muted bore.

Causing chaos in The Underworld was one thing—expected even. We were criminals; I could only hold to a certain level of standards. But when their bullshit started affecting *my* business—the business with the civilians that lined the hells out of my pockets—well, I had to make an example out of that.

Wren wasn't due in until after the first fight of the night. I'd sent him for an extra pickup. Our more popular, magically infused drug was running dangerously low for a night expected to be packed. Traffic had picked up recently. Atlas was back in Chan for the third time this month, and Zane had gone home after handling business here most of the day. The Mercers were useless in this scenario, even if they had been here when I arrived hours ago. They usually sat back and enjoyed the show, limited skin in the game when it came to the propriety of the club and all.

Which meant this was mine to deal with. If I allowed things to get too rowdy, the gangs and every other lowlife who came here would start using my place as a battleground. So we tolerated a dispute or two every week. Nothing that resulted in death over vodka cranberries. That was classless. Shit that belonged inside of some back alley dive bar. If you really wanted to hash shit out, it belonged in one of the sterilized rooms or over in the ring.

The bass hit harder with every step I took out of my office, a deep, relentless thrum that rattled through my ribs. Strobe lights cut the room into jagged frames—screaming civilians on the staircase, predators in the shadows, all watching the chaos bleed from The Underworld into The Vortex. I rolled my sleeves up as I pushed forward, the crowd shifting without a word. Faces turned away, bodies bent sideways, entire groups breaking apart to give me the aisle.

The air was thick—hot breath, the tang of adrenaline, the sharp rot of spilled liquor—and under it all, that sour note my *Chikchan* senses warned me meant fear. Theirs. Not mine. And soon enough, it would only increase.

I took the stairs slowly, one step at a time. Let the weight of my presence crawl ahead of me. The shouting above faltered in little drops, awareness rippling through the bodies crammed shoulder to shoulder until they realized I was coming. Every head in my path turned away. Every voice died. All but the ones that needed the warning the most.

It was two versus three—Lobos Negros versus Cuchillas—normally kept to their respective ends of The Underworld. Blades flashed between fists. No magic. Typical for this crowd. We preferred to feel the damage we inflicted before resorting to more...hands-free techniques.

Well, they did. Me personally, a nice mix of magic and brute made for the most thrill.

I stood behind them for a second, watching, utterly unimpressed. The rhythm of the fight was no symphony. It was all brutality and breathless grunts.

Grabbing one by the back of the neck, I yanked him off his feet and slammed him into the wall. The thud silenced the hallway—and the stairs.

"Who started it?" My voice was a harsh whisper in his ear.

No one answered. Eyes darted anywhere but me. Pussies.

I scanned their faces, raising my brows, then shrugged with my signature smirk. The one the tabloids loved plastering on their covers. "Then you all started it."

The first idiot made his move. As expected. The machete was a surprise, however. Had to hand it to him. My respect for him went out the window at the sneak attack. Going after a man from his blindside was for the weak.

My *Chikchan* senses picked up on the vibrations through the air. I snatched his arm mid-swing, twisting until his knees hit the floor. The blade clattered in the uncomfortable silence.

Being challenged like that, in front of others, hit a switch I hadn't flipped in a long time. Pre-Sienna. Back when I was nothing but rage and the desire to be the scariest creature they could conceptualize in only their worst nightmares. It was how I'd earned respect in a world that thought I was just another entitled prick who'd had life handed to him and turned away from reaping the 'benefits.'

They'd all been testing me since the engagement announcement—assuming I'd softened and that Cynod politics would pull me out of this world. They were wrong. I had no plans for retirement. And I was about to make sure they remembered it.

I clicked my tongue, staring down at the sorry bastard on his knees, and picked up the machete. "I thought I said, no weapons."

The blade spun in my hand. I let it whistle through the air and kiss the tips of his fingers, clean through. His scream tore across the room, blood spraying. The sound grated worse than the mess.

Maybe Wren's way of doing business had rubbed off on me. There was education to be found in every dark corner of the world, or so they said. "Knives. I can forgive knives. Hells, I wouldn't step into a tense situation unarmed either.

But a machete? Used against *me*?" My hand clamped on his throat, his pulse hammering against my palm. "That violation simply cannot fly."

I crouched until my mouth was next to his ear. "I've buried better men for less."

His head bobbed, frantic, though I hadn't asked for agreement. I let him go, only to drive my boot into his ribs. He folded in half and tumbled down the stairs, choking on air.

Luke, leader of Lobos Negros, hadn't moved. I'd heard the whispers—my loyalty questioned, my name dragged through dirt. I stepped toward him, catching Nola's smirk in the corner of my eye. *Cut the shit,* etched into her mouth.

I closed the distance until my shadow drowned him. Five seconds in his space and I'd already stripped him clean of steel, passing each blade to Nola. She melted them down, molten glow staining his face before fading. His swallow was loud. His hands trembled. The air between us stretched thin.

"I hear you've been speaking on my name, Luke. Questioning my integrity. Using my house while you do it. A fine one, at that." I swept a hand at the patrons pressed against the wall, wide-eyed, silent. The criminal side of the crowd leaned in, listening. "You're scaring the paying crowd. Allow me to remind you that in this very moment, you *breathe* because I allow it. And when I walk away—it is in your best interest to not forget that."

My eyes slit open, *Chikchan* pupils narrowing, locking onto his.

His world split apart.

Blood-slick walls closed in. Shadows crawled over stone. His wrists, raw, bound. The stench of burnt flesh filled his lungs. From somewhere distant, muffled cries tore at his mind—children's sobs, desperate and broken. His chest heaved, lungs burning, heart pounding like a drumbeat of doom.

Luke collapsed, gagging, scrambling across the floor of his mind. Nails split on stone. Desperation stretched his face tight, his chest heaving.

The nightmare didn't loosen its grip.

I would never hurt a child. Of course, Luke didn't know that.

He disappeared down the stairs, lost in his own terror. I had no intention of pulling him free. Not until he found his own way to the door and out of the sanctity of my establishment.

The hallway hung corpse-still. Only the bass from The Vortex bled faintly through the air, a dull, pulsing heartbeat. The sex workers stood frozen, their clients half-hidden behind them. I flicked my fingers toward the private rooms. They moved quickly, heels and boots clicking against the sticky floor.

"Downstairs." My glance cut at the bottle girls who'd tried to help Nola earlier. They went without a word.

That left me, the last two who'd been stupid enough to keep swinging, and the one I wanted most. Plus a slew of onlookers who needed a gentle reminder to stay in their godsdamn place. The first two learned fast—bone meeting wall, flesh tearing on steel, pain enough to etch me into memory. They limped off, clutching themselves, swallowing curses.

"If I find out you've been to a healer to address your wounds, I'll send an Ikari to handle the rest." The threat followed them on their way out as I turned back to the last man. Someone I'd had more than a fair share of issues with and never quite trusted. He was thirsty for power in a dangerous way. Always starting shit, even with his own. "Walk."

He didn't ask where. He followed. Eyes glued to my back as I led him down the narrow hall toward the Death Room. Nola trailed behind. The air was frigid. The cooler was on—it was occupied after all. Usually, it was as if the Ikaris were in town.

A body was stretched out across the table, limbs at odd angles, the skin carved in clean lines. Wren's work was messy; this was Atlas. Always particular in his craft. He may have been a hot-head, he didn't kill out of rage—he carved joy into flesh.

The man with me froze. I shoved him forward until his knees cracked against the metal table, until copper and rot clawed down his throat. "Any interest in becoming the next one to lie here?"

His head snapped side to side so fast his teeth clacked. Begging, stammering. Pathetic.

I grabbed a fistful of his hair and forced his gaze onto the corpse. "Then remember where you are. This is *my* floor. You want to bleed, you leave that shit away from civilians."

If I allowed more than the minor brawl every week, this place would be a madhouse. You want to fight? Take it to the ring. You want to kill? Book a room. You want to engage in bullshit behavior in front of my patrons? Don't expect to walk away without a fucked-up face.

His breath hitched, a wet choke, and I waited for him to vomit.

Nola slid between us like she'd been watching for the exact moment I'd stop holding back. I was dangerously treading that line. My imagination was...taking me places.

"Koa," she snapped. "Enough."

One of the few people alive who could give me an order and walk away intact. I respected her enough to let her. But my eyes stayed locked on Remi, pulse still rising.

"Remember what happened the last time you lost yourself," Nola reminded me.

That broke through. I released him and stepped back until the distance between us felt too wide. My shirt hung rumpled, sleeves shoved halfway up my forearms. My knuckles throbbed.

"Get the club straightened up and back in order. Every glass replaced, every table fixed. I want it spotless before Sienna arrives. She's to have a good time tonight. I'm going to shower and change."

I left him with Nola and pushed through to The Vortex. The upper level had what I needed. A shower. Distance. The crowd split down the middle at my approach. Heads turned away, eyes dropping as if meeting mine might burn.

49

WREN

Mira rolled over, the sheets draping across her naked body with her textbook still open beside her. She must have stayed up to study after I went to sleep. I chuckled, running my thumb across her jaw. She was so fucking beautiful.

I grabbed my phone from the nightstand and adjusted the blinds to let a little bit of sun in. The warm rays fell over her skin, the oil she'd put on before bed still shimmering. Curls spread across the silk pillow case, the curve of her waist and hip exposed between the folds of sheets.

Mira wanted me to put up more art. Next time she was here, she'd find this picture plastered above my bed. Fucking masterpiece.

My phone buzzed in my hand, pulling me away from admiring her. A text in the group chat between my brothers. I had to get going or Zane would be an obnoxious ass.

"Love," I whispered, kissing her nose, "I've got to go. Just lock up when you leave."

"Mmm," she responded, still half asleep.

"I've got to meet my brothers," I said.

Mira wrapped her hand around my wrist, trying to pull me closer, and fell back asleep. I carefully moved her hand back to her pillow, even though every part of me wanted to get back into bed with her. I scribbled down a note in the kitchen, letting her know I'd be gone for a while, and placed the spare key atop the paper.

My keychain was on the hook by the entrance, and I carefully closed the door behind me so as not to wake her. If she was up studying and *that* tired, she'd probably been up late. It was Saturday, and she rarely let herself sleep in. Today was the day for it.

I took the empty elevator all the way down to the parking garage. My car sat in the first row, and the moment the engine revved, Zane called.

"I'm on my way," I said.

"Better be," he responded and hung up.

Blowing air between my lips, I pulled out of the parking garage and onto the street. I was running late. Stared at Mira for longer than I thought I did. The engine purred as I pressed onto the gas, speeding up to make up the time lost.

My phone rang again, and I almost cussed out Zane before I saw who was calling.

"Hey, Ma," I said.

"Hi, baby. Is Mira around?" My mother asked.

"I'm doing well. How are you?" I joked, my tone light.

She laughed. "Oh, I'm sorry, honey. Mira mentioned that she liked my hand cream when she and Sienna came to help with my garden. I was going to see if she wanted me to pick her some up at the store. I'm heading there now."

"I'm sure she'd love that. We can come swing by later today or tomorrow," I responded, switching lanes and punching it as traffic cleared.

"Oh, good. I'll make you both some snacks to take back to campus," she said, and I could hear her rummaging through the shelves to decide what that snack would be.

"Alright, I've got to go. Love you," I said.

"Love you!" she exclaimed and ended the call.

She was thoroughly enjoying having another woman around. Mira had brought out a side to her that we'd never really seen. My mother was tough as nails, but there was a soft side that Mira had exposed. They'd gotten along so well that there'd been a few times I was *almost* entirely sure they both forgot I was there. I didn't mind one bit.

There was surely some bias there, but my mother really was the fucking best. Mira deserved to feel that, and my mother had always wanted a daughter. It all worked out.

I rolled down the windows, needing to clear my mind for the job. It was best if I tucked away these things until I was done. Especially when I was around the Cynod shitheads. If there was any hint at something to exploit, they would.

They already had my family. Aantaj knew about Mira, but none of the others had ever mentioned her. Outside of her parents, that was. They hadn't said anything else to her about me, and we weren't hiding anymore. Probably wanted to keep enemies close. If that's what I was considered. More like an employee. Regardless, they weren't actively trying to tear us apart. Too busy with Sienna and Koa, maybe.

Today's job was for security at a sponsored event. *Sponsored* in the sense that they'd paid for everything and ensured their name would be the one given praise. This one was to 'Feed Inecha,' and was a pretty hands-on event. They never showed up to these unless there was some sort of speech to be given, but with the last rebel attack, they wanted extra security. In my opinion, it was less to protect the volunteers and more to make sure there was no bad publicity.

In the last touchpoint with Zélia and Thaddeus, they'd mentioned rebels would be there. Just for intel, I was assured, and not to start anything. They knew where my loyalties lied, but they also knew what I'd have to be. Who I'd have to be in that circumstance.

I pulled into the back alley of the building to find my brothers. Zane stood with his arms across his chest, and Atlas leaned against the wall.

"Bout fucking time," Zane said. "We've got to do a perimeter check in less than a minute."

He was nowhere near as intense as Atlas, but he took jobs seriously. We all did, but when it came to being on time, he was a stickler. I couldn't give the excuse that Mira's beauty had caught me in a trap like a fucking moth to a flame.

"I know. I'm here, aren't I?" I asked.

Atlas turned his nose up to the wind, his *Ok* sense of smell a touch better than our *Ix*.

"People are arriving," he said, pushing off the wall.

I put my guns into their holsters and fitted my jacket over top of them. Zane led the way, and we ensured there was nothing suspicious around the perimeter of the building. Once that was clear, we entered inside. It was only staff so far, but the place would start filling up soon. The stations were almost set up, spots for people to bag the various foods and create baskets.

Mira mentioned that this was one the Cynod liked to throw when they needed a quick uptick in positive PR. It involved a lot of people, which in turn gave lots of opportunities for people to talk and take pictures. She said it was actually cheaper for these things to be mailed directly to the communities in need, but they shelled out extra for this setup.

Zane spoke with the security detail inside while Atlas and I made sure to keep scanning the room.

"Talk to Wolfe lately?" I asked Atlas, loud enough for only him to hear.

He shuffled, giving me a side-eye. "Why would you ask that?"

"No reason. You two seemed...close at the beach."

"This is hardly the place to discuss anything that happened there," he snapped.

I put my hands up in surrender. "Alright."

I'd barely seen him since the beach house. He'd been on job after job, all overlapping our usual Sunday family dinners. My mom said he'd stopped by during the week, but just for a couple hours. Atlas was a closed off person, even to us. If I knew him, he was beating himself up for falling into this situation with a Mercer of all people.

"Normal security, no threats or people to be aware of," Zane said as he came back.

I adjusted the gun on my left side and nodded. Atlas pretended he wasn't being awkward as fuck two minutes ago and took off down the hall.

"What's up his ass?" Zane asked.

I shrugged. "No clue."

Zane would never let him hear the end of it. He was the type to fully lean into all the rivalry shit. If someone didn't give him a reason *not* to be an ass, he was going to be an ass.

Volunteers filtered into the building, filling up each station. From my quick count, it was at least three hundred people in this space alone. The head of volunteers stepped to the stage with a mic, always cheery as fuck.

She was someone I'd seen in passing plenty of times at things like this, but had never actually talked to her. People at her level didn't have the clearance to request our...help. That was only Cynod members.

"Thank you all for being here!" she said, her voice squeaky and grating. "Each station has a lead volunteer, so listen to them for how your station works. The Cynod really appreciate your time and effort. Make sure to take pictures and use the hashtag Feeding Inecha!"

#FeedingInecha popped up on a screen across from her. I realized then that the hashtag had been placed all over the room. There were also codes to scan to drop photos into a specific online folder. Those could be used by the Cynod social management team. It was a well-oiled machine. People ate it up.

I did another lap, some of the staff shrinking away from me as I passed. Some of these people had heard of me, I was sure. They were close enough to the Cynod to know. Could have even been threatened by me at some point. Someone I recognized from the rebel fish warehouse walked across the hall, only a small dip of their chin an indication they knew that *I* knew who they were.

"Situation outside," Atlas said through my earpiece. "Left side."

We'd always been told to keep the drama away from the patrons, not make a scene. So, I walked leisurely out the door and around the building. Even stretched my arms like I just needed some air.

A woman was on the ground, leaning against the building. Deep lines stretched across her sun-damaged skin from her eyes and mouth, her clothes worn and tattered. My brothers weren't out here yet, just a volunteer.

"She thought she could come for food. I told her we aren't distributing," the volunteer said.

Bullshit.

"I've got it handled," I said to the volunteer and into the earpiece to my brothers.

She attempted a smile, the skin cracking around her lips. She wore lots of layers, but I was certain a skeletal figure would be found beneath it.

"When's the last time you ate?"

"I can't remember," she replied.

I shook my head. Wasn't usually the charitable type, and I could probably blame Mira for this...desire to help. "Come with me."

Taking her to the back of the building in the alley, I popped my trunk quickly and handed her a box of snacks my mother gave me last week. Then, I took out a couple hundred solits and put them in the box.

"Oh, the food is all I need. It's okay," she said, trying to fish the money out.

I stopped her hand and insisted. "Go find a place to stay on Broad Avenue for a couple days."

She teared up, but I didn't know what to do now. I stood there awkwardly until a few tears fell from her eyes, and she thanked me again.

Felt kind of good.

Scurrying at my back had me turning, and I found someone with their face covered trying to get into the building. It wasn't super common, but every now and then it happened. Their jacket shifted, and the glint of a weapon glimmered in the sun.

I sighed, taking out my gun and firing a warning shot at their feet. Of course, they pulled their firearm. Their hand shook as they aimed it toward me. Really wasn't in the mood to kill someone right now.

Tucking my gun away, I pulled out a knife. Wouldn't be fatal, but enough to stop them.

I pressed a hand to my ear piece. "Got another situation out back."

The person hadn't fired a shot yet, only held it up as if that'd be enough to scare me. I let my knife fly, and it embedded into the shoulder of the arm holding their gun. It fell to the ground just as Zane kicked the door down and tackled them.

"I'll take him in," my brother said.

I nodded, but a car pulled in across the alley. An all-black, tinted car, I was all too familiar with. Aantaj's personal detail exited the vehicles, all fuckers I'd dealt with before. My heart beat faster in proximity, worried he'd know what Mira had done.

Atlas jogged up to us. "What's going on?"

"I need to go," I said.

Zane whipped his head to scope out the scene. "What did you do?"

Aantaj's eyes set on me. They narrowed, but this far, I couldn't tell if he was trying to see or if he felt the absence of the bond. He took a step toward us, but someone shouted for him. On his side, windows looked directly into the building where the event was happening. Volunteers pounded against the window in what I assume was excitement that he was here.

"I'll take this one down to the station," I said. "I can't be near him."

"You're going to fill us in. *Tonight*," Atlas demanded.

"But we'll cover for you," Zane added.

"Meet at Mom and Dad's at 8," I said, yanking up the assailant and tying their hands.

Aantaj was still staring, but finally turned with a smile to wave to the crowd. My gut told me he knew. Mira said we wouldn't know until we were physically close. I had no idea what he'd do with the information. Not only was it broken, but someone close to me had the ability to break it.

I was happy it was gone; it meant he couldn't force me to hurt Mira or bring him her blood...But I hoped whatever might happen wouldn't be worse.

Atlas and Zane paced our parents' living room. Our mom and dad had gone to the garden after dinner, but my brothers had to debrief. Including explaining what happened with Aantaj.

Zane's body tightened, veins popping near his temples. "Why didn't you tell us?"

"We could have helped you," Atlas followed up.

"I didn't want to put you two at risk," I admitted. "If he found out, he would have blood-bonded you, too."

The last thing I wanted was for all of us to be in this situation.

"We would have gotten rid of him together," Zane said.

"That was what I was worried about," I explained. "But it doesn't matter now, Mira got rid of it."

My brilliant girl.

"It still matters. If he's flexing his dick around with power like that, we're all in danger," Atlas asserted.

I scratched the back of my head. He was right. This was only the beginning; if he did it once, he could do it again to someone else. Probably already had.

"We need out of the contract," Zane said under his breath.

"They'll kill everyone we care about," I responded, my gaze landing on Atlas.

Zane didn't have anybody. His work was his life. He loved us, our family, but there was no other way to hurt him. Atlas had operated in a very similar way until recently. Whether what he had with Wolfe was just carnal or if it was something real, it didn't matter. If they found out, they'd use him against my brother.

"Fine," Atlas said. "What you said earlier...it's true."

"What's true?" Zane questioned.

I looked at Atlas, wondering if he wanted to be the one to say it. He tilted his chin for me to go ahead, and I bounced on the opportunity. Been sitting on this joke for hours.

"You asked what's up his ass?" I responded with a grin. "A Mercer. Wolfe, specifically."

Atlas sneered, his lips turned down as he snapped, "You take me for a fucking bottom?"

Hadn't really thought about it, truthfully.

"That's hardly the point here. How could you do that with a *Mercer*?" Zane spat.

Atlas plopped down onto the couch. "Things didn't happen the way we think. He's shown me the proof. The Cynod did and said what they needed to ensure we were separated and not communicating."

Which was exactly what he said at the beach. Even made it known that our contracts were identical.

I, for one, had a lot of fucking questions. Starting with, "How'd you even end up together?"

"Job. He had to cover for one of the twins, and, yeah..." Atlas trailed off.

It sat in the air for a few beats. To be a fly on the fucking wall for that conversation. I couldn't imagine my brother and Wolfe working together, let alone saying enough words to find out they didn't hate each other. Had to have been Wolfe who brought it up.

Zane fell into a loud, rumbling laugh. "Dad is going to fucking kill you."

"Dad has been misinformed. I'll tell him the truth. If it even comes to that, we aren't like a *couple*," Atlas said.

Couple or not, shit was complicated. I checked the time. I had to get back.

"Look, if Aantaj tries to corner either of you alone, don't do it. We can figure out how to deal with him, but right now I'm going to do my best to avoid him. I don't know if he's aware my bond is broken."

My brothers nodded. My father came into the living room, and Atlas perked up. There was no indication that he heard what we were talking about; he just went to the bathroom without a word.

If there was one thing the Ikaris were good for, it was making a bad situation worse.

50

KOA

I'd been driving for three hours. Sienna was sulking in the passenger seat with her arms crossed and a pout that had been trying—and failing—to scare me into giving away all my secrets. I admit, one hand running up the leg of my pants and settling over my dick almost had me coming clean.

"Really, snake?" she finally muttered, twisting the air vents toward her. "Kidnapping? I knew you enjoyed being associated with the rebels, but I thought this beneath you."

"It's not kidnapping if you willingly got in the truck," I said, glancing at her bare legs tucked up on my dash. "And no, nothing is beneath me when it comes to you, Venom."

She snorted and shifted the vent again. "I got in because you promised me crepes an hour after I woke up craving them. And yet"—she gestured toward the endless blur of the mainland jungle flying past the windows—"we passed Kinich Kafe ages ago. Spill it, Koa."

"Twenty minutes." I reached over, resting my hand on her thigh, the warmth of her skin slipping under my palm as I squeezed. "Sit back. I promise to make this worth your time."

Her eyes narrowed, the brown flecked with gold in the sunlight. "You'd better. If I fail my *Elemental Manipulation Theory* final because of missing this valuable study time, it's on your conscience."

I barked a laugh. As if I had one. For anyone else, maybe not. For her, though? Abso-fucking-lutely. I tapped the console, pulling up the app I'd had built, and the familiar monotone of her study guide spilled through the speakers. Her face shifted from a stubborn pout to startled, then softened into something that made my chest tight. She leaned into me, resting her head against my arm. The weight of her body eased me from all the bullshit waiting for us come end of semester.

Twenty minutes on the dot, I turned into the narrow streets of Cobá. Downtown unfolded around us—stucco walls painted in oranges and aquamarines, balconies dripping with bougainvillea, vendors calling out over baskets of fruit and meats on sticks. The air carried the scent of roasted corn and sun-warmed stone.

Sienna glanced up from her phone, her entire body jolting. "Oh my gods." She pressed her hands against the window, and I rolled it all the way down, watching her fingers go with it. "That's the Cenote Azul Gallery. I was saving—"

"Up to take the trip before you got to Kuxtal," I finished for her. She'd mentioned it to me once, and that was all it took. I'd made a mental note and decided at that moment that I would be the one to take her. Now, the final weekend of the photographer Quixil being in town had come, and I was determined to hold true to my silent promise. "I know."

I pulled into a side street, killed the engine. Her gaze darted from the gallery's arching entrance, back to me, then back to the building again. "Shut up."

"I don't think I will."

"You didn't."

"I obviously did." I crossed my arms, letting the smugness drip from my tone.

Her mouth parted, then shut again. She tugged at her t-shirt that hung right above her knees. "I can't go in there dressed like this."

"Why not?" I asked, feigning confusion.

Her hands flicked over her outfit. "See *Quixil's* exhibit in this? They'd never take me seriously in the art world."

"It offends me that after everything, you still manage to underestimate me." I jerked my chin toward the backseat.

Her bags were already there—with the dress she'd bought months ago, she claimed she was manifesting the chance to wear it here would finally come. Sienna blinked at me, eyes glossing, then covered her mouth with her hand, whispering, "I love you."

"I know."

She hesitated, "You're not coming, are you?"

I smirked, murmured the glamour spell we'd become so comfortable with, and felt my features ripple. When I turned back, the reflection in the glass was a plain man in a polo, hair cut short, face forgettable. "No, *I'm* not."

Sienna burst out laughing. "No offense, but I wouldn't give that version of you a second glance."

"That was the point, yet it still wounds me." I placed a hand against my chest, taking a few wobbly steps back.

"It's just...very, normal." Her fingers toyed with the collar of my navy polo. "But I'll take you any way I can."

I tilted her face toward mine, fingers brushing along her jaw as I pulled her close. My lips met hers, hard enough to steal her breath, teeth grazing her lower lip before pulling away. "Go get changed. She's waiting to give you a tour."

"S-she—" she stuttered. "As in Quixil?"

I nodded, smirking at the excitement she couldn't contain. Sienna bounced on the tips of her toes.

She darted into the café on the corner and came back minutes later, curls fluffed and framing her heart-shaped face. The white dress she'd chosen perfectly silhouetted her body, stopping right at her calf, a small brown bag in her hands. She bit into a muffin, nose wrinkling, and waved the bag. "Made me buy something to use the bathroom. I hate places like that."

I stole the muffin, took a bite, and grimaced. "The crumble's too sweet."

"I know. And they didn't bother to brown the butter." Her face pulled into a tight, teasing smile. "I've turned you into a pastry snob."

"Don't tell anyone, or I'll deny it."

She tossed her bag inside the truck and rose to her toes, pressing a kiss against my mouth, muffled by her grin. "I'm so excited."

Her hand fit into the palm of my hand as we walked toward the gallery. She nearly skipped. The space was quiet but buzzing with soft footsteps. Sienna pulled me forward. One frame after another caught her eye—portraits, landscapes, shots of strangers frozen mid-motion. She tilted her head, analyzing shadows and angles, muttering about composition. Sometimes she wrinkled her nose, dismissing a photograph within a single breath.

I wasn't half as focused on the art. My attention stayed on her. The fire in her eyes when she explained how a photo lied or died by its lighting, the way her voice softened at the image of a child playing in the rain. She could've been speaking another language, and I still would've followed her through every room as we waited.

Quixil drifted over, and Sienna's face lit up. They wandered deeper into the gallery, hands waving expressively in the air. I leaned against an archway, arms crossed and watching her. She had her spark back. The same one from when we met—where she made the room come alive and I couldn't look away.

She finally came back, cheeks flushed, eyes wild. Didn't even make it past the doorway before she let out a squeal that nearly ripped my eardrums apart.

"Ow," I muttered, yanking at my ear, smirking despite the sting.

She latched onto my arm. "Apparently, Quixil has a friend with an opening at their summer showcase, and she wants me to submit my Midnight Bloom piece for consideration."

"Finally," I said, unable to hide the grin of swelling pride.

"Finally, what?"

"The world gets to see how beautiful you make it seem."

She leaned forward and kissed me, hard, teeth clashing just a little, pulling me in. I pressed back, hand in her hair, thumb brushing her jaw. When she pulled back, breath heavy, I tugged her along toward the truck. There were only so many daylight hours I had left of hers to steal.

By the time we rolled out of the city and onto the hill overlooking the outer skyline, the sun was low, flames of orange and rose spilling over the horizon. We grabbed subs on the way, planning to eat them in the bed of the truck. Sienna hopped out the second I backed in, standing far too close to the edge for my taste.

The wind tossed her hair around her face, the city spread out below, golden and endless. A car next to us squeaked, its rims taking a beating to whatever was happening inside. She threw her head back, laughing like a wild thing.

"Can you blame them? This sunset—no painting could touch it," she said, eyes shining.

"You could," I said as I leaned close.

My hand fell to the small of her back, holding her tight against me. Her laugh mixed with a gasp, and I pressed forward, teeth to her neck, lips to hers, heat coiling between us.

"Thank you," she breathed.

"For what?"

"For today. I needed this. We needed this."

I buried my face into her neck, holding myself there, allowing myself to simply exist in this moment only. We'd fallen into such a routine of sneaking around, and while it was comfortable for now, it was also emotionally exhausting. I didn't want to pretend we were over any more than I wanted to fake a relationship with Alanna. Seeing what it did to Sienna, how it dampened her soul, her light—it fucking wrecked me.

Studying every inch of her face, I crashed into her, a slower kiss than before. She reciprocated, opening her mouth and dancing her tongue around mine. She tasted of oat and honey from our coffee stop along the way. Sienna wrapped her arms around my neck, and I hoisted her up, her legs locking behind my back.

Placing her gently on the edge of the bed of the truck, I dropped my hands to cup her ass. She moaned under my touch, scooting closer, her body heat sending blood rushing to my dick. As if our minds were connected, she reached down, hand dragging over the zipper of my trousers. I nibbled along her collarbone, then slid my tongue down the center of her chest, stopping at the low dip of her dress. Her body jolted.

'So eager,' I teased.

I gave her no opportunity to respond. I spread her lips in the same movement, my fingers pushed her panties aside, and slid into her. Her hand fell over her mouth to catch her moan.

"What's wrong, Venom?" Two fingers curled inside her warm, clenching, pussy. "Don't want anyone to hear you scream?"

This had every bit of a chance of becoming a PR nightmare for my parents. I'd dropped my glamour halfway up to the lookout point. Problem was, when she squirmed like that and tipped her head back, hand squeezing her breast—I couldn't bring myself to care.

An engine to the left of us roared to life, and the truck that'd been caught in a far more incriminating act pulled away. I fell onto her, chuckling, but she found no humor as she ground into me. Using my fingers to pleasure herself. I kissed the tip of her ear, then along her jaw, landing to place a firm one on her lips. She pressed harder, leaving herself there as she found relief.

The sun had dipped further beyond the horizon, and the shadows of the night crept in. Stars poked through the light pollution, the moon trying to make an appearance. We were all alone up here now. And I knew exactly how I wanted to use our time.

So did she.

I tilted her chin up with my hand, our lips meeting again in a slow, greedy kiss, tasting, savoring, claiming. Her hands roamed my shoulders and back, pulling me closer. Sienna rolled over, pressing up from the truck and onto her knees. She licked her lips, pulling at my belt and sliding it free from my trousers. Her dark eyes held my stare. I unbuttoned the top and unzipped, daring her to make the next move. Her lids lowered.

She reached for the hem of my boxers, pulling me closer with one finger, and leaning back against the comforter we'd tossed in the bed. I finished climbing into the truck and lowered myself atop her again, cupping her face and using the remaining light to really take the moment in. Sienna's lips curled into a small smile—her hand brushing my hair back from my face.

"I'm going to marry you one day," I said. "I promise."

One slow tear fell down her cheek. All tenderness lost way to pure passion. I kissed Sienna until my mouth burned—felt raw.

She pressed a hand against my chest, pushing me to my back and switching our positions. I explored her body with both hands, one settling against her waist, another cupping her breast as she hoisted herself up, and glided down my cock.

A gasp left her throat at the same time as mine, and we both stilled. Sienna fell forward, her forehead resting against my shoulder. I gave her a moment before pressing my hips up and further into her pussy. Shuddering, I pushed the thought of coming at the first stroke out of my mind. It was far too easy to let go around her.

She adjusted to my width, her body finding a comfortable rhythm as I allowed her to control the pace. Her hips moved at a steady pace, grinding in circles. Sienna's body moved against mine, heat and shivers coiling between us. Every brush of her skin, every gasp, every press of her hand sent a jolt through me. I could feel the pull of her, the way she wanted me, and it drove me harder, deeper.

I traced my hands along the curves I knew by memory, memorizing again the way her body fit against mine. Her breath came in ragged, soft moans, and the scent of her—warm, sweet, and hers—wrapped around me. I let myself be pulled into the moment fully, every thought narrowing down to her, her, her.

Her lips brushed my neck, a gentle bite, a whisper of teeth that made me growl low in my throat. I tangled my fingers in her hair, holding her closer, guiding, responding to her rhythm. There was no rush.

"Fuck, Sienna," I swore under my breath, lips brushing hers, a promise that there was no one else, no place else, that mattered.

Her fingers traced patterns over my inked chest, over my arms, until the world contracted to just the two of us, the way her heartbeat matched mine. I pulled her closer, whispering her name like a prayer, and she shivered against me, falling still as we both found our release.

A week out from the spring equinox, and the campus felt like a pressure cooker. Finals were sneaking up, everyone's nerves were fraying, and I had exactly zero patience for the chaos that always came with this time of year. The semester had been...boring, if you could call it that. Classes, club duties, keeping the *Noctis Fraternitas* from staying too much up my ass—routine. The rebels hovered in the background. Everything was too quiet. Nothing had exploded, nothing had gone sideways, and that alone made me twitch.

I was cutting across campus, eyes half on the path, half on my phone, when I caught him out of the corner of my eye. Taran. First time I'd seen him since that day with the rebels. His posture was that same effortless arrogance, like he owned the sun and the shade it cast.

"Mr. Canek," he said, casually, and kept walking.

I froze, gave him my best incredulous glare. "Really? We're just going to pretend— Never mind." I scoffed, jaw tight, and shoved the thought down as I walked off.

He didn't stop. "I'm as up-front as they come, Mr. Canek. Perhaps it's the fact that you failed to ask the right questions that's bothering you the most. No." He clicked his tongue. "I think it's rather the fact that you never bothered to ask questions at all. I've given you what you need to find answers. It's up to you to do the rest. Enjoy your *vacation*. I look forward to hearing all about it once you return."

Cryptic bastard.

This calm wasn't real. Nothing ever was.

51

MIRA

I unplugged my laptop and selected three of the sharpest pencils from my drawer. I had already finished my finals for *Symbolism in Literature*, *Combat*, and *Inecha 102*, and only had my final left with Professor Marco.

My spell work was clean and concise. I didn't normally get test anxiety, but something about the fact that it was all in my performance, and not solely in *having* the knowledge, was bothering me. You could know every step, how to say every word, but if you didn't have that magical connection and the right intention, it didn't matter.

The list of spells played on my mind in a loop as I made it outside, and the sun warmed my cheeks. Wren was waiting for me on the path, his shades on and a toothpick in his mouth. Someone dodged his body, and I didn't miss the little smirk that graced his lips.

"Ah, my big scary boyfriend," I said, catching his attention.

"I'm harmless, truly," he responded as he handed me an iced chai latte.

I took the cup, our fingers brushing. "Is that why you have blood under your nails?"

"That's...I was cutting...strawberries?"

"Yeah, disgusting." I threw my hand sanitizer at him. "Clean that up, you psycho."

"Oh, love, you wouldn't be so interested in me if I weren't a little crazy," he retorted with his canines on display.

I held my hand up. "Aht, you're not going to throw me off my game. I have spells to practice."

Wren grasped me by the wrist and brought my hand to his lips. He pressed a kiss to my knuckles, his eyes glowing with mischief. *My* eyes narrowed at him in annoyance, but I couldn't keep the facade up. He knew that. We walked down the path together, the campus bustling with energy.

People gawked at us less now. There was a short period when we'd been out in public, not hiding, when people would stare or take pictures. Invited Atlas and Zane to the campus to walk behind us once, and that cleared up pretty quickly. That, plus we were just normal students going about their days most of the time. No attention-grabbing headlines to be found after the initial shock. Could only snap a picture of us with books walking to class so many times before people got bored. Especially when there was Alanna eating that shit up left and right.

If my parents really wanted to, they could fabricate some sort of lies or false headlines, but they had enough on their plates at the moment. World domination and all. My mother had seen the picture I took in front of the Jundi senate and gave me some kudos. Had a couple more photos planned participating in the community service program for when the effects of that accolade ran out. She might have known she was being handled, who knew? I did know that I'd take advantage of the fact she wasn't hounding me for anything.

I ran through the list of spells again, making sure not to forget any important parts.

"Let me know when you're done reciting in your head," Wren said into my ear.

There were two spells left, and I finished practicing them and turned to him with a smile. "All done."

"I have a surprise for you. I don't think you've told me if you like surprises," he said.

I tapped my finger on my chin. "Hmm, not normally. I think I'd enjoy a surprise from you, though."

"You sure? I can tell you now?" Wren offered.

I thought about it, tilting my head in deliberation. "No, you can surprise me. You should know how much trust I'm giving you," I teased.

"Oh, I do. I hold it gently and close to my heart," he responded with a wink. "We're here. Kick ass, love."

We'd made it to Maize Hall, and I hadn't even realized. A seed of panic bloomed, but Wren wrapped one arm around my back and pulled me close.

"You're going to do great," he whispered onto my forehead.

His magic caressed my back, soothing in a way only he could. I let everything around us melt away, the people, the pressure, all of it. Wren only let me go when my heart rate evened, and the panic was gone.

"I'll let you know when I'm done," I said, smiling up at him.

Wren took my empty cup and opened the door for me. I felt his gaze still on my back until I walked up the stairs out of his view. Letting out a deep breath, I wrote my name down on the list outside Professor Marco's door. We all had time slots to come in and test, but it looked like I was the first for this slot.

Professor Marco opened his door, checked the list, and called out my name. I shuffled over to him, trying to keep some of the confidence Wren had just given me.

"Okay, Mira. Thank you for emailing ahead with your inquiry. You now know exactly how this works. Any other questions before we start?"

I was sure I had at least one, but I couldn't think of any, so I shook my head. He placed a few items on his desk. From my email, I knew that there would be three spells to perform. The only thing was, they were chosen from a list of about ten.

"First spell is silencing. You will need to silence yourself, silence me, and then move about with a silencing spell intact," the professor said.

Perfect. Easy.

I did as he said with ease. I had been putting the moving silencing spell to use since I learned how to do it. Performing it now was as mindless as breathing. It was one of the spells I hoped he would choose for the test.

"Very good. Now, an illusion." He lifted a bowl. "Make this anything else."

He'd said that certain spells he'd avoid if they were things your nahual excelled in. For instance, a Kaban or a Chikchan wouldn't be asked to do an illusion. That was something they didn't need to cast a spell for. For me, he didn't know my nahual, so anything was up for grabs in my test.

I touched my finger to the bowl, trying to familiarize myself with the texture and material. It was easier to make an illusion when you knew what you were changing. Make a hard thing soft, make a rough thing smooth. Once you got to a certain point, touching wasn't necessary. I wasn't quite there yet. Thankfully, that wasn't something tested until junior year. I'd searched the syllabus.

The bowl vibrated as I recited the spell, the raw magic molecules around it shifting, changing, and camouflaging. I kept my intention intact, fluffy tufts replacing the hard sides of the bowl. A heart-shaped pillow emerged and settled.

"Excellent. Interesting choice, might I add," he said with a chuckle.

No idea where that came from, but, shit, I'd take it.

"Last one. A protection spell."

My mind spun. This was the hardest for me. It was the one my tía used to safeguard the *Eb* file. I'd spent countless nights breaking the protection spell to the point of pain. My chest warmed, a comfort I couldn't explain. Like my nahual, but...different. As if my tía was reaching through the spirit world and reminding me I could do this.

Professor Marco placed a stack of papers in front of me. Biting my lip, I put my palm atop the stack. The flashbacks of my hand removing the spell ran through my mind, but I tried my best to focus. *Deep breath in, deep breath out. Inhala, exhala.*

The raw magic around my hand buzzed, activated by the spell. With my intention settled, a desire to keep this stack protected and unopened.

My professor reached, tugging to flip through the stack, and it didn't budge.

"Passed with flying colors. You'll see this reflected in your online gradebook by tomorrow evening. Congratulations, Ms. Canek," he said.

I smiled. "Thank you."

I practically floated out of the room. My joy was thwarted when I walked into a crowd of people exiting the class across the hall. The nervous energy in the space was suffocating. I took the back way, down the staircase and out the courtyard instead of the front entrance.

Birds greeted me from the trees, and I tapped into my magic while no one else was around. I located them on a branch in the middle of the tree, their souls small, but noticeable. It was my intention to use little spurts of my magic every day, just to keep flexing the muscle. Locating birds, squirrels, or fae bodies around me was typically the easiest way to do that. My senses snapped across the courtyard because there was another person out here. Not uncommon, it was the middle of the day and quite busy, but this soul felt...ill-intended.

I sent Wren a quick text to let him know I had passed and was walking over to the smaller library nearby. Once I made it to the blacktop, my nahual eased a bit. With so many people surrounding us, I didn't sense danger. Until that sensation tingled once again. Someone was following me, and they wished me harm. My nahual knew it.

Sienna, Wren, Koa, and Katia all had my location, but I dropped another pin as to where I was, and that something was off. Until someone responded, I'd stay in clear sight in the library.

The head librarian smiled at me, but her eyes narrowed slightly. My energy must have been noticeably different; I needed to calm down.

"Having a good day?" I asked, hopefully covering enough.

"Just got a new shipment of books, so I'm having a wonderful day," she responded.

She went back to cheerfully sorting, and I went to one of the shared studying spaces. They were built in a way that was supposed to resemble studying together, even if none of us spoke. It was a good place to come if you were lonely.

Apparently, not many people were feeling lonely, as only two people sat at the desks. I set up between them and pulled out my laptop. A few grades had posted, a couple of blogs on the school forum, and one of them was a reminder that the spring equinox was coming up.

There would be a few school events available to attend. There were some spells that were strongest on the spring and winter equinoxes, so there would be a big group of people performing them in various places. Of course, we'd be performing our own spell of sorts. Everything we needed was stored in the cave, ready for us. I just had to hope we were ready for whatever came from the night.

Someone popped up in my periphery, a familiar head of dark hair and blue eyes. *Iris.* What the fuck was she doing here? My phone buzzed, indicating that Wren had finished his final and would be coming straight to me.

I tried to ignore her presence, but she kept waving at me non-stop. She was going to draw attention, so I looked directly at her. There were two other times I'd seen her appear this frazzled, once with my tía, and another time after she died. Her hair wasn't brushed, dark circles bracketed her eyes, and her skin was dull. She was normally someone who didn't leave the house unmanicured.

"Come here," she whispered.

I saw that she was about to get louder. In an attempt to avoid that, I left my things behind and went into the aisle of books where she stood.

"What do you want?" I asked.

"I need to show you something in this room," she said, still twitchy and sketchy.

Not falling for that.

"Yeah, I'm okay. Thanks." I made to turn, and she moved in front of me.

"I need you," she said.

"Wren is on his way. We can wait until he gets here," I responded.

He must have ran, because he popped up behind me just a few seconds later. The moment he saw Iris, his hand went to his side.

"Care to fucking explain?" he snapped at Iris.

"I fucked up," Iris admitted, turning to the study room behind her. "I need Mira."

Wren went ahead of me, and we followed Iris into the room. She'd been trailing me for some time, so she had to be lugging around whatever it was with her.

A man sat at the table, staring ahead as if we weren't even in the room. Something was missing, and I tapped into my magic to see what it was. I gasped as his soul grated against my senses. It was all types of wrong, incorrect in a way I'd never seen before. The colors didn't blend together, didn't form the usual shape. The lines were harsh, colors missing in some spots, like they'd plucked parts right out of him.

I moved into a defensive position. "What did you do to him?"

"I tried to avoid using your blood, so we did something a little more..." She bit her lip, searching for the word. "Manual."

She'd spoken with such clear confidence before, but whatever she'd done to this man wasn't her intention. It scared her, and that meant she was either worried about how this would be leveraged by Aantaj, or that what she'd done was irreversible. I snapped my fingers in front of him, and he didn't respond.

"I can't help you. What you've done can't be fixed," I responded. "Last time we spoke, you made it clear you owed me nothing. That goes both ways."

It was clear. Deep within I knew that this was the case.

"I need a vial of blood. I think it could reverse this with the proper medication," Iris pleaded with me.

She had lost her fucking mind. I shook my head, and Iris put her hand on my arm as I tried to walk away. Wren snarled, but I did what I'd done before. I held her soul. Iris' eyes went wide, shock filtering through her as she felt the tug. I didn't let her off right away, let her panic.

"It can't be undone," I said. "Those gaps are permanent. Now, let go of me before I kill you."

Iris shut her eyes tight, whispering a single word, "Retrieve."

The man shot up, his veins pushing against his skin. He jumped for me, but in a flash, Wren shifted into his jaguar and had the man by his throat. He went limp in Wren's mouth, and I watched as his soul sputtered. Not the normal ascent to the spirit world I'd seen before. A fizzling into the ground, just...gone.

"*That's* what I did, Mira. If I give this over, Aantaj will have an army. I *need* your blood," Iris said, barely above a whisper.

My foot bounced as my fists balled tight. It wasn't my job to fix what she'd broken. When I brought these concerns to her before the beach trip, she brushed me off. Telling me that she'd be the one to cure a terrible disease. Didn't care who it hurt. This wasn't on me. As much as I hated what she'd done.

"Tell him you failed and your evidence is dead now. You made your bed, now you fucking lie in it," I responded.

I couldn't give my blood. Not when it would be used to create something like that. All I heard was my footsteps as I rushed out of the library with Wren on my heels, my things I'd left behind in his arms.

"Should I have given it to her?" I asked him before setting up a silencing spell.

"I don't know," he answered truthfully.

"My blood is needed to stop what she's done, and in order to make something to strip people of their souls. It doesn't feel right. Not to mention, she's acting on a theory. She wouldn't know unless I gave it to her."

Neither would I.

"You're right. None of it is on you," he said.

I sighed, looking up at the sky. "But if she makes more of them, we're fucked."

"We're going to have to hope she doesn't..." Wren trailed off. "We deal with what we have the power to. One step at a time. We're going to be in another fucking dimension in a couple of days."

That could have made me feel better, but all I thought was, what if she made some sort of move while we were gone?

"I just want to go back to the beach house. I want to live in those few hours of peace," I said, resting my head on his chest.

"Me too, love. Me too."

52

KOA

"I'll be anywhere but there," Alanna said, dismissing herself and tucking into a corner of The Underworld. "I'll find you when the Mercers and Katia have the area secured."

The rest of us maneuvered through the crowd. It being a Friday night was almost too perfect. The crowd was massive for it not being a First Friday. Crushed cartilage and disturbing grunts sounded from the center ring. I let my hand fall to the small of Sienna's back, pushing her through the sea of fae who clearly hadn't been threatened by me enough in the past. She and Mira led the way up the stairs with locked arms.

Dimmed lighting filtered through the sconces between doors that not even soundproofing could quiet the pleasure coming from within. It was part of the charm. I felt eyes on us and peered over the girls' heads. A tall woman with long, dark hair sauntered down the hallway—Cleo, one of my first hires when I opened the place a few years back. Her green eyes held steady on my sister. I cleared my throat. A lot of people looked at my sister like that, Ikari the most—and I hated it every fucking time I was forced to witness.

She noticed Ikari glaring and smiled softly, holding her hand over the imprinted keypad at the side of the staff door, offering both of us a polite nod.

The crowd thickened as we neared the end of the hallway. Meems and Sienna tried weaving through the drunken mob, but it was pointless. I slipped ahead of them, Wren at my back, and carved a path toward the main room bar. I forgot the beauty of The Vortex at times. I didn't spend much time up here. Why would

I, with all the real fun happening downstairs? Red beams of light shot upward, tethering the ceiling to the circular bar. Bartenders spun bottles, snapped canisters shut, and shouted orders over the din from every section.

They were efficient, I had to hand it to them. Nola's girlfriend caught my eye and strolled over.

"Boys," she said, dropping napkins onto the counter, though her smile clung to the girls. "Y'all look hot."

"Thanks," Sienna flipped her straightened hair over her shoulder.

Mira reached across the bar, her hand brushing Ophelia's wrist. "So do you."

"Shots!" Sienna twirled her finger in the air. "Fun and fruity. Double for the men—they're in a shit mood." The whisper was loud enough for half of the room.

Ophelia laughed, wiping her hands before she disappeared into the bottles. I let my eyes drift, surveying the room that was mine in every way. Cream and gold walls, ornate molding, red light slicing upward toward the ceiling. The bass throbbed through every corner, making the shelves of glass hum. Dancers twisted in cages across the floor, their shadows stretching long against the walls. Wren doubled over at whatever Mira said, his laugh ringing above the music.

Four shot glasses slid across the counter, and Ophelia moved on down the line of waiting patrons. We grabbed them, pulsed them through the air in four smooth movements, then tapped them on the counter, tossing them back after the drinking ritual was complete. I fought off the sour squeeze of Ophelia's concoction, which was followed by the euphoric buzz of the tequila she'd used. Another bartender brought over our routine drinks, Mira and her friends spending enough time here on the weekends to be known. You'd think they ran the place with the presence they'd built around The Vortex.

We drifted toward the section reserved for me, the Mercers—lately permanent fixtures—the Ikaris, and also, as of late, the girls. Black velvet seats waited for us like thrones. Nola had already stacked the table: cigars, a feyfog lined-tray, twin ashtrays sitting heavy at either end.

Wren and I sank back, watching our women climb onto the tables to dance. Rap bled into house, one of Sienna's favorite DJs. He wasn't much. But with her hips swaying to his beat, I'd call the bastard a genius.

Eyes found us, not enough yet. That would change. Patience always paid.

I downed my drink and reached for her hand. I couldn't hold out anymore. She tossed her head back, laughing as she wrapped her hands around my neck. My palms slid down the line of her body, settling on her hips, and I lifted her from the table, setting her down in front of me.

At first, we kept it clean. Amiable in the public eye. We danced facing each other, my gaze dragging over every sharp angle and soft line the lights caught. She slid her hands up my chest, fingertips teasing over the fabric of my shirt, then spun around and pressed back against me. Sienna's hips rolled, slow, swaying in time with the bass, and I matched her rhythm without thought.

The crowd blurred into heat and shadow. The music wrapped around us, all pounding drums and syrupy synths, every beat vibrating through her body into mine. She tipped her head back against my chest, sweat beading around the halter of her short, black dress. One hand reached up to cup the side of my neck in a dare. I leaned down, close enough to catch the mix of her perfume and the sharp burn of tequila on her breath.

I wanted her. Not later. Now. Here. The most dangerous part was how close I was to losing control in front of everyone. Our game depended on restraint but, fuck—it was torture. The night had only just begun. I could feel the attention snapping our way now, a hum of stares sliding over us like static in the air. Exactly what we wanted.

By the time the bartender slid more glasses onto the table, the spell cracked.

"More shots?" Sienna asked, breathless, her smile sharp, lips glossy.

I aimed to change that.

Mira cheered, straddling Ikari from the side of the booth that was thankfully not in direct eyesight. The two of us had an awkward dance ourselves, figuring out a way to be true in our relationships without making the other want to fucking gag. It never worked. "Yes! Four tequilas—make them burn."

We needed to pace ourselves if we wanted clear heads later. Midnight was still hours away, which meant at least another hour before Alanna came to collect us. Why not let the night carry us? Especially when the gods had gifted me the ability to heal to sobriety.

The shots hit hard. Fast. Heat ran down my throat and settled in my chest as we tossed two more back. Shit. We could be dead a few minutes after midnight for all we knew. The music surged harder, bass grinding through the floor, lights strobing in crimson and violet. Sienna grabbed at me, pulling me against her, her mouth claiming mine in a kiss that stole the damn air out of the room. Her lips were soft, with the sting of tequila still fresh on her tongue.

I answered with both hands on her hips, dragging her closer until her body fit against mine. We'd been waiting for fucking months to be able to do this. To love each other loudly. The crowd shifted around us, voices rising. Attention was no longer drifting—it was locked. And none of them could say a damn thing until compelled.

Her nails grazed the back of my neck, dragging a shiver out of me. She kissed me again, slower this time, owning me completely. The heat from the lights blended between us, sweat dampening my shirt where her chest pressed tight to mine. The DJ threw in another drop, a filthy rap verse cut with synths, and Sienna matched it beat for beat. Her hips rolled hard against mine as she turned around, hands running up and down her sides.

I could've drowned in her. In the heat, the rhythm, the pull of her mouth—until the icy splash down my back shattered everything.

Liquid dripped down my shirt, trailing cold down to the floor. I spun. Alanna stood there, her glass tipped, eyes locked on me. The surrounding chatter spiked instantly.

I blinked at her once, slowly. My voice dropped until only she could hear. "Did you really need to toss a drink?"

"Oh, I'm going all in on this bit," she muttered quickly before pitching her voice loud enough to cut through the music. "Dramatic? Ha, I'm the dramatic one?"

"It's not what it looks like?" I said, feigning a guilty edge. A script would've helped, but improv was apparently the move.

"Not what it looks like?" Alanna's tone sharpened as she planted her hands on her hips. "I can't believe you."

"I can," Sienna murmured under her breath, her smirk a dagger.

I shot her a glance. *'Not helping, Venom.'*

'Wasn't trying to, snake.'

"Are you seriously *mind-speaking* with her right now?" Alanna flung her hands up, exasperation echoing through the room.

"Hey," Mira cut in, her body draped across Wren's arm, voice slurred in the way that only sounded drunk. "Can you please stop overreacting? You're ruining the fun. All I wanted was one night out with my brother and my best friend for my birthday. Is that so much to ask?"

That was a lie. Her birthday wasn't for another two weeks. But I doubted the paparazzi I spotted tucked near the wide open doors at the entrance would fact-check that small detail before hammering away at their keyboards tonight. Little Rowan Rainwater had delivered. Well, would you fucking look at that. I gave Alanna a subtle nod.

"Yeah, *babe*." I slid into my drunk-asshole act, letting the words slur. "What's wrong with that?"

Her arms crossed tighter before she spun toward the door. "Urgh. Don't even think about talking your way out of this when you sober up."

The crowd parted, giving her a path out. Even the DJ cut the volume down, feeding the spectacle.

"There goes that," Sienna sighed, tossing her hands in the air as her hair fell back over her shoulder. "They bought it." Her voice dropped. "Go. Follow the plan."

"Sorry, Si," Mira said, grimacing. "See you at midnight?"

I gave a single nod, then cut through the gap in the crowd, chasing Alanna into the storm outside.

The street exploded in flashes. Alanna stumbled forward, face hidden behind her hands, sobs racking her shoulders for the cameras. Shouts of my name came from every direction, shutters firing so fast the noise blurred into a frenzy.

Alanna knew how to put on a show. I had to hand her that. The girl worked a crowd in a way that made me think even my mother might come to fear.

Sienna shoved me in the chest as she passed, her expression sharpening into fury. "At least play your part well."

Anger was easy to summon. My face tightened into a picture of betrayal, and the crowd roared with satisfaction, feeding on the spectacle. I lunged after Alanna while Sienna stormed off in the opposite direction, the perfect split.

The black SUV waited at the curb. Alanna climbed in as her security held the photographers back, giving them one last shot of me diving in after her. Perfect fuel for every gossip column by morning.

Inside, the door slammed shut, sealing us off from the noise.

"We're going to pay for this," Alanna said as she drove us into the dark and toward a side street with no cameras to pick up Sienna.

Our owners, is what she meant. Her grandfather. My parents. The chains we'd never chosen. The one that demanded we fulfilled obligations that benefited few besides ourselves.

"Neither of us wants this anyway," I said, jaw tight. "Maybe it's time we fight back."

The back door slammed. Sienna slid into the seat, her arms crossed, fury radiating off her.

"Venom?" I asked carefully.

"Oh, don't *Venom* me." Sienna's voice snapped like a whip, her stare cutting across the back seat.

Alanna let out a low laugh, shoulders shaking as she steered one-handed. The sound only sharpened Sienna's glare in the mirror, a look that promised she'd carve her alive if given the chance.

"Don't be so sensitive. We all have a role to play." Alanna's grin stretched wider, the wheel tightening under her grip.

"Whatever. Shut up and drive the car like a good little wife."

The corner of my mouth twitched, pressure building in my chest. I pressed my tongue hard against my teeth to choke back the laugh threatening to escape. Alanna's knuckles whitened on the wheel.

Alanna nosed the SUV into the garage near the dorms, headlights slicing across gray concrete before she killed them and rolled into the far corner. Her hand lingered on the gearshift.

"Well, my job here is done," she said, eyes still forward. "I'll run one loop around campus, flush out any tails, then swing back for the Mercers and Katia when they're ready."

Sienna didn't answer. She shoved the door open, heels striking sharp against the cement as she cut toward the stairwell that funneled back to campus.

"Hey," Alanna called, stopping me at my departure. "Make it back."

I nodded, closing the door. The sound of the SUV faded behind us until the garage swallowed it whole. Sienna walked in front of me until we reached the mouth of the caves. The opening was wide and jagged, stone silk under the dim orange glow of magically lit sconces, the *Xtabay* placed leading up to their hideaway. Her shoulders were sharp with tension. I caught her wrist and pulled her back.

"Sienna." I waited for her eyes to lift to mine. "Don't let her get to you. We get what we need, and maybe this ends sooner than either of us thought."

Her lips parted, breath catching with a humorless laugh. "How optimistic of you." She shoved lightly at my chest, putting distance between us that felt like a pitz field away. She paused, stopping herself from walking away, rising to her toes. Sienna brushed her mouth against my cheek—quick, warm, and gone before I had a chance to relish in it "I'm sorry. You're right. Let's go."

The words lingered longer than the kiss. She stepped away, her hair swinging as she led the way down the path deeper into the caves.

53

MIRA

Wᵉ'd had enough time in the public eye for plausible deniability, and Wren brought us down the hallway that connected The Vortex to The Underworld.

"Okay, love. We have two options for where the rest of the night goes. Remember, this is your decision, and I'm only here for what you want to do," Wren said.

I nodded, confused, but curious.

"You told me your regret. If you'd like, we can go down that hall and rectify it—the way you said you prefer, or by yourself. The last couple of times we were here, I saw you looking at Cleo. She's waiting in the gold room." He pointed in the other direction. "Or we go this way, we have a couple more drinks, and I give you a few thousand singles to distribute among the ladies in there."

My eyes widened slightly. It shouldn't have come as a surprise that Wren remembered, or that he was making me this offer. He'd shown me time and time again that he said what he meant. There was never a time he'd done otherwise since I found out about the blood bond. There was also something…grim about it. Or maybe clarifying. That this truly could be our last night, and that if I said I had a regret, it should be rectified now.

It wasn't a trick question.

"That way," I said, pointing toward the direction where Cleo waited. "With you."

"Again, only if you're sure you want me to be part of this."

"I do," I responded, wrapping my fingers around his and leading us in that direction.

Every step I took echoed, and I'd barely finished two mixed drinks, but it wasn't from intoxication. The music boomed even up here, enveloping the noises coming from these rooms. Each one had a biometric reader, so only the people who were supposed to enter did. Security guards were stationed throughout, all paid very well to ensure the men and women were safe.

I'd learned that the gold room was the highest tier available here. This room in particular was only rented out once a day, and people paid high dollars to be in there with a Vortex fae.

We made it to the door, security at either side of the hall. I could tell Wren was about to try to give me one more out. I grabbed his thumb and put it on the reader before he could ask.

"Well, alright," Wren said as the door unlocked, and I pushed in.

As its name would suggest, much of the room had golden embellishments, but not in a gaudy way. It was clean and sleek with low light, just bright enough to garner a glimmer against the gold. A gigantic bed was flush against the wall, an ornate headboard framing it. A couple of mirrors, a table with two chairs, and a mini bar sat to the right.

Some of my bravado slipped when my eyes landed on Cleo. Wren was right, she was the one I stared at the most. It wasn't just her *Xtabay* call that pulled me in; it was...everything about her. She had a confidence I admired. Every room she walked into leaned a little closer to her. She was kind, one who tended to check on me if Wren or Koa had to handle something and leave me at the bar for a few. I'd thought they asked her to do so, but I realized now, as she looked at me, maybe that wasn't the case.

Cleo had the most beautiful green eyes, and the smoky eyeshadow she wore accentuated them like jewels on display. Long, dark, wavy hair fell down her back and over her breasts. The robe she wore was sheer, and the embellishments on the lace appliqués shimmered in the light. A silky belt pulled her waist tight, the fabric cascading down the curves of her hips.

"Hi, Mira," she said, her pretty pink lips pulling into a smile.

I somehow managed a weak, "Hi."

Wren chuckled behind me, rolling up his sleeves and taking a seat in one of the chairs. "This is your show, love. Why don't you get to know Cleo a bit first?"

She stepped forward and reached out a manicured hand. I took it, her golden brown skin so soft and supple.

"You want a drink?" she asked.

I cleared my throat. "Yes, please. I'll take—"

"Wren already brought up your favorite," she said, lifting a pitcher and pouring a drink.

"Thank you," I said as I grabbed the glass and took a couple of big gulps.

Cleo watched me down it, a small smile pulling at her lips as if finding me interesting. "You nervous?" she asked.

"A little, but I'm just anxious in general," I admitted with a laugh, loosening up a bit.

Probably didn't need to admit that here. Too late.

"Wren was right, this is your show. We only do what you want to do. At any point you may be uncomfortable, you just say the word. But if I'm being honest..." She twirled one of my curls around her finger. "This isn't the first time I've thought about doing this with you."

I couldn't help leaning closer. "Really?"

"You're a beautiful woman, Mira. I've watched you when you weren't watching me." She smirked, looking over at Wren. "Sorry, boss."

"Make no apologies. I know the prize I have," he said as he sat back and crossed his ankle over his knee.

"Well, thank you," I blushed, thankful for the low light.

Cleo pressed forward, her scent wafting toward me as her hair shifted. She helped me out of my jacket, tossing it over the chair. I felt as she returned to my back, her hands sliding my curls to one shoulder. The anticipation of her next touch drove me crazy. Her hands loomed over my body, barely making a brush of contact.

I sucked in a breath as she finally ran a finger down the side of my neck and across my shoulder. The touch was still light, but it set my skin ablaze. Her lips followed the same path back to my neck, and I just about melted when her tongue ran up to my ear.

My back arched as she pulled away, her heels clicking against the stone floor. Condensation from my cup startled me, the liquid running down my fingers and dripping to the floor. I chugged the last of it and set it on the table beside Wren.

He watched me, not an ounce of jealousy in his gaze. I placed my palm on his cheek, guiding him toward my lips. There might not have been jealousy, but I certainly felt restraint. His dick was already hard and pushing against his pants.

Wren pulled back, his eyes glowing and hair falling over his forehead. "She's waiting."

I gave him one more kiss and made my way back to Cleo, unsure of what I should do next. As if reading my mind, she leaned up onto her knees atop the bed and held her hands out. Her heels were on the floor, so I slipped out of my shoes and joined her.

"How do you feel about magic in this setting?" she asked.

"I like it," I responded.

She smiled, and her *Xtabay* song unfolded around us. It was quiet and subdued at first, a low hum vibrating beneath my skin. I heard the moment it hit Wren, his breath catching as he sat forward. Anyone could be entranced by a siren's song, but *Xtabays* only fed off men. I was sure that many booked time with her for that reason alone.

The hum intensified, deep notes ringing out as the tempo picked up. My heart seemed to match the rhythm, a crescendo on the rise. A drug made for pleasure alone, forcing my entire body to tingle. I knew my pupils would be wide. It was as if a filter had been lowered over my gaze. Everything was a bit hazy and slow. I pressed my finger to my bottom lip, and even that touch set me ablaze.

Cleo appeared satisfied, and her song hit a plateau, still there, but not blaring against my senses as I adjusted. She moved slowly, both of her hands sliding around my body to unzip my top. I was sure the zipper was a mile long as my face rested in the crook of her neck for what felt like forever.

My top fell off, just the thin lace bra I wore beneath it between us now. She pulled back, her eyes low and heavy as her hands fell to the contour of my waist. They slid down to my hips, dipping into my skirt to slide it off.

I realized there was a hint to this evening when Wren had this matching underwear set and outfit ready for me. The dark purple lace, complimented by skin, and I'd told him it was a color I felt confident in.

Cleo stopped there, laying me on my back with a push of her finger. Her legs straddled my hips, and she lifted my hand to the belt holding together her robe. I pulled before I could overanalyze, the weight of the fabric sliding right off her body.

Her skin was riddled with tattoos, but my eyes fell to the moon phases she had across her sternum. Cleo's lingerie had more thin straps than lace, hugging every curve and dip in her body. Beautiful. I could have been convinced she was a goddess in this moment.

She leaned down, and her hair fell like a curtain around our heads. In the already dim light, it forced us into the dark, only a glint or two filtering between the strands. Then, finally, our lips met. At the moment of contact, her siren song bloomed louder, an explosion in my mind and from where we were joined. It rattled my senses, the only thing running through my head being *more*. More lips, more skin, more anything. My hands lifted to grip her thighs on instinct, and I felt her smile in response.

Cleo moved to kiss my neck, her body sliding lower until her face was between my breasts. She teased my nipples through my bra, her teeth squeezing enough to pebble them. My back arched and my head tossed back when she slid the fabric to the side and wrapped her lips around one. The pressure of her thighs around me and the euphoria spreading from my breasts could have made me come immediately.

Wren was still, even more than his usual predatorial stillness. My mouth fell open, a sound escaping that broke his position and pulled him just a bit closer. Good. I wanted him to see it all, replay it in his mind. Remind me of it the next time he was inside me. Cleo hummed as she continued her descent. Her long fingers pushed, spreading my legs wider as she ran kisses from my knees to my inner thighs.

One finger hooked my panties, the cold air harsh against the wetness she found. She teased, running her knuckle up and down my lips. I squirmed with need, apparently, that was what she was looking for. Cleo glanced up at me, and I knew she saw it in my eyes. I would have begged. If it went a second longer, I would have pleaded for her to touch me. She kept those green eyes locked on me as she stuck out a pierced tongue.

Even knowing she could have stretched this out longer, could have brought me to the point of whimpering, she didn't make me wait. The warmth of her tongue enveloped me, just a hint of a cool bite from her piercing. She ran up to my clit, swirling around before her finger rubbed over the bud. My pussy throbbed as she devoured, my nipples so tight they damn near hurt.

Suddenly, I felt Wren's presence beside us. "She likes it when you put your finger." He guided her to my entrance, finding the spot I did indeed like. "Here."

Whether it was the caress of the spot, her mouth, or Wren being the one to show her what I liked, I wasn't sure. But I came, starbursts sparkling everywhere around me. Cleo consumed every shake of my body, every drop that rushed from me like it was her favorite meal. My eyes rolled back, finding Wren with his bottom lip tight between his teeth.

Who knew where exactly the assuredness came from, but when Cleo climbed on top of me, I flipped her onto her back. Her hair cascaded around her shoulders as I mimicked the way she straddled me before. My core was slick against hers, the pressure almost too much to bear.

I leaned forward, but Cleo's hand around the back of my neck propelled me even faster than I intended. She crashed her lips into mine, and I loved that I could taste myself on her tongue—how we tasted together.

My hips moved, grinding, but when our nipples brushed against each other, I knew where I wanted to be next. The rosy brown buds were tight as I unfastened the snap at the front of her bra. I sat back to fully appreciate what I was looking at, caressing each breast in my hand with care. There was no doubt I could have stayed here, playing with them and testing their weight. Instead, I brought my lips to the one on the left, sucking and squeezing until I felt her body squirm.

Huh, maybe I do know what I'm doing.

I kissed over the tattoo on her sternum, and across her stomach to her hips. Cleo moved, propping herself on her elbows to watch me. As I pressed my lips to her pussy through her underwear, I flicked my gaze up to hers. Her eyes were full of so much pleasure and desire that it made me pause. The lust in the air was thick enough to swim in.

I didn't break eye contact as I slid my hands under her ass and pulled her panties down her legs. Wren made a noise, a groan that he was trying to keep contained, but didn't have the power to. It didn't add to the pressure; it only made me want to please both of them.

Cleo's pussy gleamed, wetness already dripping down her thighs and onto the sheets. Before I could overthink it, I dove right in. I knew what I liked, and I could test that until I felt a positive response from her.

The moment my tongue made contact, Cleo pushed her hips closer to my face, asking for more. I couldn't tell if it was on purpose, or if she lost control, but her siren song boomed, blasted through the air. It pushed through me from my head to my toes, and every time it got louder I took it as encouragement. Fuck, the taste of her was...incredible. Nothing that I'd experienced or expected, but I wanted more and more. I worked my tongue up and down. Each writhe and moan made me want to earn another.

I teased her entrance with my finger, feeling her pulse around me when I plunged inside. My thumb pressed against her clit, and I could sense her release. She contracted around me as I wrapped my lips around the bud of nerves and sucked. The sensation of it—of her body releasing had one building in me, and I wasn't even being touched. *Fuck, I could do this all day.*

Wren was at the edge of his seat, like he could feel what I was about to ask. I reached my hand toward him, and in the blink of an eye, he was out of his clothes and at the bed.

He pulled me up to my knees, kissing and running his hands from my neck to my ass. Then, I felt Cleo join at my back. Her lips trailed up my spine and over my shoulder blade. I leaned back to kiss her when Wren dipped to my breasts. Touch and pleasure blanketed me, found everywhere their bodies clung to mine. They were passionate in their desire, as if my delectation would win them some prize.

Cleo's siren song blared again, impossible to do anything except melt into. It was almost a dance, the way we moved. Wren's hand replaced Cleo's when it shifted, her lips found the places he just retreated from. I tried to return the favor, a kiss for Wren or a pinch of Cleo's nipple, but I didn't know up from down in this sea of pleasure.

Wren leaned onto his back, Cleo moving my body to straddle him in reverse cowgirl with her right in front of me. Before I knew it, Wren was inside me, and Cleo's lips were right where we were joined. I didn't even have a moment to feel too exposed or embarrassed, because Wren thrust into me like he'd been thinking about it for days.

Cleo ran her tongue over my clit at every push, venturing up to suck my nipples every few moments. My body was on fire, and the flames were only growing. I undulated my hips to the pace Wren set, his hands squeezing my ass so tight I was sure to bruise. The scream that tore for me was sure to test the barriers of the silencing spell, and I couldn't have stopped it if I tried.

I retreated, slipping Wren out of me. He looked dazed and confused, but I leaned over to his lips.

"Cleo deserves another, don't you think?"

Wren's gaze turned wicked. "She did take such good care of you."

Both of us turned to her, conveying that the next part was, in fact, her show.

Her dark, swollen lips pulled into a smile as she sat up. "Hm, you." She grabbed Wren's hand and stood him up at the end of the bed. "Here."

Cleo got on to all fours, her face inches from Wren's dick. "And you." Her sultry stare landed on me. "Back here."

Oh, this is advanced. I was always up for a challenge.

She arched her back, opening up and giving me full access to her pussy. Cleo stuck her tongue out, mouth wide and ready. Wren gave me one more look, as if this would be the thing that crossed the line.

"Put it in her mouth, baby," I said before I put *her* in *my* mouth.

I heard Cleo gag, felt the contraction in her pussy where my fingers pushed and pulled already. Wren fucked her face, and I anticipated each jolt of her body, flicking and running my tongue up to her clit. We were all already so close, and it wasn't long before I felt Cleo tightening. Wren's grunts had my pussy throbbing, knowing Cleo was tasting me on him.

Her orgasm was full body, Wren's coming at the same time. I kept my mouth on her for every aftershock, until I was sure she was repaid for all she'd done for me. We fell into a pile, all three of us linked and in contact in some way. Our chests heaved, her siren song faded, but the ecstasy that rushed through my veins and over my skin stayed.

I pulled myself closer to Wren, wanting to end this with my lips on his. The kiss was slow and gentle, his hands reaching into my hair.

I didn't know how I got so lucky, but fuck if I ever let him go.

54

KOA

They showed up later than I preferred. I didn't need to check my watch for the third time to know it. Ikari knew how I felt about tardiness on the job. It made me...trigger-happy.

"You're late," I said once Mira and Wren slipped through the mossy entrance.

Mira barely caught the bag Sienna lobbed at her, still distracted by whatever happened back at the club. "We're here before midnight. That's not late."

Sienna pointed a finger at her, a smile tugging one corner of her mouth as she caught onto the same vibe I was getting from both of them. "Oh, we're going to talk about this when we get back, babe."

I turned away as they stripped out of their clothes, keeping my eyes on Sienna instead. She'd already changed—black cargos, black tee, hiking boots laced tight. Smart. She resembled someone who expected the ground to shift under her and wanted to be ready when it did. It was hot as fuck. I'd gone with the same—dark clothes, sturdy gear, pack over my shoulder heavy with everything we might need. Wherever we were going, comfort would not be part of the plan.

Still, part of me wondered if we'd stand out. If they even wore cargos on the other side. Or would we walk through that portal looking like idiots in a land full of people with capes and shit?

"How long do you think we'll be gone?" Mira asked, tossing her dress and heels from the club into the corner.

Sienna shrugged, tightening the straps of her pack. "Kan didn't say. Feels like an 'until we figure it out' kind of deal."

"Fantastic," I muttered

"Lovely," Wren chimed in at the same time.

Mira tapped my shoulder, and I turned back around. She matched us in black everything, hair pulled back sharp, eyes as steady as a Tecun-Canek. Our parents may have been shit, but that didn't mean there was no pride in our family name. We could be the ones to change it all.

It was at that moment I realized that was the first time I'd felt proud—eager even—in the understanding that one day, that seat could be mine. And I could make a difference. *We* could. We only needed to get through this test to do so. That was an obtainable goal. One that no longer seemed daunting.

"Portal's tied to the equinox," Mira said. "That kind of alignment means time distortion is almost certain. Days can pass by there, but here? Barely a day. Don't stress."

Sienna chewed her lip. "Did your textbook tell you that?"

"Let's hope you're not wrong, love," Wren said, tone lighter than I trusted. "Are we ready?"

She nodded once.

Sienna shifted her pack, the weight of artifacts and the spell papers pressing against her back. "We've got everything. Katia says the quad's been empty for twenty minutes. No eyes or movement."

Despite the attention we caused at the club, this portion of the night was best left unseen from the public eye.

"Then we move."

Mira reached for Sienna's hands before we stepped out. "We got this."

The cave spat us into cold night air. The campus lay quiet between the lake and the tree line, black water reflecting the stars like shards of glass. The velvet sky was so sharp it could cut through bone. Our boots whispered over gravel, past shadow-soaked buildings, until the arch came into view. Stone teeth against the dark. Waiting.

Figures slid from the shadows. Katia first, shoulders squared, eyes catching faint moonlight, molten glass in her stare. The Mercer twins flanked her, moving in perfect sync, a quiet current of readiness.

"Thought you'd never show," Katia teased, her long hair tucked into a bun at the base of her neck.

Sienna snorted in response. "Wouldn't miss opening a portal for the world."

Jed clapped my arm with a stupid ass grin on his face. "Koa, black really suits you. Gives you that whole brooding antihero thing."

I let it slide, gaze sweeping the edges of the quad. Darkness could hide anything. Tonight, everything had a reason to move.

"Don't feed his ego," Adler said, scanning the tree line as if it had teeth. "We'll cover the perimeter while you work."

Jed's grin stretched too wide. "For a mission this high stakes, things are going smoother than even I predicted."

Adler groaned. "Don't say that. You'll curse the whole thing."

Sienna's lips twitched. "It's like saying 'at least it's not raining' on a hike."

Jed raised his hands in mock solemnity. "My apologies. If we're doomed, it's on me. I take it back, oh great universe."

Sienna flipped him off.

Jed caught it like a trophy, spun it in his fingers, and tossed it back. "See? Reversible curse. Balanced universe."

Katia cackled, slicing through the night's quiet. My pulse picked up, the incessant teasing of our group suddenly feeling fragile against the dark.

"Focus," Adler snapped, his eyes narrowing.

The twins' heads snapped in unison behind the Chen Library. Wren's nostrils flared in the same direction. My stomach dropped. They sensed something.

"What is it?" Sienna whispered as she squinted in an attempt to see what had them alarmed.

Katia's dragon eyes glimmered, pupils narrowing as she briefly shifted parts of her face. A face of nightmares. "Company."

Shadows stretched, split. Two tall figures stepped into the open, a wall of soldiers folding behind them—at least twenty, maybe more. I'd take that as a compliment.

My pulse thundered at the sight of the silhouette on the left. I knew it all too well. Jed and Adler glanced my way in the same brush of air that Katia directed her stare to my sister.

Mira's chest heaved, her fists clenching, unclenching. She knew before the rest of us. I saw the confirmation break across her face.

"Say the word, Mira." Wren's hands curled, night flame flickering to life. His voice snapped with lethal promise. "I'll kill them."

Dr. Aantaj. And our father.

"I'm afraid this is where your...extracurriculars end, my children," Emeric said, voice slick with control, dripping contempt.

A tear slipping down Mira's cheek caught in the moonlight before it fell. Sienna moved instinctively, stepping in front of her, posture rigid, her arm subtly outstretched like a shield.

We'd tried to deny it. Give them the benefit of the doubt. The Cynod putting a hit on us was old news. We'd just held out the moronic fucking hope that our parents hadn't played a role. Our mother's tears were a lie. Her concern over the last few months, a lie. The sorry attempts to reach out and connect with us lately, perhaps the greatest lie of them all. My father's silence had been the only truth. He didn't give a single fuck about us.

"Dad?" Mira whispered.

His gaze cut through her, colder than steel, emptier than the loyal soldiers at his back. No recognition. No warmth. A stranger to us now as much as he was during our childhood. I hadn't called Emeric "dad" to his face in years. It never felt appropriate. Not when he made his distaste for us so clear.

There had been a time when I couldn't imagine him as anything but. I found there was a great difference between a "dad" and a "father". Before our parents had become the Cynod, they were a mom and dad.

I forced open the mental bridge, driving the thought into every mind I trusted. *'Get Sienna to the arch. We need a distraction. Now.'*

We edged back. Our formation shifted, boots dragging against gravel, shoulders brushing as we angled toward retreat. I had no clue if the Mercers and Katia would make it through the portal, but they were so outnumbered, it didn't appear we had a fucking choice in finding out.

"Not another step," Emeric commanded.

Our father's voice was smooth but harsh. It always had been. He never stuttered or wavered in tone. He was as solid as they came in every aspect. As much as I hated the man, there was no denying the amount of influence he'd had over who I'd become.

I was him in every light, yet his opposite when it mattered the most.

And I was pretty sure he hated me for the same reason I found fault in him. I hated that he'd had no weaknesses other than to protect his legacy; that was his fault. Mine had always been Mira—now, it was Sienna too. It was all of them. Danger surrounded us. Which meant my weaknesses officially outweighed his in an undeniable way.

I raised my chin, the defiance burning in me hotter than fear. "Or what?"

His eyes locked with mine. Unflinching. "Don't stick around to find out."

"Mira." Beside our father stood Aantaj, his hair and skin an oddly similar shade, his mouth twisted.

"Do *not* talk to me after everything you've done! Celeste considered you family!" Mira shouted, her finger pointing at him with more disgust than I'd ever seen her display.

And pain. It made me want to kill him.

He had the nerve to allow guilt to flicker over his face—faint, brittle, gone in the span of a breath—yet perceptible. "We don't have time for sentiment. Mr. Ikari—bring Mira and Ms. Hayes to me." His fingers snapped once.

Wren didn't move. His eyes cut through Aantaj, the weight of his stare saying more than words could. Wren Ikari was marking him for death.

It may be today. Right now. Or tomorrow. Shit, three years from now. But Aantaj had ordered harm to my sister and my mate. He had to answer for that. To both of us. The price of his crimes would cost him in blood.

Aantaj tilted his head, studying him with fascination. "So. You severed the bond. Impressive. It makes no difference. None of you will surrender the artifacts. None of you will come willingly. I won't waste my breath persuading you."

"Why?" Sienna stopped moving back, holding her ground, clutching at her pack.

His lip curled. "Why? A thousand reasons. A million solit question that I have no obligation to answer." He flicked his hand toward the soldiers. "On with it."

The line of soldiers spread wide across the grass, their formation flawless. Robotic. Shadows pooled in their armor, black bleeding into black. Mira's eyes widened, but not in fear of the fight. Something deeper hollowed her expression, draining the color from her face.

'Meems?' I pushed through the bond, chest tightening. Shit was so off plan, I wasn't sure there was a way to course correct.

'Their souls.' Her words sputtered through the link, raged. *'They've been tampered with. There's nothing to grab.'*

The taste of iron filled my mouth.

'Iris,' Wren hissed, his anger pulsing down the tether.

'Oh hells no,' Jed muttered, blades swinging free of their sheaths.

We pulled together, backs aligned, weapons ready. Empty husks didn't scare me. They were targets. Easy targets. The soldiers advanced. Aantaj and Emeric stood still at the center of it all, our father unaffected by the horror Aantaj had commanded on his own children.

"Dad?" The word tore from me before I could stop it, raw and ragged, scraping my throat raw. Foolish. I felt like a broken child, stripped down to nothing. And maybe at the end of the day, that was exactly what I still was. "Look at me!"

He didn't. His eyes cut past me, empty, glassy, locked on something I couldn't reach. The man I'd known, the one who had once been capable of pride in me, was buried under decades of cruelty. And I was left clawing at a shell.

"Look at me!" I roared again.

It ripped open something inside me that I thought was solid as iron. My body jolted forward, desperate to force our eyes together, to drag him back into the world where he was a father. One who had ever loved me.

His jaw tightened. A twitch rippled down his cheek, like a storm caged under skin. His hand hovered near his weapon, fingers brushing it like a promise. "Give us what we asked for. Refuse, and we'll have no choice but to make you watch us take it *her*. That will not be a gentle process, her kind are...volatile." He looked Sienna over with dismissal, nose turned up. "I promised your mother Mira would not be harmed, but I cannot control the outcome if you choose to foolishly escalate the situation more than need be. Now hand over the artifacts, Koa Benício Canek. I am no longer asking as a father, I am *commanding* as Commander-in-Chief and sitting Cynod of the Canek line."

The words gutted me. I did not fear my own death. My father knew that—had just sharpened his threat as a weapon. I saw Sienna and Mira's futures burning out like candles, and the image alone hollowed me.

"Don't," I rasped, my chest heaving, a desperate animal cornered.

I could take a bullet. I could bleed out in the dirt. But them? My sister. My mate. My whole damn heart. The world could tear me apart in a hundred different ways, but if it touched them—if it stained them—I wouldn't just break. I'd vanish. My chest rattled uncontrollably. The shift coiled in me, threatening to erupt. I forced it down, hard, because if I shifted now, I'd miss the portal. Might miss everything. If we even got that far.

Sienna edged forward. "Tell us why."

I caught her arm, fingers digging in. She twisted her head as her voice brushed our bond that I always left open.

'Trust me. Please. I'm buying Mira some time to figure out the whole soul sucking thing.'

My grip loosened. I stepped behind her, every muscle taut, ready to tear her away if it broke bad. Mira's eyes met mine, wide with warning.

"You want the artifacts?" Sienna swung her pack forward, her voice steadier than her shaking shoulders. "I have them. Right here."

Aantaj raised his hand, halting the soldiers. His eyes gleamed with suspicion.

"Tell us why you want them, and I'll hand them over. Honest. I...I'm weak. My conscience won't allow me to rest without knowing the 'why'." She extended her hand.

He scoffed, but stepped forward, palm catching hers. Sienna's charm might be her greatest fucking strength. Power surged. Purple light seared across their skin,

Sienna's glow burning through the crack between palms, threads of truth digging into his bones.

"*Tell us why*." It was no longer a request.

Emeric lunged, fury tearing his mask. I was already there with my gun pressed to his chest. He stilled, barrel close enough to burn shadow into his ribs. One mirrored off my own chest.

I bit out a laugh, humored, truly. Because the fucking irony of it all was too sharp not to taste. "You gonna shoot your only heir, old man?" The only reason I hadn't ended up discarded years ago—time ran out to make another spare.

His weapon lowered. The fury in his eyes burned hotter than a flame. I'd seen rage in him before, but never this. This was different. There was a stranger staring back at me. This was war.

"We cannot let the Veil between worlds drop." Aantaj's voice cracked under its own strain, his jaw clenched so tightly the tendons in his neck stood out. He looked like he was wrestling with shackles no one else could see.

"A bond," Wren called out. He would know. "He's tied to someone. He can't say any more than that."

Everything fell into place. It was why our father hadn't pushed Sienna aside or interfered. He didn't need to. Aantaj couldn't reveal anything, even if he wanted to. He was physically unable—not even under extreme duress. So he let her do her thing, letting Sienna test, prod, and plead without resistance. This was entertainment to him. A book he already knew the ending to.

"No. But he can let us know when something we've said is correct and talk around it," Mira said, creeping closer.

Sienna's hands trembled. Fingers flexed. "What happens if the Veil falls?" she demanded.

Aantaj's eyes narrowed, cold and black. He leaned down slightly, tilting his head so his gaze sliced over her as if she were nothing but a bug on the floor. Pure disgust dripped from every line of his face. "Lessons will unravel. The artifacts will fall where they shouldn't. And your gods...your precious journey? It will undo us."

Moonlight hit the metal at his side. A blade. He raised it, angled toward Sienna.

"Sienna!" I shouted, lungs burning in desperation.

Her reaction was instantaneous. She yanked at Aantaj's wrist, and the ground erupted. Stone and dirt ripped upward, swallowing Aantaj and my father to their knees, dragging them off balance.

I caught her arm, lifted her off the ground, and felt her heart hammer against mine. Boots skidded across gravel, chunks of stone ripping up under our momentum. Fire roared above us—Katia. Her wings unfurled as she blasted the nearest dragon soldiers into screaming showers of sparks. A torrent of water surged from the left. It smacked the dirt wall and hissed the moment it touched flame. I pressed Sienna against me, eyes forward, moving faster than I thought possible.

"Hold on!" I barked. Her hands dug into my shoulders as I pushed, surged, skipped over debris. *Etznab* shards tore the air around us, flint and obsidian ripping past, snapping stones underfoot.

Mira's chest heaved as she stumbled with her fingers twitched and hovered. She wanted to rip the soldiers' souls out. I could see it in her eyes. Could see the determination clawing at her throat.

"Meems, now would be a *really* great time for you to suck out some souls," I teased, pressing her back and putting Sienna down next to her.

She offered me an exasperated look that reminded me that, life or death, we were certainly siblings. "Can't you see I'm fucking *trying*?"

Sienna bit her lip, mud smeared across her face, eyes wide but unafraid. She grabbed Mira's hand and squeezed. My sister wasn't going to give up when she knew a wave of her hand could kill them all—if they were still fae, that was. Whatever fucked-up shit they did to their souls might have taken that title.

My mate's attention focused on getting them behind the shield of forceful wind the Mercers had tossed up to buy some time. The twins were a blur beside us, wind slicing shards of debris from the battlefield, forcing attackers off balance. It took their attention from Katia fighting it out—and objectively losing—against one of the water *Ix's* in the sky.

Wren was already moving. Quiet. Precise. A soldier surged toward Sienna's flank, trident swinging, teeth bared. Ikari dropped low, stripped the weapon from his hands, and twisted it through the soldier's shoulder, spinning him into the mud. Mud spattered. The soldier's scream cut short, swallowed by the chaos.

"Sienna, get to the arch. No matter what happens, go," I demanded.

Her head snapped up. "Not this shit again. We don't split up. That's not a route I'm interested in exploring."

"We can't split up if no portal opens at all," I said, flicking my gaze to the sigils. "Mira, help her."

Mira nodded, eyes narrowing. Wren moved with her shadow, covering Sienna while clearing a path, blades flashing, pivoting. He sliced through a shard of obsidian that flung too close, hissing as it struck the ground.

"Look at me, you sorry motherfucker," I growled as I snapped toward my sorry excuse of a father. I shoved every ounce of all the years into those words. Every scar, every betrayal, every sleepless night. My father had the power to stop this. To intervene. Instead, he had no care. No care that Aantaj had his daughter and her best friend at the edge of death. And I—his son, the one he had sworn to raise—was on the brink from his own orders. "For once in your life, face me like a man."

Above us, Katia roared, wings cutting through the storm of fire and rain. Claws shredded at anything that moved. Sparks flew—deadly fireworks across the wet air. The smell of ozone and burnt hair stung my nostrils.

"It's for the good of Inecha, son," he said, calm, measured, like he was explaining the weather and not about to watch his own bloodline decimated.

Cornered. Trapped in a bubble of false security. Between him and the arch, with seconds bleeding toward midnight. Chaos pressing in from every angle, soldiers scraping at the edges, wind whipping shards of debris into our faces. I risked a glance behind me. The Mercer wind shield was thinning under assault, moments from collapsing.

Sienna's hands hovered over the arch, fingers trembling. The sigils pulsed faintly as they fought against the storm of magic, fire, and water raging around them. I could hear her struggle. The low mumbled curse, the uneven rhythm of her breathing, the way her shoulders tensed with every misaligned piece.

"Think about Mira," I barked at Emeric, voice tight, every syllable raw. "I know you don't give a shit about me—but what about Mira? Your daughter?"

Something in him softened, a flicker behind those empty eyes. Then he turned, stepping past the edge of the battle, shoulders squared, drifting toward Aantaj. "Do what needs to be done to protect the integrity of Herta. That Veil cannot fall."

I could feel it in my chest, the hollow, gnawing realization: he didn't care if I lived or died. Not really. Not like I had imagined.

Wren shifted closer, blades slicing through the air, a silent guardian between Sienna and the world crumbling around her. The twins carved arcs of wind. Debris skimmed off in deadly arcs. Katia's fire roared above. Every second counted.

"Since you want to be difficult, then," I muttered, drawing my pistol.

The first soldier lunged before I could even aim. I fired twice, iron screaming, cutting him in half mid-charge. The next came from the left; I slammed my shoulder into him, twisting, and the sound of his spine snapping was deliciously final. A third lunged, teeth bared, trident raised—gone before it even touched the air. The blade of my knife buried itself through shoulder, flipping him like a rag doll into the mud.

My pistol barked again, taking two more before I kicked the nearest soldier into his brothers, crushing them together. Blood streaked the gravel, slick under boots, and I moved through the carnage. The wind tore at my face, cutting through fire and smoke.

55

MIRA

I could barely see Koa anymore through the wind and debris rushing around us. Sienna was fitting together the pieces of stone like a puzzle, each one glowing and linking as she whispered something I couldn't quite understand.

The twins were still wielding a wide dome, and I could only do so much to help Sienna here. She was the one who was given the message from Kan, and with every thud that hit the ground outside of the shield, I knew I needed to help.

"Do you need me?" I asked.

"No," Sienna mumbled, attention wavering between my brother and the task at hand. "Go help them. Every gun fired, I'm imagining a bullet lodged in Koa's chest, and I can't fucking focus."

Jed was the Mercer twin closest to me, so I ran over, making sure not to disrupt his focus on protecting Sienna.

"I'm going to go out there, make me a pocket?" I asked.

Behind us, a small doorway opened in the hardened wind. I ducked out of it without a second thought. Katia just landed, and I gave her the hand signal that meant to keep eyes on Sienna.

Wren, where are you, baby?

It was fucking chaos out here. Aantaj and my father had to have completely cleared the entire area to feel confident enough to do this in the middle of campus. I tried to focus on what was happening in front of me, and not the myriad of soldiers out there holding a perimeter.

Koa and my father fought, their guns now empty and discarded to the ground. They battled like the fae were meant to, before technology and weapons—fist to fist. Katia screeched, the sound sending the hairs on the back of my neck on end. Or maybe it was the electricity that pulsed from her mouth like fire.

Wren. He fought in his shifted form, his shield there, but only a couple of blows away from vanishing. I lifted my hand again. Whatever Iris had done to these poor fae altered their souls. It made them slippery, like trying to hold on to an invisible netting. The holes in their aura didn't just stay in one place, so as soon as I thought I had a good grasp, it shifted.

A feline roar burst from Wren's throat as he dragged his claws across the face of a voided-out soldier. They fell to the ground in a pool of their own blood, one of their eyes blown from the socket.

He must have felt me coming because he turned his head, not threatened by my presence. We were on the far right side with nothing at our backs currently, and I took the time to reinforce his shield.

I recited the spell with my hands running up and down his back, watching as the raw magic melded into a hard, green, glimmering guard. Wren rubbed his cheek against my side as he pounced back into the action and toward Aantaj. The Doctor had too many people protecting him, but Wren went after each of them with ferocity. Payback.

My gun was heavy and steady in my hands. I aimed, fired, and three of the soldiers went down in a single round. I doubted that's what they really were. The chance that they were just at the wrong place, at the wrong time, and turned into these...zombies was pretty fucking high. They could have been taken from prisons or ripped from the street. There was no way of knowing. What I knew for certain, they'd remain this way until they died. I still felt it in my chest.

Every time I took one down, another popped up like a fucking flower in this growing graveyard. My magic was still not cooperating, but it worked enough for me to freeze a soldier coming for me. The woman twitched as she fought against my hold, her body frantic with nothing behind her eyes. I gripped the fragments of her soul as best I could as I yanked the knife from my side and cut through her throat.

The blood splattered across my face, warm, but not the 100 degrees it should have been. These fae were barely alive. The gods made us perfectly balanced in body and soul. Mess with one, and the other was sure to be impacted. If I had to guess, what I'd marked previously as twitching was shivering. An attempt from whatever was left in their bodies to raise their internal temperature.

One of the twins shouted, but with all the noise I couldn't decipher what they were saying in time. Debris from their wind hit me in the back, toppling me down to the ground face-first. My elbows cracked in the dirt in an instinctive move to save my head. It was a pointless effort. Whatever it was that hit me was too heavy for just my arms to save. A tree branch, I realized as I rolled over and got my bearings.

My head spun, my vision a little blurry. When I looked out into the distance I saw double, triple. Each step was more like a shuffle—a battle not to allow my knees to buckle. I spared some magic to heal, making sure that I didn't let a potential concussion set in. Not now. I needed to keep a clear mind. Within seconds it spread through my body. It eased the pain, brought my eyesight back crystal clear.

Wiping some of the dirt from my face, and blinking a few times, I launched a smaller knife at the back of a soldier. It hit between their C2 and C3 vertebrae, and their body froze like I had used my magic. Paralyzed. Everyone else was dead here. The ones that hadn't met that fate were running to save their creators.

I found a loaded gun that someone had dropped and picked it up, scanning the field to determine where Koa and Wren were. They were fighting beside each other now, just a few feet apart, between Aantaj and my father, on the complete other side of the field. My brother ducked, and Wren was right there to deliver a lethal blow. The moment Koa rose from his crouch, a blade spun through the air and buried into a soldier lunging at Wren. He intercepted another hit aimed for Wren's head, twisting the soldier aside with the fluidity of someone who had lived in battle for years. They moved in sync, matching battle cries cracking through the air. A beckoning to their next victims.

Katia blasted the area from the sky, flames sparking against the dirt and grass. Koa stumbled back to avoid being burned. A wall of fire separated him from my father and pushed him back toward Wren. Katia's wings eclipsed the moon for a second, and I watched my father searching for her among the stars. The red of her scales was dark enough to blend in at her height. The glow from the raging fire had him appearing unnaturally diabolic. The very picture of a demon in the ninth level of hell.

His shoulders rolled as his fists balled. He was preparing for a shift. I could see it in his stance. My heels kicked up dirt as I ran toward him. The distance between us was too great, too far to warn. I screamed, and that caught Wren's attention. He twisted as his gaze followed the direction I pointed. Steam billowed from my father's nostrils, scales forming at his neck.

Wren tackled and pulled him down to the ground, hard. He didn't give my father a chance to focus on releasing his dragon. Wren delivered punch after punch to his face, his stomach, his side. Manically, he poured all of his anger out. He fought for his grandfather, for his father, for his brothers. Generations of hate between his family and the Cynod manifested in blows. Even if my father wasn't the one who forced the contract, he'd upheld the system of oppression. Not only for the Ikaris, but for the Mercers and countless other families.

A soldier made to tackle Wren, but Koa emerged through the flames midair, shooting him in the head and stopping his procession. Aantaj was nearly alone now. Only a few of his soldiers remained, the ones alive all appearing to be wounded. I ducked as I heard a gun go off at my back. Katia dove from the sky and swallowed whoever it was whole.

"Wren!" I yelled, only a few feet away now.

My father was still on his back, but his hand had made its way to a handgun. Wren was too lost to rage to see anything but red. His hair fell over his brow, the chain around his neck swinging recklessly. I reached out my hand, not fast enough.

The blast reverberated in my chest as a bullet went straight through Wren's arm. I felt the pain as if it was my own, and I gasped, gripping my bicep. Wren stumbled backward, and Koa's head jerked up at the sound. He'd had enough of Dr. Aantaj's shit and knocked him out cold.

My feet slid in the dirt as I stopped. Emeric Canek was unrecognizable. So much blood pouring down his swollen face. He still found the strength to stand. Mustered the energy to lift his gun again at Wren, even if his wrist shook.

"Dad, stop," I said.

He didn't. There was no indication that he even heard me. His finger tightened against the trigger.

"Please," I begged.

I didn't want to do it. I pleaded with the gods to make him stop. They didn't listen.

A tear rolled down my cheek, hot and burning. It cut through the blood, through the dirt and the grime smeared across my skin. It was my only tether to my physical body, the only thing I felt as I slowly lifted my now onyx-dipped hands, and my nahual bloomed in my chest. I didn't wait a second longer.

My father ceased his attack. He didn't move a muscle. I lifted him away from Wren, forced him to drop the gun, and hung him in the air before me. His soul lacked the color of most. Spots of brown, splotches of white, a hint of green and red, a dot of purple, but there was so much black. As if someone spilled a pot of ink over it without bothering to clean it up.

"Mira, no. Not you," Koa didn't plead in fear but with fury. I held my other hand up.

I didn't hold his soul the way I had our father. Just a warning to leave me be. Everything inside me wanted to tear our father's limbs from his body. To make him feel a molecule of the pain that he caused me by having my tía murdered. I wanted to take something he loved—if such a thing existed. Himself. He loved himself. The only thing he preserved and cared for.

"You..." Emeric Canek tried to get out.

I let up around his throat to allow him to speak. If nothing but for my own curiosity.

"What are you?" he croaked.

My smile was hellish as everything around me faded away. "I am the balance between life and death. *I* am the barrier between you and your success. I am power incarnate."

"Death," he said, his voice shaking, and not from my hold on him.

I feasted on the fucking fear in his tone. I could stick a fork in it and savor the tart terror. My nahual was overtaking me. A beast finally let out to devour. It wrapped around me like a serpent, swaying and ready to pounce.

Whatever Koa saw on my face scared him. The onyx wasn't only fingertips this time. It reached down past my elbows, to my shoulders, and across my chest.

"Meems," Koa attempted to reason. "Put him down. This is my fight, one I should have ended years ago. This isn't yours to carry."

A light burst from the wind dome. A beacon straight to the gods. That wasn't my concern. Not right now. The hands of the dead reached for me. No, it wasn't just any dead. The souls of fae my father had sent to the afterlife. They pushed me forward, encouraged me. It was all I heard.

"This," I said as my feet lifted from the ground, my voice mine yet foreign, "is resolution."

Our father's body bent at unnatural angles, his spine moments from snapping. He wouldn't hurt anyone ever again. Every single time he laid a hand on Koa, every time he forced Wren to hurt someone innocent, every time he told me I was worthless, when he'd threatened Sienna. It marked him for this moment. He didn't see me as a threat, and that was his final, lethal mistake.

His soul was ripped from his body, and instead of letting it join me right away, I held it. Toyed with it like a ball of yarn. I inspected the essence, wondering if there was ever a time that it held bright colors. If there was a time, it was vibrant with orange for happiness and familial love. Wren joined me at my side, a warm hand at the base of my spine.

I barely saw him. Not when the deceased begged for me to send them my father's soul. They wanted retribution too. My movements were choppy; it was all overwhelming. Wren moved directly in front of me. He made me see him, forced me to look at him through my own eyes. Koa appeared behind him, and the voices of the dead fell to whispers.

I blinked as my nahual slithered away, only leaving my hands and forearms dark as the night sky. Koa's shoulders were sagging—too many emotions to be able to read him. I expected a weight to be lifted as I watched my father's lifeless body.

Was this what I wanted, truly? This power, this gift from the gods, should I have used it this way? Was I better than him? Most importantly, did I care?

Balance is what I'd said I was. What the textbooks called those of my nahual. Right now, I was teetering too far. It wasn't only me in my head. Every step I took toward my father's body battled against my heart. Half of me wanting to crumple his soul into pieces and give it to the dead. The other half wanting…something else. Ultimately, it wasn't a choice I was prepared to make.

I fell to my knees, the man who brought me so much pain unnaturally still. Not a flutter of his lashes, not a lifting of his chest.

A wet cough across the field had me looking up, finding Aantaj slowly raising to his feet and turning toward me. I locked my gaze with his as I held my father's soul, willing everyone to see what I held, not leaving any room for misinterpretation. I was Death. He would know who he made an enemy of.

With more force than probably necessary, I slammed my father's soul back into his body. He didn't wake immediately, but I felt his soul filling the empty vessel that was this corpse. I stood, pointing one finger at Dr. Aantaj. He was next, and I wouldn't be so kind. The hope that my father would take this second chance as just that filled me, but I wouldn't be holding my breath.

Wren dipped down to rest his forehead on mine. It was the last thing I needed to let Death go.

"I need you all, *now*!" Sienna shouted through the wind barrier.

We refused to give Aantaj our backs—Wren, Koa, and I moved toward Sienna. My father finally took a deep breath, not strong enough to stand yet. Katia's mighty body hit the ground, grabbing him by the shirt and dragging him over to Aantaj. Her mouth opened with the threat of death as she let him go, and neither of them moved.

She took off to the sky, circling around the beam of light still shooting into the clouds.

"She's staying up there as our eyes," Koa said, relaying a message she must have mentally relayed to him.

Jed created another doorway, letting us in. The arch was glowing, a web of power connecting piece by piece like a mosaic. Sienna kept her hands raised toward the formation, her eyes closed as she kept repeating the same line over and over.

The air changed in the dome, and not from the Mercers' magic. It was heavy, ancient, a taste in my mouth I couldn't place. From the column of light, a shadow unfurled. Wren and Koa reached for weapons that were long lost to the battle, but I held up my hand. This soul I felt was above anything I'd yet experienced.

Sienna finally took a deep breath and opened her eyes. The shadow slinked across the arch, wrapping around it like a serpent. It hit the ground, no corporeal form, but enough to shift the grass around our feet, growing and growing until it matched Koa's basilisk in size.

Cool scales brushed against my side, and Wren and Koa both recoiled.

"Hello, Kan," Sienna beamed.

She held her hand out to touch him, and from the place she made contact, glowing scales formed above the shadow. One by one, all linking until Kukulkan in his full shifted form shimmered. Wise eyes flashed at all of us as he let out a mighty cry. It exploded like a bomb, vanishing the Mercers' shield and sending all the dead bodies around us flying across the field. I saw the faint form of my father and Aantaj shooting into the air and at least thirty yards away, but I kept my focus ahead.

The lights on campus all went out; the only thing illuminating us was the glow from the magic. Without a word, Kan shot through the arch. He didn't come out the other side, only leaving behind his magic and essence.

"The last piece of the ritual," Sienna said.

It was the same room we'd seen in the vision Taran showed us. A corridor with many doors and passageways lining either side. The stone on the arch blinked, and the light from one of the bricks faded.

"When the last brick fades, the portal closes," Sienna said.

Jed and Adler stood at our backs, guns raised and ready to fight. Nobody else moved; from the looks of it, they were still unconscious from Kan's blow. By the time I glanced back at the arch, almost half of the stones had faded.

"Let's go," Sienna said as she stepped in, reaching back to grab Koa.

They disappeared into the arch, the surface rippling like liquid. The impact of what I'd done hit my body at that moment, and I began to shake. Wren scooped me up with one arm and pushed through the arch. A thunderous snap went off in the distance as we made our way through. Wren turned back as a thud we were all too familiar with sounded—loud in the quiet night.

Adler went down. His twin screamed, a ragged sound that tore through the night, swallowed only by the roar that split the sky. Katia's fractured pulse of painful terror hammered through the liminal space. Koa's face crumpled then quickly recovered as he held on to Sienna.

"The portal is about to go out!" Sienna yelled.

Wren's body tensed with the desperate need to save our fallen brother. One that he'd only recently mended relations with. Across the field, Aantaj still held the gun. I reached out, straining to touch, to keep his soul tethered. The last brick began to fade, and Koa yanked us through the portal. My effort was futile, anyway. There was nothing left to save.

56

Sienna

Silence stretched across the void, heavy and suffocating. My chest heaved against it.

"What...what just happened?" My voice cracked, shattering the stillness, quivering in disbelief.

"We have to go back. Katia—" Mira's words broke in half, carried on sobs that shook her to the core.

Our friends needed us. Jed...Adler. They were there, alone—bleeding, fighting our battles. They couldn't die for us. That wasn't supposed to happen.

"That isn't possible." Koa's words landed sharp as steel striking stone. His face had hardened into something I didn't recognize. He knew something. Something he did not intend on sharing. "We need to stay focused."

Wren's eyes flicked between them, his jaw taut with grief he refused to voice. He stepped close to Mira, brushing the wetness from her cheeks with the pads of his trembling thumbs, a tender desperation anchoring her. "He's right, love."

"What's wrong with you?" Mira's hands jerked violently, her body straining with anguish. "That's *Adler*! Our friend, hello? He needs us!"

The world tilted. The only thing I could focus on was Mira's arms. Her veins were dark and spreading across her skin like a violent constellation. Black and purple danced among the streaks of her pain in an array of lightning strikes. My own hands itched to reach, to hold, to fix. But I couldn't.

Our world had become so irrevocably fucked by a few bad decisions and forced situations in a matter of months. None of it felt real. I wanted to pinch myself.

To wake up from the horror show that had somehow become my life. I wanted off this ride...I wanted off—

"Look around, Mira!" Koa's answer thundered. "We're in another dimension! We physically cannot help anyone but ourselves at this very moment."

The truth hit me in waves. Mira blazing fire, Koa solid as stone, both spilling grief in their own language, and I was just stuck in the middle, chest aching, hands trembling. I wanted to grab them both and shake some sense into the universe, but the universe didn't care. It was deaf to pleas, louder than my heartbeat, louder than my grief.

Jed's face swam before me. Katia's roar still echoed through my bones. Adler's fall seared the inside of my eyelids when I blinked. Everything in me screamed to turn back, to rip open the portal and drag them all through by sheer force of will. But reality was a cruel thing.

Kan's letter flared in my memory. *Instinct. Follow it. It will lead you where you must go.*

Not grief. Not fear. Instinct.

I pressed my palms together, the way I always did when I needed to quiet the noise. Not fists—never fists. I breathed into that space between my hands, into the ache in my chest, into the hollow Adler left behind. The air tasted heavy, but I drew it down, deeper and deeper, until it sank into my belly and settled me.

Grief still pressed against me, restless, clawing, but I let it move through instead of choking me. Roots stretching into soil. Wind weaving through branches. I found the pulse underneath it all—ancient, steady, calling me forward.

Kan called on *me*. All the gods did. I would not fail them. Not today.

When I opened my eyes, I knew where to go.

The corridor stretched ahead, endless stone arching above. On both sides: windows that weren't windows. Pieces of everywhere and nowhere stitched into the walls.

A storm swallowing a desert in sheets of gold fire.

A jungle city alive with green metal and neon leaves.

A sky split open, dripping red flame.

Frozen mountains humming with veins of light.

A meadow that refused to wilt, blossoms bowing and rising again.

And one more—the one that stopped me cold.

A world with mountainous walls. Gardens inside. None of the buildings matched in architecture, yet there was a strange cohesion to the way they flowed. Too perfect. Too staged. The place where soil was worked until it obeyed. Where beauty covered something ugly. I knew that kind of mask.

The pull hummed there, waiting for me.

"Si?" Mira's voice cracked as she caught up, tears streaking her cheeks.

When our gazes tangled, something inside me gave out. The breath between us was shaky, uneven, but we let it fall. Silent tears slipped, and neither of us hid. We reached for each other in the same heartbeat, palms brushing away the wetness, fingertips clinging longer than they needed to. As if skin to skin could stitch us together across the split that was coming.

Everything was about to change. Whether it was for better or for worse—that part was up to us.

"You feel it too?" My voice wove into the quiet.

She nodded, breath shaking. "Yeah."

"I think this is where we split."

Her grip tightened, nails pressing into my skin. "I don't think I want to do that."

A tear slipped from me, hot down my jaw. My throat shook with a laugh I didn't mean to make. "Me neither."

Koa drifted to my side, his hand sliding in mine. It was time to go. We all knew it. It just fucking sucked that the time had finally come.

I watched the two siblings fold into each other, a brief shelter against yet another sorrowful goodbye. Wren stepped toward me, his hug firm. The boys didn't shy away or soften upon their turn to part—Wren promising Mira's protection with the weight of someone who meant it. Owned the duty and would put down their life to uphold it. I only hoped it wouldn't come to that. We'd already lost far too much, and I was certain when we returned, there would be more to lose.

Mira and Wren moved down the hallway, pausing at a window that shimmered with Mira's presence. Beyond the glass stretched a world I barely recognized—rolling hills blanketed in wildflowers and dense forests, untouched by buildings or signs of civilization, like something pulled straight from the Astral-Codex.

I turned toward mine, a lump in my throat that was impossible to swallow.

It appeared a garden awaited us. Oh, the sweet, sweet irony. Green rows. A glimmering lake. Something in me recoiled. Beauty with teeth hidden underneath. Trouble crouched there, trouble I couldn't yet name. Koa's thumb traced lazy circles against my hand.

"Together," Mira's voice echoed back through the chamber.

I breathed deep—through my ribs, through my belly, down into the soles of my feet. Roots and stone and pulse. Then forward.

The earth swallowed us whole.

The tunnel clung close, damp with mineral. Crystals in the walls pulsed, glowing soft and strange. The ground hummed, earth singing beneath our steps, spiraling us down and around until there was no up or down, no air or stone, only the current of power carrying us.

The earth tossed us out hard. Dirt in our shoes, damp smell clinging to everything. I grasped at the world around me, trying to gather my senses, figure out where the hells we were. *Hello, paradise.*

It was beautiful. If I had the kind of money Koa had at his disposal 24/7, I'd buy a plot of land if only to build myself such a space. Crops were lined in perfect symmetry, the smell of citrus wafting in the air, a strong breeze coming from the direction of the crystal clear water just out of reach. A lake.

And we weren't alone.

Three palms full of power threatened our safety.

"Hi," I said, palms free, facing the one who appeared to be the oldest, attempting to deescalate the situation. "Um, not sure what to say here. We come in peace?"

Idiot. If only we'd thought this far. We'd made sure we were prepared physically, but I suspected slacking on the mental aspect was going to bite us in the ass.

Then again, how bad could this place actually be? Kan said to follow my instincts, yet, no alarm bells rang now that I was here. Despite them being quick to hop on defense, they weren't the most threatening-looking bunch. A woman in a pink sundress with a child and a teenager wasn't exactly a sign of danger, no matter the magic swirling at their fingertips.

The teenager spoke up, her voice a naturally ferocious tone that made me believe maybe looks here were *not* to be taken as an indication of a hard life. "Really? You come in peace?"

If I had to guess, she was around eighteen, nineteen, around Mira's shade, and her golden curls sat lopsided on top of her head. She stepped over a blanket on the ground littered with yarn and crochet hooks. The air in front of her moved fast, a small tornado nearly formed; it joined in from a smaller, yet mighty one from the small blonde girl at her left.

"How'd you know about the slide?" Her ice colored eyes were the hardest of them all.

I immediately took back all preconceptions and reverted to my original conclusion. These people had clearly been through some shit. And they were...small—even the adult. She was taller than me, but her bone structure was not as dense. Something was off about them, down to their scent. They were like fae...yet, not. I backed away, running into Koa, who took the cue to do the same.

My foot stepped on something thick on the ground, and I fought to keep my balance. Koa reached out to steady me. Our bags. Every weapon we had and item we packed was spread out everywhere, a repercussion of their 'slide' apparently.

"Wasn't really a choice," Koa grumbled, inching toward his pistol like three fae-like creatures ready to jump us with magic.

They tracked him with uncanny efficiency. Yet it was so subtle, Koa mistook it for ignorance. I could see the threat not register; his inability to see past what he perceived to be a civilian with two children. After the fight we'd just escaped, the alarm bells that should have been singing were merely whispers. It was my distance from distraction that allowed me to see what he could not.

"Okay," the tallest girl drawled, pushing the youngest behind her and the teenager. "Emma, behind us, please."

I reached for Koa through the bridge, but the bond was not there. A jolt of panic hit me as I glanced down at my arms—my mate mark had vanished.

"Where are we?" I said, risking a tentative step forward, their attention shifting back toward me.

Grass filled the soil at my feet, and comfort swept in. Some of my magic remained. Some was good. Some was manageable.

The small blonde's lip tugged upward, "Um, Earth?" She peered up at the bright blue sky, then back at us.

The adult's palm shimmered with water magic, responding to what she perceived as a threat. I stopped in my tracks. It was unintentional. I'd simply panicked—reached for what I could in hopes that something within me would wake up. And it did. Nature still called to me here. Wherever *here* was. Earth was a soil...a gift from Herta and nature itself. Not a place.

Eyes that resembled the sea stormed as she took me in. She was pale in an environment that seemed to be beaten down by the sun. "You're the smallest *Supra* I've ever seen."

Her hair fell in a mess of brown waves across her shoulder as she tilted her head, stepping closer. I backed up instinctively, shaking my head with confusion. I wasn't sure what a *Supra* was, but the inspection in her gaze made my chest cramp. Every instinct screamed to run, but Koa's hand gripped mine, steady and heavy.

I squinted at her, heart hammering. Her desire to get close allowed me to study her all the same. *Their ears.* They weren't pointed. My mind tried to catalog, analyze, and survive, but adrenaline shoved reason aside. Koa moved faster than he thought, gun raised as he came to the same conclusion.

"Reina! Gun!" Tiny, but fierce, the voice of the youngest ripped through the air.

Betrayal of what I could only perceive was fragile, curiosity-based trust doused, and the storms within her eyes raged. A wall of exhaustion slammed into me. Aggressive, a brute force that threatened to break me.

"It's okay," 'Reina', cooed. "Sleep."

Every fiber of me screamed, run, fight, *do something*, but in no universe did I stand a chance. Darkness took over. Absolute.

Hi...Again

Surprise! If you haven't caught on by now, Koa and Sienna have just wandered into State of the Union. That's right—a multiverse is happening between Mikayla D. Hornedo's Elements of Iteria series and Nelle Nikole's State of the Union.

For the most immersive and fun experience, we highly recommend checking out both series as they build toward Book 3. That said, we want to reassure you: nothing in either series will ever be dependent on reading the other. Each story stands fully on its own. Our promise is that no plotline will be compromised, and you'll never be required to read across series to understand the heart of the story.

But if you do choose to dive into both, you'll uncover an extra layer of depth that simply cannot be matched.

ABOUT THE AUTHORS

Mikayla

Mikayla grew up on the east coast, and has always been a fan of anything fantasy related. As a Latina, she always wanted to see her and her family represented in these stories. She focuses on Mesoamerican/Caribbean mythologies, and hopes that her readers feel represented in every story. Mikayla is happily married and has two beautiful daughters who inspire her to be better daily.

For more about her books, use the qr code below.

Nelle

Nelle Nikole was born in Corona, California, spent time in the battlefields of Virginia, and now lives in Atlanta with her husband Ben and their furkid Sophie. A lifelong reader, she began writing thrilling stories to share with her classmates as early as elementary school. Having lived a little bit of everywhere, Nelle decided to take her studies international and completed her Anthropology degree by researching abroad in Rio de Janeiro and throughout Cuba. Driven by an insatiable appetite for knowledge, Nelle pursued a Master's degree in Public Policy, specializing in Global Affairs. Never one to know downtime, Nelle decided to pursue her lifelong goal of becoming a published author where she is inspired by all things fantasy, apocalyptic, and anything in between.

For more about her books, use the qr code below.